When *Loving You* Is Wrong

A Novel

Dywane D. Birch

This is a work of fiction. Names, characters, places, and incidents are the products of the author's imagination or are used fictitiously. Any resemblance to actual events, locales, or persons, living or dead, is entirely coincidental.

Published by Soul Publishing, Inc.
P.O. Box 1285
Eatontown, NJ 07724

ISBN 0-9704652-3-8

Library of Congress Control Number: 2006920336

Cover design by: Candace Cottrell

Printed in the United States of America

1 2 3 4 5 6 7 8 9 10

This novel is dedicated to all my beautiful sisters who have loved and gotten hurt in the process; and for those who continue to look for love in all the wrong places and faces. May you one day realize your self-worth isn't contingent on having someone else love you.

Also by Dywane D. Birch

Shattered Souls

From My Soul To Yours

Anthologies

Breaking The Cycle

Fantasy

Acknowledgments

First and foremost, I give thanks to the Almighty Father for loving me despite all of my flaws. I am—because of Him. I will continue to be—because of Him. It is through His grace and mercy that all things flow in abundance. I am truly blessed.

To my mother, Alice: You are my light at the end of every tunnel, and my sunshine in every storm. I love you!

To my siblings: Melissa, Jason, Yolanda and their children: We are all very different, yet very similar. The fabric that keeps us together is intricately woven with love. Follow your hearts and always stay true to yourselves.

To my aunts, Mary Jones and Eleanor Minus: Thank you for always loving me as if I were one of your own.

To my cousins Pam & Pat: Thank you for all of your support. I love you both!

To Cynthia Manning: I hope you know I love you immensely. Thanks for always being in my corner.

To Lonjeté Garland: Thank you for the laughs, the friendship, and for always spreading the word.

To Val-Val: We share more than a friendship. It's a genuine love. Something no one will ever understand. Welcome home, my sister!

To the Parks family, especially Trena and Tradawn: Thank you for the love, support and for always adding a splash of color to my storytelling.

A special shout out to my girl Nakea Murray of the Literary Consultant Group: Thank you for your never-ending support. Much love to you.

To my email buddy, Danita Carter: Continued success in all of your creative endeavors. Congrats on the new book. You are a beautiful woman, and a true gem. Love ya!

To Zane: What can I say? I remain in awe. You are truly a remarkable woman. Thank you for being my biggest fan.

To my agent, Sara Camilli: Thank you for continuing to believe in my creative flow. Your patience is greatly appreciated.

To Lonnie and Joyce Railey and the rest of the Ujima-Nia Book & Social Club: Thank you for everything.

To Cashana Seals: Your undying love, support and encouragement remain breathtaking. I am forever grateful.

Special Shout outs to: Deep in Thought Book club (NJ), Illuminations Book club (NJ), Imani Book club (AL), Ebony Expressions (DE), In The Company of My Sisters Book club (DE), As The Page Turns (PA), Club Mimosa Book club (PA), Minds in Motion Book club (MD), and the many other book clubs that continue to embrace me as one of their favorite authors. Thank you! Your support of my literary endeavors is greatly appreciated.

To all my YDC peeps (you know who you are): Thanks a bunch for your support!

To Tru Books/Café and the rest of my Hartford, CT family: Thanks for always showing me love!

To all the readers, and my "special" fans: Thank you for continuing to spread the word, and supporting my literary work. Your emails and words of encouragement are sincerely valued. It is because of you that I remain encouraged to write.

And finally, to the one who continues to make this journey what it is: Collen Dixon. We continue to ride this wave of literary madness and travel uncertain terrain and climb to higher grounds without losing our sanity. I can't fathom this voyage without you by my side. Thank you!

Soulfully,

Dywane D. Birch
Email: bshatteredsouls@cs.com

When *Loving You* Is Wrong

One

Nia

Let me ask you something. Have you ever loved someone so deeply that you thought you couldn't do without them? Have you ever loved someone so much that it hurt? Have you ever allowed someone into your life who slowly chipped away at your stonewalled heart, teaching you how it feels to love, to only strip you of all of your senses? Rendering you incapable of thinking clearly? Have you ever loved so deeply that it emotionally crippled you? Have you ever tossed and turned in the middle of the night clutching your pillow crying yourself to sleep, wondering when the pain would ever end? Feeling like you just wanted to curl up and die. Well, let me tell you. I have. And it ain't a pretty sight.

I found myself doing and saying things I would have never considered had I been in the right frame of mind. But I had allowed someone—a man—to get all up inside of my heart and mind, confusing me. Distorting my judgment. Forcing me to believe the unbelievable, to think the unthinkable. And to see shit that truly didn't exist. I loved him to the point that nothing else mattered. Not the numerous phone calls I got from my girl telling me she had seen him somewhere he had no business being, with someone he had no business being with. Not the condoms I found in his trashcan; not the slew of phone numbers found on strips of paper, or the late night "do-you-know-where-your-man-is" calls from unfamiliar female voices. Not even the thousands of lies I caught him in. The only thing that mattered was that he kept telling me he loved me; that I was the only one who would ever have his love. And I believed in my heart, in the pit of my burning soul, that no one else would do. *Please.* What a damn fool I was!

I'm telling you. I almost lost my damn mind over him. No, seriously. I really thought I was going to have a nervous breakdown or something behind him. Well, in reality I did. He had me so wrapped around his thick fingers that there were days I didn't know which way was up. But, unfortunately, I didn't know any better. Actually, I did. I was just stuck on stupid. Blinded by the thrust of his big, black dick. And too damn caught up in the false belief that one-day he'd change. That one-day all the years that I had held him down would pay off, hoping that one-day all that I had given would be reciprocated. That I'd be all he'd ever need. Because the only thing we needed was each other. Wrong answer! I was truly living in the Land of Make Believe. But once reality kicked in, I quickly learned that the only thing I needed was to get as far the hell away from him and his madness as fast as I could. And I tried. But every time I fled, he'd hunt me down, snatch me by the heart and drag me right back into his drama.

He was to me like crack is to an addict. Addictive. Dangerous. Every time I took a hit of his love, he was slowly killing my spirit. Every time I heard his voice, I'd be lured right back into his craziness. Every time he kissed me, I weakened. Every time I allowed him to slide himself into the depths of my being, he stole a piece of my soul. And I knew this. I felt it. But the pain of being without him was so unbearable. So, I gave in. I surrendered my will. However, if I were to ever survive this, I knew I would need to stay away from him. I would need to not let him into my space. I would need an escape.

I can remember a time when I didn't need a man. I didn't want one. The only thing they were good for was sex, good times and shopping sprees—and not necessarily in that order. Nothing or no one defined me, or limited me. I was my own woman. Carefree. I lived life on my own terms and made up rules as I went along. Those were the good 'ole days: The days of Greek Picnics and Labor Day Beach Fests, South Beach escapades and Cancun trysts. Girl, I'd wave my "Love 'em and Leave 'em" banner with pride. Oh, how sweet life was. But, then came . . . a man. And love. Need I say more?

Now, I'm left with the remnants of my heart scattered all over the damn place. And as a result, I'm hurt, angry, and have no belief in love. No belief in dreams. And no belief in anything a man says. Bottom line: Niggas ain't shit.

Well, let me rephrase that. The man *I* fell in love with ain't shit. I can't and won't speak for any others so let me clear that up now. Because my man—um, I mean my *ex* man—was so full of shit it's a shame. But you live and learn. It's just too bad I didn't figure it out sooner. So, now I have to pick up the pieces of what's left of my life, put them back together and go on. And let me tell you. It hasn't been an easy task. If it wasn't for my girl Nygeria, and at times my cousin Autumn who has her own drama—although she doesn't like to admit it—I don't know what I'd do. They've both been my sounding board. And, believe you me. They've gotten me through many crying spells. I can say this: Some days are better than others. Some days I don't think I'll ever get over him. Other days I know I can and will. Thank God, today is a good day. But tomorrow is another story.

If someone had told me, long before I fell, I'd experience this kind of heartache I would have run from love a long time ago. If I would have known that the man I would give my heart to was a damn snake, I would have steered clear of him. I just want to know, why can't people just be honest? Shit. Why lie? If you wanna do you just keep it real. If you're gonna have another chick, or two, or three, on the side at least be man about it. Don't play games. And don't be sloppy with your shit. 'Cause when you do, I have to get ugly. Which is what I had to unfortunately do. Of course, I'll go into all the details later. But for now, I'm venting. So please, bare with me.

Anyway. Looking back, I have no room to be mad at him. He was just being who he is/was. A liar. Umm, correction—I mean, a chronic liar. Just lied about anything and everything to the point he's not even aware he's doing it. The kind who believes everything that comes out of his mouth to be truth. He'll look you in your face with a smile and convince you that you are the only living being worth loving. And all the while, he's giving his love to you and everyone else willing to receive it. And, no matter how many times you confront him. No matter how many times you catch him, he squirms his way out of it. He flips everything on you. Having you to believe you're the problem. That's what my man—excuse me, *ex*—did to me. Girl, he thought he was so damn slick with his fast talk, trying to convince me I was overreacting, exaggerating, or being dramatic anytime I confronted him about shit. Like I didn't know what the hell I was talking about. And, it almost worked. Almost. But once I took off those damn love blinders I wasn't trying to hear nothing else he had to say. He had to go. I saw him for what he really was: full of shit!

Sadly, people like him never change. So, I have no one else to blame but myself, because I didn't have to put up with his crap for as long as I did. And, I damn sure didn't have to take him back, time and time again. But, I did. And each time, he played me like a fiddle. Strumming my pain with his fingers. Just killing me slowly with all of his This-time-I'll-be-sweeter bull.

How long were we together? Hmm, let me see. It's 2005, so a little over five years. And, most of that time was done with him being behind bars. Why did I stay? Chile, that's like asking a chocolate lover who's allergic to chocolate why they ate the whole box of Godiva, knowing they were going to break out. Let's just say, I had a sweet tooth for him that finally rotted out. Right down to the damn gums. And believe me. It was painful. But, at the time, I just couldn't get enough of him. Honestly, it's not like I'm hard on the eyes or anything, so desperation isn't/wasn't the reason why I held on. Hell. Men have always checked for me on the sly. I just never took the bait. Out of respect. Out of love. And, now I see. Out of damn stupidity. But, had I known I would have gone through all this aggravation I would have scooped up a couple of numbers for myself. Not that two wrongs make it right. But it damn sure would have made it easier to swallow. Like they say, what's good for the goose is good for the gander. I'm convinced having a plaything on the side just might have . . . never mind. The fact is, being the good woman that I am I stayed true to the game. And got shitted on in the process.

So, you'll have to excuse me if I come across a little bitter. No. A whole lot bitter! I feel betrayed. Used. And fucking abused. Being honest with you. My first instinct was to get even. Yes, a sweet revenge is what I considered. I had crazy thoughts of sleeping with one of his boys, doing one of his brothers—or better yet, his father—who, by the way, happens to be a very attractive, sexy man who just happens to have a penchant for young women. But once I came to my senses, I realized that in the end the only person I'd be playing was myself; and, a ho I'm not. However, I will admit, that in the past I have done some spiteful things. I'll be the first to say that on occasion I held true to the saying, Hell Hath no Fury Like A Woman Scorned 'cause I have definitely done some malicious shit out of anger. But, that was the past. However, looking back, it wasn't worth it. But, at the time, I felt like he got just what he deserved for trying to play me.

Consequently, this time—after being shitted on for the fifth time—I decided that the best way to get back at him was to get over him. To move on with my life, never looking back. And, slowly, that's what I've been trying to do. Like the saying goes, three strikes and you're out! Well, in his case, five strikes. But, like I said, it damn sure hasn't been easy. There are times when I just want to hear his voice. Sometimes the loneliness gets the best of me and I want him in the worse way. There are nights when I just want to be wrapped in his arms. But I know, I can't. And I won't. No matter how much I still love him; no matter how much I miss his touch I will never take him back. Not this time. I will never give him the opportunity to hurt me again. I will never spend another restless, sleepless night crying over the likes of him. You can believe that.

You know. Through this whole ordeal, I have come to accept that there are two types of people in this world: givers and takers. The givers will unselfishly bestow to others all that they have out of love. While the takers will seize any opportunity to drain you of everything you have out of selfishness. They will use you, manipulate you and try to destroy you in the process. Not always purposefully. It's just their nature. I know firsthand. Because I loved that fool so much that I allowed him to take and take and take. And I was eventually left with nothing but empty dreams. And when the dust finally settled, I had nothing left for myself.

So, I was left to ponder the answer to a question I had asked Nygeria several months before the shit *really* hit the fan: When is it time to let go? She looked at me real serious for a moment. Took in a deep breath, then slowly said, "When you get so caught up in being what everybody else needs you to be that you neglect your own needs. When you find yourself giving more than you're getting—be it physically, emotionally, spiritually or financially—then it's time to reevaluate the nature of the relationship."

I nodded, knowingly. And then she asked, "Why do you feel the need to hold on?" And, at that moment, I honestly didn't have an answer for her so I did the only thing I could. I pitifully shrugged my shoulders. "Well, when you figure that out, then maybe you'll figure out why it's time to let go."

Well, let me tell you. My heart ached. I couldn't let go. I wanted to hold on for as long as I could, even if it meant hanging on by a thin thread. I guess I believed in the old cliché: a piece of a man is better than no man at all. Please. Whoever, came up with that bullshit must have been one lonely, miserable, butt-ugly woman because if I can't have the whole man, I don't want him. Not now, not ever. But, it took me a while to get to that point. Trust me.

Anyway. She gave me an exasperated sigh, "The nigga keeps disrespecting you, Nia." I could hear the frustration coiling through her voice. "And you still won't dump his sorry behind. You let him come right back, giving the same weak ass promises and broke down excuses. But, I can't tell you when enough is enough. You'll have to decide that on your own.

"Listen. We love who we love. So, don't beat yourself up about that. But when they continue to hurt us, then it's time to just love them from afar. And Mustafa has hurt you a thousand times over, girl. It's time you really try to let him go, *this* time. He isn't going to change. You know it, and I know it. So you need to accept that and just move on. Otherwise, he's going to keep pulling you down. Look at you. You look a mess."

I caught a glimpse of myself in the mirror. She was dead wrong. I didn't look a mess, as she had kindly put it. I looked a hot fucking mess. I hadn't slept in days. My hair was all over my head. My eyes were swollen. My skin was ashen. And I hadn't eaten in days.

"Girl, you need to pull yourself together, and get out of this house. The world is still rotating while you lie around here feeling sorry for yourself. And to make matters worse, that nigga doesn't care. He's out there somewhere doing him with some other chick, not giving one damn thought about the shit he put you through."

Sadly. She was right. Not once did he ever display an ounce of remorse for putting me through hell. And Nygeria had to keep reminding me of that. Thank God for true friends. She and I have been friends for twelve years and, like I said before, she has walked me through this train wreck of a relationship with open arms. Being the shoulder I needed to cry on; being the voice of reason when I couldn't trust my own thoughts. Through the late night phone calls, and the impromptu sleepovers, my sistafriend has helped me heal; and allowed me to painfully make my own mistakes. We agree to disagree. But it doesn't stop her from saying what's on her mind. And I admire that about her.

She bites her tongue for no one, especially when it comes to the likes of a man. Girlfriend has chased many a men away with her aggressive nature. In all honesty, her demeanor can be at best intimidating if you're not comfortable in the skin your in. Umm. In a word, She's a big girl.

Nygeria has a pretty face that reveals everything she feels. You know what she's thinking way before she opens her mouth to say it. She has smooth Hershey-coated skin, neatly arched eyebrows over beautiful brown eyes, and stands five-feet-ten-inches with big hair, big hands and big feet. And with her I-take-no-shit-from-a-man attitude she has no problem going toe-to-toe with one when necessary. I've witnessed firsthand her brawl in the middle of the street—like a dude—with her last boyfriend for forgetting her birthday. It was a terrible sight. A few times, she's threatened to *handle* Mustafa. But, somehow, I've always been able to keep her off of him.

Anyway, I hung my head low, hoping the tears wouldn't fall. I took in a deep breath. I'm telling you, had someone told me I'd be going through this level of emotional turmoil, I'd have smacked them silly. "No way!" I would have screamed. "Not me. My man loves me too much to put me through that kind of madness . . . My man would never do that to me." That's the shit I would have said with conviction. *Humph.*

"Never say never", that's what Nana—God rest her soul—used to say when I was growing up, "because you just may have to eat those words." And, believe you me. I have eaten those words— *and* choked on them—on more than one occasion. 'Cause the reality is, he was lying up with me after rolling out of bed with someone else and I had no fucking clue. Not the first time, not the second time, and not the other times after that.

Don't get me wrong. This is not a man-bashing story, although it's about a man. This is not a love story, although it is about love. And it's definitely not a pity-pitching story, although I've cried more tears than I'd like to recall. It's just my story: A story of a woman who loved a man once to the point that she lost a piece of herself in his lies, and his manipulation. It is about a woman who allowed a man to enter the depths of her soul under the pretense of a happy-ever after. Painfully learning that when loving someone is wrong, it's time to let go. Cut your loses, and keep it moving. Before it's too late. Before you end up doing something you'll regret. And so. My story begins . . .

Mustafa,

Hey sweetness. How's my baby doing? Are you missing me as much as I'm missing you? Last night, I had my first wet dream about us. I miss you so much, baby. I can't wait to feel you inside of me again. I love the way you make my insides tingle. I need your love in the worse way, baby.

If you were to ever leave me, I don't know what I would do. I think I'd just die because I can't see life without you. Please give me some reassurance that we're in this together. That you'll never leave me, not now, not ever!

I want to apologize for writing all those crazy ass letters, but I wasn't feeling the love so I had to get your attention some kind of way. I hope you know I didn't mean any of those things I said. I trust you wholeheartedly. I was just feeling alone. And I allowed my fears to get the best of me.

Physically, the baby and I are doing fine. The life we've created continues to grow inside of me. I never knew being pregnant would feel so wonderful. This baby—our baby—fills me up with so much joy. I thank you for all that you do to show your undying love for me. I love you, Mu.

Always,
Keyonna

Mustafa, baby,

When am I going to hear from you? I need to hear from you, baby. Please don't shut me out. Not now. Not with all this going on in my life. I don't think I can do this alone, baby. Please. I should be home in the next two months or so. The baby and I need you now more than ever. Please don't walk out on us. I'll be patiently waiting to hear from you.

Your Wife for life,
Keyonna

Mustafa,

You got my head spinning, baby. Every time I think about you making love to me, I get so wet. I don't think you know what you do to me, baby. I'm crazy about you. I can't be without you. You're the only one for me. I hope you know that. I still think about our first time upstairs in that empty room. And we almost got busted. Right in the middle of my orgasm and you tried to cover my mouth. I need you so bad. My insides are throbbing just thinking about your thickness. I don't think I could ever handle you giving that kind of love to anyone else, baby. Please tell me, it's all mine. I wanna get your name stamped all over my pussy because it's yours, baby. I'm never letting you go.

Your wife,
Keyonna

One, two, three letters, all from the same chick. No envelopes. No return address. No dates. But the evidence was as bold as it gets. My man was cheating on me. *Your wife,* I thought. *Oh, please!* I plopped down on my bed, reading then rereading each one, until my head started to throb. At that moment, I wasn't sure what I was supposed to feel. My body went numb, then an array of emotions swirled their way into anger. He had lied his way out of so many things. But this time I had solid proof. This time, I wanted to see his lying-two-timing-sneaky ass slither out of this one. So, there I was, in the middle of my haze, reading these makeshift—oh, baby, baby, please—love letters for the third time before it actually registered. He had gotten her pregnant. This wasn't just some quick ass. I tried to calculate when this affair/relationship could have kicked off. But came up blank. She said she loved all the things he did for her. He showed *her* his undying love. That's not something someone says if it were a one-night stand. My man—the nigga I held down for four years—had not only gotten some chick pregnant, well at least that's what she was telling him. I didn't want to jump to conclusions because I knew how desperate some women could be. Nevertheless, he'd put my life at risk by not using protection. And the deeper reality sunk in, the more pissed I got. He had really lost his damn mind this time. I snatched the phone out of its cradle and viciously punched in his cell number.

"Yo," he snapped into the receiver. "What's the deal, pretty baby?"

I cringed. "We need to talk."

"I'm in the middle of something, right now," he said. "Let me hit you back."

"I don't care what you're in the middle of. I *said* we need to talk, and we need to talk now. You got one hour to get here." I slammed the phone down in his ear. Bastard!

I love the way you make my insides tingle . . . I need your love in the worse way . . . those words echoed in my head, over and over and over, like a scratched record. I didn't want to blame this faceless woman for what I was feeling. As crazy as it sounds, I had hoped she didn't know about me because then the direction of my anger would shift. I've always hated when a woman blamed the *other* woman for the indiscretions of her mate. With all that was in me, I didn't want to fall back into that category of calling her out of her name when she was probably just an innocent victim. I hoped.

But you know how we can get when we let our imaginations get the best of us. The other woman quickly goes from unsuspecting victim to stank-ho-ass-homewrecker in a blink of an eye. In the midst of our rage we start to conjure up scenarios of finding out where she lives or works to beat her down. We'll call her house and curse her out, making all kinds of crazy threats and requests for her to stay the hell away from our man. But if he were really your man—better yet, if he were a real man—he'd have his ass home where he's supposed to be. The only person he'd be spending his time with, and giving his loving to, is you. And, if he couldn't be with just one woman, he'd be man enough to lay his cards on the table and honestly let you know what time it was. He'd give you the chance to choose—to stay or go—instead of dragging you into a bunch of foolishness. Having you come out of character, causing a whole lot of ruckus. Trust me. I know. I've stepped out of my heels and have fought many a fights over *my* man. But all that ever did was inflate his already oversized ego.

Luckily, with age, I learned that fighting wasn't worth all the broken nails because after all the scratches healed, he'd be off again—somewhere else creeping. And once caught, I'd have to go on another rampage, busting out his car windows or banging on motel doors with my baseball bat. Oh, yes. It had gotten real ugly. Instead of confronting his *jump-offs* I stepped to him.

But, when it's all said and done, I am solely responsible for how I respond to the actions of others. No matter what someone else does, I can choose to walk away or get caught up in it. It's a damn shame I chose to get sucked up in it, thinking he'd have some sort of compunction. You know, just a bit of guilt for his lying, and cheating. But he didn't. And, consequently, I was solely responsible for my own misery and worries. Whew! The truth hurts. But, it's the only way I can give it to you.

Anyway, I glanced over at the clock on my nightstand. It read: 9:30 A.M. *If you were to ever leave me.* Oh please! *You can have his dumb ass,* I thought. *After I finish slapping the shit out of him.* I knew one thing: If he didn't walk through this door by 10:15, I'd be blowing his phone, pager and everything else up. I stood in the middle of my bedroom, staring at myself in the full-length mirror. I pulled my hair back into a ponytail, then stared long and hard at the image before me, drifting back in time.

"Damn, Shorty. You fine as hell," he had said, grinning as I walked by him and his boys. I ignored the comment, and kept strolling. I had already peeped him and his friends swaggering through the mall earlier. And had summed them up to be players. I wasn't beat. I dipped into the Luis Vuitton store instead. Unknowingly, he followed behind me.

"So, what's your name?" he asked in an almost seductive whisper. He stood before me in all his fineness: Five-feet-eleven inches of smooth, cocoa-dipped skin; big, brown dreamy eyes; succulent lips, high cheekbones; and a broad nose—one of my weaknesses. He smiled, revealing a dimple in his left cheek. Another weakness.

I looked him up and down, taking in the crispness of his cologne, the spin of his waves. "Nia," I responded coolly.

"As in Long?"

"*No*, as in purpose," I corrected.

"Hmm," he said, licking his lips. "I like that." *Ugh*, I thought to myself. I hated when a man licked his lips as if it were the beginning and end to seduction. But, I had to give it to him. He was sexy. And if I hadn't been more focused on my shopping, I probably would have considered sliding him my cell number.

"So, how can a nigga holla at you?"

I slowly smiled before responding. "You can't." And with that said I pivoted on my heels, swinging my hips just enough to let him wonder. The only thing I was interested in was enjoying a day at The Mall at Short Hills without interruption, especially from a man. I wasn't pressed for conversation; and I definitely wasn't up for the game. I was out. I had made myself a promise three weeks prior that I was done with men. Especially, after the bull I went through with Phillip. Now, Phillip was definitely not my type. Which is why I don't know how I got caught up in him in the first place. One, he was too light for me. Light-skinned men have never done it for me because most of them come off so stuck on themselves. Two, he was a pretty boy. This fool spent more time in the mirror than I did. There was nothing rugged about him. Three, he was the same height as me: five-feet-eight. Which was definitely another strike. I like a man with some height to him, another weakness of mine. And, sexually, he was a flop. He had the equipment; just didn't know how to use it.

And as a sexually liberated woman, I just don't think I should have to teach a grown man the difference between *fucking* and *making* love. Sadly, the latter is what he thought he was doing. Go figure! So, you know he only got it once and that was that. Okay, okay. . . . I'm lying. Twice. Shoot, I was horny. But, I be damned if the second time was any better. And trust me. I had hoped it would be. *Not!* When he finished, I was so sexually aggravated that I had to literally take matters into my own hands once I put him out. But, then again, what did I expect other than two humps and a lousy pump. He and I had no history, no connection and no chance of building on anything. Being honest with myself, he was just nice to look at, and had a beautiful body. Which is why I wasted my time with him in the first place, besides the fact that he was always good for a dinner and night out on the town. He was also a great dancer. And he was at times fun to be around. So, if nothing else, I had thought we could be friends. Wrong!

Let me tell you what this fool did. He had the balls to ask if he could borrow my car because his was in the shop. And yes, I had the nerve to be foolish enough to let him, thinking he was going to bring it back in an hour like he said. Well, one hour goes by, then two, then three, four, five. And still no sight of Pretty Tone. Now, I'm paging him like a maniac, and biting my nails down to my cuticles. I'm fuming. Finally, he decides to call me back.

"You paged me?" he had the gall to ask. I wanted to scream on him. I just gritted my teeth, taking a deep breath, then letting a pregnant pause take its course.

"Phillip," I finally responded. "Yes, I paged you. Actually, I paged you twenty-seven times and you're just now getting back to me."

"Well, what's up?" Now, call me crazy if you will; but if I didn't know any better. This damn fool had just lost his damn mind being nonchalant with me, acting as if I were riding his damn jockstrap or something.

What's up? "Negro," I snapped, "it's ten-thirty at night. You've had my damn car since seven o'clock this morning. Now where the hell are you?" And do you want to know what his response was? Well, get ready for this.

"I'm on a date," he said. *A fucking date!* Can you believe that? This no-count nigga was out on a date in my brand new '99 cranberry Acura Legend with the beige leather interior and moon-roof. The one I scrimped and saved for the down payment, working two jobs and this . . . this stinking, Mother F'er had the audacity to be riding some female in my shit. And to make matters worse, he added, "in Connecticut."

I wanted to faint. "Excuse me?" I snapped, chest heaving in and out. "Let me get this right. You drove my damn car to Connecticut. And you're on a fucking date?"

"Yeah," he replied. "Don't worry, I'll have your car back before the crack of dawn."

"NO, Bitch!" I screamed. "You'll have my car back by midnight or you'll be locked up for car theft." I was too daggone through. Needless to say, he pulled back into my driveway at one A.M., handing me a damn doggie bag. And, then he had the nerve to ask me if he could stay the night, or if I'd give him a ride home. What did I do? I spit on him, slamming my door in his face. I was so damn sick. The lesson I learned: Never, ever loan my car to anyone else and never date another pretty-faced man.

Anyway, back to Mr. How Can A Nigga Holla. I didn't want the headache. And I didn't need the drama. Something in my gut told me he was a Drama King. But, as fine as he was, one dinner date might not have hurt. Right? I shook the thought from my head.

He followed behind me. He was like a pesky fly buzzing up in my damn ear. The minute he opened his mouth again I felt like swatting him.

"Oh, so it's like that?"

I turned to face him, looking up into his eyes a little longer than I had wanted. They were magical, and I needed to shift them before he had me under his spell.

"Basically," I said, averting my eyes from his.

"You can run, baby. But you can't hide," he snapped confidently. "I got my eye on you." He blew me a kiss, heading back to his peoples.

I laughed and continued on my shopping spree. Forty minutes later, I'm in Saks standing at the counter getting reading to pay for my purchases when I hear the richness of his voice. "I got you," he said, reaching over and handing the saleswoman six crisp, one-hundred-dollar bills. I gave him an under-eyed glare. He threw his hands up in mock surrender. "No strings attached. Just a brotha tryna be nice."

I reluctantly smiled, then came to my senses. "If you insist," I said, quickly stuffing my bills back in my purse. Please. Nana hadn't raised no fool, okay? Well, maybe she did when it comes to matters of the heart. But that's not what we're talking about right now. Anyway, she always said, "If a man wants to buy you something nice, let him. But don't ever let him buy you out your dress." So, I did, having no intentions of letting him get in my drawers. He grabbed my shopping bags before I could, then scooped up the ones that were at my feet.

"Are you always so quick to pay for a strange women's purchases?" I asked, glancing at the iced-out ring on his pinky as we strolled out of the store.

"Only for women who catch my attention."

"Okay, so I caught your attention. Now what?"

"I want the digits."

"Why?"

"I like your style."

"You don't know my style."

"Well, I like what I see."

"And what if I told you, you can't have what you see?"

His cell phone rang. He pulled it from his hip, looked at the number then put it back. "Then, I'll take it." He flashed a million-dollar smile. But, the way he said it led me to believe he meant that in more ways than one. He didn't strike me as someone who took no for an answer, not without exerting a little strong-armed persuasion.

"Is that so?" I asked, coyly.

"Yeah," he replied, flicking his tongue across his bottom lip. "But don't think I'm some sucka."

"Oh, so you saying I can't run your pockets?" I asked, faking surprise.

"Not, hardly. But if you play your cards right, I'll treat you right." His voice dipped an octave. "Let's go get something to eat."

My stomach growled. I hadn't eaten since breakfast and was famished. And I do like a man who takes charge. "What about your boys?" I asked.

"I'm not joined at the hip with them niggas. I'll get at 'em later. Right now, my focus is you."

I smiled. *So much for doing the solo thing,* I thought to myself. So, there I was sitting in Legal Seafoods, across from a strange man who had just dropped six-hundred-beans on me. Hmm. Three hours later, we were still sitting and talking. And each time his cell went off, he ignored it. I liked that. I learned he was originally from Brooklyn but had been living in East Orange for the past four years. Which was cool, because I lived in Orange. He was twenty-nine. He had two brothers and three sisters. No children, and no woman—so he claimed. *Just friends*. Which meant fuck partners. But what did I care. I had just gotten treated to a nice meal and had my purchases paid for by a cat I had only known for a few hours. One thing was for sure. I wasn't going to be clumped into that little category.

"So, tell me. What kind of work do you do?" Why I asked that stupid question is beyond me. But I didn't want to make assumptions. But, in my gut I knew. He just had the *look,* if you know what I mean.

He smiled. "Let's just say, I do what I gotta do to make it happen."

I nodded, knowingly. But, again, what did I care. I didn't intend on seeing him again, if I could help it. And if I did, it wouldn't be for long. Like I said earlier, I could tell he had a lot of game in him. And I wasn't really up for it. He glanced down at his Movado.

I glanced at my watch as well. *Eight-thirty. Holy shit!* "Listen," I said, full from my feast of shrimp and lobster. "Thanks for the meal. But I really gotta get going."

"Yeah, I can dig it," he said, grinning. He reached over and took my hand. "It's been real." He held my palm out. "You gonna be mine."

"And what makes you think that?"

"It says it right here," he answered, running his index finger along my lifeline. "Nia will fall for Mustafa." He laughed. I half-smiled, raising an eyebrow.

"Well, I suppose if I don't stand for something, I could possibly fall for anything or *any*one," I said, pulling my hand away, and shaking it as if he had smeared something foul on it. I got up. He stood as well, tossing a fifty on the table for the waiter's tip.

"Oh, you got jokes?"

"No, but you seem real sure of yourself."

"Oh, I am, baby. That's the only way to be."

"Hmm. If you say so."

"Nah. I know so. 'Cause that's how I do mine."

I rolled my eyes. "Whatever, I responded, changing the subject. "Again, thanks for the meal, and the convo. I really enjoyed it."

"Likewise," he said, licking his lips again.

This time, I grabbed all my bags. "Oh, and thanks for the purchases. Not that you had to. But a sista has no problem holding onto her cash."

"Aye, yo. Don't sweat it. I know I didn't have to. But I wanted to. I told you. I like your style." I smiled. "Let me walk you to your car."

"No, that won't be necessary."

"Nah, I insist," he responded, holding open the door for me. His cell rang. Again, he let it ring into his voice mail. I led the way, crossing the street to the parking garage, feeling his eyes on the sway of my hips. Yes, baby got back.

That I know. "Damn," he said in more of a whisper. But I heard the comment just the same. "So, when am I gonna see you again?"

I smirked. "That sounds presumptuous. What's make you think you got it like that?" When we reached my Acura, I disarmed the alarm and opened the door.

"I know I do," he said confidently, almost bordering on cockiness. "How 'bout I pick you up tomorrow around, lets say, eight and we hit a movie or something?" He licked those full, juicy lips again.

Damn, he was sexy. But I had to shake his charm. What was a girl to do? Decisions. Decisions. Decisions. Oh, what the hell. "No. How 'bout I meet you somewhere," I said throwing my bags in the trunk, then sliding behind the wheel. I started my engine allowing him to close my door. I rolled my window down. "Give me *your* number and I'll call you to set it up." And surprisingly, I did.

Well, lo and behold. The man swept me off my feet. We drove into the City. Had lunch at Mr. Chow's, then a carriage ride through Central Park. We must have laughed and talked for hours. He made me feel special. He was attentive, and thoughtful. And even bought me two-dozen yellow and white roses. It was probably one of the best dates I ever had. So, one date turned into two, then three, then four—then, before I knew it, we were dating exclusively.

Six months later, I was really feeling him. And, out of nowhere, he hit me with something that almost knocked the wind out of our whirlwind romance.

"Listen, baby," he started, after making love to me for the third time that day. "There's something we gotta talk about."

"What is it?" I responded, lusty-eyed.

"I'm going in for sentencing next month."

I had to pick my mouth up from off the bed before I could finally speak. "Say, what?"

I stared at him in disbelief. Dazed. Dumbfounded. I shook my head, peeling myself from his embrace. "Let me get this straight, you're telling me you're about to go to prison."

He nodded.

"For how long?" I asked, searching for some sign that he was pulling my leg. There was none.

"My lawyers tell me I'm facing ten years, but I'll probably only due about four."

Okay. Now I'm pissed. "And you're just getting around to telling me this shit? What kind of mess is that? You should have told me this from the door."

"I thought I mentioned it when we first started vibin'."

"You *thought?* No, Mustafa. You didn't mention shit to me, 'cause had you, I wouldn't be looking at you like you're crazy." Okay, okay. I knew what he was into but I didn't know he was cased the hell up. 'Cause believe you me, if I did, I wouldn't have been lying up with him. Okay, okay. . . . I'm fibbing. Maybe I would have been. But, I wouldn't have gotten all caught up in him. But I was. And, although six months wasn't a long time to be with someone. I liked him. Okay, I was catching feelings for him. How that ever happened was way beyond me. Despite the hustling, I thought he was a good man. But obviously . . .

"You're so full of shit," I continued. "You know damn well you never opened your mouth and said one damn thing about being cased up."

"I apologize."

"Yeah, right," I said.

He sighed. "Listen. I'm really big on you; but I don't want to put you through the drama so I'll understand if you wanna jump ship."

"Jump ship!" I snapped. "Negro, are you crazy. I'm not letting you off the hook that easy."

"So, what you sayin'?"

"I'm pissed that you didn't tell me. But, I'm gonna ride this out with you."

"You sure?" he asked, pulling me back into his arms, then kissing me on the forehead.

I stroked his dick until it stiffened, "Yes," I replied, looking him deep in his eyes. "I've got your back Mustafa. Just don't play me."

"Never, baby."

"For your sake, I hope not," I said, rolling on top of him, then slipping his dick back into my wetness. "'Cause if you do, you're gonna wish you never heard the name Nia Wesley."

"Never that," he said, thrusting himself upward. "Me and this dick are all yours. That's my word."

I closed my eyes and moaned, riding the wave of another orgasm.

The doorbell pulled me out of my reverie. I peeped out of the curtain. And there he was, standing with all his smugness. Two hours late. I rolled my eyes, swinging the door wide open. It was show time.

Two

Autumn

The season of the year between summer and winter is what we know as autumn. It is the crispness of morning song, the magnificent changing of colors, the shaking off of summer's dust, and the preparing of winter's bite. And right now, I need all the strength I can muster to prepare for the change, shake and the bite.

Here it is two A.M. in the frickin' morning, and I'm fumbling around in pitch darkness like a damn idiot, bumping into shit trying to gather my belongings without waking up the man of my life. The man I've been giving myself to for the last eighteen months. The one lying over there on that wafer-thin mattress snoring like he doesn't have a care in the world. Or the common sense to know it's time to buy a damn new bed. I don't care how many times, how many ways, I hint around it, he just doesn't get it. So, I flat out asked him.

"Baby," I had said in my sweetest voice, "don't you think it's time you get a new mattress?"

"Nah. What's wrong with the one I have?"

I had to look at him like he was crazy. *What the hell you mean "what's wrong with the one I have?"* I wanted to snap. *It's old. It's as thin as a pancake and it hurts my damn back.* I couldn't believe he'd ask me some mess like that.

"The springs stick me in my back," I shared, thinking that would make a difference.

"Oh, is that it. I'll just flip it over."

How thoughtful. I twisted my lips up in disgust, shaking my damn head. "It ain't that much flipping in the world," I snapped, "except in the trash."

"Oh, girl," he said, taking off his jeans, then throwing them across his tattered brown leather easy chair. He stepped out of his boxers, then walked over to me, leaving his drawers in the middle of the floor. I stared in disbelief—or maybe it was disgust—while he tugged at my skirt, licking his lips. "Stop all this talking and come on out these clothes. You don't be worrying about no damn springs when I'm giving you all this good dick."

Low blow. He just had to go there. I looked down at his meaty manhood, and sighed. What could I say? He was right. I loved the way he felt inside of me. And like a fool, I took off my clothes and crawled in his rickety old bed—like I always do, letting him please me in the best way he knows how—with the squealing of his springs matching the moans of pleasure escaping from the back of my throat. And, like all the times before, when it's all done, I crawl out of his bed with his musky scent lingering on my skin and his warm juices fresh in my pussy too damn embarrassed to be caught dead in his nasty place when the sun comes up.

Yes, I get up smelling real stank and get dressed *without* taking a shower or sink rinse. Well, if you seen how filthy his shower is you'd do the same thing. It would take a lifetime of scrubbing his tile and tub before I'd step foot in it. And right now I have no interest in playing Merry Maid to anyone. And, to take it a step further, I'm not even sure if I have a lifetime in me (at this point) to put up with his nasty, Neanderthal ways.

Oh, I know that's a terrible thing to say. But, it's the truth. And, truthfully speaking, had I known that he liked to slop around in squalor when we first met, I probably wouldn't have given him the time of the day. Humph. On second thought, I know I wouldn't have. Cute smile or not, I would have tossed his number in the trash and kept it movin'. But noooooooo. I let Hennessey, his sweet talk and all of his fineness trick me into giving him the panties. And *bam*. Now I'm strung. Or just stuck on stupid.

Yes. The man—my man—is fine. Which is probably why I overlook the obvious. That he's downright trifling. Just look at him over there scratching and digging in the crack of his butt. Ugh!

Anyway. Morris and I met at Brokers Night Club in East Orange. Well, actually, we bumped into each other on the way to the bathroom. But who cares. Anyway, we both say excuse me, then he grins at me. And of course, I smile back.

"You owe me a dance," he had said, checking me out from head to toe.

I gave him a coquettish grin, responding, "Oh, really. What makes you say that?" All the while, I really have to use the bathroom. But, I don't want to go. Not yet. At first, I wasn't sure if it was the drinks—or the way he was looking at me—but I could feel my body overheating. Then, I realized it was because I was standing with my legs clamped shut, about ready to piss on myself.

He stood there with his drink in his hand, grinning. "Because I said so," he finally replied, licking his lips. "It's the least you can do after tryna knock me over."

I rolled my eyes. "You ain't ready," I playfully snapped before dashing into the bathroom. So, while I'm squatting over the piss-splattered toilet his smile flashes through my mind. And now, I'm hoping I run or *bump* into him again. To see just what kind of moves he had—on the dance floor that it is. Well, one dance led to another then another and before I knew it, I was being led outside.

Oh how he sleighed me a new rhythm that night. Right under a full moon, he slid his Corona slicked tongue down my throat, reached up under my skirt and played a sweet symphony with his fingers between the folds of my flesh.

Then—without warning—he dropped to his knees, yanked my panties to the side, and lapped my nectar before turning me around, bending me over then sliding the thickest, heaviest piece of man meat inside of me, hitting places I forgot existed. I must have cum a thousand times because when he was finished with me, I was dazed. Or maybe just too backed up to know the difference. Humph. Humph. Humph. I get tingly every time I think back on it. And I also could slap myself silly for being so damn reckless.

Truth be told, I didn't clutch my pearls to the fact that I was standing outside with my skirt hiked up, and my bare bottom out for all the world to see—not to mention being penetrated without a damn condom—until *after* I got home and stood under my showerhead. I stressed for weeks hoping I didn't contract something from him. And, when he finally called—three weeks later, I asked him right off the bat: You don't have any diseases do you? Of course, it came out more of a plea than a question, and I didn't really expect him to be honest about something like that. But I just had to know.

He chuckled which made me even more anxious. But then quickly assured me he was cleaner than the Board of Health. Then he paused, and flipped it on me. "I should be asking you that," he said. "You didn't seem to have a problem giving it up or demanding I use a condom."

I had to gasp. I couldn't believe he'd make that sort of comment to *me*. Then again, I was so quick to let him hit it from the back that he had every right to go there. And of course my cousin Nia, and her loud-mouthed friend Nygeria—a.k.a Amazon.com, my nickname to describe her big, mannish self—had laughed and called me Quick Drawers for over a week after I told them about my night with him. That, of course, just added more salt to my injury.

Anyway, Nia and I are first cousins, but we're more like sisters in every sense of the word since we were both reared by our grandmother—God rest her sweet soul. Not only do we look alike, we share many of the same pains and experiences. We're even the same age, and share the same birthday month: November. I was born on the 5th and she on the 15th. Go figure. Our mothers were sisters; *were* being the operative word, since they're both deceased. Hers by an overdose; mine by the hands of her jealous boyfriend. Both died two years apart. And I think that is what tore our grandmother up. Losing both of her daughters to tragedy. I really believe if Nana—what we affectionately called her—didn't have us to care for she would have thrown her towel in, and let the good Lord take her sooner. But, Nia and I were her pride and joy. And gave her a reason to keep pressing on, as she would say. So she spoiled us rotten to the core.

Anyway, with all of our similarities we are also very different. She's what I'd call bourgeois-ghetto; but oftentimes can fall closer toward the ghetto end, especially when she's mad—which is probably why she and Amazon.com get along so well. She performs, do you hear me. I mean from neck rolling and cursing up a storm to bar fighting—over boyfriends, of course. Well, that's what she used to do. But that's another story. And she's definitely materialistic, although she'd never admit it. Okay, maybe materialistic is the wrong description. High maintenance. Yeah, that's it. Her words, not mine.

Now me, I like to consider myself low key. But, don't get it twisted. I do like to get my finger-pop and drink on from time to time, just without all the extras. If anything, I try my best to be a lady at all times. But, I'm not going to front. There have been a few times when I've had to toss my Catholic schoolgirl manners to the curb and get nasty. But, normally, I don't like drama. And I'm not going to get into an altercation with another woman (if I can prevent it) over a man. Well, okay, just that one time over Quasheem—my first love. My first bump and grind, my first kiss, my first everything. The one who popped my cherry at fifteen! And when he was done, I practically had to crawl home. And could barely walk for two days afterwards. But once I got used to it, humph . . . never mind. I'm sure I'll get around to telling you more about him. Anyway, beefing over a man, unh-uh. No how, no way, will I go there. You want him; you can have him. That's my motto.

And I like to consider myself very low maintenance. Give me a Target or Walmart gift certificate and I'm in heaven. But not Miss Nia. She wouldn't be caught dead in *those* stores. And God forbid if she thought you bought her something from out of one of them, she'd pitch a hissy fit for sure. But me: I'm the Queen of bargains, okay. I can shop inexpensive and still come off classy-looking, if you know what I mean. Clearance racks, here I come. But, Nia forget it. She has to have high-end designer wear or she won't wear it. No outlets for her. She'll pay top dollar for every thing. And, that's why she lives paycheck-to-paycheck, trying to keep up with the Jones, the Jetsons, and the damn Jacksons. But, I'll give it to her. Sistagirl looks fly as all get out every time she steps out in her Prada, Gucci and Dolce & Gabbana; the girl definitely tries to keep her finger on the pulse of what is hot, and what is not. But the poor thing is about as broke as they come. I just shake my head. Anyway—despite those differences—for the most part, we're close. Not as close as I'd like us to be, but close enough to have each other's back when push comes to shove. And that's what really matters.

Okay, back to my phone call with Morris. Now was my turn to reassure him that I was squeaky-clean. And I felt somewhat embarrassed to have to defend myself, considering the fact that doing what I did that night wasn't something I normally did. I may have fantasized about it, but it being practice was definitely not the case. For some reason I was compelled to let him know that, but then an inner voice stopped me. He'd think I was full of bull.

"Touché," I said instead, staring at myself in the mirror. "I guess I deserve that."

"Yeah, well. I guess you do."

I squinted my eyes together real tight, then sighed running my fingers through my hair. Ugh. My hair felt like steel wool. And the hair at the nape of my neck was a tight mess. I made a mental note to stop by Walmart to pick up a perm.

"I apologize for coming at you like that," I responded. "It's just that I'm not usually so careless. And with everything going on, I know I really should have known better. I don't have you to blame for anything. I take full ownership of my actions. So will you accept my apology?"

"Only under one condition," he coolly replied.

"And what might that be?" I asked, feeling almost afraid to ask. However, thoughts of our first meeting danced through my head. I sat on the edge of my bed, tightly crossing one leg over the other in attempt to shut off the warm sensation stirring between them. That one night with him was a tease for me. And hearing his voice had confirmed what I already knew each time I slid my hands between my thighs in the middle of the night. I wanted more.

Yes. Up until the moment he called me, I had been masturbating thinking about him. Imagining him hovered over me, gazing into my lust-filled eyes as he slowly entered the depths of my sea, riding the waves of my desires. I honestly welcomed the new face in my fantasies with reckless abandon. Because the one before him had slowly faded in and out, becoming a worn-out memory.

Trevor.

Tall, dark and, oh, so delicious; that's what he was. Everything I could have ever hoped for in a man. Passionate. Thoughtful. Charming. Intelligent. And, did I mention capital F-I-N-E. And to top it off, he was every bit of a gentleman. Held doors open, called to say hello in the middle of the day; sent gifts "just because"; catered to my every need and always made sure my sexual desires were fulfilled. The man knew how to make my toes curl, my eyes roll in the back of my head, and my body quiver every time he slid himself inside of me. Yes, he was the man with the magic hands, and the magic stick. I was hooked. And I almost lost my damn mind—literally speaking, when I found out he was married. *Married?!* Yes, the man whom I had been building my dreams around was with a wife, four children, a dog and a damn white picket fence.

Crazy thing. I stayed with him. Why? Because he loved me, so he said. Besides he was only with his wife for the children's sake. That's what he had said too. And, at that time, that's what I wanted to believe. How could I come between him and his children? I would have never forgiven myself. He even took it a step further by reassuring me that they shared separate bedrooms. He was no longer in love with her. No longer sexually attracted to her. That had to be true, too, since he was spending most of his nights with me. So, I remained the devoted mistress. Okay, smack me now why don't you. I was a damn fool. And I know it.

But I loved him. And, somewhere in the back corner of my twisted mind, I believed he would eventually leave her for me. Ha! What a joke. I believed he would get tired of the farce and realize he could still be a devoted, loving father out of that house, and away from his wife—with me. And stupid me held my breath waiting.

Then, gradually, things began to change. He started spending less and less time with me. Didn't respond to my pages right away. Stopped answering his cell phone or would be very short with me when he did. And when he did happen to drop by he'd stay for a few hours or so—just long enough to pop a nut, and then I wouldn't see or hear from him for three or four days; sometimes even longer. Why was *my* man doing this to me? That's all I wanted to know. Well, I got the answer to that million-dollar question the day I accidentally—okay, all right already. There was nothing accidental about it. My crazy side kicked in and I started following him for a few days. Okay, are you satisfied? Call it stalking if you want. Bottom line, I needed to find out what had him so preoccupied. And there stood the culprit who had all of his attention: A very pregnant woman. His wife.

I couldn't believe what I saw. The two of them laughing, and walking arm and arm. And then they stopped in the middle of the walkway, and he kissed her on the lips. I almost choked. My eyes burned with tears, but not one fell. I wanted to jump out of my Hertz rental and make a wild-woman dash across the street and cause a scene fit for an Oscar. But I restrained myself. Instead, I flipped open my cell and dialed his number. I watched him flip it open.

"Hello," he coolly said into the receiver.

"Bastard," I sneered into the phone.

"Who is this?" he asked, sounding genuinely confused. His wife gave him a quizzical look.

"When were you gonna tell me she was pregnant?"

He stopped in his tracks.

"Who is this?"

"Autumn," I snapped, "you lying motherfucker!"

"Uh, um. L-look," he said stammering, "I can't talk right now."

"I can see that," I shot back.

He looked around puzzled. "Meaning?"

"Meaning, I'm looking right at you." He shifted his weight from one foot to the other, looking around. His wife plopped her hands on her wide hips, then huffed off into one of the boutiques.

"Listen, how 'bout I give you a call later and we can talk face-to-face. It's not what you think."

"Nooooo!" I snapped, "How 'bout I walk up and slap you in your damn face for playing me, you lying son-of-a-bitch. Better yet, how about I introduce myself to your fucking wife."

"Where are you?" he asked in a panic.

"Don't worry about it. I'm right where I need to be. Watching you try to squirm your way out of this one."

"Come on Autumn stop playing. I don't have time for this right now."

The Mrs. came wobbling out of the door with a bag. "I gotta go," he said hurriedly. "I'll give you a call later on." *Click.*

Oh, no he didn't, I said to myself as I made my way across the street. *No good, lying-ass bastard.* My heart raced as I marched right up to the both of them, planting the palm of my hand dead square on the side of his face. *Slap!*

"What the hell is your problem, Bitch?" His wife snapped, dropping her bag to come at me. "Putting your damn hands on my husband." He grabbed her before she could reach me.

"Back off, lady," I responded. "This is between me and Trevor."

"And what is that supposed to mean?" she asked, glaring at me then him.

"Come on, baby," he said, pulling her by the arm. "She's buggin'."

"Buggin' hell," I snapped, placing one hand on my hip and twirling my other in the air. "It means you've been sharing him with me for the last three years."

"Say what?" She asked, snatching her arm away from him. "You've been doing what?"

"You heard me. Your husband's the damn problem. Not me. He's been lying to me for God knows how long, and obviously lying to you as well."

"Trevor," she bellowed, "This little girl better be fucking lying! Or we are gonna have problems." I ignored the 'little girl' remark, considering she looked like she was pushing her late forties. Just because I look younger than I am, don't hate, okay. And, yes, I was much younger than her—and him for that matter. Oh, don't get me wrong. She was cute, but not as cute as me. And her breasts clearly weren't as perky as mine. I'd almost bet the moment she removed her bra, those rolled-up titties of hers would flop down like a pair of click-clacks. And her waist would never again be as tight as mine. And I was sure she'd never be able to drop it like it's hot the way I do. So, I threw my head up, planted one hand on my round hip, and pushed my chest forward.

Pregnant or not, I thought, *she's still a fat bitch.* Damn piglet. I pursed my lips.

"Listen, baby," he said, pleading. "Calm down. I can explain."

"Calm down nothing!" she screamed. "I want to know right now what the hell she is talking about. And you got three seconds."

Now by this time, passersby are stopping and looking at the spectacles we've become. And now I'm going from being pissed off to deeply embarrassed, feeling like maybe I should have handled the situation a little differently. But it was too late, I had already pulled the cat out of the bag. I folded my arms and waited. Waited to hear what bucket of lies he was going to toss on her. Waited to see if I even mattered to him.

Long story short, I didn't. That no-good fool painted me out to be some raving lunatic. A stalker. Damn him! I was so darn furious I could have spit nails. Instead, I walked away, got behind the wheel of that blue Camry and drove off. Face forward, eyes straight ahead. And the minute I got home, I ran to my room, threw myself across my bed and cried until my chest felt like it would cave in. Since that day, I haven't seen or heard from him. Although I had heard he and his family have since moved to Roanoke, Virginia. How convenient.

Anyway, back to Morris and I. He continued, "Let me see you again."

I smiled. "Say when," I offered with more enthusiasm than I should have. But for some strange reason, I wanted to see him without being tanked up with the brown juice.

"Tonight," he replied.

My smile remained glued in place. "What time and I'm there."

"Say, eight-thirty. I'll come pass your place, so we can chill."

Silence. *My place, what kind of mess?* I had hoped he would have offered to take me out. Fat chance. I had a better chance of seeing it snow in hell.

"Hello, you there?" he asked.

"Uh, yeah," I responded in a deflated tone.

"So, what's up? We gonna chill tonight or what?" Now my head was screaming, "Girl, don't you dare bring him up in here. Let his sorry behind take you out." But, my neglected loins were shouting, "Bitch, get over yourself. You've been in a drought. The dick feels good, go for it." So, lust won.

"Eight-thirty's cool," I responded.

"Cool," he said, smiling through the phone. "Let me get your address." So after giving him directions we hung up and I straightened up, thinking that maybe him coming by wouldn't be so bad after all. Now call me old-fashioned, and whatnot; but normally when someone comes to your house for the first time they usually bring something, right? Like, a bottle of wine. Perhaps flowers. Maybe even a box of candy, right? Wrong! Cool breeze waltzed up in here an hour late, and empty damn handed. That should have been warning number one. But it wasn't. There was just something about his Colgate smile that I found enticing. So, I overlooked his oversight, chalking it up as poor etiquette or just plain ole poor home training. But one thing was for sure: he wasn't getting any panties no matter how damn sexy his smile was. And he didn't. Not that night, anyway. But eight days later, he did. And the sex was just as I had remembered it the first time. Good. Then again, I believe I was just too darn horny to know the difference.

Nia, of course, thought I should have waited a little longer; like a month or so. But of course this was coming from someone who really didn't have a good track record with men either. She could barely keep up with her man; yet, was trying to tell me the dos and don'ts of giving *it* up. Since when was she a damn expert on sex protocol, I wondered. So, of course I took her advice with a grain of salt. Now, in hindsight, maybe I should have taken her suggestion. Maybe I would have set a higher standard where this relationship is concerned. Oh, well.

Anyway, back to this fool over there in bed. Ugh! He just farted. How gross. If I can just find my damn shoes, I'd be outta here. Chile. Sometimes, I feel like I'm one foot in and one foot out of this relationship. I just for some reason haven't mustered up the nerve to completely walk out with both feet forward. I mean. He gets on my last nerve sometimes. But, between you and me, I can't get enough of that dick of his. Not that it's humongous or anything. It's average in length, but that width . . . humph. That's what keeps me dropping these drawers. Which is really another part of the problem. My problem. Because he doesn't seem to mind doing anything else but screwing 'til the cows come home.

I, on the other hand, would like more than just a good pumpin'. I mean. It would be nice to go out to dinner sometimes, catch a play or comedy show, or go to the movies instead of looking up at his paint-chipped, water-stained ceiling all the damn time. I can count on one hand the number of times he's actually taken me out without me having to badger him to death. Oh, a few times, he's called me over under the pretense of taking me out somewhere. But, when I get here, he's still in his boxers or has a towel wrapped around him. And before you know it, one thing leads to another and the only place I end up is on my back with my legs wrapped around his neck.

Then again, lying on my back is probably a better place to be than going to some of the low-budget places he's taken me. Now, I don't mind inexpensive; like I said, I am low maintenance, but don't play el cheapo all the time. Do you know the last time we went out he had me get all dolled-up, thinking we were going out for fine dining. And do you want to know where we ended up? The damn Cracker Barrel! You don't know how mad I was. Here I was decked out in my cute little black Anne Klein skirt set I had gone out and bought earlier in the day at Macy's, standing in my new Nine West pumps pissed off to the nth power. When we finally sat down he had the nerve to sit across from me and gaze into my eyes, smiling.

"Damn, baby. You one sweet cup of chocolate; I can't wait to get back home to slurp you up." He stroked my hand. I couldn't help but smile and gaze back at him, fantasizing about how he'd lick me up, down and all around. So much for being mad. We didn't even wait to get home. He paid the check and did me in the back seat of his truck, then politely dropped me off home.

Although I'd like to think our relationship isn't just based on sex, I have to really wonder exactly where it's heading. I mean. We've been seeing each other for close to two years and he's said nothing about any long-term commitment. I'll be twenty-eight in a few months, and I want to start making plans for a future—a future that consists of a husband and a new home. But every time I try to get him to open up to me—you know, express what he wants from me—he takes the easy way out by saying, "All of you."

Well, as far as I'm concerned, wanting all of me means wanting my mind, body *and* soul. Not just what's between my damn legs! He claims he has *feelings* for me. But not once—not even in the heat of passion—has he told me he loves me. Now what is that suppose to mean? Well. What it means is, I need to do another personal inventory and try to figure out why I'm still with him. 'Cause if I'm really, really honest with myself I'll see this so-called relationship for what it really is. And, probably take flight.

Between you and me. Now that I'm standing here, thinking about all this. He's stingy with his money, and is too damn stuck on dumb to know he has a good woman. It's obvious he's too set in his ways to change. And I have to wonder if he's even teachable. I mean. If he is, then he's about as trainable as an Autistic child whose blind and crippled. I don't care how many times I try to be the wind beneath his feeble wings he just seems to flutter off in the wrong direction. Yet, despite all of his shortcomings, there's a part of me that cares for him. I guess you can call him my autistic butterfly. And I'm the pitiful catcher, standing in the middle of empty promises holding out my net, patiently waiting for him to find his way in. So, when is enough going to be enough? I honestly don't know. I guess I just keep holding on, waiting for a miracle. They say, don't quit before the miracle. Humph.

After feeling around in the dark for God knows how long, I finally found my shoes, slipped them on my feet, then grabbed my car keys and purse. I glanced over at him one last time then looked around his room taking in the surroundings. Even in the dark, it was a hot mess. The gray area rug covering his dusty hardwood floors was frayed at the ends and needed a good vacuuming—better yet, needed to be pulled up and thrown out with the rest of the old shit in his four room hut.

I shook my head, imagining what Nia would say if she *really* knew how low I had stooped. I'd be the laughing stock of the town. The classy Miss Autumn Marie Brimmington strung out on a thirty-seven-year-old man who uses living room drapes as a shower curtain, has newspaper up at his windows instead of shades, and a room full of mismatched, chipped up furniture. And the only thing I can come up to say in his defense: He has a nice, fat dick.

The more I think about this whole situation, I really have to wonder who's more pathetic, him or me? I quietly opened the door, then gently closed it, slipping out into the night air with the tune "The Whole Town's Laughing At Me," ringing in my ears.

Three

Nia

"It's about damn time," I snapped through clenched teeth. I didn't even bother asking him where his key was. Nope. We didn't live together. Not that I didn't want to. But I wanted to be married. That is the one thing Autumn and I had in common, the No Shacking rule. Well, maybe not. She didn't even allow her man to stay the night. I did. Hell, he had clothes hanging in the closet, and was here at least four nights a week. And he had mail coming to the house. Anyway.

He sucked his teeth, walking by me. "Yo, what you tryna beef about now?" I slammed the door behind him. He grabbed me, trying to get a kiss.

I pushed him back. "Who the hell is Keyonna?"

He scrunched his face up. Standing there, looking like he just stepped off the cover of *Source,* sporting a black Yankees fitted cap, and a black Sean Jean jacket over a white Tee and black jeans. The diamonds from his two-carat earrings and thirty-six inch encrusted chain flickered in the light. "Who? I don't know no Kenya."

"I didn't say *Kenya.* I said, Keyonna. Now who is she?"

"Oh, her," he said without blinking an eye. "She used to mess with one of my mans. Why?"

Okay, so he was gonna play games. I felt the urge to slap him wash over me like a tsunami. I willed myself still, slamming my hand on my hip. Now, normally, I'm ladylike in my daily approach to life. But when I'm mad, I can get as ghetto as they come. And you best believe cursing becomes a prerequisite. And right about now, I was feeling ghetto to the highest power.

"Don't fucking stand here and try to insult my damn intelligence Mustafa."

"What you mean?" he asked.

"Don't play games with me. I'm not in the damn mood."

"I'm telling you," he said, tripping over his thick tongue. "I don't know who you're talking about."

"Just a few minutes ago you said she used to mess with one of your mans. Now you don't know who I'm talking about. Now, I'm gonna ask you again. Who the hell is she? And don't give me that 'I don't know shit'. And she damn sure wasn't *messin'*, as you say, with one of you damn mans. So don't give me that shit either."

Silence.

I reached into my back pocket, yanking out two of the letters. I threw them at him. He quickly glanced down at his feet. But didn't budge.

"'Cause from where I'm standing, you seem to know her pretty damn well since she's carrying your baby."

"What the fuck you talking 'bout?" he retorted, quickly scooping up the letters, then crumbling them up. "That chick ain't pregnant. Not by me."

"So now you know who the hell I'm talking about," I snapped back.

"Yeah. I told you I know her."

"Oh, but just a few minutes ago you didn't. Now you do. Which is it?"

"Are you gonna let me explain?"

"Go, 'head," I said, planting both hands on my hips. "I'm listening,"

"She and one of my mans was dealin' for a minute; but then they started beefin' and shit—"

"What the hell does that have to do with you and her?" I cut in, rolling my eyes. "If she was dealing with your *man,* as you say, then why the hell is she writing you?"

"Are you gonna let me talk," he snapped, "or are you gonna keep jumping to conclusions?"

I gritted my teeth. "I'm not trying to hear your half-assed bullshit. I want a straight damn answer from you, Mustafa. And I want it now."

He sighed, rubbing his chin, and shifting his eyes. "The truth?"

"That would be nice," I responded sarcastically. "If you can ever get to it."

"Can you promise to hear me out, and not start snappin'?"

"Go 'head, Mustafa."

I folded my arms, and waited.

He sat on the arm of the sofa. "It ain't nothin'."

"What do you mean 'it ain't nothin'?" I asked, trying to calm myself before I tore my living room up.

"Just what I said. I hit it a couple of times and that was that. It didn't mean shit to me. It was just sex. Then she started buggin'."

This fool had the nerve to be nonchalant about it. Like, oh well. I sucked my teeth, rolling my eyes so hard I thought they'd snap out of their sockets. I felt like bashing him in his face. "Well, not judging by those damn letters. Seems like a whole lot of something to me. And how the fuck you know she's not pregnant by you?"

"Because she's not. The ho is crazy."

"Oh, now she's a ho? That's so damn typical."

"Well, she is. She let several cats run up in her."

"But that didn't stop you from letting her wet *your* damn dick and you getting her pregnant, now did it?"

"Will you stop saying that shit, I told you I didn't get her pregnant."

"So, you're gonna sit here and tell me you used condoms?"

I paced the room. One hand on my hip, the other balled in a fist.

He didn't answer. Now call me crazy if you want; but the ultimate disrespect to me is not the actual act of cheating; it's cheating on your mate and *not* using a damn condom. How dare you put someone else's health and life at risk, or bring a child into the relationship, all because you have some self-serving need to fulfill wanton desires!

I screamed on him. "How the fuck you gonna raw dog this chick, and then come up in here and have me sucking all over your fucking dick like shit is sweet?! That's some real foul shit, Mustafa." I snatched my crystal vase off the end table and threw it at him. He ducked. It smashed against the wall, leaving a big hole and an imprint of my anger.

"Damn. Why you buggin'?"

"Negro, I'm buggin' because I feel like you fucking disrespected me. And I'm not feeling that. You stuck your damn dick in some chick who claims she's knocked up by you. And then you gonna tell me, she was a damn ho. Like that's supposed to clear the damn air. You must be out of your fucking mind."

"Listen, okay," he pleaded, sounding like an ass. "I was wrong. I got on some impulsive shit, and wasn't thinking. It was a mistake."

"Bullshit!" I snapped. "You knew just what the fuck you were doing." I stared him down, trying to get my thoughts in order before I busted up everything in the house. I caught a glimpse of the 16 x 20 portrait of my grandmother hanging on the dining room wall. For a split second, it felt like she was shaking her head at me. I erased the image out of my mind. "And, now you got the audacity to sit here and tell me it was a mistake. How fucking convenient."

"I'm telling you. I deaded it when I realized she was a nut."

"Yeah right! Well, you should have kept your nut to yourself and we wouldn't be having this conversation. But you didn't. You get caught up in some relationship with some other chick. And I was the one holding your stupid ass down. What kind of shit is that?"

"I wasn't in no *relationship* with her," he reasoned like that was supposed to make a difference. "So, stop saying that shit. We just fucked."

"Oh, really. Well, when'd you start fucking her?"

"I don't know."

"What do you mean you don't know?"

"I don't remember."

"Bullshit," I snapped. "So, don't sit there and give me that shit."

Silence.

"I'm waiting," I said, tapping my foot against the carpet.

He let out a deep sigh. "Like around April."

"April of this year?"

"Nah, last year."

I squinted my eyes, then started counting in my head. Jan, Feb, Mar. Wait a damn minute! He had left the Assessment Center for the halfway house in the beginning of January and was able to get out to look for work around March. Most times, I was picking him up, and we were getting our groove-on on those days he was *supposed* to be out looking for a job. And supposedly he couldn't get out on the weekends. And, I didn't do the weekend visit thing. But, every Tuesday and Thursday, I was there at the corner gas station waiting for him, faithfully. However, there were a few times he claimed he only had two hours to return. So, on those days, he went out on his own. Hmm. Probably to fuck. But when he finally did get a job, I was picking him up every damn night. And we went to either a motel or back to my place where we fucked, screwed, made love and everything else in between, then I'd drive him back to the damn halfway house.

"Where'd you meet her?"

"At the halfway house."

"What, she was coming up to see you?"

He shook his head. "Nah."

"Well, then how'd you meet her? At work?"

"I told you. At the halfway house."

"So you were screwing one of the counselors?"

He shook his head. "Nah."

"Wait a minute. You mean to tell me. She was up in there with you?"

"Yeah."

Now, you know I was really disgusted. Of course I wanted to know how and when he was able to get with her in the building if there were counselors there. He explained how the male and female residents attended certain groups together and how on certain shifts the counselor's were too busy doing their own thing, and weren't really too beat to pay attention to what was going on in the building. So a few times, he and this chick were able to sneak off to one of the empty rooms and do their thing. Other times, they got it off when they went out on their weekend store runs. The counselor would just drop everyone off and tell them what time to meet back. So, they'd hit the motel. Ugh! I was hot, to say the least.

I did that whole fucking four-year bid with him, never missing a beat. From collect calls to visits—running up and down the damn highway—to making sure he had money on his books. I put my ass on the front line for him. Not once cheated on him, or denied him anything. And he gets out and screws some chick in a matter of months.

Slap!

He jumped up, shocked that I had slapped his face. But he took it. I raised my hand to slap him again, but wasn't fast enough. He grabbed me by the wrist. "Come on now. I know I was wrong. But, you're not going to be putting your hands on me."

"Get your damn hand off of me," I snapped, yanking my arm away.

He stepped back further, giving himself more space between us. He rubbed the side of his face.

My jaws tightened. "How many times you fuck her?"

"What?"

"You heard me. How many times did you fuck her?" I repeated, glaring at him.

"A couple of times."

"What's a couple of times, Mustafa, three, four, five times?"

"Look. I fucked up. Does all that really matter?"

"Yes it matters," I snapped. "I wanna know how many times you stuck your damn dick in her?"

"I don't know," he said. "I didn't keep count; maybe five or six times. Why? I said it wasn't nothin'."

"Fuck that. It *is* something. Maybe not to you, but to me it is. You up in the damn halfway house sleeping around then got the nerve to be all up in my face."

"Come on Nia, listen," he pleaded. "I fucked up."

"You already said that," I replied nastily.

"Listen, baby," he responded, lowering his voice.

"Don't fucking 'baby' me."

"I didn't mean to do it. It just happened. She was feelin' me, making passes and shit and I just got on some 'let me knock her back out real quick'. That's all. I got caught up in the moment. Then shit got out of hand. I'm telling you it was a mistake."

The more he talked, the crazier he sounded to me. "Nigga," I screamed, "mistake my ass! A mistake happens one time. Not three, four, five damn times. That sounds planned to me. You knew what the hell you were doing. So, don't give me that shit, talking 'bout you didn't mean to do it. NO, you didn't mean to get your dumb ass caught."

"Listen. You got a right to be mad—"

"You fucking right I do," I interrupted.

"But, you blowing shit out of proportion. You're going off about something that happened over a year ago."

"Over a year ago my ass. Where'd those letters come from then?"

"Those letters are old. I was still in the halfway house when she wrote them. I forgot I even had them shits. Do you see any dates on them?"

I rolled my eyes. He just never ceased to amaze me. Though he did have a point. No matter how moot. But I didn't care. He cheated on me and that was all that mattered.

"So, why the hell you keep them then if she didn't mean nothing, huh?"

Silence.

"Just what I thought." At that moment, a tear slid down my face. "You ain't shit Mustafa. That's real fucked up."

"Yo, come on, baby. I'm telling you the truth. I mean. I have no reason to lie to you. Like I said, those letters are old. I just didn't get around to throwing them out. Hell, where'd you find them any way?"

"Why the fuck does that matter, where I found them? The fact is I found them, and you were cheating on me."

"But, it's old news."

"So what!" I yelled. "I'm finding out about it now."

"But, it didn't mean anything," he reiterated for the umpteenth time. "I only cheated once. That's it."

"Bullshit! You cheated more than once."

"Okay. You right. But she's the only chick I slept with," he reasoned.

I rolled my eyes. "And that's supposed to make it better?"

"I'm not sayin' that. I know I was wrong. I fucked up. But since I left the halfway house, you're the only one I've been with. Real talk, baby." He grabbed me, trying to wrap his arms around me.

"Don't 'baby' me," I snapped, pushing him off of me. I paced the room. "I can't believe you were fucking playing me." I wiped the tears from my eyes, trying to catch them before they fell.

"Come on, now. Don't cry. That bitch didn't mean shit. It was just a nut. If anything, she got played. That's why she started buggin' and shit. I fucked up."

I glared at him.

"And, I'm sorry." He lowered his voice, and looked at me with pleading eyes, reaching for me again. This time I didn't move. "Don't you know I love you? You're my heart. I just really moved off of impulse. After being locked up for four years, she was throwing the pussy at me. And I took it. I was wrong for that. But you gotta know I wouldn't do anything to fuck up what we have, baby." He kissed me on the forehead, then my nose. He kissed my tears away. "You're my everything, baby. You hear me?" He brushed his lips against mine, then kissed me. I stood there stone still.

He kissed me again. "You hear me?"

This time I nodded, getting lost in his tongue. I closed my eyes, slipping. Believing. Then I came to my senses again. I pulled away from him.

"What's her last name?" I asked.

He frowned. "What?"

"You heard me. What's her last name," I repeated, looking him in his eyes.

"Why you wanna know all that?"

Please. If Miss Lady was up in there with him, I wanted to know what she had done time for, and for how long. I wanted to know what type of criminal he had stuck his dick in. And I wanted to know what the hell she looked like. That's right, I was going on the Department of Corrections website and pulling up her damn info. Believe that.

"What's her last name, Mustafa?" I asked again, tilting my head.

"Come on, Nia. You really buggin', now. I said it was nothing."

"If it's really nothing, then you shouldn't have a problem telling me her last name."

"I don't know what her last name is. I told you all we did was fuck."

"You're lying," I said, crossing my arms over my chest.

"Damn," he snapped defensively. "Why do I have to be lying? I'm telling you. I don't know what her last name is."

"Hmm. Hmm. Yeah, right. You screw her five or six damn times, lying up in a motel room, and I'm supposed to believe that. Give me a damn break, Mustafa. I know you and her spent time swapping war stories. So, don't give me that. And until I get her last name, you and I are going to be beefing."

"What the fuck you need to know that for?" he asked again, allowing frustration to etch his forehead.

"Because I want it. That's why. Now what is it?"

"I don't remember," he retorted. "But, I'm sure you won't believe that either."

"You're right. So where is she?"

"I don't know. She bounced on parole."

"Humph."

He shook his head, staring at me. "What the fuck you snooping in my shit for anyway? You real fucking sneaky."

"Oh, hell no!" I yelled. "Nigga, you are not going to try to flip this one on me. I'm not the one who got busted. You did. And for your information, I wasn't snooping. I just happened to come across it. So, don't even go there." And that was the truth. Now let me think. How did I come across those letters anyway? Oh that's right. I was cleaning out the hallway closet, throwing stuff out and came across a box he had left here when he first paroled from the halfway house. So I started going through it. And voilà! I come across letters stuck in a black and white composition book.

He sucked in the air around him.

"You know what, just get out," I snapped, storming over to the front door, then swinging it open. "I'm done going around in circles with you. I want her damn last name and until I get it, I'm done with you. Now get the fuck out!"

"I can't believe you really fuckin' taking this shit to the extreme."

"Extreme, my ass. I want her last name, and that's that."

He tsked, shaking his head. "Whatever!" He snapped, snatching his jacket off the arm of the chair. "I'm out." He brushed past me, leaving behind a trail of unanswered questions. "I ain't beat for this shit right now."

"Well, you don't ever have to be beat!" I yelled, slamming the door behind him, then leaned my back against it and slowly slid down to the floor, pulling my legs up to my chest and wrapping my arms around them. I heard the faint sound of his car door slam, then the purr of his engine before the tires screeched out of the driveway. I rested my chin on my knees, closing my eyes. I needed to think about what my next course of action was going to be. Bottom line: I wanted answers. I needed to know who this chick was who would die if he ever left her.

I wanted to know who *my* man had been giving his dick to, making feel good. Giving her the pleasures that should have only been mine to enjoy. I was honestly jealous. And hurt. That he had served her, and served her well. Because if nothing else, Mustafa Abraham Peters was capable of making a woman see the stars and the moon in one orgasm. He is longwinded, and long and thick and knows how to hit all the right spots. Yes, I was fucking jealous!

Then my mind started wandering. And the tears started falling. Hard. My mind really started playing tricks on me. I imagined her with her legs up over his shoulders, and him deep thrusting her the way he does me. I started seeing images of her on her side, and him slipping himself inside of her from the back, slowly gliding in and out of her. I tried to find her face in a crowd of faceless images. But came up blank. I needed to know what this ho looked like. Oh, excuse me. I know I said I didn't want to call her out of her name because I hated when we did that. But, right at that moment, I was too damn mad to call her anything else other than that. A damn ho! My mind was swirling a mile a minute.

And what about this baby, what if she really was pregnant by him? Then what? I honestly I didn't think I could handle knowing he fathered a child outside of this relationship. It just would be a constant reminder of his infidelity. I burst into tears, again. I knew how bad he wanted a child. Just before he went for sentencing, he had asked me to have his baby. And I sort of laughed it off to myself, never really saying "no" but never officially agreeing either. The thought of going through a pregnancy by myself wasn't appealing to me. Besides, I felt like that was more of a way to ensure I didn't flee when the going got rough. Not that I intended to. I had promised him I was going to do that bid with him, and I did.

And, since being home, he's made it very clear how bad he still wants to spawn. I know the way I said that sounds almost like preparing for mating season. Sometimes that's how I feel. Yet, it remains something I haven't been ready to do. One: I 'd like to go to Law School, and do something a little more exciting than what I'm already doing down at the Court House. Working in the child support division of Family Court, listening to dumb ass chicks lie about the whereabouts of their babies daddies, and working around a bunch of ghetto bitches isn't my idea of a rewarding career. But for now it pays *most* of the bills.

And, two: He's only been home from prison a year. And, although he's working, I'd like to know he's committed to holding down a job for at least two years. Preferably three, considering he's someone whose never held down a job for any long period of time. Well actually, before getting knocked, he never had a job. Not a real one anyway. I mean . . . Ugh, forget it. I don't know what I mean. All I know is if I'm going to have a baby with him, I need to know he's done with the streets. And right now, I know he still has a run in him. Although, he tells me he doesn't. However, a part of me doesn't believe him. Call it woman's intuition. Call it a gut feeling. Call it whatever you want. I just know I'm not interested in lugging a baby up to a prison to visit its father. But I love him. And I do believe, if nothing else, that he loves me as well.

The ringing telephone disrupted my one-woman pity party. And instead of ignoring it, I jumped up and glanced at the caller ID, then picked up. It was Nygeria.

"Hey," I said, dryly.

"Damn, who pissed in your Cheerios this morning?" she asked.

"I just got finished jumping in Mustafa's shit," I replied.

"Uh-oh. Anything you wanna vent about?"

"Girl, I don't even want to get into it."

"Okay. Say no more. I was just calling to see if you wanted to hit the Mall."

"Nah," I said, sighing. "I'm not in the mood."

"Whaaat, *you* not in the mood? Humph. He must have really wrecked your nerves."

"That's putting it mildly. But, I'll get over it."

"Well, you know, if you wanna talk about it, I'm here."

"I know, thanks. Hold, on," I said, rolling my eyes at the caller ID. "It's Mustafa's ass on the other line."

"You go 'head and deal with him. I'll get up with you later," she said.

"Alright. I'll hit you later." I clicked over.

"What?" I asked, nastily.

"Yo, what the fuck is wrong with you?"

"I don't fucking appreciate what you did. That's what the fuck is wrong with me. Trying to fuckin' play me."

"I wasn't playin' you," he replied. "I just got caught up in some real dumb shit. That's all."

"Yeah, right. And, I'm Boo-boo the damn fool. So you can kiss my natural-black ass 'cause I'm not trying to hear shit you gotta say unless you're given me that chick's last name. Period."

"So you gonna be a real bitch about this, right?"

"Exactly."

He sucked his teeth. "I don't know why you gotta be so fucking dramatic about shit."

"Ohhhh, well," I snapped. "The same reason you're fucking full of shit."

"Listen," he said, lowering his voice. "I don't wanna beef with you. I made a mistake. And I'm sorry. But, you don't have to blow it up to be something more than what it was."

"Excuse you?"

"Stop overreacting," he replied.

"Whatever, Mustafa." *Click.*

So maybe, I was going overboard. Maybe. I mean. Other than that one little incident, he'd never given me any reason to doubt him. So why should I start now. Perhaps he was right. I was overreacting. After all, he did say it happened last year. And, maybe it was just a slip-up, right? Hell, he's a man. And men are notorious for thinking with their dicks. Not that it makes it right. It's just what it is. No ones perfect. And I'm certain it was just what he said: a mistake, and an isolated incident. Humph. Maybe. Anyway, that's what my heart was telling me. After all, I'm the one he's with. I'm the one he's coming home to. Well, that's what I wanted to believe, and that's what I did believe. Stupid me.

Four

Autumn

"Damn, baby. This pussy's good," he moaned in my ear, thrusting his eight-inches in and out of me. "Oh, baby."

I closed my eyes real tight, and held my breath, trying to suppress a moan. Girlfriend was dog-tired after working all day, and had a sudden splitting headache from his hot breath in my face. But the way he was pumping inside of me sure did feel good. He had my legs up and spread wide open with the palm of his hands on the inside of my thighs, watching himself slide in and out of me. Hitting that spot just the way I liked it. Finally, he lifted his left hand from off my thigh, licked his thumb with that long tongue of his, then pressed on my clit. Immediately, I felt the surge of an orgasm swell and swirl. I bit my bottom lip, relenting. Forgetting about the pounding in my head.

"Hmmm. Hmmm. Uh."

"Yeah, you like that, don't you?" he asked. I moaned again. "That's right. Show daddy how you like it," he chanted. I moaned louder; this time grabbing on to his ass. He was already knocking the walls just right. I just wanted him deeper in me. Needed him to bang the headache away. Here it was ten, forty-seven on a Thursday night and I was once again lying on my back on his damn paper-thin mattress. But I knew if we didn't hurry this up, it'd be one in the morning. And I needed to be up at seven. There was just no way I could handle another long-winded session. Especially with the springs of his bed stabbing me in my back. Ugh, I swear I'm gonna end up with spine injury by the time this is all over.

"Let me get on my knees, Daaaaady," I begged in between shallow breaths. He loved it when I called him that, especially when it's drawn out—as do most men. And I knew if he hit it doggie-style it would only be a matter of moments before he let loose his love juices. That was just one position that was sure to get him to blast off without much effort. He loved watching my soft bubble-butt bounce and shake while he pumped in and out of me.

Truth be told, I could kick myself for leaving the comforts of my own home. When he called me at five-thirty asking if I was coming over, I told him *no*. Told him I'd see him tomorrow. Told him I had things to do. Nothing pressing. I just wanted some "me" time. I wanted to finish watching Shaka Zulu—again for the sixtieth time, then take me a long, hot bubble bath. I wanted to light a few candles, listen to Will Downing and Gerald Albright's, *Pleasures of the Night* CD while fantasizing about Shaku sliding his Mandigo dick in me. From the neck down, that Zulu warrior was one sexy man. He was hard on the eyes, but I loved his body. So, I'd replace his face with Morris' and drift off into a self-induced orgasm. Umm . . . question: is fantasizing about someone you know you'll *never* be with a form of cheating? If it is, then I've been one unfaithful soul. Because, between you and me, I've had affairs—in my head—with not only Shaka, but L.L., Jayson Williams and—scream on me if you want—Lloyd Banks. There's just something about that man I find so daggone sexy. Anyway, that was my plan. To fantasize and masturbate, but Morris wouldn't take no for an answer.

"I wanna see you," he had said in a low, husky whisper.

"Not tonight," I replied. "I'm really beat."

"Come on, baby. Just for an hour; then you can get some sleep."

"No."

"How 'bout I come over there," he offered knowing daggone well I wasn't going to allow him to lie in *my* bed and get in my panties. If a man wants to lay up with me, he'll have to do it at his own place. That's my house rule. Of course, Nia thinks it's crazy. But crazy or not, it's a rule I refuse to break. Well, okay. Alright, already . . . I'm lying. I broke it with that cheating, lying behind Trevor. Had him all up in my place. He even had a key. He sure did. Came in and out of here anytime he wanted. And took the pussy—oh, I hate using that word. It sounds so nasty. Oh, well. Anyway, he got in these panties anytime he wanted. That's how strung out I was. Humph. On second thought, I was just young, dumb and hot in the tail.

Nana had made it very clear it wasn't ladylike to court a man in your home. But I didn't listen. *Don't ever let a man lay up on you. Make him put a ring on your finger and take you to his place.* I let her warning go in one ear and out the other. Here I was twenty-two, going on twenty-three, messing with a forty-three year old man. I just knew I was the shit. Please. I should have known better. Should have recognized something wasn't right with his sorry behind when we first started seeing each other and the only contact number I had for him was his cell number. Anytime a man I'm dating or seeing can't give me his home number, warning bells ring loud and clear. But with Trevor, I ignored them. Why wouldn't I? Everyone has a cell hooked to his or her hip, so who needs a home phone, right? Please. I should have known he was up to no good when he'd never invite me to his place. He always had some excuse. And I brought it hook, line and sinker.

Like I said, once he told me he was married I still stayed with him. Out of pure stupidity. But the minute I stumbled onto the truth—about him *still* fucking his wife, and her being pregnant—I had my good cry, then had my door locks and the alarm code changed. Sure did. So, you better believe, no other man will lie up in here. Boyfriend or not, I don't care. I don't want any man getting too comfortable here. And, since there's still no ring on my finger, it's a rule I will live and die by. No matter how bad I'd prefer to be in my own plush bed. So until Morris puts a rock on my hand, I'll suffer through nights at his run down place, and on his raggedy-assed bed. Anyway . . .

"No," I said with an exasperated sigh. "Not tonight. I'm too tired."

"Too tired for your man?" he asked, sounding like he was about to lose his best friend.

"Yes," I replied. "I don't feel like driving to Newark tonight."

"I'll come get you."

I sucked my teeth. "Morris, no."

"Fuck it then," he snapped, slamming the phone down in my ear. My sentiments exactly, I said aloud. Sometimes, I'm just not in the mood to be around him. As much as I care about him, sometimes he just rattles my last nerve with his complacency. I mean. At thirty-seven, how can any man be okay with not owning his own home. How can you not want more with your life. And how can you be okay sleeping on that damn bed. But, Morris just seems so content. I mean. He's a hardworking man. I'll give him that. But, like I told you, he's cheap. Just works and hordes all of his money. Truth be told, I don't know exactly what he does with it since he spends very little on me. Or him. But I told him, when he dies he can't take it with him. So why not spend it—well, at least some of it. Invest. That's what I tell him. But he looks at me like I have two heads or something.

Here I am, almost twenty-eight-years old, and I own my own home. Thanks to the insurance money Nana left Nia and me, and the sale of her house. At twenty-one, I bought me a two-story, cute fixer-upper in Orange (New Jersey that is) and have watched my investment almost triple over the last six years. And I still have a few dollars tucked in a Money Market account for emergencies. And a portfolio of stocks that continues to grow. But he doesn't know that. Shoot. Never let a man know all of your finances. That's another rule of mine. And never loan a man you're seeing money, no matter what the circumstances. Another rule I live by. One I learned the hard way. Messing with that damn Marcus, another *ex* of mine.

Marcus wasn't the finest of men. And he didn't have the greatest body. But he was the sweetest, gentlest man I'd ever known. And a damn con artist like no other. Had me thinking he needed money to fly to California to see his ailing mother. The one who was dying from cancer! Now, my instincts were telling me to let him scrape up the money somewhere else. So I told him no. But when he broke down in tears, I caved in. How could I deny him? Picture a six-foot-four, strapping man balling his eyes out, okay. Ugh, it was . . . hmm, let me see. An incredible damn performance that's what it was. But, I fell for it just the same.

"Baby," he had said, with wet eyes and slob and snot flying everywhere. "I really need your help. I got to get out there before it's too late."

"Can't your family send it to you?" I asked still feeling skeptical.

"Everyone's strapped," he replied, wiping his face with his sleeve and blowing his nasty nose. "With all my mom's hospital bills, things are really tight. I need you to trust me on this. I wouldn't be asking you for the money if I really weren't in a bind." He broke down again. "I need you to have my back, baby."

I gave him a hug filled with compassion, and empathy. We had been dealing with each other for six months, and he had always treated me like a lady. Always wined and dined me. So, like a fool believing him, I gave him the thousand dollars for his emergency plane ticket with the understanding that he'd give me my money back the minute he returned from his trip. Well, minutes turned into hours. Hours turned into days. Days turned into weeks. Weeks turned into months, and the fool never came back. No phone call. No postcard. No see ya when I see ya. I was too through.

Finally, five months later, I'm coming out of the Washington Mutual on Market Street in Newark, preparing to cross the street when I think I hear my name being called. I look around but don't see any familiar faces, so I keep up with my pace trying to avoid getting hit by traffic-goers and buses. Then someone catches up to me, and taps me on the shoulder.

"Excuse me," she says, trying to catch her breath, "is your name Autumn?"

"Excuse you?" I say, swinging around to face her with attitude. Her doobie was tight, and her face neatly made-up.

"Autumn, right?"

"Yes," I reluctantly respond, looking her up and down, frowning up my face then looking around to see whom else was with her. Although girlfriend looked harmless, I wasn't going to underestimate her. Shoot a sista can never be too sure with these Newark chicks. I wasn't in the mood for a fight, and I definitely wasn't feeling up to getting jumped by a bunch of thugettes, if you know what I mean.

"I knew you looked familiar," she continues. "I'm Janelle."

"Okay," I reply, trying not to lose my patience. "How can I help you?"

"Well, I was wondering how you were holding up?"

"Come again."

"I'm so sorry to hear about your mother," she says with sincerity. My eyes bulged, and my mouth dropped open as she continued. "I wanted to go to the funeral but Marcus told me it was only for close family." *Marcus?* Oh hell no, I thought to myself, it's about to be on. *Marcus and I losing our mother; what kind of games?* I felt my nerves start to rattle. But I kept my composure. I had no idea what this child was talking about. Honestly, I thought she might be a bit *touched*, if you know what I mean. But the look she gave me was that of genuine concern so it led me to believe she didn't know any better.

I close my mouth, then open it to speak. "Sweetie, I lost my mother years ago. So I have no idea what you're talking about."

She tilts her head. "Aren't you Marcus' sister?"

"Where in the world did you get that idea?" I ask incredulously. "And how do you know him?"

"From the pictures of the two of you," she explains. Well, come to find out, he was dating her and me at the same time. And gave her that bull crap story about me being his sister when she questioned him about all of the pictures he had of me, and the ones we had taken together at Six Flags. "He told me you were his sister. I'm his girlfriend."

"His girlfriend?" I repeat.

She nods her head. "Well, I mean, I was."

"Is that so."

"Yeah," she says, pausing for a beat. "He never mentioned me to you?"

"Not at all," I reply. Now my nostrils are starting to flare. This shit was starting to get too much for me, but I decided to give it to her straight. "I don't know what kind of lies his fake behind has been feeding you, but I'm not his sister. I *was* dealing with him, too, up until he took off with my damn money. I haven't heard from him or seen him in months. So, if he is or was your man, when you see him let him know I'm looking for him."

This time her mouth drops. "Oh, shit!" she snaps, holding the side of her face in disbelief. "You've got to be kidding." The look on her face told me she too had been on the receiving end of his bull.

"Let me guess. He broke down in tears and told you he needed money to see his dying mother."

She nods again. "Basically. Told me he'd give it back—"

"As soon as he got back," I finish for her. "And that was months ago."

She nods, again. Stunned. "I can't believe that nigga played me."

"Welcome to the club," I say, giving her a knowing look. "How much did he get you for?"

"Three thousand dollars," she says. I shudder at the thought of giving him that much. She goes on to tell me how she gave him a thousand for his plane ticket, and spent the other two thousand on a suit and shoes for him. Right then, I decide my loss was definitely not as great as hers. Poor thing.

I shake my head. "Well, he only got a thousand out of me, but he'll get a beat down to go along with that if I ever run into him again."

"Make that from the both of us."

Silence. We stare at each other. Feel a kinetic bond forming.

"Niggas ain't shit," we blurt out in unison. We give each other a sympathetic smile, then exchange phone numbers just in case one of us ever happens to run into him again.

Well, that's been well over four years and we still haven't seen or heard from his punk-ass. I'm sure he's somewhere else milking some other unsuspecting soul out of her hard-earned dollars. So, thanks to that awful experience, no man can ever get another dime out of me. I don't care who he is, or what it's for. Death, medical emergency; it doesn't matter. Bottom line: His intestines could be hanging out of his ass, and he'd just be shit out of luck.

Anyway, one hour goes by, and Morris calls back and tries to cajole me into coming over. Again I say no. Then another hour goes by, and he still hasn't gotten the hint: I don't want to see you tonight. *Click.* Well, this fool hops in his Grand Cherokee and drives over to my house and starts ringing the doorbell, and banging on my door like he has lost the rest of his mind.

"What are you doing over here," I asked, opening the door.

"What you think," he replied, walking in, then closing the door behind him. "I told you I wanted to see you tonight." He stared at me real hard for a minute, knitting his brows. "Why you got that on?" he asked, gazing at me in my black-laced teddy and matching robe.

"I felt like being sexy," I said. Damn. Can't a girl have a moment to herself? Sometimes I like to come home and slip into my silky lingerie and just chill, by myself. Like I said, "me" time.

"Oh, but not for your man," he snapped with an attitude. I caught him scanning around the living room, searching for God knows what. Humph. He probably thought I had another man up in there. I could see his nostrils flaring as he took in the ambiance of the room. Sandalwood candles burning; jazz in the background. Yeah, he thought I had company all right.

He walked up on me, grabbing me by the waist. "Who you getting all sexy for?"

"Me," I said, rolling my eyes. "I told you that already." He pressed himself into me. Damn he smelled good.

"Yeah, aiight." He let me go, walking through the house blowing out my candles. Then with the press of the remote, turned off my stereo.

"What do you think you're doing?"

"I'm shutting this one-woman party down," he replied. "That's what. So, go get your coat and let's go." Well, alright daddy, I thought to myself, smirking. And, yes, I like it when he *thinks* he's taking charge.

"Morris, come on now," I said, feigning a pout while tying the belt of my robe around my waist. "I told you I'm tired."

"Well, I can't tell," he snapped. "Prancing around half-assed naked like you waiting for some dick." I rolled my eyes in mock disgust, walking past him. He grabbed me by the arm. "Who you waiting for?"

I sucked my teeth. "Will you stop bugging," I replied, snatching my arm from him.

"Oh, I'm bugging?" he asked, unzipping his pants and pulling out his dick. He grabbed me with both hands practically pushing me up against the wall, then pressed himself into me, while shoving his tongue in my mouth. I responded, letting him find his way between my legs with his fingers. *I should have made him wash his hands first,* I thought. But I let him rub and tease me down there anyway, brushing my spot with his rough hands. I was already wet from playing with myself so it didn't take much. *Forget Shaka*, I thought as he yanked the string of my teddy. I opened my legs just enough for him to slide in me, then gasped. Oh, his dick feels so good in me. Damn him! So, he popped that first nut in me up against the wall, and would have gotten ready for another round had I not stopped him.

"Lets go back to your place," I said, trying to collect myself before he started taking off his clothes to get comfortable.

"Why can't we just chill here?" he asked, nibbling on my neck.

"Because," I stated, moving my neck away from his mouth. I freed myself from his grip, readjusting my lingerie. "I told you, I'm not allowing you or any other man to lay up in here. Period."

"I'm not just *any* man," he snapped. "I'm *your* man."

"Well, *my* man. I suggest you put a ring on *my* finger, 'cause until you do you won't be laying up in here."

He sucked his teeth, mumbling under his breath. "Yeah, whatever. You and these stupid ass rules."

"You right, whatever," I snapped. "But if you want to crawl up in this pussy it's a rule you'll have to live by." I really hated when I had to use that P word. It's so unladylike. Oh, well.

He shook his head, letting out a sigh of frustration. "Let's go." Humph. I guess I was supposed to care about his little attitude. Not.

"Lets," I responded, opening up the hall closet and pulling my black trench off its wooden hanger, then putting it on. So, here I am. Back at his filthy place wondering when the hell he's going to clean up. Surprisingly, he does change his sheets weekly; but anything else, forget it.

Anyway . . . Finally after begging and pleading in soft moans for him to take me from behind, he does. Sweat dripped from his face, splattering on my back. He pounded me like an overheated locomotive. I arched my back, dug my nails into his springs and bit into the pillow. I could feel his throttle thicken. I squeezed my vagina. And within minutes it was over. Thank goodness. Three minutes later, he rolled over and started snoring like he had just been hit with a tranquilizer. Ugh. Men.

Silently, I watched him sleep. Listened to his light snore, then jumped out of his bed and onto his dirty floor, standing on the balls of my feet when the chirping in my purse alerted me that someone has just called, and left a message. I spotted his slippers, then slid my feet into them, flip-flopping over to my purse to retrieve my cell. It was Nia. I listened to the message, then pressed the option to call back. She picked up on the third ring.

"Hey skank," she said playfully. "Where are you, or do I even need to ask? I don't know why you just don't move Mattress in."

I sucked my teeth. Sometimes I wish I never told her about the state of his bed because ever since, that's been her nickname for him. "Shut up," I whispered into the phone, walking into the kitchen—I mean, kitchenette. "What are you doing?"

"On my way home?"

"From?" I asked.

"Flavas, Mom," she responded. I chuckled. She's such a smart aleck sometimes. Flavas is a soul food spot over on E. Park Street in downtown, Newark. Her mentioning that place made me realize just how long it had been since we'd seen each other. Two months. It's crazy but, we live only minutes apart; yet, we see very little of each other, particularly now since Mustafa's come home. We talk on the phone almost every other day, but it's not the same. Sometimes we'd meet up at Flavas after work to get caught up and grab a quick bite to eat. It has a cozy atmosphere and good, inexpensive food. And, Thursday nights is open mike for all the aspiring singers, including Nia.

"So, how was it?"

"What?"

"Open mike, fool."

"Oh, it was the usual. There was some serious competition; but I won."

"You go girl," I responded. "Now come get me."

She sucked her teeth. "And why didn't you drive over there? I'm already on 280."

"Because he kidnapped me," I replied, sarcastically. "Now turn around, and come get me."

She smacked her lips. "I'll be there in fifteen minutes."

"I'll be waiting," I said before hanging up. I walked over to the refrigerator, and peeked in. Hoping to find something safe to drink. I was parched. But I'd die from thirst before I drank anything that wasn't sealed. *Bottled water. Good.* I opened it then guzzled it down. But stopped in midstream when I saw a roach crawling on his wall. The sight of this critter gave me the creeps as I thought of the possibility of carrying one of those things home with me. It was definitely time to go. I made a mental note to encourage him to bomb this place, or else I wouldn't be coming back.

"Damn!" she exclaimed when I hopped up in her new Lexus truck. "You could have at least wiped your ass down before coming out!" *Chile, if you only knew*, I thought. Now, I told ya'll before how horrid his bathroom was. So you know showering is out of the question. The only thing I did was use a few baby wipes to clean myself off with, then roll some toilet paper up and stuff between my legs just in case remnants of our sex started to seep out. I know. Nasty. But, hey, it's better than nothing. Besides, every time I go into his bathroom, I get nauseous. Between him not flushing the toilet after using it, to his toothpaste splattered on the mirror, it just drives me crazy. And, I won't even talk about the dirty bar of soap in the soap dish for you to wash your hands with and the dingy towel he has hanging up for you to dry them on. How trifling is that? Just too cheap to invest in paper towels and pump soap. Humph.

"I didn't have enough time," I lied.

"Well, reach in the backseat and see if I have a towel back there."

"For what?" I asked, scrunching my face up.

"For you to sit on," she snapped. "I don't want your nasty behind funkin' up my leather seats."

I sucked my teeth. "Nia, shut the hell up, and drive." She pressed on the interior lights, cracking the back windows, then burst out laughing. "What the hell's so funny?" I asked, feeling myself getting irritated. And partially embarrassed that she had to see me like this. Oh well. I needed to get home.

"You smell a mess," she commented, holding her nose and twisting up her lips as if she had just kissed a skunk.

I rolled my eyes, "You're so darn dramatic." I flipped down her visor. "Ugh," I said, trying to fluff up my matted hair. I looked a mess. "I needed to get out of there quick, fast and in a damn hurry before I woke him up, and he'd want more."

She laughed. "Oh, Mother put that snapper on him. Knocked him right out, huh?"

I chuckled. "You know how we do."

"Well, seems like that's all ya'll like to do."

"Girl, please," I stated, flicking my hand at her. "Wrong answer. That's all *he* likes to do."

"And you don't seem to mind?" Although, it sounded more like a statement than a question, I took it for the latter.

"Actually, I do. It's really getting played out." She glanced over at me while we were stopped at a red light.

"Meaning?"

"Meaning, I'm getting really tired of him and this routine. I want more."

"Uh, oh. Sounds like you're getting bored with him?"

"I'm not sure what it is," I responded, giving my left temple a three-finger massage.

"So, are you thinking about ending it?"

"I don't know," I said, sighing. And I honestly meant that. I mean. Despite everything I've already told you about him, I truly would like to believe he has the ability to be a good man. And you already know we women are always so quick to say it's hard to find a good man. So when we see a man who we *think* has potential we get so blinded by the fear of being alone that we settle. Sadly, sometimes, we don't even know who or what's good for us. Lord knows I don't want to turn into one of those women. Stuck. And I definitely don't want to turn into an old spinster either. Nor am I interested in playing spin-the-bottle with a hundred different men, hoping I get the right one to grow old with. "I care about him," I continued. "But, it just doesn't seem like enough. I'm really not satisfied."

"Satisfied how, mentally? Sexually? Emotionally?"

"All the above." She cut her eyes at me, giving me a sideway glance. "Okay. Maybe not sexually . . . then again . . . " I shook my head, allowing my thoughts to drift. Although, he feels good inside of me, he doesn't do a whole lot to get me hot and popping, if you know what I mean. Basically, he's real stingy with the foreplay. And he's usually rough. Which is not how I like it, *all* the time. Sometimes, I want it slow and gentle. Sometimes, I want to be caressed. Sometimes, I just want to be licked and kissed. But, Morris seems to have trouble executing that consistently. He'll rub a little bit here and lick a little bit there, then start sticking when I'm only lukewarm, if you know what I mean. It's almost like trying to deep-fry a whole chicken in warm grease. However, once that oil heats up, it cooks the hell out of that bird. But before it gets to that point, it's just sitting in a big-ass fryer waiting to cook. That's how I feel sometimes when we're having sex. And my pan of oil takes a while to get hot, if you know what I'm saying. But, once he's in me, and moving just how I like it, my pussy—oops. There goes that P word again—starts to snap, crackle and pop, and his dick starts to feel so good in me. Humph. If only he'd be more open in the bedroom. I mean. He could start by traveling south with his mouth more frequent. I remember when we first started seeing each other his tongue visited the clit and coochie quite regularly. Not that he really knew what he was doing. But it was the earnest attempt that mattered. But now, forget it! He seems to have misplaced the road map to that part of my body. Yet, he's quick to want me to suck him off. Not! I lick every now and then, but as a common practice—forget it. That's a treat for someone who's willing to reciprocate.

" . . . On second thought, there's definitely room for improvement," I finally admitted. "It could be so much better if he was willing to be adventurous."

"Hmm. I feel you," she said, glancing over at me. She knew exactly what I meant since we're both Scorpions. "Not that I have that problem."

I rolled my eyes. "*What*ever, heifer."

She pressed on, ignoring my remark. "So, sexually he leaves you hanging."

"Not all the time," I explained. Okay, okay. I was contradicting myself. But, I didn't want her to know too much of what does or doesn't go on in the bedroom. "I mean. He can put his thing down when he wants to."

She chuckled. "Okay, so he rocks your world some of the time. But emotionally, he still leaves you feeling deprived. All the time."

"Something like that," I acknowledged.

We were quiet for a few minutes and then Nia asked, "Do you love him?"

I shook my head. "I don't know. I mean, I feel something for him; but, I'm just not sure if it's really love. I mean, the kind of love that can sustain a relationship. I just don't feel like we're on the same page. And I'm getting tired of trying to get him to turn to the page I'm on. I want a family Nia, and I really don't think that's what he wants. Like I said, the sex is good—some, I mean most, of the time. But, it's just not enough for me. I want a man I can wake up to every night, knowing that he loves me. Knowing that we're building a future. With Morris, I always have to guess what he's thinking.

Wonder what he's feeling. Sometimes it feels like I'm standing in quicksand with him. And it's exhausting trying to keep from being sucked in to nothing." Okay, after saying all that, I guess the writing was definitely on the wall. The question was: Was I really ready to read it for what it was? I really needed to do another self-inventory and soon.

"Well, have you asked him what he wants from you?"

"Sure I have. But, I can never seem to get a direct answer from him. He seems to know how to say the right thing just to appease me for the moment."

"Autumn, let me ask you something. Was Morris just a rebound for you?"

"What do you mean?" I asked puzzled. "We've been together almost two years."

"Girl, don't play stupid with me," she said, turning onto my street, then pulling up in my driveway. She turned her engine off, facing me. "I don't think you ever really gave yourself enough time to get over Trevor."

I rolled my eyes. "Please. I've been over that fool."

"I'm sure you're over him *now*. But he hurt you really bad."

"And?"

And maybe you used Morris to fill a void."

"Oh, okay, Oprah," I said sarcastically. "So you're suggesting I used Morris to get over Trevor?"

"Maybe."

"Not hardly," I responded. "Trevor hurt me because he lied to me; not because I was in love with him."

"Oh so now you're saying you didn't love him."

"I didn't say I *didn't* love him. I said I wasn't *in* love with him. There's a big difference."

"Okay. For argument's sake, maybe you weren't *in* love with him; but you loved him enough to stay with him when you found out he was married."

"No, I was I crazy."

"Well, that too," she agreed. I sucked my teeth. "But, you had hoped he'd leave his wife for you."

"No, well, yes," I stammered. " But, that's what *he* said he wanted to do. And I believed him."

"And you were willing to wait for him to do it. Even if it meant waiting for his kids to go off to college."

"Now, I wouldn't go that far," I said, rolling my eyes. "But, yeah. I would have waited."

"Why?"

"Because . . . I don't know," I replied, feeling foolish. "At the time I thought he was worth the wait."

"Because you loved him."

I shrugged my shoulders. "Yeah, I guess." She gave me a don't-even-try-it glare. "Alright, I loved him. Damn."

"And you loved him enough to consider keeping his baby."

Ouch. She just pulled the scab off of a very ugly wound. Yes. I had gotten pregnant by Trevor. And, yes, I would have kept the baby—even though he played me—if I hadn't miscarried. Not because I had hoped for anything else. After I caught him with his wife and found out she was pregnant, I had already made a conscious decision to cut him off. And when I found out I was pregnant I had no intentions of telling him about it. I intended on raising the baby on my own. "Don't even go there," I snapped. "You already know the circumstances behind that. So what's your point?"

"My point is: if you feel what you and Morris have isn't going anywhere, why stay with him?"

Because I'm dick whipped. "Good question," I responded in between a yawn. "Oh, excuse me. I'm beat. You wanna come in for a while?"

"No, I need to get home before Mustafa puts an APB out on me."

I chuckled. "Speaking of Mustafa. How is he?"

She paused. "He's fine."

"Is he still working?"

"Supposedly," she said. I stared at her, tilting my head. "Don't even start."

I raised my hand in mock surrender, leaving it alone. When she was ready to talk, I'd be there to listen. But, I knew better than anyone. There was no way homegirl could afford the payments on that LX 470—which to me was just an overpriced, carbon copy of the Land Cruiser—pay rent in that expensive behind apartment of hers in West Orange, and shop the way she likes on her salary. And, I know she didn't have a Sugar Daddy on the side, so Mustafa had to be doing *something* to help her make ends meet. But, if she wanted to be evasive, I'd play along.

I smiled. "Well, thanks for rescuing me," I said, bowing out gracefully while glancing down at my watch. It was 12:47 in the morning.

"No problem." We gave each other a hug. "Love you."

"Love you, too," I said getting out of her truck, then shutting the door. She rolled her window down.

"Umm. Excuse me, Sex Kitten. But, you still didn't answer my question."

"I know," I said, purring. She backed up, rolling the window up and shaking her head at the same time. I waved her on, then went inside trying to conjure up a plausible reason for why I stayed with Morris. Other than for the sex—that wasn't always the best, nothing tangible came to mind. How ridiculous. Bottom line, we definitely needed to have a serious talk, and soon. And I had better be ready for whatever the outcome.

When I got upstairs to my bedroom, I immediately spotted the flashing red light of my answering machine. I walked over and hit PLAY MESSAGES. There were three and not one from Morris to see where I was, or if I had made it home okay. Maybe he was still asleep, I reasoned, slipping out of my clothes, then heading for the bathroom to hit the shower. After I showered, I dried myself off then covered my body in Frankincense and Myrrh body butter, rubbing it into my skin. I loved the way it smelled, and made a mental note to visit the POOKA PURE & SIMPLE website to order a few more cans. By the time I slipped my nude body into my bed between my crisp white sheets and goose down quilt it was almost two in the morning. I closed my eyes. Then wondered why I was still holding onto Morris, before drifting off to a sound sleep.

TGIF! Thank the good Lord for Fridays. That's all I can say. As much as I hate my job, I hate Mondays even more. Because that means I have to come back up in this place, and listen to a bunch of irate customers whine and complain about anything, everything and nothing. Something I dread every damn day. But it pays the bills, so I get over it. I know you want to know what I do for a living, and where I work. But that's irrelevant at this point. Bottom line, I was worn out and could not wait to get out of these clothes, and out of these heels. My feet were throbbing. I had been standing on those bad boys for most of the day, making daggone copies because the darn secretary—oh, excuse me. Administrative Assistant—had called out, claiming she had an emergency and wouldn't be in for the rest of the week. Suddenly I mused myself with the notion that my feet wouldn't hurt as much if I broke down and bought a more expensive pair of shoes. Nia swears her feet never hurt in those four, and five-hundred-dollar heels she wears all day. I erased that craziness out of my head the moment my cell rang.

"Hello."

"What you doing tonight?" I shook my head. No hello. No how was your day? No nothing. It was definitely time to draw the damn line.

"Nothing," I said with a slight attitude. One I'm sure he detected, but didn't feed into. "Why?"

"Well, how 'bout you go home and pack an overnight bag. And I'll be by to pick you up around seven. I've made plans for us this weekend."

"What kind of plans?" I asked half-interested.

"I've planned a getaway for us. So, just be ready when I get there. And try to get off Monday."

Take off Monday? Didn't this fool no it was quitting time, and too late to put in a vacation request. Oh, well. I'd just call out sick. "Okay," I replied. "But, can I know where we're going?"

"It's a surprise."

"Well, can I at least know what I should pack?"

"Just pack light," he said, sounding excited. He hung up before I could question him any further. Needless to say, he had piqued my curiosity. Maybe I was wrong after all. Perhaps, despite the ambivalence and second-guessing, there was still hope.

Five

Nia

As close as I am with Autumn, I didn't have the heart to tell her about my argument with Mustafa, or the letters. I just didn't feel like getting into it right then with her. So, I played it cool like things were all good between us. Besides, hearing her talk about her flimsy relationship with Morris had me thinking about all of the relationships I've been in and out of. Not that I've had many. I can count them on one hand. But I know enough to say that they definitely weren't the ones for me.

Humph. Like Glenn; my first boyfriend. All the girls loved them some Glenn with his fine, sexy self. He was a senior and star quarterback for Orange High School, and I was a sophomore Varsity cheerleader. At seventeen, he stood six-feet and weighed two-hundred-twenty-pounds. The boy was as solid as an oak tree. We had been dating since my freshman year and had been named "best-looking couple" two years in a row. We were inseparable. Well, that's until he went off to Morgan State to play football, and experienced the joys of campus coitus. He'd come home on the weekends, pressing me for sex and since I wasn't giving it up—yet, we slowly drifted apart. I was crushed for about two weeks. That's right, two whole weeks. Please. I was too fly to cry over spilled milk when he broke up with me, stating he needed time to spread his wings and to find himself. As far as I was concerned, he could have all the time he needed and spread whatever he wanted; he just wasn't gonna be wasting my time, or spreading himself inside of me. Interestingly, I ran into him a few years back in Penn Station begging for change. I didn't even recognize him when he called out my name. *Oh, my*

God. I couldn't believe my eyes. *What in the world happened to that thick frame of his,* I wondered to myself. He was as thin as a rail. And was filthy. He even had the nerve to crack a chipped, three-missing-tooth smile. Ugh, what a damn shame. All that body and talent wasted. I stuck a ten-dollar bill in his cup, and kept stepping before he tried to get his rap on. There was definitely no need to stroll down memory lane with him looking all busted and beat down.

Jeremy was my first *real* man. He was twenty-five and I—hmm. Let me see—had to be about eighteen. And—boy, oh boy—did he introduce me to the joys of cunnilingus. He loved eating my "young, tender pussy" as he called it. Chile, the first time he put his tongue on my clitoris and started licking and sucking on it like it was dipped in sugar, I thought I was going to lose my mind. He had my head spinning. This new encounter had nothing on the bumping and grinding Glenn and I used to do in our underwear down in his basement. I got to shaking and screaming and my eyes rolled up in the back of my head like I was possessed. It felt so damn good. And when he dug his tongue inside of me, I really lost it. From that moment on, I was hooked on having my pussy eaten. I truly understood what Pavlov's dogs went through every time they heard those bells. 'Cause any time he licked his lips, I'd get wet. Talk about classical conditioning. Strangely, he never wanted to kiss or do anything else. Just eat the pussy. But, hey, if all he wanted me to do was lie back and wrap my legs around his neck, and back, it was fine by me. Sadly, our love affair only lasted eleven months when I found out he was also eating out cross-eyed, fat, bald-headed Tasha down the street from me. I knew Tasha from around the way with her funky, trifling self. In school, we were in the same gym class; but the bitch never undressed since everyone teased her. The one time she did, her drawers looked like the bottom of a sewer. She was the type of chick who'd wipe her ass from the back to front. And wash her pussy, then her face—with the same washcloth. So when she made it her business to throw it up in my face that my man was eating her shit-stained pussy out, I beat her down right there on the corner of Berwick and Lincoln, then dumped him like a hot potato. How dare he try to play me with something like that! I don't think so. Then, a year later, I saw him in Tunde Dada's bookstore. And he had the nerve to try 'n holla at a sista—*me.* Please. Not hardly. There was nothing he could do with me, or for me, with big ass bumps all around his lips. He definitely looked like he had gotten a hold of something rotten. Although he hadn't had his lips locked on my love box in over a year, I still ran my behind down to the clinic and got tested for every thing under the sun. Just in case. Luckily, I came up with a clean bill of health.

Mason was my Adonis. The nigga was extra fine, and was a fitness fanatic. Spent three hours a day in the gym. And the fruits of his labor showed every time he took off his clothes. He had the body of Hercules, and had the stamina of a stallion. And I loved every inch of him, literally and figuratively speaking. He taught me the true meaning of Kama Sutra. And basically opened up Pandora's box for me. He would sex me out from sunup to sundown, in every imaginable position. And it was with him that I learned how to suck a dick. And once I got the hang of it, I'd suck him blind. I just could never bring myself to swallow all that white, sticky gook. Basically, sex with him was off the charts. Anything went. The only problem was outside of the bedroom he wasn't playing with a full deck. The brotha would do some of the craziest things. Like fart and belch, then start giggling. Ugh! Or we'd be on the phone talking about *nothing*, and out of the blue he'd say something like, "You know you want to suck the cream out of this Twinkie." Now, I don't know about you—but any man who refers to his dick as a *Twinkie* has got to go. Needless to say, our little love affair didn't last long. Eleven months, and it was a wrap.

Leon. Leon. Leon. What can I say? Nice brotha. But just not for me. He was a manager down at Checkers on Route 9, not that there's anything wrong with that. Hell, it's a job. He was hard working, and definitely thoughtful. He always made sure he brought me a bag of their banging apple pies. And, had no problem spending his bi-weekly paycheck on me, buying me flowers, taking me to the movies, out to eat or shopping—not that he could afford to buy me anything too expensive on his salary. But, it was the thought that counted. And I appreciated the gestures. The problem was—his sex game. It was whack! He didn't like to kiss. And I understood why 'cause he didn't know how. It was like sticking your face in a dishwasher. His tongue just sloshed all over the place. Ugh. And he didn't eat pussy. And when he tried, he gnawed it to death. And he didn't like his dick sucked. Not that I had any desire to—although, sometimes, I do like to please my man orally. But, he had nothing to worry about 'cause I had no interest in sucking something that looked like a damn snake. It was long and skinny. And every time he stuck it inside of me, it felt like he was shoving a broomstick in me, stabbing up my uterus. Bottom line: He and his serpent dick had to go.

Then there was Charles. I wasted six months of my time with this deadbeat. He was a walking charity case if I ever saw one. He still lived at home with his mother—and *she* paid all the bills and bought his clothes; he didn't have a car; and he never had any money after paying child support for his four crumb-snatchers by three different women. And to top it off, he had a cell phone that was in some chick's name. The only reason I knew that is because I had Autumn trace the number to tell me whose name it was under. Yet, he'd go out with his boys frontin' like he was the damn man. Please. When I met him lampin' in the passenger's seat of his "peeps" Escalade, I should have kept it movin'. Instead, I had to entertain his lame behind. We'd chill at my place, watching movies, and cuddling. Which was fine by me 'cause I had no interest in giving him any. He was nice-looking and had a nice body; but he just didn't wet my panties like that. I thought we could be cool. And, *maybe*, one day I'd hit him off with a taste. That's until the night he called himself taking me out to eat—although, *I* drove—then had the nerve to pull out a fake Louis Vuitton wallet and only have thirty-dollars in it. And the bill came to ninety-eight dollars, not including the tip. I was too through. I snatched *his* change out of his hand, put the rest of the money toward the bill, then got in my car and left his broke ass right there in the City. I told him to get home the best way he knew how. I sure did. After I cursed him the hell out. There was no way he was riding back with me, okay. Anyway, I still see him around every now and then. And he's still living at home with his mama, and still riding in passenger seats, frontin'. Damn bum!

Basically, what I'm trying to say is, all of my past relationships were inconsequential compared to what I've shared with Mustafa. He came to the table with something, other than baggage and baby mama drama. He's able to hold his own. And I have loved him like I've loved no other. And I've been in what I *thought* was love before, but nothing like this.

Once Mustafa got sentenced and went to prison, what started out as a physical attraction bloomed into a very emotional and mental connection; our relationship developed through letters, phone calls and visits. And as crazy as it may sound, I looked forward to his letters. Every time the mailman came, I'd run to the box hoping there'd be something from him, and catch an attitude when there wasn't. Even though I knew I'd hear from him later on that night. And the phone calls. I eagerly waited for those collect calls. And would tell him to call right back just before our fifteen minute timeframe was up. Please. It didn't matter to me that each call was nine dollars a pop. We'd burn the phone lines all the way up to count. Everything I did was surrounded by count. If I had to step out, I got to the point where I had all my calls forwarded to my cell phone just so I wouldn't miss him when he called. And when those six, seven, and eight-hundred-dollar phone bills came in each month, I never blinked an eye. Just wrote my check and kept it moving. Hearing his voice is what got me through the night. And the visits—I lived for them. Couldn't wait for them. And I made every one, religiously. Wednesday nights. Saturday and Sunday mornings—no matter the weather or road conditions, I was there for my man, faithfully. It didn't matter that I drove over a hundred and thirty miles each way. And it definitely didn't matter if some of the CO's were nasty and treated us like *we* were the ones who broke the law. I was there to see my man, and could take whatever their miserable behinds dished out. Nothing was going to deter *me* from tasting his lips, from being in his arms, okay? No matter how brief. That's the storm we weathered, and built our relationship from.

Anyway, the minute I got home, I checked my messages. There were four from Mustafa in which he just said, "Hello, hello" into the machine, then hung up when he realized I was either not home or wasn't going to pick up. He had even tried calling me on my cell several times; but I had deliberately left it home on the kitchen counter, and brought my other phone with me—the second phone line on my Family Plan. It's what I call my backup phone. A phone I used to use when I was single and going out regularly. I'd give out that number to the goons I never really had any special interest in. It was also a phone line Mustafa knew nothing about. No particular reason. It's just something I never felt the need to mention to him. Umm, no I don't consider that keeping a secret. Well, not really. Is it?

Oh, forget it. Anyway, after talking with Autumn, I realized my situation wasn't as bad as hers. At least I *knew* my man loved me. At least I *felt* like we were building something together. I just wasn't sure what. And I wasn't sure when it'd be finished. I just knew we had something to stand on, a foundation. For some people, four-and-a-half-years isn't a long time. But it's long enough when you've invested all of your heart and time into someone. Which is what I did with Mustafa. As far as I was concerned, we had a history together. And I wasn't going to throw that all away over one indiscretion. Would I knowingly share him? I truly hoped I'd never have to, or want to. What would

I do if I found out he cheated on me, again? I really hoped I would never find out, or put up with it for that matter. But, somewhere in the back of my mind, I was smart enough to know, Never say never.

I jumped in the shower, allowing my mind to drift into the future. I stood underneath the showerhead and saw life with Mustafa flicker before my eyes. I'd have my law degree and a prosperous practice. And maybe even a record deal. 'Cause you know sistagirl can *sang*. He'd have his money stacked the way he wanted it, opening up some kind of business. We'd have three beautiful kids: a daughter, and two sons. And live happily-ever-after. That's what I crawled into bed believing before sleep had its way with me.

Then somewhere in between having children and a successful law practice, my visions of life with Mustafa shifted to flashes of my mother. I hadn't dreamt of her in years. I could clearly see her face: Smooth, beautiful skin the color of caramel, warm brown almond-shaped eyes and full lips that always revealed a thin gap between her two front teeth every time she smiled. She was always smiling, and singing. Oh, how I have missed her. Sometimes in the still of the night, I've often wondered what life would be like if she were still alive; if drugs hadn't taken her from me. "I'll always be with you, baby," she whispered, then reached out and wrapped her frail arms around me, and started singing her favorite song in my ear, the theme from *Mahogany*.

Do you know where you're going to? Do you like the things that life is showing you? Where are you going to, do you know? Do you get, what you're hoping for? When you look behind you there's no open door. What are you hoping for? Do you know?

I thought I was still dreaming when I heard the ringing in my ear. I jumped up when I realized it was the phone. I glanced over at my clock on the nightstand: 3:50 AM. I rolled my eyes, snatching the phone off its base. "Hello."

"Yo, what's good?"

"Nothing," I said, then covered my mouth to stifle a yawn. I rubbed my left eye, and allowed another yawn to escape from me anyway. I didn't feel the need to excuse myself so I didn't. "Why you calling so late?"

"Oh, now I need a time schedule when I can call you?" he asked.

I ignored the question. "How can I help you?" I responded sarcastically.

"Oh, word?"

"Yep."

"Yo, where you been? I've been calling you all night."

"Out," I replied.

"Oh, word. It's like that?"

"Basically," I replied, finally sitting up then propping two pillows in back of me. I leaned my head back on the headboard, folding my arms across my chest. I wasn't really upset anymore. More disappointed than anything, but definitely not mad. "I told you, I want that chick's last name."

He sucked his teeth. "Yo, you still on that shit? I told you it was nothing. Damn."

"And I told you I wanted her last name. So if it was nothing, then you'd have no problem doing what I asked."

"I can see you still wanna beef so I'm gonna let you go."

"Yeah, you do that," I retorted, still holding the phone in the crook of my neck. Between you and me, I was hoping he'd call. And I didn't really want him to hang up. Yet, I wasn't going to let him know that. I wanted to drag him over the coals a little while longer just to see where his head was.

Silence.

"Well," I said.

"Well, what?"

"I thought you were hanging up."

"Yo, won't you fucking quit it," he snapped. "I said I fucked up. Damn. So why can't you let it go?"

"Don't try'n pop no attitude with me," I snapped back. "I'm not the one who was out fucking around."

"I don't have an attitude. But, damn. You act like I did the shit a few days ago, or something."

"Well, it feels like it."

"Well, it's not. It's a year old."

Silence.

"Where you calling from?" I asked.

"I'm at my man's spot."

"Oh, really. Humph."

"Damn. Why you say it like that?"

"Like what?"

He sucked his teeth. "Nothing."

Silence.

"Listen, baby. If I could take what I did back, I would. But, I can't. I'm really sorry for what I did."

I rolled my eyes. "Yeah, right."

"Damn. Can we move on from this, or are you gonna keep harboring the shit?"

"Who else you fucking?" I asked, dismissing his question.

"What?"

"You heard me."

"Yo, come on. Do you even have to ask?"

"Obviously, I do. So I am. Now are you going to answer the question or do I have to give you the dial tone? Because I *thought* I was the only one you were smashing until recently."

"You are," he said, sighing. "I did some real dumb shit. And I apologize."

I grunted. "Humph. Well, let me ask you this: Would you like it if you found out I had fucked around on you?"

"Nah," he responded, lowering his voice.

"How would you feel?"

"I'd be heated."

"Exactly. So how 'bout I go out and fuck some nigga after you've had my back, and let you find out about it so you can tell me how you feel."

Again, silence set in allowing images to come to mind. Him fucking. Her with her legs wide open. His ass muscles flexing as he sleighed her with his dick. The expression of pleasure on her face. I pressed my eyes shut.

"Can we get past this?" he asked, shattering my imagery. I brought my knees up to my breasts, hugging myself.

"Was it good?"

"Was what good?"

"The pussy."

"Not as good as yours," he replied. *Hmm. Good answer.*

"So why'd you keep fucking her then?"

"Because I was being stupid," he reasoned. "I wasn't thinking."

"Puhleeeze. You weren't *thinking* you'd get caught."

"That too," he admitted, lowering his voice. "Can you forgive me?" he asked, sounding remorseful.

"Maybe," I stated, glancing over at the clock. It was now 4:45. Luckily, I had nothing to do, and no place to be in the morning.

"What can I do to make it right, baby?"

I removed the pillows from behind me, then lied back down. I closed my eyes, clamping my legs together, then opening them. I slipped my hand in between my white, laced panties. I loved him so. "Well, you can start by coming over and blowing my back out," I finally responded.

I could see him grinning through the phone. "I'm on my way."

Thirty minutes later, Mustafa was slipping out of his clothes and hovering over me with his weight on both his arms. There was no need for talk. I saw it in his eyes. And he saw it in mine. Lust and love neatly wrapped around a ton of "I'm-sorry-and-I-forgive-you's. He slid his tongue in my mouth and kissed me passionately. Then took my left nipple in his mouth and swirled his tongue around it, then the right one. I moaned, reaching up under him and stroking his already hard dick. I spread my legs wide open; wet and ready to receive him, and guided him in. And, right at that moment, whatever apprehension I may have had was immediately lost with the thrust of his hips.

It was eight in the morning when I realized Mustafa had slipped out of bed. I was sore but exhilarated at the same time. I could still feel the heat from our passion between my legs. And I wanted more. But suddenly I ignored my horniness, and listened intently. Mustafa was in the master bathroom. And it sounded like he was having a whispered conversation. I laid still, trying to determine if he was talking to himself, if I was imagining things, or if he was actually on the phone. Being Miss Inquisitive, I decided to get out of bed and place my ear to the door. But, he had flushed the toilet, then ran the water before I could get to the door good. I quickly jumped back in bed, pulling the covers up over my head. When the door opened, I closed my eyes. Pretended to still be asleep. Mustafa quietly crawled back in bed, pressing up against me.

"Wake up, Sleepyhead," he said in my ear, then kissed me on the back of my neck.

"Hmmm," I moaned, faking a stretch. "What time is it?" I asked.

"A little after eight," he responded, cupping my right breast. He kissed me on my shoulder, then on the back of my back. "Listen, baby. I gotta go out of town for a few days."

I craned my neck around to look him in his face. "Where?"

"Maryland."

"For what?" I asked, twisting my lips up.

"My sister wants me to go to court with her on Monday; my niece got herself in some trouble and she asked me if I'd go down with her."

"Which sister?" I asked, suspiciously. For some reason, I thought all of his sisters lived in Jersey. But I could have been mistaken.

"Janice."

"I didn't know she moved to Maryland."

"She didn't. Her oldest daughter lives out there with her father."

"Oh," I responded. "So, when ya'll leaving?"

"This afternoon."

Now, why would you need to leave on Saturday to go to court on Monday? That's what I asked myself; but I kept it to myself. Although, I didn't want to start getting paranoid, my gut was telling me there was something fishy behind this story; but I didn't have anything to base my skepticism on so I decided to just go with the flow. I knew for a fact that he and his family were all very close so even if it weren't true, they'd never give it away.

He explained that his seventeen-year-old niece, Shari, and two other females were arrested and charged with aggravated assault and possession of a weapon. Apparently, they had gotten into an argument with some thirty-five-year old woman, then came back to her house, and knocked on her door. When the woman came to the door, they dragged her outside then commenced to stomp and beat her. One of the girls pulled out a gun, and beat the woman in the face with it. He stated the prosecutor was trying to waive them up.

I shook my head. These damn teenagers today are too damn bold. Going up to someone's house to fight. "Damn, that's crazy," I said, feeling stupid for thinking he might be trying to pull a fast one on me. There was just no way he'd make something like that up.

"Tell me about it. I told Janice she should have never sent her down there to live with her punk-ass father."

"Well, I hope everything works out."

"Yeah, me too. Janice has been stressed out over this."

"I can imagine," I responded sympathetically. "So when will you be back?"

"Probably Monday night; if not, then Tuesday. We have some cousins in Upper Marlboro who we haven't seen in a while, so we're gonna crash at their spot and just make a weekend out of it."

"That's cool," I stated, looking him in his eyes.

He kissed me on the lips. "We straight?"

"Yeah. Why wouldn't we be?"

"Just checking," he replied, pressing his stiff dick up against the crack of my ass. I twirled my hips a tease. "'Cause I know how you get."

"And, how is that?"

He sucked his teeth. "You know."

"Whatever, Mustafa," I replied, reaching in back of me, and rubbing the head of his dick.

"You want some more of this big dick, don't you?" he asked, reaching around and rubbing my clit. I threw my leg over his thigh so that he could have all the access he wanted.

I smiled. "Maybe."

"Yeah, I got your maybe," he snapped in a tone filled with desire, pulling open my butt cheek then letting the tip of his dick touch my slick spot. I lifted my left leg up, and allowed him to slide it all the way in me. I moaned. It was like a hand sliding in a glove. A perfect fit.

Two hours later, I was in the kitchen whipping up breakfast. I fixed walnut pancakes, turkey sausage, cheese grits, and scrambled eggs. The stereo was on, and Amel Larrieux's CD *Infinite Possibilities* was playing in the background. Mustafa walked in freshly showered, and dressed in a navy blue Roca Wear sweat suit and crisp, white tee. Damn, he was fine. We sat across from each other not really saying much; just gazing into each other's eyes.

"Why you so quiet?" he asked.

I shook my head. "Just thinking."

"About?"

"You," I responded.

He smiled. "Oh word. Anything you wanna talk about?"

"I just want you to know that I love you."

"I love you too, baby."

"And I really hope you don't try to play me."

"Come on now," he said, getting up from the table, grabbing our plates, then placing them on the counter. "I fucked up one time. And it was the worse mistake of my life. I'm not going to do nothing that's gonna jeopardize what we have. That's my word." He walked over to me, kissing me on the top of my head. "I gotta get going." I glanced up at the wall clock then looked at him, nodding my head. He leaned in and kissed me on the lips, then slid his tongue in my mouth before saying, "I love the hell out of you, girl. I'll call you when we get to Maryland."

I held my hand out. "Aren't you forgetting something?"

"What?" he asked, slapping it five.

"Wrong answer."

He sucked his teeth, shaking his head. "You somethin' else," he said, digging in his front pocket. He pulled out a wad of money, then handed me five, one-hundred-dollar bills.

"That's all?" I asked, rolling my eyes.

"Damn, girl," he responded, peeling off another three hundred.

"Drive safe," I said, smiling.

"Most def," he replied, snatching his keys off the counter, then heading for the door. I remained glued to my chair for another thirty minutes, wondering if my mind had really been playing tricks on me. Was he in the bathroom on the phone talking to someone else? Another chick. I decided to let it go before I drove myself crazy. I needed to believe that that Keyonna shit was over, and that he was gonna stay true. *Lord help him,"* I thought as I got up from my seat, slipping the crisp bills in my pocket, *if he doesn't.*

I started washing the dishes with a million questions surfacing the forefront of my mind. For some reason, I just couldn't let it go. What if this Keyonna chick *is* still in the picture? How can I find out who she is? What the hell is her last name? Where the hell is she from? What did she have, a boy or girl? Is it his? Why the fuck did I have to find those damn letters in the first place? *Because what's done in the dark always comes to the light,* I answered in my head. What if that was her he was on the phone whispering to? "Girl, get over yourself, I said aloud. "He said it was over, and that's what it is. You'll just have to trust him." Since when did you start worrying if some nigga was cheating on you, anyway? *Since I fell for his ass,* my mind answered. "Well, if he wants some ex-convict skank, then just let him have her," I continued. "If that's the type of chick that floats his boat, then fuck him, and her. You're better than that." Then why the hell am I feeling so uncertain?

The doorbell disrupted my monologue. I dried my hands wondering who in the world was coming over here unannounced. 'Cause you know a sista don't play that, especially two o'clock on a Saturday afternoon.

I looked through the peephole, and smiled. It was Nygeria, standing with one hand on her wide hip, blowing huge bubbles with her grape gum. Bazooka, I bet. I shook my head at the sight, swinging the door open.

"Girl, what brings you over here this time of day? I asked, stepping aside to let her in. She waltzed in wearing an ankle-length, faded denim wrap dress and a pair of brown leather box-toed boots with the four-inch stiletto heel. Her shoulder length hair was pulled up in a big twist. I gave her the once-over, then gagged when I spotted her brown Bottega Veneta draped on her arm. It was slammin'. "Oooh, bitch," I yelped, pointing at her bag. "I hate you!"

"Boo-boo," she snapped, "don't hate the playa; hate the damn game. "Now, get your ass in gear so we can go get our hair and nails did. My treat."

"Oh, shit," I snapped, tossing images in my head of what I'd wear. There was no way I was going to let her upstage me. "You know how I like treats," I said, jokingly. "Let me get showered, and show *you* how a real diva does it."

"Yeah, you go do that," she shot back, grinning. "'Cause right about now you look tore up from the floor up in that Ma Rainey get up."

I laughed. "Fuck you," I responded, pulling my blue and white polka-dot scarf off my head and tugging at my pin-striped housecoat."

"And that looks like just what you've been doing. Speaking of which, where's your man?"

"On his way to Maryland."

"Aaaah, shit," she said, plopping down on my sofa. She crossed her legs, opening up her bag. Her split opened up, revealing smooth, thick legs as she rummaged through its contents. When she found what she was looking for, she pulled out a mirrored compact and tube of M.A.C lipstick, lip-gloss and a lip liner. She neatly applied a splash of Plumwine to her lips, then carefully contoured the edges with liner. I watched as she blended it in. Afterwards, she added gloss to the center for an exaggerated effect. She puckered up, admiring her image, then snapped the compact shut and looked over at me. She was definitely in Diva mode. I rolled my eyes. She ignored it, and continued, "That means the mice can play while the cats away. AC here we come."

I shook my head. "Not, hardly. I got things to do in the morning. Atlantic City will have to wait another time."

"Girl, the Tropicana has this bangin' spot called T.S.O.P, and if they're not poppin' there's the Cuba Libre. We'll be home by seven."

"No, thank you," I said. "I have no interest in going to AC with you. The last time it costs me almost six-hundred dollars."

She laughed. "Yeah, but I won it all back for you."

"I'm still not going."

"No, gambling tonight. I promise."

"Nope."

"Aww, come on, Party-Pooper," she whined. "Let's just go get our finger-pop on."

I sucked my teeth. "You mean to tell me Devon is going to let you out?" Devon was her new flava of the month, a six-six, brown-skinned, burly nigga from Newark. Just how she liked 'em.

"Please, he's in Miami doin' him."

I shot her a look, but said nothing. I figured, he was down there making moves, if you know what I mean. Since drug-dealers were the only type of guys Nygeria seemed to attract. Not that I had much room to talk. But, at least my man had gotten out the game. Well, that's what he told me.

"Well, I don't know," I said, hesitantly. "See if Autumn wants to go."

She gave me an "oh-no-you-didn't-go-there" glare. "Girlfriend, I know that's your cuz and all; but those bargain basement wears just won't do, okay. Besides, you know me and her don't roll like that."

"Whatever, heifer," I snapped, heading for the stairs. "Let me go jump in the shower." When I got to the top of the stairs, I asked, "Where we going, anyway?"

"Weaves and Wonders," she yelled up at me. Weaves and Wonders was a posh hair, body and nail salon with locations in the Village and on Fifth Avenue—and about a year ago, another spa opened in Connecticut—owned by one of the wealthiest black females in the Tri-State area. Her face had been on the cover of at least four magazines in the last year. From hair, face and body products all over the place, she was a young sista doin' the damn thing. Now *she* was a Diva.

"The one in the City?"

"No, Chile. A spot just opened up in Somerset."

"Oh, really," I said impressed. "I didn't hear about that one." I had read an article in *Sister 2 Sister* that two additional salons were scheduled to open. I just didn't know when, or where. "They're just popping up all over the place."

"Hmm, hmm. I hear it's *fierce.*"

"And you would know," I responded, taking off my robe. "I'll be right down."

"Well, don't take too long. I wanna catch the Champagne sip before it ends at six."

I chuckled knowing good and well bubbly was one of her weaknesses. "Don't worry Queen Lush, you'll get there in time to get your drink on."

Twenty-five minutes later, I came downstairs wearing a red Chantilly lace blouse, my beloved faded Cavalli Jeans with matching jacket and a red pair of Manolo Blahnik lizard pumps. When I sauntered into the living room with my red Hermés leather Birkin bag on my arm, Nygeria almost shitted on her self.

"Touché, wench," she snapped, getting up from her seat. "You didn't tell me you had *that*."

I smiled, satisfied that I had one up on her. She and I loved hitting the other with some of the fly wears; and would go to no end to out do the other; all in fun, of course. Truth be told, I'd practically spent up all of my savings trying to keep my finger on the fashion pulse. And that bag had cost me dearly. Luckily for me, I had a man who appreciated a woman who liked the finer things in life, and didn't mind hitting me up with cash to stay up on things.

"Well, I can't let you know everything, now can I?" I flipped down my Prada shades, giving her stance. "You ready?" I asked, opening up the door, allowing her to exit. She shook her big booty outside, disarming the alarm to her black Infinity QX 56.

"Weaves and Wonders, here we come," she said. I slid in the passenger side, and smiled. The interior was heaven with its plush leather and DVD navigation system.

"You musta sucked the hell outta his dick to get this," I said, buckling up.

"Hmm, hmm. Sucked his ass silly," she giggled, slapping me five. "Spit-shined and swallowed him into tomorrow." I burst out laughing.

"You so crazy."

"Yep, I sure am," she replied, putting on her Gucci shades, then backing up. "But, I keeps it real."

"You ain't never lied," I said, cracking up. "That you do." And, between you and me, I was thankful to call her a friend.

"Hey, Sexy," Mustafa sang into the answering machine. "Just wanted to hit you up and let you know we made it to Maryland. It's about seven-thirty. I guess you're out spending money mad crazy. Anyway, I think we're going to some spot in D.C. tonight. So, I'll hit you up later on, or sometime tomorrow. I love you."

I checked my watch. It was 7:45 P.M. *Damn,* I thought, *I just missed his call. I wonder why he didn't call me on my cell.* I picked up the phone and called him. His voice mail picked up. I hung up, and tried again. Same thing. *Hmm. That's strange. He always has his phone on.* "Whatever," I said aloud. "I'm not gonna stress myself over it."

I was feeling good, and looking absolutely radiant. So the last thing I was gonna do was try to figure out why the hell Mustafa had his cell phone off. Nygeria and I had had a great time at Weaves and Wonders. The salon was all that. It was a three-floor paradise. With tropical plants and exotic flowers throughout the building. Lit candles were everywhere, while soft music filled the air. Everyone who worked in the Salon was beautiful. Practically model material. I was truly in awe.

Anyway, in between the flutes of Veuve Clicquot and the shrimp, I ended up getting a Sea Salt Body Polish and Hot Stone massage. Followed by a deep pore-cleansing facial, then had my hair highlighted and wrapped.

"Who you in there talking to?" Nygeria asked, plopping down on the sofa.

"No one. I was just checking my messages." I came back out from the kitchen with two glasses of white wine. "Here," I said, handing her a glass. "To friendship."

"And sisterhood," she added, clicking her glass against mine.

"And sisterhood," I agreed.

"And niggas with good dick and long dollars."

I chuckled. "If you say so."

"Oh, Bitch. Don't act like you don't know. 'Cause I know damn well if Mustafa wasn't putting his thing down right, and he was a broke-ass nigga you'd have left him in the dust a long time ago."

I smiled. "Maybe."

She sucked her teeth. "Yeah, whatever, heifer. I know you."

"True. But things have changed. I mean. Money doesn't really matter to me anymore. I'm more interested in honesty, and trust."

She pursed her lips, giving me an under-eyed glare. "But you didn't cancel out the dick."

I flicked my hand, sipping my drink. "Well, no. But I'd rather know I'm loved, and that I can trust my man than be concerned with all that other stuff. Like I said, that's not what's important to me now."

"Humph," she said, gulping down the rest of her wine. "If you say so. Just let me be loved by a big dick nigga with money. As long as he can wear my back out right, and I'm spending his loot, I'll worry about trusting him later."

"I heard that," I replied, pausing. "Let me ask you something. What would you do if you found out your man was cheating on you?"

"Drop his ass like a bad habit. *Next,*" she said, snapping her fingers. "But, I don't worry about all that with Devon. We've been talking for almost six months and I know he's probably doing him; hell, there's no ring on my finger, and luckily I'm not all caught up in him. But I tell you what. As long as I don't hear about it, it's fine by me. 'Cause I *will* beat him the fuck down, then whip his ho's ass."

I shook my head, half-smiling.

"Why you ask me that, anyway? Don't tell me you caught Mustafa out there."

"Unh, uh. I was just wondering," I said, lying.

"Oh, 'cause I was about to say. Let me find out Mustafa's out trying to get his creep on."

My stomach churned. "Girl, please," I said, dismissing her comment. The thought of him laid up with another chick, blowing her back out, sickened me. I shifted my eyes around the room as Nygeria stood up and looked at herself in the mirror.

"Enough talk about cheating niggas, and what ifs. You need to come on out and shake that tail feather tonight," she said, admiring her reflection while still trying to convince me to go to Atlantic City with her. "After all that pampering, you look too damn fly to be sitting up in this stuffy ass condo."

"Well, I am looking good, if I do say so myself," I replied. "But, no can do. Not tonight. I just wanna chill. And finish reading this book, *Every Shut Eye.*"

"Humph. Suit yourself," she said, grabbing her bag off the floor. She glanced at her timepiece. "Hopefully, I can get Chandra's silly ass to go. If not, I'll go it alone. I'm out."

I got up from my seat, and gave her a hug. "Thanks for the treat. Next time it's on me."

"Hmmm, hmm," she responded, rolling her eyes up in her head. "Later."

"Have fun for me."

"Don't I always?"

"That you do," I said, smiling. "Be safe."

"Always," she responded, heading for her truck. I stood in the doorway and waited for her to get in safely. She started her engine, then blew the horn as I waved to her as she backed out of the driveway and drove away. "That girl's a piece of work," I thought aloud, closing the door behind me.

Six

Autumn

I glanced at my watch and noticed that it was five in the morning. We had been on 95, heading south for close to six hours and I was getting restless, and becoming agitated. It's bad enough we didn't get on the road until almost eleven-thirty because Morris wanted to get up in my hips, first. Which would have been cool if he had served me right. But, once again, he had half-stepped, leaving me sexually frustrated. If he could just get the foreplay right, I'd be in heaven. I'm constantly trying to redirect him. No, kiss it like that. Lick it over here. Rub it like this. It seems like the longer we're together the more lax he's getting in the bedroom. And I'm slowly getting tired of it. Bottom line: the scorpion in me needs to be satisfied, completely. Consistently. But, that's neither here nor there. At the moment, I just wanted to get to wherever we were going. So, when we passed King's Dominion, I decided I had had enough of this secret road trip and asked, "Morris, where the heck are we going?"

He cut his eyes at me, sucking his teeth. "Yo, will you just sit back and chill. I told you, it's a surprise."

I rolled my eyes. "Well, how much longer before we get to this surprise? I need to stretch. My legs are killing me."

"Let me rub them for you," he said, looking at me and reaching over and slipping his hand on my thigh. He squeezed. I slapped his hand off me.

"Keep your hands on the wheel, and your eyes on the road." I clamped my legs shut. *Damn him!*

"There's a rest stop coming up," he said, grinning as if he were reading my mind. "We can stretch, then I can blow that back out for you. How's that?"

"Whatever," I snapped, staring out the window. When he called me at work telling me to pack a bag because he had planned a weekend getaway I thought he might have been taking me to the Pocono's, or some other spot. As cheap as he is, I knew it wouldn't be anyplace *too* expensive, or extravagant. But going south, I had no clue where our destination would end. And more than anything I really had no idea where this relationship was headed. Just like this road trip, I was tired of being in the dark.

"You alright over there?" Morris asked, squeezing my knee. "Looks like you're somewhere deep in thought."

"Actually," I responded, turning to face him, "I was. Umm. I need to know where we're going with—"

He sighed. "C'mon, can't you just wait to see?" he said, interrupting me.

"I'm not talking about where you're taking me, I'm talking about this relationship."

"What about it?" he asked, taking his eyes off the road to glance at me.

"We've been *dealing* with each other for almost two years, but I don't feel like we're on the same page."

"And what page is that?" he asked, placing both hands on the steering wheel, and returning his attention to the road. I could see his hands gripping the wheel tight as if he was bracing himself for whatever might come out of my mouth.

"I need to know what you want from me, and this relationship. If that's what you want to call it."

"What do you mean by that?" he asked, looking over at me.

I matched his stare. "I mean, I need to know how you feel about me, about this relationship. What do you want from me?"

"You know I'm big on you."

"What does 'I'm big on you' mean?"

"It means I'm feelin' you."

I raised my eyebrow. *I'm feelin' you.* Oh, hell. That basically says, "Look ma. I like you. You're a good fuck but that's it. Let's just go with the flow." Well, if that's what he meant, then I wasn't *feelin'* that.

"I think you need to elaborate on this *I'm feelin'* you mess," I stated before I screamed on him.

"You know what I mean."

"Actually, Morris. I don't. So, please help me comprehend."

"It means I have feelings for you." Okay, so maybe I was just more than a good fuck. I pressed further.

"What kind of feelings, Morris?"

"Feelings," he repeated, sounding annoyed.

"Just feelings? That can mean anything. How 'bout putting a label on what those feelings are so I can understand? 'Cause life is too short for me to be trying to play guessing games. If you love me, then say it. If you don't, then say that. I'm a big girl. I can handle the truth, Morris. No matter what." For the life of me, I don't know why it's so hard for a man to just say how he feels instead of dancing around the subject.

Silence.

"Morris?" I snapped.

"I heard you. Damn." He sighed heavily. "Aiight, look," he finally stated. "I don't know what I feel. I can't tell you it's love because I don't know if that's what it is. I know I enjoy you."

"You enjoy me how?" I asked, trying to keep this from turning into a heated conversation. But he was starting to wear my patience thin with his evasiveness. I knew if he didn't start giving me some direct answers—and soon—it was going to turn ugly.

"Just what I said. I enjoy you. Spending time with you. Sexing you."

"Is that it?"

"Yeah. Why, is there supposed to be more?" Well, then. Maybe I was wrong. Maybe I was just a good screw. A convenient piece of tail 'cause anytime he wanted it, he usually got it. No questions asked. Whenever. Wherever.

I took a deep breath, then slowly blew it out. "That's what I'm tryna find out. But you keep giving me these half-assed responses. Talking about you enjoy me like I'm some damn Call girl or something. If that's how you see me, then you need to start coming out your pocket for my company, *and* my services."

He sucked his teeth. "That's not how I meant it."

"Well, how did you mean it? 'Cause that's just how it sounded to me."

"Don't put words in my mouth."

"I'm not tryna put words in your mouth, Morris. I'm tryna understand what it is you're saying. That's it. But you can't seem to give me a straight answer."

"Where's all this coming from anyway?" he asked, scratching his forehead. "What you need to do is stop watching all those chick flicks. They got you ready to lynch a brotha."

I rolled my eyes. "That's a crock of bull. Chick flicks have nothing to do with me wanting to know where I stand with you."

"I want you standing beside me, in front of me, on top of me. How's that?" he remarked trying to be a wise guy.

"Whatever" I said, clucking my tongue. "I see this conversation is going nowhere. So forget it."

"Well, where did you want it to go?" he asked.

"At this point, it really doesn't matter. I'm done with holding my breath with you."

"So what you sayin'?" he asked. "You not happy?"

"What the hell do you think? Hell no, I'm not happy!" I wanted to snap but I flipped it on him instead. "Are you?"

"Yeah, I'm cool."

"'I'm cool', what in the world does that mean?" I asked, smacking my lips.

"C'mon, now. Why you tryna turn this into an argument?"

"I'm not. I'm trying to get some clarity on a few things so I know how to proceed."

"Proceed?"

"Yeah, proceed," I repeated. "As in going forward. And if necessary, moving on. Because I'm not gonna sit around and wait for you to figure out what it is you feel for me. I need to know that you want the same things I want. If not, then it's been real. No need to waste any more time."

"So that's what you think you've been doing, wasting time?"

"I'm starting to wonder," I replied.

He shook his head. "So what *do* you want?"

"I already told you. I want to know where I stand with you."

"If I'm with you, that must mean I want to be with you, right?"

"Not necessarily," I stated. "It could just mean you're with me until something better comes along."

He shrugged his shoulder. "Well, if that's how you feel."

I cut my eyes at him. That was not the response I was looking for. "Is that how I should feel?"

"Not at all," he replied.

"Hmm."

Silence.

"So what is it you *really* want?" he finally asked.

"I want a family."

"Okay. So do I. But not now."

"Morris, you're thirty-seven years old when do you think you're gonna be ready?" I felt like asking more. Like don't you think its time to move out of that nasty four-room apartment and purchase a home? Don't you think you need to get yourself a banking account, instead of going down to the Check Cashing place every time you need to cash a check? Don't you think it's time to establish some credit? The man didn't even own a major credit card. My goodness. What kind of man is comfortable living the way he does? I already knew the answer to that: A man with no ambition or motivation, basically. I decided to keep my thoughts to myself. I waited for his weak response.

"I don't know," he replied. "I guess when it hits me." He gave me a puzzled look as if he thought I might be crazy enough to poke a hole in a condom or stop taking my birth control pills.

"Don't flatter yourself," I snapped, clearing the air. "I'm not that desperate or pressed to try to trap you. That's a real bird move. I don't want a baby or a husband that bad." *Particularly, one like you,* I thought.

He shook his head. "You something else, you know that? Shit. I missed the turn for the rest stop."

I crossed my arms over my chest, and pursed my lips. *Humph,* I thought. *If he thinks I'm giving him some roadside pussy, now, he's in for a rude awakening.*

"I guess you got an attitude now."

"Not hardly, I said, dryly. I reclined my seat all the way back. "Wake me up *when* we get to wherever you're supposed to be taking me." I turned toward the window, throwing my jacket up over my shoulder.

He snickered. "Yeah, my baby got an attitude." I rolled my eyes in my head and stared out the window, into nothing.

He turned off at the next exit, and drove to an Exxon Service station. "You getting out?" he asked, opening his door, then getting out. I ignored him. "Suit yourself." He slammed his door shut. While he was paying the attendant, then coming over to pump the gas, I thought about my conversation with Nia a few days prior. And, in all honesty, I really had no reason to catch an attitude with him. If anything I was mad at myself for having mixed feelings. On the one hand, I wanted to be with him. For what real purpose other than not wanting to be alone was beyond me. However, I knew I definitely wasn't interested in keeping things as they were. Truth be told, I felt so unfulfilled. Like something was missing. And I couldn't put my finger on it. Well, maybe I could. I just wasn't ready to. Nevertheless, I knew I couldn't blame him for not knowing what he felt for—or wanted from—me when I didn't have any idea what it was I really wanted from him. I know I wanted—needed—to be with someone I felt intimately connected to. Someone I could have children with. Someone I could spend a lifetime with. I just wasn't sure if he was that someone I could spend my life with. Maybe I was just stuck in my self-centered, schoolgirl fantasy of being in love. And a part of me was disappointed that he couldn't fulfill that dream. Maybe. However, whatever the reason, I think I was just looking for an out. And he wasn't making that easy for me. I watched him through the passenger side mirror as he pumped the gas. He was really a nice-looking man. And there were some things I truly liked about him. Like . . . umm. Well, let me come back to that. The bottom line: I needed to evaluate—correction, I mean, reevaluate—this relationship and identify what was good and bad about it, then decide the benefits and costs of trying to maintain it. When he finished filling the tank, he tapped on the window, licking his lips and motioning with his head for me to get out and follow him to the bathroom. I rolled my eyes, flicked my hand at him, then closed my eyes in search of sweet dreams.

It was eight A.M when Morris woke me up, announcing we were there. I squinted my eyes, then rubbed them trying to figure out where we were. There was nothing but woods.

"Where are we? " I asked, interlocking my fingers then stretching my arms out in front of me. I sat up straight.

"Ahoskie"

Ahoskie? "Ahoskie, what?"

He sucked his teeth. "North Carolina," he said as if I was supposed to know that already. Truth be told, I knew nothing about the Carolina's. I pursed my lips. The farthest south I had ever been was Maryland. And was vaguely familiar with certain parts of Virginia. Like Norfolk and Richmond; and, of course, Hampton. And that was only due to the trip we made to the historically black colleges in those areas when I was in the eleventh grade, and we spent three days touring their campuses. Other than that, I was clueless. As far as I knew, I had no roots in the South. My great-grandmother was born in Brielle, New Jersey and my grandmother and mother were born in Harlem. And I grew up in East Orange. So the North was all I knew.

"And who lives here?" I asked.

"My moms."

"You're mother?" I asked in surprise.

"Yeah," he responded, turning down a long, winding road. There were several houses—more like shacks, if you ask me—scattered across acres and acres of land, basically, in the middle of nowhere.

"How long has she been living down here?" I asked, hoping she had just had enough of the hustle and bustle of city life and decided a more rural way of living was what she needed.

"Nah. This is where my family's from, and where I was born," he announced. I looked at him amazed. "I know," he said, reading my mind. "I don't have an accent. That's because I moved to Newark to live with my pops when I was ten."

"Oh, 'cause I was wondering," I said.

"Yeah. Well, I don't really talk about. It was only supposed to be temporary," he continued. "But, she never came back for me so I ended up staying. Which was cool." I looked at him not really sure what to say. "My moms was pretty wild so I guess she still wanted to run the streets. But, it's all good." *More like the woods,* I thought, looking around and seeing nothing but open fields. He explained his mother had met his father when she spent a summer in Newark with relatives. She was fifteen, and he was eighteen. When she returned to North Carolina she found out she had gotten pregnant. And wanted to keep the baby. Her mother whipped her, but allowed her to have him. His parents never married but continued seeing each other until he was two years old. However, their relationship deteriorated when his mother found out he had fathered four other children by two other women. Well, actually, it ended when his mother caught him in bed with her first cousin. She stabbed him with a steak knife, and fled back to North Carolina with Morris in tow to avoid criminal charges. Shortly, thereafter, she started drinking and partying. And running with different men, leaving Morris with her mother, and anyone else who'd watch him. When Morris's grandmother passed away; his mother decided he should go live with his father until she could get her life together.

"Hmm." That's the only response I could give. I guess it goes to show just how much I really didn't know about him. I just assumed his family was from around the way. Come to think about it, we've never really talked about his family or mine, for that matter. And neither of us ever felt the need to ask, I guess. I wondered what kind of woman would just ship her child off hundreds of miles, and never come back for him. "So, I take it you're her only child."

"Nah. I have two sisters."

"Oh, really."

"Yeah. And between the two of them they have about fourteen kids."

I gave him a surprised look. "Get out of here."

"Yeah. My youngest sister has nine; four boys and five girls, and the next to the oldest has five; three girls and two boys. "

Damn. "How old are they?" I asked, trying to figure out how they took care of all those kids with today's economy the way it was. *Humph. Public Assistance*, I thought.

"Peaches is twenty-seven. And Princess is thirty." *Ugh,* I thought. *How trifling is that. Twenty-seven with nine kids, ugh. She's just pushing babies out like kittens. Humph. And those names?* Who in the world would name their daughters Peaches and Princess? I wondered. I guess I should have felt honored to finally be graced with the knowledge of his family tree. But, for some reason I wasn't. And the fact that he wanted *me* to meet his family should have been a big deal for me as well. It wasn't. Frankly, I was a bit annoyed that he hadn't prepared me for this. I mean. First impressions are definitely lasting ones. And I wasn't sure if I was going to be up for trying to impress this clan; or if I would be impressed by them for that matter.

"Well," I said, trying to sound excited. "I wish you would have told me that this is what you had in mind. I would have packed more appropriate clothes. I would like to make a good impression since this is the first time I'm meeting your family."

"Yo, don't sweat it. You'll be fine," he chuckled.

I wasn't too sure how true that was, but I accepted it since he would know better than me. "Well, do they at least know that you're bringing me to meet them?"

"Yeah, they know. I should warn you, though. They're a bit wild."

Humph, just what I need. "Oh, really?"

"Yeah," he paused. "So, if my moms starts running off at the mouth, just ignore her."

Oh, trust me. "Why?" I asked puzzled.

"She has a drinking problem."

Oh, great, I thought, *he's bringing me to meet his drunkard mother who likes to talk slick. And this is what I've been waiting for. Lord, help me.*

He made a right turn on another winding road, then made a left at a blinking light then another right. "Here it is," he said, turning down a gravel road. It was the only house on a dead end street. Which I guess was supposed to be a cul-de-sac. Go figure. It was a white, ranch-style with black shutters. And had a long porch with a big wooden swing hanging from it. From the outside it didn't look too bad. There were three little girls, playing outside in their bare feet. One of them was in her pamper. And a little boy with a head full of unruly curls was riding a tricycle. *These kids must get up with the roosters,* I thought to myself. The little girl peeled off her pamper, which was shitty. Ugh. Suddenly the door swung open and out came a big-boned, chick in a pair of jeans and a too-tight, white belly-shirt that exposed her gut, and stretch marks. Humph. The words, TOO FINE TO BE BOTHERED were stretched across her big breast. She wasn't bad looking; but she was definitely *not* fine. Everything about her was big. Big lips. Big Eyes. Big stomach. Big ass.

"Ella Mae git yo' self up in here fo' I tan your rear." She scrunched up her face, trying to see who was in the truck. When Morris got out, she jumped off the porch and screamed. "Well, look what the cat done dragged in." She turned toward the house, and yelled, "Mama, Big Baby done made it in. And he done brought his gal with him." Big Baby? Gal? I knew then, this was going to be the longest damn weekend of my life. *If* I survived.

"What's up, girl?" Morris asked, giving her a hug, then looking over at me. "Autumn, this is my sister Peaches. Peaches, this is Autumn."

"Nice to meet you," I said, cordially.

"It sho' is," she replied, staring at my extended hand before finally deciding to shake it. Limply, that is. The bare-bottomed little girl raised her arms to be picked up. "I ain't fixin' to pick yo' stinky tail up," she responded, grabbing her by the hand. She cut her eye over at me. I gave a fake smile, glancing down at her black Chinese-slippers with the fake red rhinestones. How Bama is that? "Antwan," she yelled at the cute boy on the bike, "come pick up this diaper and put it in the can?" He shook his head, and kept riding. "Don't you shake yo' head *no* at me, boy. Come get this diaper fo' I beat the skin off you." He pouted, getting off his bike and dragging his little feet toward her.

"Where's everybody at?" Morris asked, grabbing our bags from out the trunk.

"Mama's up in the house," she drawled. "And Princess is—" Just before she could get the rest of her words out, the door swung open, again, and out she came. Wearing a white knit mini-skirt and pink tube top. She was another big girl. But had a smaller waist from what I could tell. And she had a cute face, cuter than Peaches' with skin the color of pecans. But that behind . . . Ugh! It was out of control in that three sizes too small skirt. There were just no words to describe it. She had to be carrying at least a hundred pounds of ass. No lie. *It must be from having all those babies,* I thought.

"Well, now," she said, coming down the steps to give Morris a hug. When she smiled, I noticed her two-front teeth were trimmed in gold. Humph. The bottom of her ass cheeks peeked out from under her skirt when she reached up and wrapped her arms around Morris. It was obvious she didn't have on any drawers. I looked down at her feet and noticed the back of her heels needed a pumice stone across them. I frowned, turning my head the other way. "Ain't this a sight for sore eyes? You done got plum skinny in your old age ain't ya boy."

"Nah," Morris replied. "Just staying fit. Princess, this is Autumn. Autumn, Princess."

I smiled. "Nice to meet you." This time I kept my hand to myself.

She returned the smile. "Well, ain't you right purty," she commented. "A bit thin. But purty just the same." I wasn't sure if she was trying to come for me or not, so I just smiled. "I gotta run into town for a bit, so I'll see you when I get back."

"Aiight," Morris said.

She opened the door to her Ford Explorer then said, "Mama's been drinking since sunrise so she might be in rare form."

Morris shook his head. "Some things never change," he replied.

"Have fun," Princess said as she closed her door, revved up her engine then sped off, kicking up dust all around us.

"Come on, let's go in," Morris said, looking at me. He must have seen the look of displeasure on my face. "Don't worry. You'll be fine."

"I hope," I mumbled, following behind Morris, and his big-booty sister.

Well looks are definitely deceiving. Like I said the outside of the house didn't look bad. But, the inside was nasty. And smelled of old funk. The wood floors were in desperate need of a good stripping and waxing. Not to mention, having a broom across it. And the walls were filthy from handprints, grease stains, and crayon and pen markings. There were three floral sofas in the living room, and a rocking chair. Now, I know I said I was a bargain queen. But everything in their place looked like it was straight from a cracked-out Salvation Army.

"Mama," Peaches called out, walking down the hall toward the back of the house. "Big Baby's here."

"Well, hand me my wig," I heard a voice respond. "And shut my door." A few minutes later, a string-bean thin, brown-skinned woman with big breast came out of the bedroom wearing a black-fitted wig cap. It was a spiked cut, and was cute for her narrow face. She had on a pair of black leggings and an extra-tight, white T-shirt with no bra. Her large, dark nipples poked through her shirt. Humph. I glanced down at her feet and noticed she had on a pair of strappy sandals. And her toenails . . . Oh, Lord . . . they were about three inches long, and painted red. *What kind of mess,* I thought, trying to keep a straight face.

"Well, looka here," she said, grabbing Morris and kissing him on his cheek. She smelled like she had just finished guzzling a twelve pack. He hugged her.

"Hey, mom. How you feelin'?"

"Just ducky," she replied, turning her attention to me.

"Mom, this is Autumn. Autumn, this is my mom."

"Nice to meet you ma'am," I said, extending my hand. She shook it.

"I know you ain't fixin' to get my son to put no ring on yo' finga. Is you?" his mother asked, smacking her ruby-red lips.

I cringed. "No, ma'am," I politely said.

"Well, that's good 'cause I ain't fittin' to have another daughter-in-law. Sugar Mae is my only daughter-in-law." Now who the hell is a Sugar Mae? I wondered. I made a mental note to ask Morris about her when I got him alone.

"Come on Ma," Morris interjected. " Don't start."

"Well, you know I don't bite my tongue. I love me some Sugar Mae. But you had to run off a break that girls heart. I still think that youngin of hers is yours."

I raised my eyebrow, glaring at him. *Don't tell me he has an ex-wife and a child that he just forgot to mention to me,* I thought before responding to her remark.

"Well, I have better things to do with my life than trying to get your son to marry me," I said. "If that's what he wants to do, then it'll be on him. But I'm not pressing him." I stopped myself from saying, "You must be out of your cotton-picking, wig-wearing mind if you think I want to walk down the aisle into this mess." I smiled.

"Is that so?"

I nodded. "Yes it is."

"Ma, don't start that. Suga and I been over for years."

"Well, it mighta been over; but I know you was still creepin' with her the last time you came through a month or so ago. And she still loves you." I didn't recall Morris mentioning taking a road trip anywhere. I raised my brow. *Oh, no this fool didn't*, I thought, *sneak down here to screw some buffalo named Suga.*

He sucked his teeth. "Here you go."

We hadn't been in the house a good fifteen minutes, and I was ready to make a dash for the door and burn rubber back to Jersey. I cleared my throat, parting a phony smile. It was obvious there were a few things Morris and I needed to discuss. Pronto! "Well, sounds like Morris has some loose ends he needs to tie up before—"

"What kind of weave is that?" Peaches interrupted, reaching over to put her hands in my hair. I moved my head out the way, scrunching up my face.

"This is *not* a weave."

She grunted. "Yeah, right. If you say so."

I forced a tight smile, running my fingers through my hair. Who the fuck did she think she was getting ready to put her ape hands in my damn hair? That was a no-no.

"Ma," Morris, interrupted. "You and Peaches aren't gonna start giving Autumn the third degree?" He glanced at me, then over at his mother and sister. "We haven't even got in the house good, and the two of you are already starting."

"It's okay," I stated with a strained smile. "Can I use your bathroom?"

"Third door on the right," his mother answered flatly.

"Thanks," I said, slowly walking down the hall. I heard his mother ask Morris if he planned on calling that Suga chick. His response was, "Nah." Then she asked him, "Where'd you find that one?" Meaning me, I guess. I heard him say, "Don't start." *Don't start what?* I wondered. When I found the bathroom, I flicked on the light and almost passed out. It had a pissy stench, and the floor was covered with strands of hair and dirt for days. And I was too through to find someone hadn't flushed the toilet. There was no way I was going to drop my drawers and squat over that filthy bowl. *Humph,* I thought. *I can see where Morris gets his poor cleaning habits. The apple doesn't fall too far from the tree.* Then on top of all that, I shrieked when I spotted roaches crawling on the wall.

"Is everything alright?" Morris asked, coming down the hall. I took a deep breath. I felt myself getting sick.

"I can't use that bathroom," I whispered, backing out of the door.

"What's up?" I stepped to the side so that he could come in to see. He walked in, shaking his head. Then walked over and flushed the toilet. I pointed to the roaches crawling on the wall, which he killed with the palm of his hand, unfazed by the state of the bathroom. He ran water over his hands. I stood there, disgusted.

"Morris," I said in a hushed tone. "I appreciate you bringing me down here to meet your family. But, we're not staying *here* are we?"

"Yeah. Why?"

I took another deep breath. And calmly stated, "I can't stay here."

"Why not?" he asked, twisting his face up. I couldn't believe he had the audacity to ask that simple-behind question. Then again, what did I expect?

I didn't know any other way to say it, other than straight. "I don't mean no harm, but this place is filthy. I thought you said, they knew we were coming."

"They did."

"Well, obviously, from the looks of things they didn't make much preparations," I stated, cutting my eyes over at another roach crawling on the wall. "You're gonna have to find me a hotel to stay at, or take me back to Jersey 'cause I can't lay my head here."

"It's cool," he said, sounding disappointed. But what did I care. There was no way I would be able to close my eyes in that place. "I'll ask my moms for the name of the closest one." When we got back to the living room, his mother and sister were sitting down across from each other. "Ma, we're gonna stay at a hotel."

She and Peaches glanced at each other. "Hmm. Hmm," his mother said. Morris shot her a look. "What, you too good to stay here with yo' family?"

"Ma'am no disrespect, but I would just feel more comfortable in a hotel."

"I ain't speakin' to you," his mother sneered.

Instead of being disrespectful, I simply said, "Morris, I'll meet you outside." He handed me the keys.

"I'll be out in a minute," he said. Peaches rolled her eyes at me as I walked toward the door.

"Snotty heifer," I heard her say under her breath. But I let it go. But inside, I was ready to set it off.

"Where'd you find that uppity gal," I heard his mother ask.

"C'mon, Ma. She's good people."

"Humph. She seems a bit too high up on that horse of hers if you ask me," Peaches remarked. "Stuck-up bitch. Turning her nose up, like she ain't never seen a damn roach."

"Peaches, you watch your mouth for I put my foot in it," his mother snapped. "Don't go calling Big Baby's gal stuck-up." They laughed. I clenched my teeth. I know Morris wasn't going to let her crusty tail get away with that. His mother slick-talking was one thing, but that knotty-haired, weave wearing, Troll-doll of a sister calling me out of my name was another. Now, I wasn't raised to be disrespectful, and I definitely wasn't raised to talk about someone's mother; but damn, them. Coon bitches! I was a split second from forgetting my manners and barging back inside to slap the soot off her when I heard Morris open his mouth.

"Yo, go take your stinking ass somewhere," he said. "You always running off at the mouth. You need to take your nasty ass home and take care of those bad-assed kids of yours instead of worrying 'bout somebody else. With your trifling behind."

"Aww, look Mama. He done got his nose wide-opened for that high-yella wench of his. Ain't that cute."

"Peaches, knock it off," his mother snapped. "She ain't that yella." They laughed again.

"You know what?" Morris snapped back. "Both of you are fucked up for that. Ya'll not gonna be disrespecting her like that, and definitely not in front of me. "

"Big Baby, we just messin' wit you. I reckon she's alright, if that's what you like," Peaches said.

"The gal ain't nothing but a bag of bones," his mother replied. "And comin' up in my home actin' all high 'n mighty. Like she too good for my hospitality."

"Well, maybe if you cleaned up around here," Morris retorted. "She wouldn't feel that way. Damn! You knew we were coming."

"Now, don't you go sassin' off at me," his mother snapped. "I think you done got a bit too big fo' yo' britches. I keep my place the way I like it, and if you don't like it, you and your bony-high-yella-heifer can let the door knob hit ya."

Morris sucked his teeth, walking toward the door where he saw me standing. His jaw dropped. I glared at him, as I swung the door open. Steam was coming from every which way. I didn't care how far away from home I was or whose mother she was. I went off. Essex County came flying out of me like there was no tomorrow.

"Morris, get me the hell out of this place, *now,* before I go the fuck off!"

I could tell he was embarrassed. "Yeah, let's go," he said, looking at me, then at his mother and sister. "I should have known better any damn way to drive all the way down here."

"The next time you crusty, porch-monkey bitches have something to say about me, say it to my damn face!" I yelled.

"Who you talking at like that?" Peaches asked.

"You, you fat moose."

"Gal, you bet watch ya mouth in my house," his mother said, banging her hands on her hips.

"Well, you watch your mouth. You and your fat-assed daughter don't know me to be talking shit about me."

"Yo, what the fuck!" he yelled. "This is why I don't bring no one around ya'll ignorant asses." He snatched up our bags. "Let's get the fuck up outta here," he snapped, pushing the door open. I followed behind him, pacing in circles. I was ready to whip up on either one of them. And dared one of them to step to me.

When we got in the car and drove off, he stated, "I'm sorry about that. I really thought this was gonna be a good idea. This is why I don't fuck with them." I could hear the humiliation and hurt in his voice.

"Humph," I grunted, turning my head toward the window.

"I should have never tried to surprise you with this shit."

You're right about that. I turned to look at him, then turned my head back toward the window. I was wordless. If I didn't know before, I knew after meeting his niggerish, countrified kinfolk that thing's between him and I were definitely not going to work out. There was just no way I'd ever marry into a family like *that*. Ugh. Whatever thoughts I might have entertained were quickly dismissed. Whatever reservations I might have had were long gone. There was absolutely no hope for us. The minute we got back to Jersey, I was axing him.

Seven

Nia

"Girl, I'm telling you," Nygeria said, talking fast into the phone. "I saw him dancing with some mixed-breed chick at Cubra Libre. The skinny bitch was wearing a halter type mini-dress, and she had her big basketball ass all up on his dick. And he was riding it like he was ready to slam-dunk it."

"Are you sure it was him?" I asked, not totally convinced.

"Well, if it wasn't, he damn sure has a clone somewhere out here. And he's getting his freak on like no other."

"Well, did you say something to him?"

"No, because I was on the upper level and it was packed as hell." She said when she looked over the railing she spotted Mustafa on the dance floor getting his bump and grind on with some light-skinned chick with long, wavy hair. By the time she fought her way through the crowd to get downstairs, he and the chick were gone.

"Well, it couldn't have been Mustafa. Because he's in Maryland."

"Well, that's what he told *you*. But I know what I saw."

"How many drinks did you have?" I asked, flipping through my latest issue of *Bazaar,* half-listening to her try to convince me that my man was at some damn club with some half-naked hooch.

"Bitch," she huffed. "I had enough, but not *that* many. You know I have eyes like a hawk. Trust me. It was him."

"What time was this?"

"Like two, maybe three, in the morning."

"Nygeria, are you absolutely, positively sure it was him?" I asked again, hoping her eyes had been playing tricks on her. I closed the magazine, and held my breath.

"I'm telling you, the nigga I saw was the same height, body build, color and everything as Mustafa. I'm almost one hundred percent certain it was him."

I exhaled. Being *almost* certain wasn't good enough for me. Unless she was absolutely sure, and had spoken to him, there was a great possibility that she was mistaken. I know Nygeria when she's tanked up. She probably saw somebody who resembled him and just assumed off the bat that it was. There was no possible way. Besides, Mustafa doesn't even like Atlantic City. He'll go to Vegas before he goes there. And even if that wasn't the case, there's no way he'd play me like that after I just confronted him about that chick from the halfway house. There's just no way he'd be *that* crazy. Nygeria was definitely seeing things.

"Well, trust and believe. I will ask him," I said, certain her eyes were playing tricks on her. But just to be on the safe side, I was going to check it out.

She smacked her lips. "Ugh, do you really think he's gonna admit to it. Get real, girl. You need to just keep an eye open, that's all. Trust me, he'll slip up again." She sounded so sure of herself. Those letters flashed through my mind, and suddenly my confidence began to waver.

"Yeah, you're probably right," I agreed. But, in the back of my mind, I knew I was going to ask him just the same. "Listen, let me call you back," I said, pacing the kitchen. My nerves were starting to get rattled. *That motherfucker better be his ass in Maryland.*

"Don't tell me you're getting ready to call him?"

"No," I lied, "I need to run an errand real quick." I glanced up at the wall clock. It was eleven o'clock in the morning. I frowned, wondering why the hell she was just now calling me if she saw Mustafa around two in the morning. She should have called me right then. Whatever.

"Let me let you go then," she said, yawning. "Oooh, excuse me. I'm whipped. We didn't get up to the room until seven this morning." She and Chandra decided to rent a room at the Tropicana instead of taking that long ride back up to Orange. Plus, she had hit the blackjack table, and won five hundred dollars. Knowing her, she'd play a few more hands before heading back up the Parkway. "Call me later. Better yet, I'll stop by later on this afternoon when I get back."

"I'll be here."

"And remember what I said. Just keep what I told you under wraps."

"I sure will," I said, before clicking over and speed dialing Mustafa's cell number. He quickly picked up.

"Hey, Baby," he said, sounding half-asleep. "What's up?"

"You," I responded, keeping my tone in check. I pulled out a kitchen chair and sat down. "I got your message last night. How come you didn't call me on my cell?"

"I started to, but my sister started beasting about some dumb shit; and I got sidetracked. I figured I'd just hit you up today."

"Oh, 'cause I tried calling you back but your voice mail picked up. You must have turned your phone turned off."

"Nah, I thought I had put it on vibrate," he explained, "but I accidentally turned it off."

Yeah, right. Then again, it could have been an honest mistake. So I didn't press it. "So ya'll went out?"

"Yeah, we ended up going to this spot in Temple Hills."

"Who all went?"

"Three of my cousins, and two of their friends." Asking if his cousins were male, or if their friends were female or vice versa didn't even matter.

"Oh, yeah. So where'd ya'll go?" I asked trying to sound like I was really interested instead of coming across like I was trying to interrogate him.

"The Legend, or some shit like that," he responded, yawning. "Damn, sorry 'bout that."

"How was it?" I asked, sitting on the edge of my chair. I blew a silent sigh of relief that he *was* in Maryland where he said he'd be.

"It was aiight."

"Well, you go on back to sleep. I just wanted to give you a quick call."

"Yo, it's all good. I need to be getting up anyway. So, what you gonna be doing today?"

"Not much," I stated, getting up to look out the window. It was unseasonably warm for October. Felt like summer. "I'll probably just clean up around here. Do some laundry."

"Oh, yeah?"

"Yeah."

"What you got on?" he asked, lowering his voice.

"A tee-shirt."

"What else?"

"That's it."

"Damn," he replied. "You got my dick hard."

I sucked my teeth, plopping down on the sofa. "Yeah, right."

"Real talk. You know what your sexy ass does to me."

I crossed my leg, bouncing my right leg over my left. "Hmm. Hmm. I know what you say."

"Oh, what. You don't believe me?"

"I didn't say that."

"Aiight, then. Act like you know."

"Humph. When you coming home again?" I asked, changing the subject.

"Wednesday," he answered.

Humph. First it was Monday night, or Tuesday. Now it's Wednesday. Suddenly it dawned on me that he hadn't said anything about his job.

"So when you going back to work?" I asked.

Silence.

"Mustafa?"

"I'm here."

"Well, when do you have to be back to work?"

"I don't," he replied. "I quit that piece."

I frowned. "When?"

Silence. I could hear a muffled sound in the background.

"Mustafa, what are you doing?"

"Nah, nothing. My sister just walked up in the room."

"Oh. So, when'd you quit your job?" I asked with attitude. "And when were you gonna mention it to me?"

"Yo, I don't feel like getting into it right now," he told me. I sucked my teeth. "Yo, come on, Baby. Don't. We'll talk about when I get home, aiight."

"Yeah, whatever." I said. "Well, let me get off this line so I can get some work done. Call me later."

"No doubt. I love you."

"Hmm. Hmm. Me, too," I said, squeezing my eyes shut as if I could see him through the phone, lying in bed in his boxers with his hand on his dick. Or perhaps . . . scratch that. I'm not even going there.

"Give me a kiss." I blew a quick one through the phone. "Come on you can do better than that." I gave him a longer one this time. "That's wassup. Be easy, baby. I'll hit you later."

"Yep," I responded, slamming the phone down. *I knew that wasn't him Nygeria saw. But if this nigga's not working that only means . . . I'm not even going there,* I thought to myself, fuming.

When he got home from prison I told him straight from the gate, reminding him, I wasn't going to tolerate drug dealing. Been there, done that. Granted, when I met him that's what he was into. And I accepted it. Well, not really. I just turned a blind eye to it. And it's also what got him bagged. And had me running up and down the damn highway. But, I made it very clear I wasn't beat for that shit again.

"I'm not doing another bid with you," I had told him.

"Nah, don't even wet it," he reassured me. "I'm done. I'm just gonna squat on a job and chill. I got enough dough to hold me over for a minute." Well, it sounded good. But, so far, since he's been home, he's only worked five out of twelve months. I understood it was hard at first getting a job because of his criminal record. But I kept encouraging him. He must have filled out sixty applications, and got turned down countless times before he finally landed the job at Home Depot in Elizabeth. Fortunately, one of his boys was a manager there, and hooked him up making twelve dollars an hour. Oh, okay. So it's not a lot of money for a baller. But it's legitimate. And it beats looking over your shoulder every damn day. And it keeps his parole officer off his back. Plus, he had benefits. And now, he tells me he quit. *Yeah, we'll definitely talk when you get back,* I thought, heading up the stairs.

"Okay, Bitch," Nygeria screeched. "Tell me you didn't call him."

"Nope," I said, keeping a straight face.

"You're such a liar," she snapped. "So spill it. What did he say?"

I sucked my teeth, rolling my eyes. "You think you know so damn much."

"I know you, girlfriend."

"Well, you're wrong this time," I stated, sticking to my little white lie. There was really no need to tell her that who she *thought* she saw wasn't Mustafa. "I decided to just keep it tucked for now."

"Humph," she grunted, smacking her cranberry-red painted lips. "Well, what's up for tonight?" I shook my head. Girlfriend was always down for a good time. She was laced in an ankle-length cranberry Emilio Pucci frock dress. And was killing me with her Gucci flat shoulder bag, and four-inch T-straps. Oooh, I could just scratch her eyes out.

"Not a damn thing," I replied. "I'm just gonna chill."

"Later for that," she sighed. "Let's grab a bite at the Olive Garden, then hit a movie. I wanna see *The Diary of A Mad Black Woman;* that Tyler Perry is just doin' the damn thing—with his rich self."

I chuckled. "You stupid. Let me get a rain check."

"Damn, girl. What you gonna do, sit around the house all weekend, waiting for Mustafa to roll back in."

"Not at all," I responded defensively. "I just don't feel like going out." My stomach growled. Then again, going to get something to eat didn't sound like a bad idea since I didn't have any food in the house, and I really didn't feel like cooking, anyway. "Let me go throw something on," I stated, relenting. "Your treat."

"Bitch," she snapped. "I treated your ugly ass yesterday. Or did you forget?"

I gave her the finger. "Today's a new day. So get over it. And for your information, this ugly ass is cuter than you."

"Whatever," she said, waving me on. "Just hurry up. I'm starved."

When we got to the Olive Garden on Route 22 in Springfield, it was a twenty-to-thirty minute wait. The place was packed with heads. But we decided to wait it out. So while we were sitting outside on one of the benches, this Oriental blue 745i pulled up to let out this nondescript chick. I caught a quick glance at the driver before he drove off to park. *Damn, he looks familiar,* I thought. A few minutes later, this chocolate-colored cat comes boppin' in our direction, wearing a sky blue Phat Farm sweat suit with white Tee, and a crisp pair of white Air Force Ones. I had to admit, his swagger was sexy as hell.

"That nigga's fine," Nygeria whispered, nudging me with her elbow. "But he could have kept the old-maid home." I glanced again. As he got closer, he definitely looked like someone I knew. But I wasn't for sure. He shot a look in our direction.

"How you ladies doin'?" he asked, opening the entrance of the door.

"Fine," we responded in unison.

He grinned, catching my eye. "Oh snap. Nia?"

"Yeah," I said, tilting my head with attitude.

"Damn, it's been a minute," he said, letting the handle of the door go. "I thought that was you." For the life of me, I couldn't figure out who he was. He must have read the look on my face. "You don't even know who I am, do you?"

I took the 'tude down a notch. "I can't say that I do. You look familiar, though."

"Qua. I mean Quasheem."

"Oh. My. God!" I snapped, getting up to give him a hug. "It's been years."

"True that. You still looking good," he stated, checking me out from head-to-toe.

I smiled. "Thanks. Damn, you've changed. Got all tall and thick." He stood about five-feet-eleven and had a broad chest and shoulders.

He grinned. "Yeah, something like that."

Nygeria cleared her throat. I rolled my eyes, shaking my head. "Oh, Qua. This is my girl Nygeria."

"What's up?"

"You, Playa," Nygeria replied, coyly.

His plain Jane came back out just as he was about to respond. I'm sure to see what was taking him so long. But, I'm not gonna front. As fine as he was, I'd have done the same thing. She looked over at us, then parted a phony smile, before turning her attention to him.

"They said it's gonna be a thirty minute wait," she said.

"That's cool. Yo, this is Nia. We went to school together. Nia, this is Nicola. And, my bad. What's your name again?"

"Nygeria," she said, twisting her face up. I chuckled to myself.

"Hello," his companion said. We returned the customary greeting with fake smiles. "Baby, I'm gonna wait inside. It was nice meeting you."

"You too," I said. Nygeria ignored her, turning her head in the other direction. Knowing her, she'd have something to say once we were alone.

As soon as the door closed behind her, he quickly stated, "She's just a friend."

"That's what they all say," Nygeria replied, turning her attention back to us. I shrugged my shoulder.

"I can tell you a real piece of work," he commented, pointing over at Nygeria. She batted her eyes, licking her lips. I was certain she was only being flirty because of his ride. And she probably thought—or should I say, assumed—he was a hustler. She even had a bit of an attitude when he didn't feed into her. "What's up with Autumn?" he asked, ignoring her. His eyes lit up when he asked about her.

I could almost see Nygeria's eyes rolling up in her head when he asked about my cousin. Nygeria could say whatever she wanted 'bout my cuz's gear, but she knew not to press it any further than that. Girl or not, blood was still thicker than water. "She's chillin'."

"Oh, yeah. Well, let her know I asked about her."

I smiled. "I'll definitely do that."

"Better yet," he said, reaching into his back pocket, then pulling out his leather wallet. He pulled out a card, flipped it over, then wrote his number on the back of it. "Give her this. Let her know I'd really like to hear from her. If she can't reach me at the shop numbers, she can hit me on my private line."

I glanced at the card. It read: SIGMA CUTS. "I'll make sure she gets it." Our little round puck lit up, alerting us that our table was ready.

"Come on," Nygeria said, getting up abruptly. "Our table's ready." He held the door open for us.

"It was good seeing you," I said.

"Yeah, you too," he agreed, walking in behind us. His date was sitting in one of the chairs with her legs crossed and her arms folded tight across her chest. I smelled attitude. "Make sure you do that for me, aiiight." He put his hand to his ear gesturing a phone.

I smiled, nodding. Nygeria threw her head up, poppin' her hips towards the hostess.

Once we were seated, and the waitress had brought us our salad and garlic breadsticks—which I love, I gave Nygeria the 411 on Quasheem. I gave her the condensed version of how he and Autumn messed around in junior high and part of high school. I left out the part about him getting two other chicks pregnant while they were together. And how this chick from Irvington tried to have her jumped by her girls over him at a basketball game. But, little did they know, that if they fought Autumn, they were gonna have to fight me and my clique, too. And then after we fought 'em, my mother and my aunt—Autumn's mother—would end up going to their school and beating them up. Because, that's how those two rolled. If you touched one of their kids, you were gonna have to deal with them as well. And then, they were going to find the mothers and slide them too. That's why no one from the Oranges messed with us. They knew our mothers were crazy. Miriam and Muriel, the Dangerous duo. That's what they were called. So, to eliminate all the drama, I told the chick to fight Autumn a fair one. And the dumb trick did. And got mopped. I guess she thought Autumn couldn't go with the hands because she was all quiet and whatnot; sort of nerdy, if you know what I mean. Ha! Autumn wore that tail out, then the next day broke up with him. Girlfriend cried for almost two months over him. He tried everything to get her back; but she refused, stating, "If I gotta fight over a man, I don't need or want one."

"Humph," Nygeria grunted, in between bites of her salad. "I see his taste in females hasn't changed much."

"And what's that supposed to mean?" I asked, giving her my "bitch-don't-start" look.

"I'm just sayin'."

"You're sayin' what?" I tilted my head, waiting.

"Nothing. Forget it."

"Hmm. I thought so," I snapped.

She turned her lips up.

Ny was my girl and all, but in one quick breath I was about to bring it to her. I counted to ten in my head. "You know, I don't know what your problem is with Autumn but you really need to chill."

"I don't have a problem with her. She's just not my cup of tea."

"And you're not hers. But she doesn't spend her time trying to dis you every chance she gets. The shit's getting really played," I said, putting my fork down. "I keep telling you to stop tryna come for my cousin. Keep your underhanded comments and remarks to yourself. And I mean *that.*"

She put her hands up in mock surrender. "Damn, you don't have to get your panties all in a bunch. I don't mean no harm."

"Actually, I think you do. But that's my blood and you're not gonna be disrespecting her. Playing or not, especially around me. I got mad love for you, but please don't ever think I'd side with you over my own flesh and blood. 'Cause if push comes to shove, I'd jump on you like the next bitch on the bricks, okay."

"And you should. But you don't have to go there."

"Well, then, don't take me there. And we won't have to get there." The waitress returned to our table, looking at the both of us. I guess my voice was louder than I had wanted it to be because it looked like she wasn't sure if she should ask if we were ready to order, or ready to rumble. I looked over at her before she could open her mouth. "I'll have the chicken scampi," I said, handing her my menu. "And a glass of the Montevina white Zinfandel."

"And I'll have the seafood Alfredo, and a glass of Pinot Grigio—Bottega Vinaia.

"I'll be right back with your order," the young waitress said. Between you and me. I really wanted to read Ny's ass, but I think she got my point, 'cause for the rest of our meal girlfriend kept her conversation light. Not that that's something to brag about, but when you don't have a lot of female friends you do what you must to keep the only one you have on your side. Needless to say, the rest of the night was uneventful. And by the time we walked out of the movie theater, it was all love again.

"That movie was good as hell," Nygeria commented as we walked out of the theater toward her truck. "That was some real foul shit Charles did, dragging Helen out of her own damn house. Then movin' his jumpoff in. He treated Helen like a fuckin' dog."

"Worse, if you ask me," I agreed. "He was just a fucked-up individual."

"Like most niggas."

"Mmmhmm. They'll have a good woman who stands by their side through thick and thin, then blow up and turn around and give her their ass to kiss. Go figure."

"Just straight up doggish."

I nodded. "Well, it couldn't have been me, that's for sure. I'll never let myself be put in a position where a man puts me out of *any*thing, or treats me like that."

"I know that's right," she said, flying down the highway. She ran a red light. "I would have beat that nigga down, then took him to the cleaners."

I chuckled. "Well, she did the right thing. And he got just what he had coming to his ugly, big-lipped behind."

"They always do," she stated.

"You ain't never lied," I responded, glancing at my watch. It was a little after ten. I checked my cell to see if I had any messages. None. Then I called my house to check my answering machine. Nothing. *Hmm. Why the hell hasn't Mustafa called me back yet?*

"Trust and believe. In the end, payback is always a bitch."

"It sure is," I replied, snapping my cell shut. "It sure the hell is."

Eight

Autumn

Morris apologized profusely for about ten minutes, trying to get me to respond to him. But I just stared ahead. Finally, he gave up and just drove. You could hear a pin drop. I just zoned out the window of his truck, acting as if he were invisible. Wising I could fold my arms, blink my eyes and be home. A few times, along the way, he tried again to strike up a conversation but I was not feeling it. He got the hint and just left me the heck alone. The more I thought about how rude and trifling his family was, the more sure I was that it was a wrap between the two of us. Truth be told, it should have been over before it got started. Especially once I realized how trifling *he* was—like the time he pissed in a cup and left it sitting on his nightstand. How nasty is that? Humph. Too damn lazy to get up and go to the bathroom. Or like the time he blew his nose on the end of his bedspread because he didn't have any Kleenex nearby. Just leaned over, grabbed the bottom of his blanket and blew snot like it was nothing. What did I do? I just turned my head in disgust, then got out of bed, put on my clothes and went home. Right then, I should have left for good. But, I didn't. Silly me. Well, it's better late than never. Bottom line: I was finally throwing down my net, and letting this ghetto butterfly flutter on its merry way. And the only reason I didn't let him know that while he was driving was because I didn't want to run the risk of being put out on the side of the road. At least, not until I got closer to home. In all honesty, a part of me felt as though my anger was a bit misdirected. It's not like he could have known his little attempt to introduce me to his countrified family would have turned out the way it did. Not that we get to choose whom we're related to. But daggoneit! He knew how darn trifling they were. And he had no business subjecting me to that kind of drama. *Then again*, I suddenly thought, *I should be thanking him for giving me the out I'd been looking for.*

When we finally got to the Delaware Memorial Bridge I relaxed, glancing at my watch. Home was right around the corner. Two more hours, and I'd be done with his lame behind. I decided once we hit the New Jersey Turnpike that I was staying clear of men, once and for all. I stretched my arms over my head, then clamped my legs shut. I had a decision to make: Sit in my stubbornness or let him know I needed to use the bathroom. I swear, if I hadn't been wearing my good panties—the ones I bought at Macy's—I would have just sat in piss the rest of the way home. Unfortunately, my obstinacy was slowly drowning in an overflowing bladder.

"Can you do me a favor and stop at the next rest stop?" I asked, keeping my face toward the passenger window, pressing my legs together tighter.

"No problem," he responded. "I need to get gas anyway."

I reached down on the floor, grabbing my pocket book. I opened it, then pulled out my wallet, taking out a fifty-dollar bill. I handed it to him.

He looked at my hand, "What's that for?"

"My half of the gas," I replied, cutting my eyes in his direction.

He gently pushed my hand away. "Come on, you know better than that."

"I insist," I stated, stuffing the money in his front shirt pocket. For the first time since we left North Carolina I looked at him. Hard.

He matched my stare, pulling the money out of his pocket and stuffing it in my lap. "I don't need your money."

I rolled my eyes, tossing it up on the dashboard. "I didn't say you did." He shook his head, shifting his eyes back on the road and veering over to the left toward the Service area entrance.

Finally, we were pulling up in my driveway. Before he could get the truck in park good I had the door open, preparing to get out. "There's no need to turn your ignition off," I said, grabbing my purse.

"Oh, it's like that?"

"It sure is," I replied, opening up the rear door and grabbing my bag, then closing it.

"Damn! Why you trippin'?" he asked, getting out of the truck.

"I'm not, *trippin'*. I'm not beat. That's what I'm not. So, get back in your truck and press on. Because, I'm done."

"Excuse me?"

"You heard me," I stated. "I *said* I'm not beat."

He walked around the truck, staring at me dumbfounded. "Yo, just like that?"

"Yes, Morris. Just like that. You and I have come to a fork in the road. And, it's time we go our separate ways. I don't want there to be any hard feelings. So, be safe in your travels."

"And what is that supposed to mean?" he asked, coming closer to me.

"It means. It's over. It was nice knowing you. But this is where it ends for us." I turned on my heels and started toward the door.

He yanked me by the arm, swinging me around. "What the fuck you mean, 'it's over'?"

I snatched my arm away from him, dropping my purse. "Have you lost what's left of your good senses, putting your damn hands on me?" I snapped. "I said it was over so get back in your truck, and go on about your business."

"Not until you give me some kind of explanation."

Maybe I should have been more tactful. Oh, well. I wasn't. And maybe my tone should have been a bit softer. Well, it wasn't. I had held so much in with regards to our dead-end relationship that I figured I might as well go out with a bang. So, I did. "You want an explanation, Morris. Fine, I'll give you one.

Better yet, I'll give you two. One, I'm tired of you. And, two, I'm tired of being tired of you." Now that I was on a roll, I kept going. "And if that's not good enough for you, I can give you two more. Starting with the fact that you're cheap. And trifling. And ending with the fact that I no longer want to waste my time, emotions or energy into a relationship—or man, for that matter—that is not going anywhere."

He looked at me stunned for a moment, then frowned. "Why didn't you tell me this before?"

"Well, I'm telling you now."

"Well, you should have told me this shit before I drove your silly ass all the way to North Carolina."

I laughed, "Silly? Ugh. Please. For your information, I didn't ask to go. And I definitely didn't ask to meet your uncivilized family."

His jaws tightened. "Say, what?"

"You heard me," I stated, stooping down to pick up my purse. I stood up. "Now, do us both a favor and get off my property."

His lips tightened. "Fuck you, Autumn."

"Whatever!" I snapped, flicking my wrist at him.

"Yo," he snapped, getting up in my face. I dropped my bags, preparing for what might come next. "Don't you ever, fuckin' flip your damn hand at me."

"Whatcha gonna do. Hit me, Morris?"

He backed up, "Fuck it! You not even worth it."

"I'm glad I'm not."

He walked back toward his truck. "Stupid, bitch!"

That did it. The ghetto came out of me, and before I knew it, I went off. "And so is your drunk ass, bald-headed mother and fat-ass, Magilla Gorilla-looking sister. And you're right, I *was* a stupid bitch for putting up with the likes of you."

He jumped back out of his truck, rushing over to me. "What did you say?" His face distorted, and his eyes narrowed. But, I ignored the signs that danger was approaching.

"I said, so is your mother. So go take your trifling, can't-eat-the-pussy-right behind back to your roach-infested, shoebox of a place. And get the hell off my damn property before I . . . " *Slap!* Before I could get the rest of my words out, he backhanded me.

"Don't you ever fuckin' disrespect my mother. Or talk shit to me. You hear me, bitch!" He slapped me again. I screamed, fighting him in the middle of my driveway with all my might.

By the time the police arrived, blood was everywhere. We both had busted lips. My eye was swollen shut. His face and neck were clawed up. His nose was bleeding. And my neighbors were standing outside, getting an eye full. I was too through. Two of the officers had Morris in handcuffs and were placing him in the back of their patrol car.

"Miss, are you sure you don't want us to take you to the hospital?" A white officer with a gap-toothed asked.

I shook my head, holding an icepack to my eye. "No. I'll be fine. I just want to lie down. What's going to happen to him?" I inquired. Why, I don't know.

"We're taking him down to the precinct," he answered.

"I don't want to sign a complaint or see him get arrested," I stated.

"I'm sorry, but any sign of injury in a domestic violence situation requires us to arrest the perpetrator. Whether you sign complaints or not." *Domestic Violence.* I couldn't believe my ears. This wasn't supposed to be happening to me. Not Autumn Marie Brimmington. But, with the blink of an eye, I had become a statistic. I was a victim of partner abuse. And had become my mother. She and Bradley—her boyfriend of twelve years—would fight like cats and dogs. She'd be arrested. He'd be arrested. Her face would be all beat up. Ribs broken. He'd be all stabbed up. Or cut up. Then two weeks later, she'd be right back with him. And anytime someone said anything bad about him, she'd defend him. Or tell them to mind their business. I couldn't stand him. Or their craziness, and finally went to live with my grandmother. But, in between the fights she would always say, "Autumn, don't you ever let no man put his hands on you. You hear?" I'd nod my head. "If he does, you beat him with everything that's in you, then leave him. And never look back. Promise me." I'd make her, and myself, that promise. And, each time, I'd ask her when *she* was leaving. Her eyes would water and she'd say, "When I stop loving him." Then one day, I guess she stopped loving him. Or maybe she just finally loved herself enough to want to leave—realizing she deserved better—and he killed her. He wrapped a telephone cord around her neck and strangled her to death, and if that wasn't enough—in his wild, rabid attack on her life—he bit her in the face, then stuffed her body in a closet. It was eight days in the middle of July before anyone found my mother's corpse. Wide-eyed. Decomposed. She was thirty-three.

Hearing that my mother had been killed was the worse day of my life. I had heard the words, clearly; but still could not grasp that the woman who had given me life was gone. Taken away by rage, and insecurity. By hatred and hostility. She had become a tragedy. A target in a war where there was no beginning or end, just the overwhelming need, and desire, to love. I knew, but did not fully comprehend this. In my mind, I recognized it. Tried so hard to deny it. But the day had come, the final hour struck and, suddenly, I had become motherless. It felt like my life had been tossed in the air, and blown away. My world had become a jigsaw puzzle without all its pieces. And no matter how many times I tried to put everything back together, something would always be missing. My mother. And, I honestly didn't think I'd ever get through it. Sometimes, I don't think I completely have because she was taken from me without any closure. Or understanding.

I was eighteen when I drove to East Jersey State Prison—formerly Rahway—and confronted my mother's murderer during a window visit. I needed to know why he did it. Why he couldn't just let her go. And, he looked me straight in my eyes and said, "Because she belonged to me. I know it was wrong. But, it was right for me. And I'd do it again if I had to." There was no apology. No remorse. No value for human life. "I hope you rot in hell!" I snapped before hanging up the phone and walking out, knowing then that I'd never let a man try to control me or treat me as his property.

I grimaced, holding the side of my face. "What are you going to charge him with?"

"Assault," the officer said. "I think you should file for a temporary restraining order just to be on the safe side."

"That won't be necessary. I just want him and his truck off my property."

He nodded. "Well, if you change your mind, you can always come down to request one."

"Thanks." I could overhear Morris arguing with one of the patrolman, claiming he was only protecting himself. Just lying through his teeth. I shook my head. "Are we done? I'd like to go inside now." I caught Morris' stare. It was vacant. I shifted my eyes.

"Bitch!" he yelled out.

"Officer, you have my numbers. If you need me for anything else, call me." He nodded, heading back to his car. I got up from the step, and went inside, locking my door. I caught my reflection in my wall mirror. A tear slid down my face. "That was the first and last time a man will *ever* put his hands on me," I said aloud as I made my way to my bathroom to run a hot bath to soak my aching body.

Nine

Nia

"He did what?!" I asked, not believing what I'd just heard.

"Morris, and I got into a fight," she repeated, "and he slapped me."

"Oh, no the hell he didn't!" I snapped. "When?"

"Late Saturday evening."

"And what possessed him to put his hands on you?" I asked, slamming my hand on my hip while pacing the kitchen floor.

"I guess I said some things he didn't like," she offered. It sounded like she was trying to minimize what he did, or place the blame on herself.

"And that excuses him for slapping you?"

"Not at all. I'm just saying. Maybe I should have ended it differently. That's all."

I rolled my eyes up in my head, blowing out a breath of frustration. "No, maybe he should have kept his damn hands to himself."

"You're right about that."

"You damn right I am," I snapped. "Why didn't you call me?"

"I didn't want to get you in the middle of it," she said. "Besides, it's over."

"Oh, no the hell it's not. He put his damn hands on you. He slapped the wrong sista. Trust. Me and Slugger are going to pay that bitch-ass nigga a visit and bust his ass up." Slugger was my nickname for my baseball bat.

"Nia, don't. The police arrested him already. I just want to get on with my life. Let me handle this. Promise me you won't do anything crazy." I rolled my eyes again. Promise, hell. Autumn and I are the only family we have. And I'll be damned if some nigga will get away with slapping her. Police or not, I don't care. You fight one, you fight us both, and that's that. She must have read my mind.

"Please, Nia. Let it go. Promise me you won't go after him."

Silence.

"Nia," she repeated.

"I heard you."

"Then promise me."

"I can't"

She sighed, "I don't need you to fight my battles."

"I didn't say you did. But you know how we get down."

"But that's when we were kids. We're grown women now, and we can't go around jumping people who have wronged us. Just let the police handle it. I don't want you doing anything crazy, then getting arrested and losing your job behind him. It's not worth it." Flashes of my Aunt Miriam's black eyes and swollen face came to mind, then images of my mother's rage. My mother would throw on her sweats, pull back her hair and lace up her sneakers, then go over to my aunt's apartment and wait for her sorry-ass boyfriend to come back in. And when he did, she'd fight him like there was no tomorrow. The police would be called, and my mother would be arrested. But she didn't care. That was her blood. And she'd kill for her. "I don't give a fuck about jail. No one puts their damn hands on my sister, and gets away with it!" she'd snap. Sadly, aunt Miriam kept going back to his abuse. And my grandmother would have to bail my mother out of jail every time he put his hands on her. I could never understand how anyone could stay in an abusive relationship. Then again, I'd never been in one. So, maybe I'd never comprehend.

"Don't worry," she said, bringing me back to the present. "I'm not going back to him. It's over."

I blew out a sigh of relief, hoping that was so. "Well, did you at least fuck him up?"

"And you know I did. Clawed him up real good."

I chuckled. "That's what I'm talkin' about. So how are you doin?"

"I'm fine. Sore. But I'll live."

I pursed my lips, not totally convinced. "I'll be right over."

"Nia, you don't have to. I'm fine, really."

"Well, I'll be over to see for myself. Bye." I hung up before she could try to talk me out of it.

I jumped in the shower, threw on my clothes and hopped in my truck. But before I left the house, I pulled Slugger out of the closet and slipped him in the backseat. Just in case.

As I waited at the stoplight, I flipped down my visor and checked myself. *Let me catch that punk*, I thought, flipping the visor back up, *I'm gonna smash his grill in.* All of a sudden, a burgundy Lex sped through the light going east. I assumed to catch it before it turned red. *Idiot*, I thought. *That's how someone gets killed.* The light in front of me turned green, and I proceeded. Then it hit me. The car that had just rode by looked like Mustafa's. And it looked like there was someone on the passenger side. I flipped open my phone and spoke, "Mustafa", then waited for his number to dial.

"Yo," he answered. "What's good?"

"You," I responded. "Did you just come down Main Street?"

"Nah. Why?"

"Oh. I thought I saw you ride pass me."

"Nah, wrong guy baby."

"Hmm. Where you at anyway?"

"Up Top."

I sucked my teeth. Again, he was in New York. "Doing, what?"

"Tryna stack this paper, Nia. Why?"

No this fool is not tryna pop an attitude. "Forget it," I snapped. "Do you."

"Yo, what the fuck!" he cursed. "I'm tryna make moves, and all you wanna do is ride my damn back."

Now where was this hostility coming from? *Guilt*, I answered in my head. I calmed myself before I went off. "Mustafa, I don't care how many moves you tryna make. We already went through this. And I told you. I'm not beat for that shit. What you need to do is look for another job."

He sucked his teeth. "Look, a niggas tryna eat. You knew how I got down when we met so stop trippin'. Damn. Relax. I got this"

"I'm not trippin', Mustafa."

"Then back up off me."

I blinked real hard, then spoke. "Understand this, if you get knocked, you're on your own. I meant what I said. I'm not doing another bid."

"Oh, word. But it's all good when I'm lacing your ass in Gucci and shit, right? Or when you're ridin' around in that fuckin' truck, right?"

"Whatever, Mustafa." I snapped, pressing the END button, hanging up on his stupid ass before I said something I'd regret later. Mustafa got back from Maryland late Tuesday night. Took his behind to NY early Wednesday morning, and now, here it was Thursday, and he's there again. And the crazy thing is, I haven't seen him since he's been home. We've talked. But that's it. You would have thought that I'd be the first person he'd want to see once he got back in town. Not! I pulled up in Autumn's driveway. *I'll deal with him later.*

I rang the doorbell, then knocked three times. No response. I pressed down on the bell, and banged. Finally, the door swung open. "Gosh. Pump your brakes. What'd you do, fly?" she questioned as she stepped aside to let me into her house. The right side of her face was swollen. Her eyes were puffy. I felt something inside of me snap. I wanted to turn around and beat that nigga down. She must have read my mind. "Let it go, Nia. It doesn't feel as bad as it looks." She spread her arms in the air, forcing a smile. "I'm still standing."

I frowned, raising my brow. I blinked the snapshots of my aunt Miriam out of my head. Instinctively, I walked to her and hugged her. She returned my embrace. "Promise me, you won't go back to him," I said to her in almost a pleading whisper.

"Trust me," she said, pulling away. "If I didn't know before. I know now. It's over. And there's no going back." I pulled in a deep breath, then exhaled. "I know what you're thinking. And you don't have to worry. You only have to raise your hand to me once. I'm not my mother."

"I didn't say that." I replied, tilting my head.

"You didn't have to. It's in your eyes, Nia."

I reached out and stroked her cheek, feeling my tightened expression slowly soften. "I just don't want anything to happen to you."

"It won't," she said, reassuringly. She smiled, then looked me square in the eyes, lowering her voice. "I'm not responsible for Morris putting his hands on me. But I am responsible for what *I* do about it. And let me say this: I am nobody's punching bag. No man will ever put his hands on me, and I turn around and go back to him. Believe that." She kissed my cheek, giving me another hug. "You hungry?"

"Starving," I replied, following her into the kitchen.

Over grilled salmon and a tossed salad, Autumn gave me the run down on her road trip and of the events that transpired before Morris lost his damn mind. I bust out laughing when she told me what she had said about his mother and sister.

"Girl, no you didn't go there."

"Yes, I did. He came out of his face wrong, calling me out of my name. And I let him have it. I probably would have said more if he didn't get happy-handed. And you know me. I'm not the one to talk about anyone. But, he asked for it when he called me a 'stupid bitch'. Wrong answer."

I smiled. Unlike me, Autumn has always tried to be ladylike no matter what the situation. Even in high school when chicks would try 'n talk slick, she'd rarely raise her voice. But when she did. *Watch out!* You knew it was about to be on. Little Miss Prissy would flip into ghetto-mode, read you with the quickness, then flip right back into being the belle of the ball without blinking an eye. And the only way she'd fight was if you put your hands on her—first. She and I were definitely opposites in that regard. I'd kick off my designer heels to fight a bitch, and think nothing of it. I remember this one time when this chick from Paterson tried to come for me at the Senior Prom. She started popping off at the mouth. About what, I couldn't even tell you. I think it had something to do with some he-say-she-say mess. Anyway, I put my finger up, and said, "Ho, hold that thought." I didn't want to mess up my backless, sequined gown so I stepped out of it right in the middle of the dance floor. Handed it to my homegirl, then beat her down in my G-string and heels. Once I stretched her out on the floor, I stepped back into my dress, and started dancing again. Everyone was in shock. And awe. But, I didn't care either way. I knew I had a bad body.

"Girl, he's lucky. I didn't roll up on him. It would have been ugly. They would have needed a spatula to lift his ass up on a stretcher. Slugger and I would have done him dirty. They'd be reconstructing his face."

She chuckled. "Lucky him."

Silence took over for a beat, leaving us both in our thoughts. I'm not sure where her mind drifted, but mine . . .

"Listen, baby," Mustafa had said, leaning forward in his seat and speaking in a conspiratorial whisper. "I need you to handle something for me."

"What is it, Mu?" I asked, leaning in to hear what he had to say.

He rubbed his hands together. "There's paper to be made in here. And I'm tryna make some moves . . . " I raised my eyebrow, then leaned back in my chair. I tilted my head, trying to absorb the hidden message.

"And, your point?"

" . . . I'm tryna get it poppin'. Can I count on you?"

My nose flared. *No the hell he's not!* "Count on me to do what?" I asked, crossing my arms tight across my chest.

"Before you go off. Hear me out." My eyes narrowed to slits, waiting. "My man has a package for you. And I need you to bring it up the next time you come." He stopped talking, looking around. "Let's walk over to the snack machines." We both got up. He put his arm around me, then whispered in my ear. "You're gonna have to place everything in balloons then—"

I stopped in the middle of the floor. It hit me. This fool wanted me to smuggle up drugs in balloons stuffed in my damn pussy. "You must be out of your fucking mind," I responded through clenched teeth. "You must have banged your damn head. Look around. Do you see where you're at?"

"Yeah, and?"

"*And* that's the shit that got your black ass here. Yet you got the nerve to try—"

"Yo, sssh. Lower your voice."

"Shush, hell. I don't give a fuck how much paper is up in this piece. I'm not bringing shit up here. So you can cancel me out of your scheme. 'Cause I ain't the one." I stormed back over to our seats, fuming. The nerve of him! I knew of dumb-assed chicks who transported drugs up to prisons for their men, pulling the shit out of their asses like it was nothing. But I wasn't one of them. Ain't that much love in the world.

"Yo why you buggin'?" he asked, sitting back in his chair. "You act like I'm asking you to go out and rob a bank or something."

I wanted to scream on him. Right there in the middle of the visiting hall, I wanted to curse him out like the world was coming to an end. "Nigga, you might as well. 'Cause either way, if I get popped, I'm going to jail."

"If you play it cool you can get it off," he continued, dismissing what I had just said. "I wouldn't be coming at you with this if the numbers weren't right. I'm tryna get it off for the both of us."

"Bullshit. This has nothing to do with me. So don't give me that. You're locked the hell up for dealing and you're dumb ass is in here still tryna get your hustle on." I shook my head. "I tell you what. You need to make a decision right here and right now. If hustling is what you want, then fine. But, don't pull me into your shit 'cause I'm not going to jail for you or nobody else. I said I'd ride this bid out with you. And I meant that. But I have no problem bouncin' if you still tryna be in the game. Period. As far as I'm concerned, you can go recruit one of those birds on the bricks to cluck up here with that shit." Before he could open his mouth to say a word, the C.O. announced over the loud speaker that all visits were terminated. I got up, leaving him sitting there, looking like a damn fool. And every time he called I hung up on him. Finally, after three weeks and ten letters apologizing and begging for me to come up to see him, I went. And he swore he was leaving it alone.

"For you. I'm not gonna fuck with that shit. I got enough dough on the tuck so I'm straight. I was just tryna be on some impulsive shit. Everything you said, I was feelin'. And I'm not tryna jeopardize what we have."

"No, Mu. Don't do it for me. Do it for you. 'Cause at the end of the day, you have to live with whatever decisions you make. Because I'm very clear on what I'm going to do if the hustle is what you want. And that's a promise."

"Nah, I'm done."

"Are you sure?" I asked, half-believing him. "'Cause if not, we need to part now."

"No doubt, baby."

Humph. The realization that the hustle was much bigger than truths was becoming clearer by the minute. . . .

"How's Mustafa doing?" Autumn's question drifted toward me like a raft, waiting for me to jump on. Pulling me away from somewhere deep, someplace I wasn't ready to visit.

I need a drink. "Girl, what you got in here to drink?" I asked, dodging her question. I got up from the table and walked over to the refrigerator, then opened the door.

"If you feel like champagne, there's a bottle of Moët on the door. And some wine on the bottom shelf." I grabbed the wine and two wineglasses from the cabinet, then poured us both a glass.

I shuffled back over to the table handing her a glass. "Thanks," she said, keeping her gaze on me. I returned to my chair.

"What?" I asked, feigning innocence. "Why are you looking at me like that?"

She took a sip from her glass, then sat it down. "Because I asked you how Mustafa was doing and you basically igged me."

"I did not," I lied. "He's fine."

She tilted her head, and waited for the truth. Over the rim of her glass, she watched me intently. "How's he doing at his job?"

I sipped my wine then suddenly confessed. "The nigga quit it," I said disgusted. "I think he's dealing again."

She raised her brow. "You *think*, or you know?"

"More or less, he basically told me."

"Hmm. And how do you feel about it?"

"I'm pissed," I admitted. "But how I feel doesn't really matter because he's going to do what he wants regardless." I got up and grabbed the bottle of wine from the counter and returned to the table, pouring us both another round. I glanced up at her wall clock. 4:30 P.M.

"So, what are *you* going to do?" she asked.

"I don't know yet. But I know I'm not interested in dealing with a nigga whose occupation is pushing drugs. Been there, done that."

"And he knows that?"

"Of course he does."

"But honestly, Nia, did you really think he was going to stay out the game for long?"

I shrugged my shoulders. "I hoped so. I mean. He did four years in prison for dealing. Damn. If that wasn't a wake up call, I don't know what is. Besides, he's still on parole."

She shook her head. "Have you given any thought that maybe he has another bid in him before he's ready to get out, and stay out."

"Not really. He told me he was done with it. And I believed him." I rolled my eyes. "He can have all the bids he wants. But, I tell you this: The next one, he's on his own. I'm ghost."

"Obviously the rewards are greater than the risks."

"Well, nothing good can come out of selling drugs for a living. Not for long, anyway. Eventually, it all comes to an end." For a moment, I thought about my mother; how she ran behind drug dealers. She loved the fastness and flashiness the lifestyle offered. And eventually got so caught up in it that she got . . . lost. I saw what the drugs did to her. The cocaine. The crack. And finally, dope—killed her. The last thing I ever want to do is end up like my mother. Chasing dreams, then losing them to drugs. Am I slowly becoming her? Have we both become our mothers? I wondered.

"So, then you either leave him or you stay. The question is, will you be able to live with your decision?"

The weight of her question landed on my shoulders. Was it really something I was ready to bare? Would—I mean, could—I really walk away and not look back? "I'm gonna have to," I finally replied, hoping I sounded convincing. In my heart, I didn't.

She nodded, knowingly.

I sighed, needing to change the subject. "Enough about that. Guess who I ran into the other night at the Olive Garden, looking good as ever?"

"Who?" She poured herself another glass of wine. Then slid the bottle to me. I refilled my glass as well.

"A blast from your past."

"In that case," she replied, waving me off. "I don't even want to know. As far as I'm concerned, the past is in the past. And that's where *it* and he should stay."

"You sure you don't want to know?" I asked, tentatively. "I'm telling you he looked good as hell." I got up and walked into the living room to grab my bag.

"Yep, I'm sure," she answered.

"Okay, then. I won't tell you who it was. But just in case you get curious," I said, sitting back at the table, then sliding his card to her, "he asked about you and would like to hear from *you*." She glanced at the card before picking it up. It was hard to read the look in her eyes. It was blank. She stared at the card turning it over, then putting it back on the table.

"Like I said, the past is in the past. And the last thing I need or want is to rekindle an old flame, or get reacquainted with someone I *used* to deal with."

I shrugged my shoulders, gulping down the rest of my wine. "Hey, don't shoot the messenger. I did what was asked. What you do with it is clearly up to you."

"Exactly," she replied, folding the card in half, then tearing it up.

I smirked.

"What's that for?"

"Nothing."

"Don't give me that."

I hesitated, searching for the right words. "What's the worse that could happen if you called him? I mean. It's been years since you've seen or heard from him. After all, he was your first."

"I can't answer that because I don't intend on finding out. Yeah, he was my first alright; my first love, first heartache and first mistake. Please. Thanks but no thanks. Anyway . . . what does him being my first have to do with anything."

"Well . . . maybe, you'd want to find out if there's still anything between the two of you. You know how crazy he was over you. And the way you're acting leads me to believe there *might* still be some feelings there."

She gave me an incredulous look as if she wanted to smack me, or at the very least tell me to kiss her ass. Instead she rolled eyes. "Please. He was crazy alright. Running around making babies with two different girls while he was so 'crazy' about me. Trust me. There are no feelings here."

"He was young," I defended. "Maybe he's changed. At the least, maybe he just wants to apologize for how things ended. I mean. It's not like you gave him a chance to."

"Well, there's nothing to apologize for. Shit happens. We get over it. And we move on. I've done both."

Hmm, hmm, I thought. *It sounds good.* "Well, I think you should call him," I said, ignoring her comment. "It couldn't hurt."

"And it wouldn't help. After this mess with Morris, I want nothing else to do with men. I'm done with 'em. I have my own baggage. And I don't have enough room for anyone else's. I can do without the drama, or the aggravation. I've had enough of both to last me a lifetime."

"Oh, Lord. Please don't tell me you're gonna turn lesbo on me."

She chuckled. "It's a thought."

I got up from my seat. "On that note, I'd better get going before you start licking your lips at me." She winked then blew me a kiss, laughing. "I think that wine has gone to your head."

She walked me to the door. "Don't worry, Sweetie. Your goodies are safe with Big Momma," she patted me on the butt. We broke out in laughter.

"Girl, you crazy."

She smiled wide, giving me a hug. "Thanks for coming by. I really appreciate it."

"That's what family's for. You just keep that nigga away from you."

"Don't worry."

I gave her a kiss on the cheek. "Love you."

"I love you, too."

She stood by the door and waited for me to get into my truck. I stared at her standing there looking so much like her mother. I rolled down my window, then reached in the back seat for Slugger. I waved my aluminum friend out the window. "Don't make me use that niggas head as a baseball. I'll knock a home run in his ass." She smiled, shaking her head. I backed up, fighting back tears as she closed the door.

Ten

Autumn

My phone rang at 11:54 P.M. It was Morris, calling out "hello, hello," into the answering machine. I reached over, and lowered the volume. 12:10 A.M. It rang again. Then again at 12:18 A.M., 12:22, 12:26, 12:29, 12:35, 1:00, and 1:05. *This fool has lost his mind,* I said to myself, tossing around in my bed. Yanking my comforter up over my head. *The nerve of him! Calling my house this time of night.* Why I didn't turn the ringer off is beyond me. But, when the phone rang again, at 2:17 A.M. I thought I was going to blow a gasket.

"Who is it?!" I snapped into the receiver, flicking on my lamp. I had asked that stupid question already knowing the answer.

"It's me," he responded softly.

"Have you lost your daggone mind, calling me this time of morning?"

"I've been trying to call you all night."

"What do you want?"

"We need to talk. I need to see."

"No. We don't. And, no you can't."

"Please, Autumn," he begged into the phone, "I really need to talk to you. I've been doing a lot of thinking. And I know I fucked up."

"Yes, you did," I agreed. "In more ways than one."

"I didn't mean to hit you. I feel really bad about that. It's fucked up. I've never hit a female in my life. And—"

"You made me your first," I finished for him.

"I didn't mean for that to happen," he replied. "You said some things I didn't like and I got mad. So I just lost it."

I just lost it? What kind of mess is that? He must have really thought I was a darn fool if he thought I was going to buy that crock of bull. Anyone who hits another being makes a conscious decision about it. It's not about anger. And it's not about just losing it. It's a choice. That much I do know from all of my past readings on the matter. He could have easily gotten back in his truck and drove off instead of slapping—umm, correction. Backhanding—me, and punching me in my eye.

"Well it did happen. It doesn't make a difference what I said to you, Morris. You still had no business putting your hands on me."

"I know. And I'm really sorry."

"Well, you should be. I didn't deserve to be hit on. If you didn't like what I said, you should have just bounced."

"But, you hit—"

"Don't even go there," I snapped. "I fought you in self-defense. I was protecting myself. There's a difference."

"Yeah, but I'm all scratched up. And I had to get stitches in my bottom lip."

Humph, you're lucky you didn't get more than that, I thought. "Well, again, you should have kept your hands to yourself."

"I know. What I did was some real fag shit."

"Well, you're a day late, and a dollar too short. What's done is done."

"Can I come by so when can talk?"

"There's nothing to talk about."

"I just want to apologize."

"You've already apologized, Morris."

"I want to do it in person."

"There's no need for all that. I don't want to see you. The best thing you can do is to just leave me alone." And I meant that. I didn't wish any harm done to him. And between you and me, I really didn't want to see him in trouble with the law. Which is why I didn't to want to pursue any legal action against him. But, he crossed the line. And he needed to be held accountable for what he did.

"I'd like to start over with you, if you'd let me."

I almost laughed. He couldn't possibly have been serious. As crazy as this may sound, I don't hate him for what he did. I don't like it. And I will never accept it; but I don't harbor any ill feelings. I guess I should. But, I don't. Honestly, I do care about him.

"That's not an option," I said, sighing. "You had your chance. And it didn't work out between us. So, let's just leave it at that. I think you should get some professional help."

"What, you think I'm crazy or something?"

"I didn't say you were. But you definitely have a problem that needs to be addressed before it escalates into something more serious. There's a lot more going on with you, Morris. Which is probably why you have a problem committing in a relationship."

"It was a mistake," he offered again.

"Maybe so. But, it was a lesson well-learned for me."

"Can we at least try to be friends?"

I couldn't believe him. Didn't he hear anything I had just said? Please. As far as I'm concerned, any man who hits a woman is a coward. And any man who puts his hands on me is a done deal. There's no going back. If he does it once, he's likely to do it again. And I have no intentions of ever putting myself in that kind of predicament of being someone's personal punching bag. Or worse—ending up like my mother. I deserve better.

"Friends? Morris, have you banged your head? After what you've done, I'd never consider that."

"Well, are you gonna at least drop the charges?"

"Morris, I didn't charge you with anything. The police did. So I think you should be calling them and asking them that."

"Well, can you at least come to court and tell them that you don't want to pursue it?"

"Morris."

"Unh?"

"Good night." *Click.*

Eleven

Nia

When the number flashed up as PRIVATE on my cell, I started to ignore it 'cause a sista doesn't talk to callers who block their digits, but something compelled me to answer despite my rule. "Hello?"

"Who's this?" the voice on the other end asked in a hushed tone.

"You called me," I responded. "So, who are you looking for?"

"This number keeps coming up on my man's cell and I'm trying to find out who it belongs to."

"Well, who's your man?" I asked, getting annoyed.

"Mustafa!" she snapped. "Now who are you?"

"His woman," I snapped back, "that's who. Now who the fuck are you?"

"Don't worry 'bout who I am," she shot back. "You just stop calling my fucking man, Bitch."

"Bitch?"

"Exactly. Now, stay the hell away from my man."

"Or what?" I challenged.

"You'll find out," she responded, hanging up on me.

"Yeah right," I said aloud. "You ain't real with yours. 'Cause if you were, you would have told me your name." I wasn't beat for no foolishness tonight. But I definitely wasn't going to get myself all vexed over some ho playing games. If he were really her man, she wouldn't have hung up like she did. She would have aired it out, woman-to-woman. But she didn't. So as far as I was concerned, she was just another playa-hatin' trick tryna get at my man. *But how the hell did she get my number?*

This was like the third time in the last several days that someone had been calling my phone from a private number, and I'd just let it go into voice mail. But no messages were ever left. Whatever!

When Mustafa walked through the door three hours later, I was sitting at the kitchen table writing out bills. Leela James' *A Change Is Gonna Come* CD was playing in the background. The sweet melodic sound of "When You Love Somebody" filled the room as I hummed along. Interestingly, I was amazingly calm when I looked up and saw him standing in the doorway.

"Hey, Baby," he said, walking over and planting a kiss on top of my head.

"Hey," I responded, glancing up at him. Narrowing my eyes, I stared him down as he strolled over to the refrigerator and pulled out a container of Tropicana orange juice. *No this nigga didn't,* I thought, *just go in my refrigerator without washing his damn hands.* He reached for a glass, filled it to the rim, then sat in a chair across from me. I rolled my eyes.

"What?" he asked, scrunching up his face.

"You not washing your hands," I said indignantly, "that's what."

"Oh, my bad."

I shook my head, deciding to let it go.

"What you been up to all day, with your sexy ass?" he asked, taking a swig of his drink while gazing at me.

I ignored the question, and his gaze—and got right to the point, putting my pen down and looking him dead in the eyes. "Some chick called my cell today talking 'bout you were her man," I said. "Would you happen to know who that might have been?"

Mustafa never flinched.

He answered, "You bullshitting right?"

"Do I look like I am?" I asked, tilting my head and raising my brow.

"Well, who did she say she was?"

"She didn't," I replied. "She hung up on me."

He shook his head. "I wouldn't even sweat it. It was probably some prank call."

"Hmm. Perhaps. But she said your name."

"Well she musta been looking for another Mustafa 'cause ain't no chicks checking for me like that. I'm sure it's some kinda mistake."

I pursed my lips. "Humph. Maybe."

"What's that supposed to mean?"

"It means I hope and pray you're not tryna play me. I've had this number for four years and not once have I ever gotten a call from someone trying to find out who *my* number belonged to. Now all of a sudden some chick is ringing my digits tryna pop shit, talking about you her man."

He sucked his teeth. "Come on with that. I'm strictly about you, baby."

I leaned back in my chair, folding my arms. "Like you were when you were fucking that Keyonna chick?"

He rolled his eyes. "I thought we deaded that. I told you, that was a big mistake."

"If you say so," I responded, half-believing him.

"What, you don't believe me?"

"Should I?"

"No doubt. I fucked up once. I'm not gonna do anything to disrupt what we have. Real talk." He got up from his seat and took me by the hands, pulling me up. I looked up at him, stared him deep in the eyes. Frantically peeked through the windows of his soul. "You, my baby. I'm not fucking that up. Believe that. So you have no reason not to trust me."

"And how is that, Mustafa . . . " I asked, pulling away from him, " . . . when you couldn't even keep your word that you were gonna stay out the game? I thought we had an understanding."

He sighed. "Yo, come on. Don't do that. I know I said I was done. But . . ." he paused, rubbing his chin. " . . . I gotta make this paper. And that nine-to-five just wasn't getting it for me. I apologize for not telling you. But, I know how you feel about it. And I didn't want to beef with you over it."

I gave him an incredulous look. "And, you thought you'd could chase the paper and I wouldn't catch on that you weren't working. Do I really look that slow to you?"

"Not at all. I knew I was gonna have to tell you, sooner or later. I just wanted to wait until the time was right."

"And when was that gonna be? When you were calling me to bail your ass out of jail. That's fucked up, Mustafa. I deserved to know from gate what your intentions were."

"You right, Baby. It's just that you've already made your position clear. I know where you stand, and I wasn't ready to deal with you bouncin' on me. Not after all we've been through. But, you gotta understand. This is what I know. This is who I am, baby. And I need you to—"

I cut him off. "You need me to do what, Mustafa? Sit around and worry about you getting popped again? You must be out your damn mind. And don't stand here and give me that 'this is what I know' shit. *That* is not who you have to be. It's who you want to be. For God's sake, you're on parole."

"Don't remind me—"

"Well, somebody needs to," I snapped, cutting him off. "Because you are really on some crazy shit right now."

"Look, I don't wanna beef with you."

"And I don't want to beef with you either," I admitted. "But . . ."

His cell phone went off. He ignored it. "But what?" It rang again.

I raised my brow. "You should answer it," I said sarcastically. "It might be important."

"Who the fuck is this?" he said more to himself, glancing at the display before answering. "Yo," he said, flipping it open. He listened for a moment, and then frowned. "I can't talk right now." He disconnected the call, seemingly distracted. His jaws tightened. I could tell he didn't like what he had just heard.

"Who was that?" I asked, knowing he probably wouldn't say. But, I decided to ask anyway.

Suddenly he seemed nervous. His eyes narrowed and bounced around the room like miniature golf balls. "Nadine," he quickly responded, shutting his cell off. Nadine was one of his sisters, and someone who couldn't stand me. Not that it mattered 'cause the feelings were definitely mutual. About seven years ago, I had let Nygeria drag me out to this little hole in the wall bar/club down in Neptune called the Redwood so she could meet up with some nigga—a drug dealer, of course—she was messing with from that area. Supposedly, it was one of the local spots where the wannabe-ballers, gold diggers and so-called dime-pieces hung out. The music was cute but that was about it. Anyway, I'm on their little-assed dance floor dancing with one of Nygeria's man's boys when this chick bumps into me. The first time, I let it go. It might have been a mistake. The second time she did it, I stopped dancing and stared her down. *This bitch has one more time to elbow me and I'm gonna put her ass through that wall,* I thought, moving away from her. She kept on dancing, acting like she was just doing her thing. But, the third time, I knew it was purposeful. So I cursed her ass out. Girlfriend started poppin' off at the mouth, and I slid her. Then her girls jumped in and that was all she wrote. The lights went on, the music stopped, and Nygeria and I ended up tearing that place up. Come to find out, I had been dancing with her baby's daddy. And she still wanted him. Please. I was far from interested. Needless to say, we were thrown out. But, *me* being my mother's child, I waited for the trick to come out the bar, and the minute she did I beat her down in the parking lot. Then all hell broke loose. Niggas started fighting, and shooting at each other. It was a mess. Then just before Mustafa got locked up, his boys threw him this big party at Brokers and I almost gagged when I spotted her walking toward us.

That's the bitch I had to beat up in that corny ass club, I thought, watching her hug everyone in the place. There were two things I never forgot: someone's voice pattern, and a face—especially one I fought. And I knew that face anywhere. "What the hell is she doing here?" I snapped.

"Who?" Mustafa asked.

"Her."

"That's my sister," he snapped defensively. Needless to say, my face was cracked, and so was hers when he introduced us. Crazy thing, I was ready to fight her again—sister or not—if she came wrong. Luckily she didn't. She just turned her nose up, letting out a disgusted grunt. I smirked, slipping my arm through Mustafa's, letting her know who the *real* dime was.

"So, where we at with this?" Mustafa asked, bringing me back to the present.

"With what?"

"Us."

I sighed, heavily. "I don't know, Mustafa. I honestly don't know."

"I gotta do, what I gotta do, baby."

I pursed my lips. "Then I guess that makes the two of us. 'Cause I can't do another bid with you." It seemed like he was pondering the weight of my words. For a moment, it looked as if regret was finding its way all over his face.

He walked back over to me, then wrapped his arms around me. He placed his chin on the top of my head. "I love you," he finally said.

I placed my head into his chest, and listened to his heartbeat. "I love you, too," I admitted, holding back tears. "But, if hustlin' is *who* and *what* you are, then I can't do this with you."

"Give me one month, baby. And I'm out, for good." I looked up at him, and squinted. "Thirty days. That's all I'm asking. Just let me get this last run off, and it's done deals."

I closed my eyes, wanting desperately to believe his words. "I think you should go," I finally responded, pulling away from him.

"Thirty days," he whispered, kissing the tips of his pointer and middle fingers, then pressing them against my lips. I said nothing. "You hear me?" he asked. I smiled faintly, nodding.

"Listen, I gotta go back down to Maryland with my sister tomorrow; but I'll be home on Friday. Lets plan to go into the City for dinner. It's been a while since we've gone out."

Humph, so you've noticed? Of course, I kept my remark to myself. I can't remember the last time Mustafa and I had gone out, or really spent anytime together. I nodded. "I'll see you when you get back," I replied, holding the door open for him. He stood in the doorway, waiting. For what is beyond me. He probably expected me to ask him more about his trip to Maryland. But, between you and me, why he needed to take his ass back down there was of no importance to me. He leaned in and gave me a quick kiss on the lips, then walked out toward his car. I stood in the doorway and watched him. He got in, then blew me a kiss as he started his engine. I gave him a fake smile, then slowly closed the door behind me as he pulled out of the driveway. I knew it wasn't going to be a good night for me so I did the only thing I knew to do. I picked up the phone and called Nygeria and Autumn for a sleepover. Surprisingly they were both up for a night of sisterly bonding in the middle of the week. And I was thankful, 'cause at that moment I needed them more than ever.

I walked over to the stereo, turned it on, then pressed the numbers and waited for track 14 on Joss Stone's *Mind, Body & Soul* CD to play. "Sleep Like A Child" began. I turned up the volume, then headed for the shower.

Thirty minutes later, Autumn was ringing my doorbell. The swelling on her face had gone down. But you could still tell she had been in a fight of sorts. She handed me her overnight bag, then removed her jacket. We hugged.

"Hey, girl. Thanks for coming."

"Well, it sounded important. And you know how we do. So here I am." She flopped down on the sofa, crossing her legs. "Besides, I didn't feel like being in the house by myself."

I smiled, knowingly. "Have you heard from Morris?" I asked, hanging her coat in the hall closet.

She sighed. "Yeah. He's called a few times. But, I haven't given him much conversation." I rolled my eyes up in my head.

"Humph. What does he want?"

"For me to go to court—"

"And do what?" I interrupted, placing my left hand on my hip.

"He wants me to tell them I don't want to pursue the complaints."

"You've got to be kidding me?" I asked, incredulously. "That bastard has some damn nerve."

"Please. Don't even worry yourself. I laughed at his behind. He tried to say I pushed his buttons by saying what I said to him. Can you believe that?" She turned in my direction, looking up at me; waiting for me to respond. I said nothing. I needed to hear where she was going with this before I opened my mouth. Aunt Miriam flashed through my mind. I shook my head. She continued, "He had the nerve to try to make it seem like it was my fault he got happy-handed. I told him he had no business hitting me regardless of what I said."

"And what did he say?"

"That he was sorry. And never meant to do it. But I said, 'well you did and whatever consequences you get you need to take it up with the police. Not me.' Then I hung up on him."

"So are you going?" I asked, sitting down beside her.

"Not to get them to drop the charges, that's for sure. He needs to wear that."

"When does he have to be in court?"

"I have no idea. I haven't gotten anything in the mail stating when it is."

"Well, when you do, make sure you let me know so I can go with you." She gave me one of her looks. "For support," I answered, knowing I'd be prepared to knock his block off if he tried anything slick. "I promise I'll be on my best behavior."

"Yeah, right," she laughed. "As much as I appreciate the offer, I know you Nia. The first time he said something you didn't like, you'd be ready to jump all over him."

"That's not true," I lied, feigning insult. "I just want to be there for my favorite cousin. That's all."

She smiled. "I know you do. But, I can go it alone. Thanks anyway."

The doorbell rang. "Suit yourself," I responded, getting up to answer the door. As usual, Nygeria had to be her fashionably late self. She waltzed in—in her usual diva mode—with her face beat to the nines and hair whipped in a bun, wearing an ankle-length brown knit wrap dress and a banging pair of chocolate brown Gucci high heel booties. Her matching leather hobo-bag hung in the crook of her left arm while she carried her large tote in her right hand. "Hey, girl. Glad you could make it. Here, let me get that for you," I said, taking her bag from her, closing the door.

"Please, that's what girls are for. What's up Autumn?" she asked, giving her a quick glance, sitting her pocketbook on the coffee table. She caught my glare. *Not tonight, bitch.* She read my thoughts and parted a fake smile.

Autumn returned the favor, smiling wider. "Not a thing, girl."

"You bitches are so damn phony," I responded, chuckling. "But, tonight, I'd appreciate it if the two of you can break bread without all the sarcasm. I'd like to spend a sisterly evening with the two most important people in my life, okay."

"Do you," Nygeria said, pursing her lips and pulling out a white handkerchief, then waving it in the air like a flag. "I come in peace." She sat in the easy chair across from Autumn, crossing her legs.

"I'd like to see how long that lasts," Autumn, replied snidely, running her fingers through her silky hair—compliments of Revlon.

"I've missed you too, dear."

"I'm so sure."

I sucked my teeth, sighing heavily. I went into the kitchen to fix a tray of snacks. For the life of me, I couldn't understand why the two of them didn't try to get along. It's been like this with them from the moment they first met ten years ago. It's not like the two of them ever had beef—well, with the exception of that one time when Autumn, after a few drinks, politely asked her if she were a man. Chile. I almost gagged. Nygeria was ready to go off. "Why the hell you ask me something like that?" she snapped. Autumn, shrugged. "Just curious." Nygeria responded, "No, I ain't no damn man!" And Autumn's silly behind bust out laughing, and said. "If you say so." I felt so bad for Nygeria. Luckily, I was there to defuse the situation otherwise I'm sure it would have gotten ugly. Anyway, they just never connected. And I believed Nygeria's dislike for my cousin ran much deeper than her distaste in her fashion, or lack thereof. A part of me believed Nygeria was truly jealous of Autumn's natural beauty. Her almond-coated complexion was smooth, and blemish-free. And her big oval eyes with her thick, long lashes were captivating. Like mine. And her shape was to die for. Too bad she kept her little waist, pert breast, washboard flat stomach, and perfectly round behind hidden beneath clothes that did nothing for her. If she didn't, she'd be dangerous. Even in her plain Jane outfits she still draws attention without trying. Something Nygeria has a problem with because she always has to be the center of attention—or be the "featured attraction", as Autumn once put it. Of course, that cracked me up. There was definitely some truth to that.

And I knew Autumn thought Nygeria was a loud-mouthed, troublemaker who hid her insecurities behind a bunch of make-up, and expensive designers. She felt she was always bragging and showboating which annoyed her. But, one thing was for sure. Autumn could hold her own when it came to dealing with Ny's flip manner. And Nygeria already knew just how far to go. Every now and then I chuckle to myself when I think about Autumn's nickname for her: *Amazon.com.* Humph. That would really throw Nygeria over the edge. But she's my girl, nonetheless.

"You need any help in there?" Nygeria asked.

"Nope. I got it. You two just get comfortable. I'll be out in a minute."

"Soooo, Autumn. What's new in your world?" Nygeria asked, trying to break the silence.

"Nothing much. Just staying true to myself."

"Hmm. How boring."

"I guess for you it would be since . . . never mind. It's obvious you wouldn't know anything about it."

"And what is that supposed to mean?" Nygeria asked. "I keeps it real. All day, everyday."

"Humph. Not hiding behind all that paste on your face."

"No dear. The makeup is to enhance the beauty."

"Which is definitely in the eyes of the beholder," Autumn responded.

"Exaaaactly."

"Are you girls behaving yourselves?" I asked, returning with a platter of Buffalo wings and deviled eggs. I sat them on the coffee table.

"We're just getting caught up, girl," Nygeria responded, smirking.

"Yep," Autumn chimed in, twirling her hair through her fingers. "We sure are." She pasted a fake smile on her face.

"Well, good," I said, heading back toward the kitchen. "Give me a few more minutes, then we can really get this party started. How 'bout some drinks."

"Now you're talking," Nygeria snapped. "A cocktail is just what I need."

Autumn smiled. "That's probably the one thing you and I will agree on tonight. Umm, Nia, make mine a double, please."

I laughed, hitting the remote for the CD player, then going back into the kitchen to bring out the rest of the stuff. I turned on the gas fireplace, lit the candles around the living room, lowered the lights, then sat down on the floor. "So, now that we are gathered here together, I'd like to thank both of you for coming. Because tonight, I need you both to help me make some decisions, or at least give me some advice."

"You got that," Nygeria responded.

"Anytime. You know I'm always here for you."

I smiled. "I know." I took a deep breath, then told them about Mustafa getting back in the game, his thirty day request and my suspicions that he was cheating—or getting ready to cheat—on me. Of course I didn't mention the letters I found a few weeks ago. Some things needed to be kept to myself.

"Well . . ." Nygeria started, picking up an egg, then slowly biting into it. " . . . Hmm. Girl, you did your thing on these. . . ." She licked her lips. "If you really love him, I think you should honor his request. Let him stack his paper, then spend the hell out of it."

"Well, I disagree," Autumn stated. "Love shouldn't have anything to do with this. If you feel that strongly against it, then you should just give him his space and let him do whatever it is he has to do. Obviously, he's not concerned about your feelings so don't compromise yourself, or your beliefs."

"What's thirty days?" Nygeria asked. "I can see if he was saying he wasn't gonna get out. Giving him four weeks to do him isn't going to kill you. Is it?"

I shook my head. "Not really," I answered.

"Then what's the problem?"

"The problem is he lied to me."

"But now you know. And it sounds like he's going to get out and stay out."

"Please," Autumn replied. "I don't believe him. I doubt very seriously he's just gonna step off from the grind. That drug-criminal lifestyle is what he likes. And I don't think he's going to give it up that easy. Most never do. And that's why they end up right back in prison."

"Exactly," I responded. "And I'm not going back down that road with him."

Nygeria rolled her eyes, "Girl, let him do his thing. If he doesn't get out in thirty days like he said, then you know what you have to do."

"Yep. I sure do." I knew Ny would support him getting his hustle on since she doesn't require any of her men have legit jobs.

For the rest of the night, we sat in front of the fireplace with a bottle of Grey Goose and a pitcher of chilled Pineapple juice. And poured *my* troubles into our glasses.

We drank.

We ate.

We listened to music.

We talked about the distinction of being men and being male. And how few understood the difference. Some just really believed having a dick—no matter how big or small—is what made them a man. We talked about the difference between sex and intimacy. And how men somehow believed both concepts were one in the same. We shared our views on men having female friends, and male friends who were cheating on their partners.

"I don't have a problem with my man having female friends as long as she stays in her lane, and he does nothing to step outside the boundaries of our relationship," Autumn said.

I nodded.

"Well, I don't buy into that we're 'just friends' crap," Nygeria stated. "Because nine times out of ten when men have close friendships with women, if they haven't already, they're gonna end up fucking. Period. And if their boys are fucking around on their women, you can bet these six hundred dollar heels, his ass will be cheating too. Trust. It's just a matter of time. Birds of a feather usually flock together, okay."

"I don't think that's always the case with all men," Autumn replied. "I do believe there are some men who can just be friends with a woman. That's not to say somewhere along the way he wasn't interested in her, or vice-versa. But, maybe, for whatever reasons, there wasn't enough sexual chemistry to jumpstart an affair. And just because his boys creep doesn't necessarily mean he's gonna follow suit."

"Humph. Please," Nygeria grunted. "Men having a close relationship with a woman spells trouble. And a damn beat down, okay. And we all know the majority of men out here think with their dicks. If they *think* they can get away with fucking some other chick, it'll be on and poppin'. Believe that. It's called peer pressure, honey. And men are like little boys when it comes to being down with the fellas."

"I'll admit," Autumn stated. "Men have their weaknesses for a big butt and a smile. But that doesn't mean all men will act on it."

"Well, most of them will. And you wanna know why?" Nygeria asked, eyeing us both. She took a long, dramatic sip from her drink. We waited for her answer. "Because they lack discipline. And they lack the common sense and logic to know that when they get caught it's a bitch like me that'll pull a Lorena Bobbit and take his dick clean off."

We laughed.

We drank some more.

We talked more shit about niggas not being shit. And tried to imagine a world without men, then decided they were still needed . . . despite some of their little boy mentalities and their lies and games, they were still an important species. Well, the good ones were. The ones who were abusing and mistreating women could all go to hell and burn. And the cats who were cheating on their women? Well, they deserved to get something to. I just wasn't sure what.

Nygeria rolled her eyes. "Well, if I were you. I'd check his voice mail to see who the hell's calling him. 'Cause a bitch needs to know who— and *what*—her man is doing."

"You're kidding, right?" I asked, disbelievingly.

"The hell if I am. Break that damn code, and listen to every damn message that comes in. And then when you're done, erase them bitches."

Autumn shook her head in disbelief. "Hmm. I don't know. If you need to do all of that, there's no need of being with him. That seems a bit extreme and crazy to me. Besides, who has time trying to figure out someone's pin numbers?"

"I do," Nygeria snapped. "Sometimes a bitch gotta do what a bitch gotta do to know just where she stands. If niggas didn't lie so much, we wouldn't have to go to those extremes. Hell, we wouldn't have to get crazy if they did what they were supposed to do instead of tryna be slick. Just be real with yours. But since they can't then we gotta get *extreme*ly crazy."

"Well, you gotta point," I agreed, pouring myself another drink.

"I don't know," Autumn reasoned. "I just think it's just better to confront him."

"Puhleeeeeeze," Nygeria responded. "So, he can tell you a bold-faced lie. What Planet are you on, dear? Like he's really gonna admit to being on the creep"—Nygeria deepened her voice—"'Dig, baby. I've been blowin' this chick's back out behind your back for the last six months. And, if you like, I'll bring her home so we can both bust her guts.'" I chuckled. Autumn sucked her teeth, shaking her head. Nygeria continued, "Get real. Niggas ain't shit.

Notice, I didn't say men. I said niggas. 'Cause a real man isn't gonna put you through no bull. So, if you gotta be on dick detail to know what the hell he's doing, and who the hell he's doing it with, then so be it."

"*Dick detail*, what kind of mess is that?" Autumn snapped.

"Just what it sounds like," Nygeria stated, leaning back in her seat. "Monitor who the hell he's sticking the damn dick in."

Autumn continued, "Oh, please. If you gotta go through all that, why put up with it? Just leave him. If you know, or *think*, your man is a liar, and you can't trust him; why stay? You can't baby sit no dick."

"Maybe not. But when you love somebody," Nygeria answered, "it's not always that easy. When your heart's all wrapped up in a nigga it's hard to just let go."

"Humph. And while you're sitting around stressing, the world is still rotating on its axis. And he's out doing him. Ain't that much love in the world for me . . . all that private-eye and fatal attraction stuff takes too much energy."

"Girl, don't sit there and act like you never did it before," I interjected, reminding her of the time she got a rental and followed her ex Trevor around when she thought he was tryna play her. "You almost lost your mind over him. Or have you forgotten?"

"I wouldn't go that far," she replied, sucking her teeth. "I was young and too dumb to know any better. But, you're right. I did follow his behind. And that was the craziest thing I ever did. But, I tell you this. I wouldn't do it again."

"Yeah, but if you hadn't you wouldn't have found out the truth. Now would you?" Nygeria questioned.

"Eventually. I'm sure I would have. In the end, the truth always comes out. Believe that."

"Humph," Nygeria grunted. "Who has time to sit around waiting for the damn truth to come knocking on the door when all you have to do is go out and find its ass?"

"Okay, you go out looking for it, and then what?" Autumn asked.

Nygeria bucked her eyes as if Autumn had asked one of the dumbest questions on earth. "Then you beat the bitch's ass, and his too."

"That's utterly insane," Autumn stated, furrowing her brows. "And what is beating up on his jump-off going to prove? Nothing."

"Maybe not. But I bet you every time the ho looks in the mirror she'll think twice before she fucks with your man again. Trust me. Bitches don't want it."

"And what if she doesn't know about you?"

Nygeria rolled her eyes. "You still whip her ass. Just for GP. Then you slap him up."

"Give me a break. And all he'll do is turn around and find somebody else to creep with."

"Then you fuck her up too?"

Autumn sucked her teeth. "Fix me another drink," she requested, handing her glass to me. "Cause I need to be totally drunk to buy into this child's madness. . . ." I laughed, taking her glass, then getting up to go into the kitchen.

"While you're in there bring me something darker," Nygeria yelled. "You ho's sitting around drinking this girly shit. I need something stronger."

"Like what?" I asked, sticking my head out the doorway, laughing. Nygeria's first three drinks were fixed with more Vodka than pineapple juice and she still wasn't feeling a damn thing. I, on the other hand, had a nice buzz.

"Break open that Remy XO."

"Coming right up."

" . . . Anyway," Autumn continued, "as I was saying. You're just going to spend your life beating up on all these women instead of just dumping his cheating behind? That makes no sense to me. Violence only begets more violence. And it's not the answer."

"Well, I'm just saying what I'd do. But, I'm not the one with the problem at the moment. Nia is."

"Exaaactly," Autumn snapped. "So how about giving her some healthy advice instead of this Rambo nonsense." I returned with their drinks on a tray along with a bucket of ice, and the bottle of Remy. I returned to my spot on the floor.

"Nia, girl," Nygeria said, leaning in, speaking in a proper tone. "Ask him only"—she put up one finger—"one time, and if you still think he's up to no good, then do I what I said. Check his cell every damn day for the next two weeks. If he's on the up and up, then you can put it to rest. But if he's not, then you know what you gotta do. Beat the ho down." She looked over at Autumn. "Was that healthy enough for you?"

Autumn waved her off. "I don't think you should waste your time or energy doing all that. If you do, you'll drive yourself crazy. And end up in jail."

"Please, the crazier the better," Nygeria retorted. "Then he'll know that he fucked the wrong sista. Because at the end of the day, it doesn't make a difference how good your pussy is, or how good you sucking his dick. Make no mistake. It does not immune you from him cheating on you or leaving you. Therefore, you gotta play it right or you'll end up getting played to the left. So before that happens, niggas gotta be taught."

I nodded, resting my head on the back of the sofa. "Ain't that the truth," I agreed, leaning back. My head was beginning to hurt. I'm not sure if it was from the vodka, our conversation, or a combination of both. Fantasia's, "Ain't Gon' Beg You" found it's way through the speakers. How fitting. Silence took over the room while she sang. We listened. Nygeria fingered snapped to the beat. Autumn closed her eyes, swaying. And I silently tried to figure out in my head what my next move was going to be. But one thing was for sure. I wasn't gonna do much beggin'.

Twelve

Autumn

When I got—um, let me rephrase that. Dragged—into work this morning, it was almost eleven o'clock. And my head was throbbing from my night of drinking and late night talking with Nia and that . . . never mind, I'm gonna be nice . . . Nygeria. Ugh! *Dick detail.* Have you ever heard such madness? Humph. Leave it to Nygeria. That child is a mess. That's all I'll say. Anyway, I think when we finally got to sleep it was going on four o'clock in the morning, knowing darn well I had to be at work at eight. The only reason I didn't call out was because I had used up the last of my sick days for the year after that Morris fiasco in my driveway. There was no way I was going to walk up in here with my face all banged up. The last thing I wanted—or needed—were the gossipmongers huddled around the water cooler talking about *me.* I think not. So, I missed seven days of work. And before that, I had used up about five days when I allowed Nia to convince me to go to Vegas on a whim a couple of months ago. I still kick myself for going; but it's what she wanted to do. So, I went. Now, I'm usually very levelheaded. And I try to plan things out. But Nia complained that I never wanted to do anything, that we never spent any time together, and how I needed to live on the edge a little. So, what do I do? I call out from work—sick. And ended up spending a whole week watching *her* gamble and shop her money away. And, that was her idea of us spending time together, and *me* living on the edge. Please. I could have done something more constructive with my money, like putting a new roof on my house. I really hate spending—or should I say, blowing—money that's not budgeted. In any case, I made it into the office feeling tore-up from the floor up., and not in the mood for a bunch of mess. All I wanted to do was close my office door and lay my head on my desk. But as soon as I got up from my seat to close my door, my phone rang. I rolled my eyes and let it roll over into my voicemail. *Probably another irate fool upset that their car was repossessed.* "Oh, well. Pay your damn bills on time," I said aloud, closing my door then returning to my desk.

These people act like it's my fault that their cars get taken away. I'm not the one who tells them to get in way over their heads in debt. Now don't get me wrong, things happen. Emergencies creep up and before you know it, you're robbing Peter to pay Paul. I truly try to be understanding of that; but, don't try to play me with your sob stories and think I'm not going to expect you to make some sort of payment arrangements to get yourself out of the rears. I'll work with you. But, the minute you renege on your agreement, or try to act like it's my fault you couldn't keep up with your note, you'll wake up and find an empty space in your driveway. I'll have them tow your car and think nothing of it. *Snap!* Just like that. You'll be on foot before you know what hit you. Oh, every now and then we get somebody who tries to get slick and hide their car from us; but let me tell you how we find 'em. They'll come out from the club tryna be all fly and whatnot, just knowing they're 'bout to get some after hours booty and get to their parking space to find their car gone, thinking they've just been jacked. And after they've gone through the whole police report thing, and calling their insurance companies, the next morning I kindly call them and let them know, "We have your car. We'll release it when you come down with your four payments." It just cracks me up. Like I always tell 'em: You can run, but you sure can't hide.

I decided to check my messages. None. *Good,* I thought, *I didn't feel like returning any calls any way.* I still couldn't get over that crazy advice Nygeria gave Nia. Check Mustafa's messages, and then beat up on the women he's cheating on her with—if that's what he's really doing. You should have seen her salivating, and getting all animated about fighting some other woman. That's the silliest mess I've ever heard, just downright ghetto. And I could tell Nia was buying right into that foolishness. Well, they can both act a fool if they want. But I will not have any part of it. And Nia knows she had better have some bail money stashed if she ends up in jail listening to that big-faced child because I'm not shelling out a dime for that kind of nonsense. She knows I'll have her back if someone tries to hurt her because that's how we roll. But if she's going out to start trouble, then she's on her own. I'm not breaking one darn nail getting in the middle of it. Like my grandmother always said: The tea you brew today will be the tea you drink tomorrow. And I live by that. So, I don't go looking for trouble.

My phone rang, again. Without thinking, I picked up, and answered in my best professional voice. "American Financial, Autumn Brimmington speaking. How can I help you?"

"You can help me by letting me see you."

"Excuse me?"

"Let me take you to lunch."

"Who is this?" I asked, getting annoyed.

"Morris."

Ugh. "What in the world are you doing calling me? I thought I told you I didn't think it was a good idea for us to . . ."

"I miss you," he said trying to turn me on with a low, sexy voice that was doing nothing but grating on my nerves. I was too over him. You slap me up, then think a few days, or weeks, go by and I'm going to be forgiving. Not hardly. Now before all this happened I might have been flattered. And even gotten all mushy, considering that in the whole eighteen months we were together not once did he ever call to say he was thinking about me, or to offer to take me out to lunch. Now all of sudden, he's missing me. Yeah, right. Well, I'm not missing him. I meant what I said. I'm done with him.

"Listen, don't be calling me with your nonsense. I got work to do. And, I don't want you calling—"

"Autumn. Just hear me out—*please*."

I sighed heavily. "Go 'head. You got thirty seconds."

"I really fucked up. And I know it. All I'm asking is that you give me a chance to make it up to you."

"Not possible."

"Why not?"

"Because I said it wasn't. That's why not."

"I can't stop thinking about you. You were the best thing that has ever happened to me. And it's taken this for me to realize that."

"That sounds personal," I replied.

"I love you." He said those three words in almost a whisper.

I know I just didn't hear what I thought. "What did you just say?" I asked, pulling the phone away from my ear and looking at it, then putting it back. I was completely taken by surprise. Those were words he had never parted from his lips to me. Ever.

"I said I love you."

"Well, that's too bad, Morris. Because any man who raises his hand to me can *never* love me."

"Do you love me?"

"*What?*"

He repeated himself, slowly as if I were hard of hearing or something. Bastard!

"Do. You. Love. Me?"

How dare he ask me that! "Nope," I snapped, hoping he got the point. "I could never love a man who hit me. I'm going on with my life and I think you should do the same."

"I want you to look me in my eyes and tell me that."

"I just told you."

"Well, I don't believe you."

"Guess, what? At this point, it doesn't matter what *you* believe. The fact of the matter is I could care less. I wasted almost two years of my life in a dead end relationship. And I have no intentions of spending another two minutes debating this with you." I paused for effect. "You and I had—nor do we have—nothing in common. The only thing I was to you was a convenient piece of ass. That's it."

"That's not true."

"Well, it's my truth. But I'm not blaming you for that because I allowed it. And I'm okay with it. But don't think for one minute that I'm silly enough to ever give you the time of day, again. Goodbye, Morris. And I do mean, Good-damn-bye."

"I'm sorry for what I did."

"Tell it to the Judge," I snapped, slamming the phone down. Can you believe that? The nerve of him! *He loves me.* Oh, Please. That fool wouldn't know the first thing about love if it were a pit bull and bit him in the face. He must have really thought I was born yesterday to give me that crock of bull. Then he had the nerve to try to play that 'do you love me?' mess. Like that was going to make a difference. Give me a break. The only thing he was trying to do was manipulate me into feeling sorry for him so I would go to court to ask them to dismiss the charges.

Don't you ever let no man put his hands on you. "Don't worry," I said, picking up my mother's picture from off my desk and staring at it. "I won't." I closed my eyes and tried to block out the echoes of violence that remained locked in my head.

"Miriam, where the fuck you been?"

Silence.

"Bitch! I asked you a fucking question."

"Out!" she snapped.

"Out doing what?"

Silence.

"I done told you about not being here when I get home."

"I don't answer to you. I go where I'm good and goddamned pleased. "

"What the fuck did you just say?"

Silence. Then slamming of furniture.

"Bitch, you hear me talking to you? Don't make me put my foot in your ass."

"I said, I go the fuck where I want!"

Slap!

"Pack your shit and get the fuck out. You no good sonofabitch."

"I pay the bills in here, bitch."

"Fuck you!"

Slap!

Slap!

Crash!

"I hate you!"

"I'll kill you, bitch!"

Slap!

Smash!

"Motherfucker—"

Slash!

"Owww! Shit. Bitch, you just cut me."

"And I'll cut your fucking heart out. I swear, nigga. I'll gut you and serve your heart to the dogs if you don't get the fuck out. NOW!"

Slash!

"You crazy bitch!"

Slam!

I shook the sounds from my head, staring into my mother's dark eyes. Eyes filled with pain and discontent. "Don't worry, Momma. I won't ever live like that," I whispered, wiping tears from my face. "I promise." Why didn't you leave and never look back, huh, Momma? Why couldn't you follow your own advice? Why did our home have to be a battlefield? *No momma, I will never be on the receiving end of another fist.* The reality of knowing my mother was never coming back hurt so damn bad. It was the aching kind of pain that made my heart feel like it was going to stop at any moment. The kind of pain that I knew would never let me forget. It flowed through my blood like poison. Held me hostage. Snatches of my mother's screams echoed in hollowness. Clanged on the inside of my head. Bounced. Rattled. Injured my spirit. I clutched the picture frame against my chest, and without warning . . . sobbed uncontrollably.

Thirteen

Nia

Mustafa was down in Maryland for four damn days before he finally returned, giving me some bull about his niece wanting to taking her case to trial. I wanted to ask, for what? That just made no sense to me. She and her bad-assed, wanna-be-grown friends jumped that woman and beat her almost an inch from her life, and she wanted to take up time and money going to trial when it was clear as day that they were all guilty as sin. However, I knew enough to keep my mouth shut. It was his family, and their money. Not mine. So, I left it alone. Anyway. When he walked through the door, I was watching a DVD of Season two of *Nip / Tuck* I'd rented from Blockbusters since I had missed all last season's shows. And, girl, let me tell you. I don't watch television, but . . . baby. *Nip* n' damn *Tuck* got it going the hell on. So every Tuesday night I got my channel locked on FX and I'm plastered smack in front of this flat screen, gagging from the antics of these plastic surgeons. I was watching the episode when they inserted breast implants into this writer who was doing research on cancer and mastectomy as a tribute to his wife, and of this chick who created a sex doll and wanted a more realistic vagina made from the mold of her own pussy. Anyway, I was sitting on the edge of my seat watching Sean—one of the surgeons— in his drunken stupor, sleigh this plastic vixen when Mustafa plopped down on the sofa, placing his arm around me. He kissed my neck. Then nibbled on my earlobe.

"Will you quit it," I snapped, jerking my head away from him. "I'm tryna watch my show."

"And, I'm tryna get some pussy," he replied, rubbing my left breast.

I rolled my eyes, swatting him away from me. "Not now."

"Yo, put that shit on pause. You can come back to that later," he said, reaching for the remote, then clicking it off. "I wanna make love to my woman."

"Oh, is that so?" I questioned, eyeing him with annoyance. Sean was digging that doll's back out, tossing it every which way. And I was getting into it. Chile that doll's hair was disheveled and her panties were all twisted up. And here Mustafa goes turning it off right in the middle of what I assumed was going to be him busting his nut.

"Look how hard you got my dick," he replied, grabbing his crotch area. He stood up, grabbing me by the hand. "Come on. Let's go upstairs, let daddy make love to you."

I smiled, knowing I was getting horny watching this show. *I guess he has a point,* I thought. *Why sit here getting all hot and bothered when I can be getting the real thing.* I got up and let him lead the way.

I went into the bathroom, showered quickly for some of my man's good lovin'. When I returned from freshening up my love box, Mustafa was already in bed, lying on his back with his arms behind his head, his legs spread wide and his dick harder than Chinese arithmetic. I knew what that meant without him saying a word: Suck my dick for me. I crawled in bed, and took his dick in my hand, then licked the underside of it. Slowly, I glided my tongue down both sides of his fat dick, then flicked my tongue across the head, before taking him in my mouth. Unhurriedly, I sucked him. Slurped him. Lapped him. Swirled my tongue around him. Deep-throated him. Then I gagged. I felt like I was about to throw up. I know it was all in my head—or was it?

Although he smelled freshly showered, the scent of another woman, the smell of fish, was suffocating me. Was I allowing my doubts to get the best of me? I stopped sucking and studied his dick for clues, looking for signs of infidelity. There were none.

The sounds of Dr. Blake's words were echoing in my head, *"You have a yeast infection."* The sudden itching and burning had caused alarm for me so I made an appointment to see my gynecologist. And even after she tried to explain that seventy-five percent of all women would experience a yeast infection at least once in their life, I wasn't buying it. My gut told me I had gotten it from Mustafa, and he had gotten it from someone else. I was convinced of it. But I had no proof.

"Could I have gotten it from somebody else?" I had asked, cautiously. Although I had asked the question, there was a part of me that hoped, prayed that it wasn't possible. I held my breath, waited.

"Although it is not a sexually transmitted disease," she stated. "Yes, it is possible to contract a yeast infection through sexual relations. But it is rare."

"But, *is* it possible?"

She nodded. "Though not common, yes," she said, trying to reassure me that it was highly unlikely. She prescribed me a prescription and I went to CVS to have it filled, then went the hell off when I picked Mustafa up from work, driving him back to the halfway house.

"Who the hell have you been fucking?" I snapped, tossing the medication in his lap.

He frowned. "What?"

"I just came back from my doctor's, and I have a yeast infection. And I need to know who the hell you've been fucking. 'Cause I don't get yeast infections."

"Go 'head with that," he said, waving me on. "You the only person I'm sexin'"

"Well, you need to take your behind down to the damn doctors and get checked. Because you will not get any more of this pussy until you come back with a fucking clean bill of health. And I mean that."

He sighed. "You know, you always coming up with some shit. I'm not fucking around on you, but if it makes you feel better, I'll make an appointment and get checked out."

"Yeah, you do that. And get an HIV test while you're at it."

He stared at me, then blinked. "Say what?"

"You heard me. Get tested for every damn thing because I don't know what the hell that ho you laid up with might have given you. Period."

"I wasn't laid up with no ho," he snapped, sucking his teeth.

"Whatever. You just go and get tested. And I want to see the damn results."

And for three weeks, he got nada. I meant what I said. Well, when the test results came back, he was negative for everything—except for . . . you got it, a damn yeast infection that he tried to have me believe, think, that he had gotten from me. "I'm telling you, you're the only one I'm with, and that's my word. You really need to stop trippin'. Word up. Stop letting your imagination run wild." So I let it go, half-heartedly. But, then I came across the letters. And my suspicions were correct. Fuck what the medical expert said. Mustafa stuck his dick in that Keyonna chick, then turned around and brought her pussy juice home to me.

"Damn, why you stop?" he asked in a husky voice, bringing me back to why I was on my knees between his legs with his dick in my hand. "That shit was feeling good, baby."

That was then. This is now. He's not fucking anyone else. I shook my head, then took him back in my mouth, shifting my body so he could insert his fingers in my slippery hole. One finger. Two fingers. Three fingers. I sucked him feverishly as he played in my burning pussy. I moaned when he lifted my hips and replaced his fingers with his mouth, plunging his tongue deep in me.

Licking. Sucking. Kissing. Blowing. I was shaking with an intensity I never experienced before. Groaning with delight, I begged him to take me.

"Uh. Mustafa. Uh." Finally when I could no longer take it, I swung my body around, reaching around and sliding him in me, riding the images out of my mind. "Hmm. Hmm. Hmm," I moaned galloping up and down, rubbing my clit. Bringing myself to an enormous orgasm. The dick was so *gooood* inside of me. I loved this man. Needed him. Wanted him. I could never stand the thought of him being with someone else. I wouldn't.

He grabbed my titties, squeezing them in his big hands. "Yeah, baby. Ride daddy's big dick."

"Hmm. Hmm. Uh."

Wave after wave, I rinsed the thoughts of him cheating on me out of my mind. I picked up my pace until he flipped me over, rubbing the length of his dick across my pussy. I spread my legs wide—bending at the knees, anticipating his entry.

"Who's dick you giving me?" I asked in almost a plea.

"Yours baby."

"Is it all mine?"

"Yeah, baby. All this big dick is yours." He leaned in and kissed me. And the minute he slid himself back in me—I was forgiving him, offering him a sense of redemption. I replaced the visions of him fucking someone else with moans of pleasure as he deep-stroked my essence. *If you can't trust him, then why stay with him?* I pressed my eyes shut, blocking out Autumn's voice.

"Oh, Mustafa," I moaned as he pounded the length of his dick in me. He was swelling inside of me. Thrusting. Filling me up. Stretching me. Hitting the bottom of everything I was. Alicia's Key's "If I Ain't Got You" played as I gasped.

I was ready to cum. Ready to release all of my apprehensions. Prepared to let go of any past indiscretions. I screamed his name, raking my fingers down his back. Digging my nails into his ass. Matching his rhythm. “Hmm. It feels so good, baby.” I was exploding. Contracting. Releasing a thousand ripples of pleasure. There was no turning back. I loved him like I have never loved any other. And I hoped in my heart he was capable of giving me what I required the most. Honesty. ‘Cause if he wasn’t I knew it was gonna get ugly. Mustafa Peters would see a side of me he’d never think existed.

Fourteen

Autumn

"Hey, girl," Nia chimed into the phone. "What's up for tonight?"

"Nothing much. I think I'm going to just chill."

"You have me on speakerphone?"

"Yep," I stated. "Why?"

"'Cause everything is echoing."

"Oh. Well, anyway, I went to Borders and bought this book, *Relative Secrets* so I want to start reading it."

"Who's that by?" she asked.

"Collen Dixon."

"Oh, that must be her newest book. Because I just got finished reading *Every Shut Eye* by her. It was an excellent read."

"Well, I read her book *In My Father's House,* and this one is the sequel. So, I'm dying to see what happens to those bratty Cavanaugh's."

She laughed. "I know that's right. That's how I was after I read *Simon Says*. I just had to know what was going to happen to that damn Simon who was just too damn crooked for his own good. But, he got just what he had coming."

"They always do," I responded.

"You know that's right. Well, when you're done you need to let me borrow the two books you have, and I'll give you mine."

I shook my head, remembering the condition of the last two books I loaned her. The covers were all bent back and a few of the pages had grease-stains on them. I was too through. I know reading is fundamental, but even a blind man can see she's just too hard on a book. "No. How 'bout you support the sista, and go buy your own. The last time I *loaned* you my books they came back looking like you had read them in some greasy-spooned diner."

She sucked her teeth. "*What*ever, heifer. Just let me borrow them when you're finished."

"Mmmhmm. Hold your breath."

"You're so damn stingy."

"Yep. I sure am. But I love you anyway. Now why are you calling?"

"Well, I thought you might want to go out tonight. There's this cute spot over on Route 1 & 9 in Woodbridge that has Comedy from ten-to-twelve, then downstairs they play house and club music until like two in the morning. Talent with his fine self host's the comedy."

I glanced up at the clock. It was six-thirty. "Who else is going?" I asked, knowing she only rolled with one other person.

"Nygeria is gonna meet us there."

"I'll pass," I responded. "One night with Amazon.com is all I can stomach for now. You two go ahead and get your chuckle, and drop 'n pop on without me."

She giggled. "You know you ain't right. Leave my girl alone. I thought the two of you got a long quite well the other night."

"Yeah," I remarked, pulling my hair up into a ponytail, then letting it fall back down to my shoulders. "If you say so. But let's not push it."

"Oh, come on. It'll be fun. Besides, I already know you don't have to work tomorrow. So don't try to you use that as an excuse."

"And how'd you know that, Miss Smarty Pants?"

"Duh, I called your office and it's on your voicemail."

I sucked my teeth. "It figures. Well, that still doesn't mean I want to go out on a Thursday night."

"Please, Autumn," she whined. "Come on and go. It's been a long time since we've shook things up. It'll be like old times. And you know how we do."

I smiled, knowingly. Anytime Nia and I have gone out—even with Amazon.com in tow—we've had fun. Like the time we ended up at the Brooklyn Café over in Flatbush with their jamming beats. We got our dance on that night. Pelvis thrusting. Sweat dripping. Hip grinding, thighs slipping between thighs. Backing it up to overly eager brothas getting aroused by our rhythmic moves. We turned the place out, then went on about our business. I think I must have gotten about eight phone numbers that night. And never bothered to call any of them. For me, it was just a dance. For them, I'm sure they thought it'd be a quick hit. Not. Call me a tease, if you want. But you'll never get the chance to call me a Ho.

"I sure do," I said.

"So, come on and go. I'll pick you up."

"Nope. I'm staying right here."

"You make me sick. You act just like an old Maid sometimes."

"Yep," I agreed, flipping through the novel I had just purchased. "So, where's Mustafa?"

"He just left here."

"Hmm. So, I take it you've decided to ride the thirty days out."

"I guess. But, if he's not out by the end of the month, it's a wrap."

I shook my head, unbelievingly. "Yeah, right. You and I both know how you feel about him. So, who you tryna fool?"

"I'm not tryna fool anyone. My feelings have nothing to do with this. I mean what I say. I'm bouncin' if he decides to stay in the game. And you can bank on that. I'm not sayin' I won't be hurt. But, I gotta do what I gotta do for me. If I don't stand by my words he'll never take me serious."

"You're right about that," I agreed. I wanted to believe her. But, I knew my cousin. And the way she liked to shop and spend money, walking away would be one of the hardest things for her to do. I've always told her to save for a rainy day. Prepare for life's storms. But now that she was in way over her head with debt, she'd end up at the bottom of the river. And, eventually, I'd have to be the one to fish her out. "Well, I hope you've been saving," I finally said.

"I have a little stash," she replied.

"And what's a *little* stash, Nia?" I knew it meant practically nothing since she had spent up most—if not all—of her inheritance money and the money from the sale of Nana's house on clothes, accessories, furnishings, and whatever else. Between you and me. I'd be surprised if she had a thousand dollars in savings and checking combined. I don't care how many times I've warned her to put away three-to six months worth of living expenses—just in case, it's done nothing but fall on deaf ears.

She huffed. "Look. Don't start. I know all about my spending habits and I don't need you to keep reminding me. Everyone can't be as frugal as you."

"I'm not saying that," I countered. "But, you and I both know there's a part of you who doesn't mind what Mustafa is in to because—" I paused, wondering if I should even share my thoughts.

"Because what?" she asked, sounding annoyed.

"Never mind," I said, not wanting to get into an argument. "I'll keep my opinion to myself."

"No, Autumn. If you've got something to say," she challenged, "say it."

"That's alright. It's none of my business."

She sucked her teeth. I'm sure rolling her eyes too. "Since when?"

I smiled, knowingly. "Are we about to argue?" I asked, deciding how to choose my words.

"*Noooooo.* We're having a discussion. And we can agree to disagree. Right?"

"Exactly."

"Then finish saying what you were getting ready to say."

"Well, since you insist," I said, placing my stocking-clad feet up on my coffee table. "We both know if it weren't for Mustafa's hustling you wouldn't be riding in that Lexus, and you definitely wouldn't be dropping money on two and three thousand dollar handbags like it was nothing."

"That's not true," she snapped defensively. "I make my own money."

"Of course you do; but not enough to sustain your lifestyle. Let's face it. You've always been into the guys with the fast money. And, if they weren't in the game, then they'd better have a job that could keep you in all that high-priced fashion you adore. If not, you wouldn't waste your time on them."

"You make it sound like I'm a gold-digger or something."

"I'm not saying that. But, we both know a hard-working man with a regular nine-to-five has never appealed to you."

"Okay. In the past, that might have been true. But, I've outgrown that life. I'd rather have a man with a steady job and benefits."

I laughed. "Since when?"

"Since I fell for Mustafa's dumb ass," she answered. She let silence come between us for an awkward moment, then continued. "That prison shit ain't cute, Autumn. And, it's not for me. I'm really serious. Just like you, I want to settle down one day. And I'd like it to be with Mustafa. But, I'm not beat for settling for some nigga who wants to be in the streets. Love or not, I'd rather be by myself."

"Well, I just hope he wants the same things as you because I really don't see him getting out any time soon. The hustle is too addictive."

"Then that'll be his choice," she responded.

"And I hope you'll be able to live with that," I said.

She sighed. "I'll have no other choice but to."

"I hear what you're saying—but, um . . ."

"But what?"

"Seeing is believing."

"Well, believe it."

Yeah, right, I thought, rolling my eyes up in my head.

Nia was so much like her mother it was a shame. I shook my head. Before Aunt Muriel overdosed on drugs, she was one of the flyest females in Orange. She always had to have the best of everything, from the most expensive clothes and jewelry to the sexiest guy driving the most luxurious car. Unfortunately, she had nothing of her own to show for it. No savings. No investments. Nothing. Yeah, she was known for having all the latest fashion, and getting the finest men with the fattest pockets. But, eventually, that fast life caught up to her and she wound up losing in the end. She lost her innocence, her self-respect, her dignity and finally her life. All in exchange for a fast life and a good time. What a high price to pay.

"So, Miss Stocks and Bonds," Nia said mockingly, "now that we've got that all out the way, are you gonna come out or not?"

I glanced at my watch. It was almost eight o'clock. I sucked my teeth, tossing my book on the table. "Well, Miss-I-Don't-Have-A-Pot-To-Piss-In-Or-A-Window-To-Throw-It-Out," I shot back, "how much does it cost to get in, and what is the dress code?"

"It's like ten-dollars," she stated, ignoring my remark. "And you can wear whatever you want."

I grunted, deciding to give in. "What time are you picking me up?"

"Nine-thirty," she replied.

"I'll be waiting."

I knew I should have kept my tail home—like I wanted to—and curled up and read my novel instead of gallivanting to some box of a spot with Nia. I mean. The place was okay. I guess—if you're in the mood to be jammed in like a bushel of crabs. The after-the-comedy party downstairs was just as bad. There were so many people on the dance floor that I couldn't even get my twirl on the way I wanted. And the beats were tight. Anyway, by the time we had gotten there it was almost ten-thirty and the parking lot was packed. And cars were still pulling in behind us. "Damn, Nia," snapped, trying to find a parking space that wasn't too far out. "I knew we should have gotten here earlier. We're gonna be packed like sardines in that little-assed spot."

"Humph," I grunted, flipping down the visor then checking my updo and sweeping bang to make sure it was on point. She knew how I felt about being in places where everyone was breathing over top of each other. It made me paranoid. Besides the fact if a fire broke out, the last thing I wanted was to be stuck in the middle of a blaze and everyone stampeding like wild cattle trying to get out. There were two ways I didn't want to die: An airplane crash was one; and a fire was the other. "Well, I hope they have more than one exit."

"Don't worry, Fire Marshall Bill," she said, reading my mind. "They got more than one way to get out."

I shot her a look, rolling my eyes while I opened up my purse, and pulled out my lip-gloss. I applied a fresh coat over my lips, then puckered up, flipping the visor up. I noticed she had left her sunroof slightly opened. "Aren't you gonna close your roof all the way?" I asked as she shut off the engine opening her door to get out.

"Nah, it'll be okay," she replied.

"Suit yourself," I said, closing the passenger side door.

The alarm chirped.

As we walked through the parking lot, a group a guys sitting in—and standing around—a car were whistling and yelling things like, "Damn, baby got back . . . Yo, ma. Let me holla at you." We ignored them, rolling our eyes. They continued making comments. Finally, I glanced over at Nia and noticed she was wearing a faded jean jumper that looked like it was painted over her curvaceous body. *No wonder they're acting like a pack of dogs in heat*, I thought. I shook my head, grinning.

"And here I thought they were barking at me," I said, gesturing with my eyes at her behind. You got these boys drooling."

"Please. Clown-ass niggas," Nia mumbled, glancing over her shoulder to see what they were riding in. The expression on her face told me their vehicle wasn't up to her standards. I smiled, knowingly.

When we got up to the door, there were three bouncer-type doormen, frisking the brothas and looking into the bags of the females going in. We both spotted Amazon . . . I mean, Nygeria the minute we got inside. She was also wearing a jean jumper, but hers was dark blue.

"Well, it's about damn time, she snapped, swinging her designer bag from one arm to the other. It looked like she had blown her whole savings on this mini suitcase. "I was gonna give you five more minutes, then I was out. It's too damn tight up in here."

"Oh, please," Nia responded, waving her on. "Did you at least get us some seats?"

"I tried, but everything was already taken. I told you it's crowded as hell up in here. Hey, Autumn," she said, glancing over at me, tossing me a hand wave.

"Hey," I responded, looking around the place. There was some young comedian from Chicago on the stage, and whatever he had said must have been funny because the crowd was roaring with laughter. The place was not only packed but it was small. And people were standing all over the place. You could barely see what he looked like. I found me a spot up against the wall—by the door, of course. Just in case.

"Girl, you want something to drink?" Nia asked, fishing around in her satchel for her wallet.

"Yeah."

"Your usual?"

"Yep," I said, frowning when this Spanish-looking chick almost stepped on my foot and didn't excuse herself. I let it go. But when she brushed up against Nygeria, I knew it was about to kick off.

"I know that bitch saw my big ass standing here?" Nygeria snapped, giving the girl an evil-eyed stare. The girl looked over at her, twisting her face up, walking over to a round corner table. I guess to be with her friends. Of course, Nygeria, being who she is just couldn't let it go. She walked up behind the girl and tapped her on the shoulder. "I'm talking to *you*. Next time watch the fuck where you walking." Before the girl could open her mouth to respond, Nia grabbed Nygeria and told her to chill. "No. She don't be bumpin' all up into me, and not say excuse me. Please. I am not the one. And you know this. I'll turn this motherfucker out."

"Damn, Ny." Nia snapped. "It was a damn accident."

"Well the bitch shoulda said excuse me."

The girl stared her down, flipping the palm of her hand up. "Talk to the hand, ho."

"What?" Nygeria questioned. Nostrils flaring. "I'll beat you the fuck down in here."

"I'd like to really see that," the girl responded, placing her hand on her hip. Her girls raised up from their stools, preparing for a showdown. Before the situation could escalate any further and Nygeria got any louder and started showing her behind, Nia grabbed her by the arm, dragging her to the bathroom.

I walked over to the girl and her friends and said, "Please, don't pay her any mind. Her ass is crazy."

"Trust me," the girl said, sipping on her drink. "I'm not. 'Cause if she knows like I know, she'll put the cuckoo back in the clock before I do." Her friends laughed, giving me the impression that this chick could be a spitfire if pressed.

"I heard that," I responded. "Well, I just wanted to come over here and apologize for her unnecessary outburst."

"No problem. I appreciate that." We gave each other cordial smiles, then I walked back over to my little spot against the wall. *I knew I should have kept my behind home,* I thought to myself, trying to fade into my little corner. *We just got in here and her ghetto ass is already carrying on.* I folded my arms across my chest—disgusted. And ready to go. This wide-shouldered guy and his posse stood in front of me, blocking my already minimal view of Talent up on the stage. As usual, he was acting a fool. And the audience was rolling.

Ten minutes later, Autumn returned with my drink, cranberry and Grey Goose. "Here," she said, handing it to me.

"Thanks. Where's Nygeria?" I asked, not really caring.

"Over there," she answered, motioning with her head. "I told her wild ass to stay on the other side of the room until we can get downstairs."

"She is so damn ghetto," I said, taking a sip of my drink.

"I know. But that's my girl."

"Humph," I grunted glancing at my watch. It was going on eleven P.M. "What time does this party get started?"

"Right after the show. In about another hour or so." I burst out laughing when I caught the tail end of this comedian on stage say something about some stuck-up girl he had brought home, anticipating digging her back out. And how she had his dick hard, talking about what she was going to do to him. But when she dropped her drawers they looked like the bottom of a gym mop. He then replied, "Me and my dick were mad as hell. Instead of using one condom, I'd have to waste a whole damn box. So, I got my Johnson wrapped up in on all these condoms and I'm getting ready to enter when my dick gets scared and goes soft.

"So, I look down and say 'don't worry buddy. I got you covered. Let's just bust in her guts then put her out.' But my dick is so shook that it starts shriveling up. So, I'm stroking it. She's stroking it. She's begging. I'm begging. But every time I close my eyes trying to will it hard again, I see those nasty ass drawers over in the corner burning a hole in my rug. And I can't do anything but jump up, snatch off the condoms and tell her to get her nasty ass out of my bed.

"Then she got the nerve to ask me if everything was alright. I was mad as hell. Here I got this bad-assed sista in my bedroom, buck-naked, and can't get no ass because she's too damn trifling to wash her ass and change her drawers. I snapped. 'No, everything is *not* alright. You need to take your crusty ass home and hand-wash your panties in lye. Then come back in the morning." The crowd was hysterical. Nia and I were laughing so hard are sides ached.

Someone tapped Nia on the shoulder just as she was getting ready to say something. She looked back. And smiled. It was one of Mustafa's sisters.

"Girl," she said. "I thought that was you standing over here."

They hugged. "Hey, Yvette, what's up? I haven't seen you in months."

"Hey, Autumn," Yvette said, smiling at me. I acknowledged her, smiling back. "Chile, I got the hell up out of Jersey."

"So, where you at now?"

"Scottsdale, Arizona, girl. And lovin' it."

"Well. Alright," Nia said. "I heard that. "How long you going to be in town?"

"For about two months."

"Oh, so you flew in for Shari's trial?"

Yvette scrunched her face up. "What trial?"

"The one in Maryland," Nia stated, catching the look on Yvette's face. "Didn't she and some of her friends get in some trouble down there?"

She gave Nia a confused look.

"Mustafa has been going back and forth to Maryland with Janice—"

"Oh, that," she responded, shifting her eyes. "Please. I got my own problems. They can work that out on their own."

"I know that's right," Nia said, tilting her head. "I'm sure Janice is going through it, though."

"Yeah. I'm sure she is," Yvette replied, looking around. "Well, look. Let me get back to my table. I just wanted to say hello. It was good seeing you."

"Yeah, you too," Nia said, watching Yvette scramble away. We looked at each other.

I shrugged. "What was that all about?" I asked. "She almost ran trying to get away."

"Beats the hell out of me."

"She seemed a bit distracted," I stated.

"Hmm," Nia said, raising her brow. "Maybe."

We gave each other another look. But said nothing. Either she didn't want to talk about it. Or she didn't know what Nia was talking about. But, either way, there was something more to the story. That's for sure. "I think we should order ourselves another drink," I said, slipping my arm through hers, and threading our way through the crowd toward the bar.

Fifteen

Nia

Well, they say an idle mind is the Devil's workshop. And let me tell you. They never lied because that red-faced fool was definitely poking me with his horns, stabbing at my good senses. Hammering some wicked shit in my head. I sat by the phone, contemplating. Trying to talk myself out of it. But, a force stronger than me was weakening my will. So, what did I do? Exactly. I succumbed. I picked up the phone, and dialed Mustafa's cell phone. When the voice mail picked up, I pressed the star button. When I heard, "Please enter your password," I punched in four numbers. Nothing. I tried again. Nothing. I know I should have taken that as a sign that I really didn't need to know. I should have just left well enough alone, right? But I couldn't. After running into his sister two weeks ago, I had this funny feeling in the pit of my stomach that Mustafa wasn't keeping it real with me. And I needed to find out what the hell he was really up to. I needed to put an end to this madness once and for all before I lost my damn mind. Fortunately for me, patience came when I needed it the most. 'Cause three hours later, I knew I had successfully cracked the code when I heard, "You have one unheard message . . . First message 3:50 P.M. today. Hey, Mustafa. This is Kelly. Just wanted to confirm you're still stopping through tonight. Can't wait to see you, baby . . . end of message. To replay, press one. To save it in the archives, press two. To erase it, press three. To hear more options, press zero." Of course, I pressed three. "First saved message, sent Saturday, September twenty-fourth at 7:58 P.M. Hey Mustafa. This is Kelly. I forgot to give you my address when I spoke to you earlier. It's 4312 Elizabeth Avenue, apartment two. Definitely looking forward to getting up with you. Call me. 908-555-1384." I listened to all the prompts, then pressed two to save it.

I sat on my sofa for what seemed like hours, dazed. A part of me wanted to cry. But couldn't. I was too fucking mad to shed tears. I immediately picked up the phone, and dialed his number. I took in a deep breath when he picked up, trying to steady my voice and slow my raising heart.

"Yo," he hollered into the phone.

"Where are you?" I asked, opening and closing my fist.

"With my man. Why, wassup?"

"Am I gonna see you tonight?"

"Yeah, I'm gonna try to come through tonight. It'll probably be late, though."

"Like what time?"

"Probably after one, or two."

"Why so late?" I asked, trying hard as hell to keep it together. But inside I was screaming, "You black, lying, motherfucker!"

"I gotta go up Top and I'm not sure when we'll get done."

"Hmm."

I let a deafening silence come between us.

"Yo, you aiight?"

"Yeah," I responded, "why wouldn't I be?"

"I don't know. You sound kinda distracted."

"I guess I got a lot on my mind."

"Don't worry, baby. Daddy'll be home to take care of that. Aiight?"

"Yep." I replied, squeezing my eyes shut. "I'll see you when you get here."

"No doubt."

"Later." I hung up. "Nigga you finger-fucking the wrong bitch," I said aloud, racing upstairs to get dressed.

Thirty minutes later—sporting a black fitted cap, a black hooded sweatshirt, black sweats and Timbs—I was backing out of my driveway in my hooptie, my mother's '95 black, tinted Mazda Mx6—the one I kept in the garage, heading to Newark. I was gonna bust Mustafa's ass if it was the last thing I did. When I got to my destination, I parked on the opposite side of the street a few houses down, turned off my lights and waited. The digital interior clock read: 10:30 P.M. No sign of Mustafa's car. But, I'd wait it out. And as I waited, I kept playing that message over and over in my head to the point it had me so damn upset that I was shaking. Then for some reason, as I sat in my car, I thought about my Nana. And how much I missed her, her smile. The warm smile that comforted; the wide, toothy smile that took away any hurts. The smile that greeted me in the morning, and just before I went to sleep. And I missed her hugs. She'd hold me against her bosom, against her beating heart. Filled with love. They were the kind of hugs that wrapped around me like a blanket. Warm. Comforting. I missed her more than I missed my own mother. I yearned for her strength. She had lost a husband and two daughters, and still faced the world with a smile. Understanding and forgiveness outweighed her losses. "Baby, God needed them more than me. And I trust in the Lord's will," is what she said. It was her undying faith that kept her giving, and going. And I yearned for her wisdom. "You'll never get to tomorrow staring at yesterday," she'd say. "You gotta take hold of today. And prepare for something better." I closed my eyes, and took in the memory of homemade cinnamon rolls wafting through the house Sunday mornings. Their scent and the sweet recollection sent me into reverie. Slowly, I drifted off . . . wishing things were the way they used to be. Sadly, I knew things never stay the same.

One hour later, I spotted Mustafa. He slowed in front of her building, then parked two houses down. I clutched the front of my shirt, pressing against my chest, in an attempt to keep my heart from jumping out. I watched his ass get out of his car, walk the sidewalk to her building. Stroll up to the door in his cocky manner and ring the doorbell, then the door swung open. She stepped into his arms, and then moved aside, letting him in. The door closed. I reached over for Slugger, gripping it with a vengeance. My mind was racing a mile a minute. *Crack him in his damn head, then beat her the hell up . . . Ring the doorbell . . . Stand in the middle of the street and scream for him to come outside . . . Kick the fucking the door in and set him and his bitch on fire . . . Girl, you're thinking crazy. Pump your damn brakes. You don't want to end up in jail for murder. Think, Nia. Think. You can't plan an attack sitting here getting emotional. Fuck him!*

The ringing of my cell snapped me out of my self-induced hysteria.

"Hello."

"Girl, where are you?" Nygeria asked. "You got every damn light on in your spot."

"Oh," I replied, keeping my eyes on my mark. "I had to run out real quick."

"Well, it must be one helluva errand for you to leave your door unlocked."

"Say what?"

"You forgot to lock your door. I'm standing in the middle of your living room as we speak. Luckily I'm not a fiend 'cause I'd strip this bitch down to the bare walls." She chuckled. I didn't respond. Tears slowly rolled down my face. I wiped my cheek. *Pull yourself together, girl.* "Hello, you still there?"

"Yeah," I answered.

"Girl, are you alright? You sound kind of out of it."

"I'm fine," I lied, sighing. "Just in the middle of something."

"Well, do you want me to wait around for you? Or should I cut every thing off and lock the door behind me?"

"No, just lock up for me. Thanks. Listen. Let me call you back." I hung up before she could respond. I sat in silence for several more minutes, decided what I was going to do, then got out of my car and quickly walked toward his shiny Burgundy Lexus. I was glad the street was dark. It made my mission that much easier. I looked around, noticed the coast was clear, squatted down, pulled out my awl, then went to work on all fours. When I was satisfied with my labor, I ran back to my car and hopped in, then made a quick u-turn, heading back home. *I wanna see how you explain your way out of this one, nigga.*

When I returned home, I pulled off my clothes, jumped in the shower, then called Mustafa on his cell. He didn't pick up. Not that I expected him to. I left a message for him to call me back. Of course, he never did. *That's right. Get your fuck on 'cause after tonight, I promise you, you are gonna have hell to pay,* I thought, throwing myself across my bed, crying myself to sleep.

At five minutes to four in the morning, I heard the alarm chirp. I glanced at the clock, then threw the covers up over my head, pretending to be asleep when he came into the bedroom. He went into the bathroom. I heard the heavy flow of his piss, the flush of the toilet, and then the running of water. He slid in the bed in back of me, pressing his body up against me. I felt a lump in my throat. Held it along with my breathing. *No this nigga won't press his dick up against me after being out fucking some other chick,* I thought, trying to maintain my composure. *Play it cool, Nia.*

"Hey, baby," he whispered, pressing his lips flush to my ear.

I groaned, feigning grogginess. I faked a yawn and stretch. "Hmm. What time is it?"

"A little after four," he responded, cupping my breasts. I stiffened. "Sorry, I didn't get here sooner. But I had to call a towing service and wait for fucking hours until they got there."

"What happened?" I asked, finally turning to face him, feigning concern.

"Someone slashed all four of my tires."

"Say what? Where were you?"

Lie number one: "In Elizabeth."

"Where at?"

"On Elizabeth Avenue." Well, that was true.

"Doing what?"

Lie number two: "I stopped at the titty bar and when I came out, my shit was down to the ground."

"Who were you with?"

Lie number three: "One of my mans."

I almost wanted to laugh at the ludicrousness. Instead, I took in a deep breath, willing myself from slapping the shit out of him. I continued to play along. "Why didn't you call me?"

"I was so damn vexed. It just slipped my mind."

"Hmm. Are you sure you weren't somewhere you shouldn't been?"

"Nah," he replied, looking me in my eyes. I stared at him, waited to see him flinch. He didn't. "Why would you ask me something like that?"

"'Cause I'm tryna figure out who in the world would flatten your tires."

"Beats the hell out of me. Probably some crab ass nigga." He sighed, then started kissing on my neck. *Guilt.*

"Where did you say you were again?"

"I told you. The titty bar in Elizabeth?"

"Which one, Mustafa?"

"What difference does it make?"

"It doesn't. I just wanna know."

He sighed. "Cinderella's."

"Hmm."

"Listen. I don't wanna talk about that right now. I just need you to make love to me, baby." He rubbed his dick up against me, tryna slide his fingers between my legs. "I want some of this sweet pussy."

The nerve of this nigga! "Get the fuck off me," I snapped, pushing him off of me, then getting out of bed. I flipped the light on. "Who the fuck do you think you're talking to, Mustafa?"

"What you talking about?" he asked, looking at me like I had just lost my mind. "Why you buggin'?"

"You weren't at no fucking titty bar," I challenged. "So don't give me that bullshit."

"How the hell you gonna tell me where I was? I'm tryna tell you where I was, and you standing there on some extra shit."

"No, nigga. You were laid up with some fucking bitch. That's what. And that's how your damn tires got slashed."

"Yo, where the fuck you get that? I wasn't laid up fucking no bitch."

"Liar," I yelled, slamming my hand on my hip.

"You need to stop being so fucking jealous. I wasn't out fucking. You can call my man. He'll tell you where we were."

"Give me a fucking break. Of course the nigga's gonna vouch for your ass."

"'Cause it's the truth."

"Well, did you call the cops?"

"What? Call 'em for what?"

"For a police report, asshole."

"Nah, I ain't beat for no pigs. I just had my shit towed, and got my man to drop me off here."

"Show me the tow slip. I wanna see where the fuck you were towed from."

"Yo, you fucking buggin' on the real."

"No, you're the one bugging. And, I'm gonna ask you one more time, Mustafa. Where the *fuck* were you?"

"I told you. Damn. Get off my back. You need to stop being so damn insecure all the time."

"Nigga, I'm far from insecure. So lets get that clear right now."

"So why the fuck you buggin' then?"

"Who the fuck is Kelly?" I asked, reaching for my bat.

He jumped out of bed, preparing for what might come next. "Yo, what the fuck! I don't know who you're talking about?"

I slammed the bat down, beating it against the bed. "Who the fuck is she? Don't try to fuckin' play me like I'm some dumb ass."

He stood there naked, looking at me with a stupid ass smirk on his face. "Yo, you need some help. Word up. 'Cause you fuckin' crazy."

"No motherfucker. You're the crazy one for crawling up in my fucking bed after being out with some other female."

"I wasn't with no other female!" he yelled.

"Stop fucking lying. You were fucking some other bitch. That's why your damn tires got slashed."

"I wasn't fucking."

"Well, then she musta been sucking your motherfuckin' dick. So now who the fuck is she?"

"I don't know what you're talking about." I wanted to black. He was really going to stick to his damn story. Unfortunately, letting him know I had listened to his messages was out of the question—for the moment, anyway. And I definitely wasn't going to tell him I was the one who had him flat-bedded. "Why you gotta be so dramatic all the time?"

"You know what, Mustafa," I put my hand up, pausing. "Forget it. You're a fucking liar. So get your shit and get the fuck out before I crack you in your damn face."

"And go where?"

"I don't give a fuck where you go. But you gotta get the fuck up out of here. Before I really hurt you, Mustafa. I don't fucking appreciate you coming up in here tryna slide all up in my pussy after you've been with some other bitch. I'm not feelin' that shit."

"I told you. I wasn't out fucking. Damn! Stop sayin' that shit."

"Well, who the fuck is Kelly then?"

"I don't know no damn Kelly."

I raised the bat in the air, getting ready to swing. He took a step back. I put it down, taking a deep breath. "Do you love me, Mustafa?"

"Of course I do. What kind of question is that?" he asked, walking over to me. I raised the bat. He stopped in his tracks, slowly backing up.

"Then why the fuck can't you just be honest?"

"I don't know what you talking about!" he yelled. "I *am* being honest. Damn. If I didn't love you I wouldn't be with you."

"No nigga!" I screamed, "You wouldn't be out cheating on me."

"How many times do I have to tell you? I'm not cheating on you. So stop accusing me of that shit."

His cell phone rang, then finally chirped, letting him know a message had been left. He glanced at it. "It's probably your bitch," I snapped.

"You need to stop acting so damn jealous."

"I'm not acting jealous, nigga. But, since you say I'm buggin' prove me wrong. Let me hear your messages. If you don't have any bitches calling you, then make me a believer."

He stood there, shaking his head.

"Just what I thought." I walked over and slammed Slugger onto his cell, smashing it against the dresser.

"Yo, what the fuck! You know how much I paid for that damn phone?"

"I don't give a fuck how much you paid for it!" I bellowed, throwing it at him.

He tried to sidestep it, but it hit him in the head. "Fuck, man! You happy."

I felt my nostrils flaring. My chest heaved in and out. I was going to loose it, and end up in jail if I didn't get a hold of myself. "Get. The. Fuck. Out. *NOW!* You so busy chasing paper and chasing fucking pussy. And I'm sick of it. Get your shit and get out."

"What is that supposed to mean?" he asked getting angrier by the second.

"It means I'm not going to put up with you fucking cheating on me and lying to me. So . . ."

"So, what?"

I held back my tears, trying to keep my voice from cracking. No matter what I told myself. Or him. I knew I wouldn't be able to stop loving him. I knew I wouldn't be able to get over him. But, I knew I couldn't—wouldn't put up with his lies. "It's over," I finally said, keeping my emotions at bay. "I can't let you keep hurting me, Mustafa. I can't. So, lets just end this shit before one of us ends up getting seriously hurt."

He stood there, dazed. "Yo, just like that?" he asked, pleadingly. "After all we've been through. We gotta fuckin' history together. And you just wanna throw it all away over some bullshit?"

Dawn was beginning to make its way into another day, peeking its presence through my blinds. I dropped the bat. I was emotionally and mentally exhausted. And this wasn't going anywhere. I gave him a long, pained stare. "Get out Mustafa. Call your little friend Kelly and tell her to come get your ass. She can have you and your lies. So just go do you. And leave me the hell alone. Because I'm done."

"Why you doin' this to us?"

"You did this to us. Not me." I crawled back in bed under my blankets, reached over and shut the light out. "Bye, Mustafa," I said, turning my back to him. "Lock the door on your way out." I refused to let him see me shed another tear. Not tonight. Why did this love have to hurt? Why did the truth hurt? Why couldn't he just love me, or be man enough to let me go? Those were the questions I silently asked myself as I rocked myself—fighting back disappointment, and resentment. I don't know if it was his lies, or the fact that I wanted to believe them, that fueled my pain.

Instead of leaving, this fool got back in bed. Slid over to the side of the bed where I laid stiff and gently rubbed my shoulder.

"Don't touch me, Mustafa. Just keep your hands off of me."

"I don't wanna lose you, baby," he responded.

"You already have," I said, letting the agony escape from my eyes and slide down onto my pillow. He slid in closer to me, slipped his thick arm around my waist, and pressed into my back. It felt desperate.

"I'm not letting you go, Nia," he whispered, kissing me on the back of my neck. His tone was filled with an unshakeable conviction. "And I'm not going no where." His words divided my heart; split it right down the center, as if . . . as if each half would—could—beat independently on its own without the other. He had no idea that I had cocooned myself in intense feelings. Feelings that had been intricately woven with love for him, and were now being torn open and tossed out. Splattering. He spoke as if the power of what he had said would be enough to keep what existed in the tiny spaces of my spirit from falling apart. At that very moment, it wasn't. Somehow, in my reality of knowing, but unwilling to accept, I knew I was becoming unglued. *He loves me. He loves me not. He loves me. He loves me not . . .*

Silence took over.

Loneliness emerged.

Finally I said quietly, resolutely, "Then you're a damn fool, Mustafa."

Sixteen

Autumn

I had fallen asleep on my sofa listening to Heather Hedley's, "In My Mind." I had worked a half-day and came straight home to chill. My intentions were to just take a power nap—or what the party heads called a disco nap—and then start dinner. But before I knew it, I was in a deep, dreamless sleep. A sleep that seemed to transport me to another world outside of my own, which is probably why I didn't hear the doorbell. But, when I heard the knocking on my door, I opened my eyes feeling confused. I laid there for a moment longer trying to get my bearings together. I heard the knock again. I sat up, rubbing my eyes, looking around and realizing just how dark it was inside. The vertical blinds and curtains were drawn tight so when I got up and peeked out, I wasn't sure if it was morning or the beginning of evening. That's how disoriented I was. I spotted a delivery truck in my driveway, and walked over to open the door.

"Hello," the blonde, blue-eyed man said, smiling and holding a huge, long white box wrapped with a red ribbon and big red bow. He had another box leaning up against his leg. "I have a delivery for a Miss Autumn Brimmington."

"That would be me," I responded, surprised.

"Please sign here," he requested, handing me a clipboard. I did, then he handed me one of the boxes.

"Wait a minute," I said, carrying the box in my arms. "Come in. Let me get my purse." I sat the box across my sofa, walking toward the hall closet while he sat the other box beside the other.

"No need," he stated. "It's already been taken care of." He flashed another smile.

"Oh," I said, turning around.

He was already walking toward the door. He retrieved something else from outside then came back in holding a gorgeous wicker basket in his hand. "This is for you as well."

I put my hand over my mouth, then replied, "Oh my!" I was stunned to say the least. *Who in the world would be sending me gifts?* I thought to myself, taking the basket from him. It was heavy. "Thank you."

"You have a good day, Ma'am."

"You too," I said, closing the door behind me. I felt like a kid at Christmas. I didn't know what to open first. I sat the basket on the table and looked inside for a card or something but the only thing I saw was an array of scented candles, bath crystals, body oils, a gold box of chocolates, two CD's, a bottle of Cristal, and two Champagne flutes. I decided to open one of the neatly wrapped boxes first. I gasped. It was filled with fifty beautiful red and white roses adorned with Baby breaths. And every other rose was inscribed in gold with the words: MISSING YOU. I noticed a red envelope and snatched it, then tore it open. Neatly written on a white card read: "Each petal represents my love for you. My life hasn't been complete without you." I plopped down on the sofa, rereading the card. The handwriting wasn't recognizable. I opened the other box. There were another fifty red and white roses and another card atop of them as well. I pulled it out the box and opened it. "No matter the distance or space between us, I'll never stop loving you." Then it hit me. I sucked my teeth, tossing both cards on my coffee table. "Damn you," I mumbled. "Your little gestures don't change what you've done." I picked up the phone.

"Hello," he answered.

"Hello, Morris," I said, staring at the lovely flowers. "It's Autumn."

"Hey, baby," he responded, sounding enthusiastic. Hopeful. "It's good to hear your voice."

I frowned. "I thought I told you I didn't want to be bothered anymore."

"I was hoping you'd change your mind. And give me another chance."

"I'm not. So you should have saved your money. Although the roses and gift basket are beautiful, I'd appreciate it if you didn't send me any—"

"Excuse me?" he interrupted. "Save what money? What roses?"

"The roses and gift basket."

"I didn't send you *any* roses or gift basket."

"Don't play games, Morris. I just got the delivery a few minutes ago."

"I'm telling you. It wasn't me."

"Are you sure?"

"Why would I lie about something like that? But, if it'll make you feel better, I'll take the credit if you want me to. If it means you'll see me."

I scratched my head, then picked up one of the cards and read it again. *My life hasn't been the same without you.* No, he was right. He was too low budget to spend this kind of money. And he wasn't romantic enough to come up with such an idea. It definitely couldn't have been him. "Listen. I can see I made a mistake. So just forget I called."

"Hold up," he said, lowering his voice. "You feel like some company?"

I rolled my eyes. "No, Morris."

"I miss you, girl."

"I'm sorry to hear that," I replied, pulling a rose from out of the box. I smelled it. Touched its petals. *Each petal represents my love for you.* I don't know why, but a part of me was disappointed that he hadn't thought of the gesture. But who did? I ran through my mental Rolodex trying to figure out who in my past knew where I lived. Not that there were many, but it was worth the try. There was Marcus, the Conman. No. It wouldn't be him. Not unless . . . Ugh. Not unless he swindled another unsuspecting soul out of her money and decided to make amends. Gag me. I'd slap his damn face first. No, it wasn't him. I kept searching. Julius? No, he had never been to my place. We hadn't dated long enough for him to be invited over. That was another one of my . . . yes, self-imposed rules. Never bring a man to my home unless we'd been dating for at least four months. Okay . . . okay. I know. I broke that rule with Morris. Damn him! Anyway, no, it wasn't Julius. He had missed the mark by two months. Julius and I met over the phone, and had gone out on several dates over a course of two months. And I had been over to his place a few times. And each time he was always the perfect gentleman. I was almost starting to wonder whether or not something was wrong with him. Like maybe he was gay or something because he never made a move on me. Of course I flat out asked him. And he answered, unequivocally, "Hell, no!" He said he just wanted to take it slow. And I respected him for that. Unfortunately, the scorpion in me was ready to sting his sexy behind up, something fierce. He was tall, stocky, and had these deep-piercing eyes that were downright mesmerizing. Yes, I needed, wanted, my carnal appetite fulfilled. But, I'd be the lady I was raised to be, and wait for him to make the first move. And I did. Ugh. What a disaster. When he finally did try to get his groove on, I almost threw up in his lap when he leaned in to kiss me. He had the worse case of halitosis known to mankind. It was . . . it was putrid. That's the only way to explain the invisible life form that had crawled in between all of his teeth, seeped into his gums and rotted. Even after I had him gargle and brush his tongue, his breath still smelled like hot shit. Needless to say, our interaction ended quite abruptly. Now I see why he was always chewing on globs of gum, and popping jolly ranchers. And he was such a nice guy. So no. It definitely wasn't him.

I continued, flipping through my memory bank. Then it hit me. Oh, no. I felt sick to my stomach when Trevor popped in my head. He was the only one of my exes remotely thoughtful enough—or financially capable—to do such a thing. No good, married dog! I tossed the delicate flower back in the box. But, what if they weren't from him either?

"Listen," Morris stated, bringing me back to our conversation. "Since you've called. I have court next Wednesday and I'm hoping you'll still come to speak on my behalf. You know, let the Judge know it was all just a big misunderstanding.

I sucked my teeth, rolling my eyes. Oh puhleeeze. A misunderstanding my behind; I understood all to well. He was a damn idiot and I was an even bigger fool for having wasted my time with him. "Good-bye, Morris," I said, hanging up on him. No, these gifts were definitely not from him. *Asshole!* I went into the kitchen, poured myself a glass of white wine, then curled up in my loveseat staring over at the huge basket, I sipped my wine, turning my attention to the boxes of roses. I needed to figure out who sent these things to me before I decided what to do with them. Toss them out. Or keep them. That was the question in my head. *Then, again*, I decided, *no need to waste beautiful flowers.* I got up from my seat, pulled out two large crystal lead vases from the closet, filled them both with tepid water, then arranged the flowers and set one vase on the coffee table and the other on the fireplace mantel. I smiled at the lovely display. *My life hasn't been the same without you.* Hmm. I grabbed my glass of wine and took another sip, settling on the sofa. The phone rang before I could continue shifting through my memory. I glanced at the caller ID before picking up.

"Hello, I answered.

"Hey, girl."

"Well, I'm glad you've finally got around to calling me back," I responded, feigning disappointment. "It's a good thing it wasn't an emergency. I'd be in a crap load of trouble waiting on you to get back to me." I had called her three days ago just to check up on her. And she was just now getting back to me.

"I'm sorry. I've been sort of . . . busy."

"Hmm, hmm," I responded. "But it's okay. I still love you." I chuckled, "For a moment there, I thought Mustafa might have kidnapped you or something."

"Yeah, I wish," she said, sounding dejected. I listened beneath her tone and heard what sounded like sadness. Although we don't spend a lot of our adult time together, I know my cousin—almost like I know the back of my hand. And there was something wrong. She seemed distant. But, perhaps it was just my imagination. Maybe it wasn't any more than what she said—she's sort of *busy*. But I asked anyway. "Is everything okay?"

I heard her pulling in a breath. Then I thought I heard her sniffle.

"Nia, what's wrong?"

"Nothing," she finally said. "Everything's fine. I think my allergies are flaring up."

"Hmm," I responded, half-believingly. "So what you been up to since we last spoke?"

"Not a damn thing."

"Are you sure?" I asked.

"Yeah. Why?"

"Nia, I know you. And it sounds like either you've been up to something, or you're about to *do* something you shouldn't. But I'm not going to pry. When you're ready to talk about it you know I'm all ears."

"And you promise you won't say anything. Just listen?" she questioned.

"Cross my heart and hope to die," I replied, sitting back. In my mind's eye, I saw her rolling her eyes. "I promise."

"I stabbed up Mustafa's tires," she blurted out.

"You did what! Girl, have you lost your damn mind? What in the world possessed you to do some mess like that? Don't you know you can end up getting arrested?"

She sucked her teeth. "See. I knew I shouldn't have said anything."

"Okay, okay. I'm sorry. But, what in the hell is going on?"

"Well, if you'd shut your trap for a minute, and let me get it out. You'll know."

"My traps shut," I said, sitting down. "Now talk."

She told me how she figured out the code to Mustafa's voice mail, listened to his messages, then sat out in front of the chick's house and waited for him to show up. I shook my head in disbelief.

"Instead of ringing her doorbell and causing a scene—like I wanted to, I ice-picked his tires up."

"Does he know it was you?"

"Are you kidding? Hell, no."

"Well, what did he say when you confronted him about this Kelly chick?"

"He lied. Talking about he didn't know who I was talking about."

"So now what are you going to do?" I asked already knowing the answer. Nothing. But I kept my mouth shut.

"I don't know."

What in the world? "You don't know?" I challenged. "I thought you said he slept with her."

"Well, I don't know that for certain. I just know he was at her house, and didn't come up in here until after four in the morning tryna get some pussy."

I turned my lips up. Well, if he didn't sleep with her, then what in the hell was he doing sitting up in another woman's house? And why did he feel the need to lie about it?

"And what did you do?" I asked, almost afraid to know. *Please don't tell me you gave him some,* I thought to myself. I held my breath.

"I went the hell off. Smashed up his cell phone with my bat and told him to get his shit and get out. Then I cut off the light and got back in bed, leaving him standing there in the dark."

"Did he leave?"

"Nope. He crawled up in bed with me, begging me. Telling me how much he loved me. And would never do anything to hurt me. Said I was the most important person in his life. And that he wanted to marry me."

My jaw dropped. I couldn't believe what I was hearing. I had to fix me another drink to swallow this craziness. I went into the kitchen and retrieved my bottle of wine, then poured the remainder of its contents into my glass.

I let silence come between us. Waited for her to say something else. She didn't.

"And you believe him?" I finally asked.

"I want to," she answered, pausing. "But . . ."

"But what?"

"I'm starting to think I can't trust him."

"Then why stay with him?" I asked. "Why put yourself through the heartache?"

She sighed. "Because I'm not ready to let go."

"Hmm."

"You think I'm crazy don't you?"

"What I think doesn't matter," I responded, gazing at the roses sitting on my table while taking another sip from my glass. "It's what you think, and how *you* feel about it that really matters."

"I don't know what to think. But I know I love him, Autumn."

I closed my eyes, squeezing them tight, searching for something unknown. I didn't trust myself to speak. I wanted to express to her that she deserved more. That life was too short for drama. That she was better than this. That she was worthy of being loved, and didn't have to settle. I wanted to let her know that she didn't need him, or his lies. But the words wouldn't come out. Instead, I tossed my head back and gulped down the rest of my drink. There was nothing for me to say. I knew then . . . she had it bad.

Seventeen

Nia

Over the past two weeks, Mustafa and I have spent more time together than we have since he first got home from prison. He's suddenly so attentive and passionate. And the lovemaking has been absolutely wonderful. It almost feels like the way it was. Yet, I'm still skeptical. Don't get me wrong. I love him, and I want nothing more than to trust him; believe me I do. But I'm still leery. I mean. I've checked his messages a few times since that Kelly incident, and so far there's been none from any females. However, I still haven't let my guard down—not much. I guess I need to get over it, especially now that he's asked me to marry him. And, yes, I said *yes*. Don't give me that look. I'm not delusional. I'm just a woman in love. And, if nothing else, I deserve—no, scratch that—I've earned a ring from him. That's what I wanted. And that's what I got. So let's just leave it at that. Anyway, between you and me, I'm not sure if the fact that I called and confronted Miss Kelly had anything to do with Mustafa's drastic change of behavior. Yes, I called her. And, no I don't think I played myself. I felt, woman-to-woman, we needed to have a heart to heart. I needed to be clear if she knew about me. And where she fit into the equation before I decided my next course of action. So, the next day when Mustafa left up out of my house to get his car out of the shop, I picked up the phone and dialed her number.

"Hello?"

"Hi, may I speak to Kelly?" I politely asked.

"This is her," she answered. "Who's speaking?"

I ignored the question and got right down to the meat of the matter. "Do you know Mustafa?"

"Yes," she hesitated. "Why?"

"Well, I want to know what your involvement with him is?"

"I don't know who this is. So I suggest you ask him that."

"No, sweetie. I'm asking you. Because if you know—or knew—that he has a woman, and you're dealing with him, then you and I are gonna have some problems. Because as far as I'm concerned. You're disrespecting *my* relationship. And if you're disrespecting my relationship, then I'm gonna have to disrespect *you.* "

"Excuse me?"

"You heard me."

"First of all," she said, "I'm not *dealing* with Mustafa. And, second of all, who are you? And how'd you get my number?"

"Well, I'm his fiancé," I announced. "And I got your number off his cell. And I want to know what—"

"Hold up," she interrupted. "You're telling me Mustafa has a girl?"

"Exactly."

"Oh, hell no," she snapped. "Listen. I don't get down like that. I didn't know he had a woman, or a fiancé for that matter. And trust me. If I did, I definitely wouldn't have given him my number. I don't step on no one's relationship. Oh, no. I'm not the one."

"So, then I guess you know what you gotta do?"

"Oh, most definitely," she responded, letting out a disgusted sigh. "I will be erasing his number from my phone. And when he calls me, I will check him."

"Umm. How 'bout you let me handle him?" I asked. "And trust me. He won't be calling you again. But if he does, hang up on him."

"Oh. You don't even have to worry my sista."

I smiled. "Well, Kelly," I said calmly. "I'm glad we were able to resolve this amicably. Because I was ready to be on your doorstep and I really didn't want to have to get ugly."

"I appreciate you giving me the heads up. I've been on the receiving end of that madness, so I know how it feels."

"And that's why it's important for us sistas to stick together. And respect each other's relationships."

"Definitely," she agreed. "Because I am not down for the drama."

"Well. I'm glad to hear that. Because, sistagirl, I was ready to bring it to you."

"You know," she said, ignoring my threat. "I'm really sorry to hear that."

"Meaning?"

"Having to fight to keep up with your man. That's a really sad place to be. I know because I've been there. But if it works for you, then more power to you."

"Trust me—"

"No," she interrupted. "Trust *me.* It's not a good look. But, it's obvious you're too blinded to see that right now. And that's okay. One day, you will. Hopefully, before it's too late. Now like I said, you don't have to worry about *me* talking to *your* man again. But, understand. I'm just one of many. So good luck to you, *my* sista." And with that said—she hung up, leaving me slack-jawed.

In hindsight, I didn't quite catch what she was saying. Or maybe I did, but wasn't ready to face it. So I didn't. Then again, I, too, was good at denying things—to myself that is. And, I did it well. In any case, I was glad she didn't try to jump ugly like some chicks would have. Lord knows I would have beaten her down. And I really didn't wanna have to go there. Now, you know how some females can get, so don't even give me *that* look. You know what I'm talking about. No, I don't think it's cute fighting over a man. But, when a female knows he's involved and she purposefully continues to deal with him, then it's no longer about *him*. It's about *her* disrespecting *me*—and I'm not havin' that. Anyway, I don't know if she's spoken to Mustafa or not. But if she has, he hasn't mentioned a damn thing to me about it. And I know he won't. But, what I do know. He's been walking around on eggshells, trying to smooth things over with me. Which is probably why he went out and bought this ring. But, I could careless what his motivation is, or was. Bottom line: Diamonds are a girl's best friends. And they've always been mine. And, since I'm sharing. I'm gonna tell you something else. At this point, Mustafa can keep on hustlin'. I don't even care. Because he's gonna buy me *what*ever the fuck I want. And if his ass gets knocked, he's gonna be on his own. And I mean that. I know, I know. I'm contradicting myself. Oh, well. I've had a change of heart. And as you know, it *is* a woman's prerogative to change her mind—and I have.

Anyway, Mustafa had been driving my truck and I was using his car to get around in. Hell, with the way gas prices had soared since this hurricane Katrina mess, I'd decided I'd rather have him filling up that gas-guzzler of mine than me, okay. And he didn't seem to mind. Therefore, so be it. Surprisingly, it was unseasonably warm for October, and I wanted to get out and enjoy the day before I went stir crazy. I was bursting at the seams wanting to show Nygeria my ring. So I agreed to meet her for lunch at the Cheesecake Factory in Menlo Park Mall, and then do a little shopping. Not that they have any great store selections. But I'd find something. And if not, we'd just mall hop. Of course I was running behind schedule, and was flying down Route 1, blasting *Floetry Live* and thinking about what had transpired between Mustafa and I in the last several months, and how Mustafa had managed to either deny or minimize his actions. I had cursed his ass out. I had cried. And now I was prepared to move on. I mean. I decided he wasn't going to be completely honest—particularly about that Kelly chick. Even though in my heart, I believed he had fucked her. But since I didn't have any real proof and she didn't confirm it either way, I decided to let it go. And I did.

Anyway, I was so caught up in my thoughts that I didn't notice the flashing lights on the police car following behind me. "Fuck," I cursed, glancing at my speedometer and pulling over to the side of the highway. I was going seventy-five. I watched him get out of his patrol car. I took a deep breath. I hated cops. Not all of them because I knew there were some who truly were good. But the ones who were crooked, and nasty—I HATED.

"License and registration," the police officer said in a tone that sounded like more of a demand than a request. I forced a smile, looking up at him. Of course I couldn't see his eyes because they were hidden behind a pair of metallic sunglasses.

"Good afternoon, Officer. Is there a problem?" I asked, peering over my brown Luis Vuitton shades to get a better look at him. Blonde-haired, pale-faced and square-chinned with thin red lips. Humph.

"Is this your car?" he asked, looking the vehicle over. His rudeness made the hairs on the back of my neck raise. I guess he had a problem seeing someone of color driving an expensive automobile.

"No," I responded, keeping my smile in place and my tone even. He glanced at the inspection sticker. "I'm borrowing it. Why, is there a problem, Sir?"

"License and registration."

"I would like to know why I'm being stopped," I demanded, knowing damn well why. But, I decided to play dumb. "If that's alright with you?"

"You were speeding," he finally answered.

"How fast was I going?"

"Is there something wrong with your speedometer?"

"No. But I wasn't paying any attention to it." I lied.

"Well, maybe you should have been," he snapped.

I bit my lip. I felt my temper flaring. Granted I was over the speed limit by ten miles—okay, twenty—but there was no need to take that tone with me. Just because he had a gun and a badge that gave him no right to talk to me anyway he wanted. I reached in my bag, pulled out my wallet, then my Drivers license, handing it to him, keeping my eyes straight ahead. He looked at the picture then at me. "Yeah, you miserable fuck. It's me," I wanted to say.

"Registration and insurance card."

I pulled the key out of the ignition, unlocked and opened the glove compartment, then fished around for the documents. My heart stopped when I spotted two boxes of condoms. Still, I kept my composure. Continued searching. Underneath an orange and red Kodak envelope I found the requested items, then handed them to him. I pulled out the envelope, placing it on the passenger seat next to my wallet.

He examined the papers, then walked back to his patrol car. I watched him in my rearview mirror. He made a call on his radio. *This motherfucker thinks I'm riding in a stolen car,* I thought. *No, he thinks it belongs to a drug dealer,* I decided, rolling my eyes in disgust. Okay, so it did. But he didn't know that. Granted it was shining like it had just rolled off the lot, was sitting on twenty-two's, and was tinted-out. But that gave him no reason to stereotype. I'm sure if I had been a brotha he would have ordered me out of the car, made me place my hands on top of the car and spread my legs. And I'd be surrounded by squad cars while they tore the vehicle up looking for drugs and weapons. And when they found nothing, I'd be charged with, D.W.B., Driving While Black. I sat, seething. Then decided to flip through the envelope that was packed with pictures. I shuffled through the first eight. They were photos of him with some of his boys, a few of his sisters and their children, one with him, his father and brothers. I smiled when I came across a picture of him and I in Vegas. We were standing in front of the Monte Carlo, and he had his arms wrapped around me, kissing me on the side of my head. It reminded me of a postcard. My cell rang.

"Hello," I answered.

"Girl, where are you?" Nygeria asked.

"On the side of the damn road," I snapped. "I just got pulled over by a fucking cop. I'm like five minutes away from the Mall."

She sucked her teeth. "Damn. Well, I'll be standing in front of the restaurant waiting for you."

"I'll be there."

Ten minutes later, he got out of his car. I watched him walking toward me. When he approached my window, I placed the pictures back in the envelope, then shoved them in the zippered compartment of my bag, with the intention of finishing looking at them later.

"I'm gonna cut you a break, *this* time, Miss Wesley," he said, handing me back the documents. I'm sure he would have rather been able to come back and say the car was improperly registered or something else. "But, I suggest you watch your speed limit."

I gave him a tight smile. "Thank you."

"You have a good day."

"You do the same," I said, dryly, tossing everything back into the glove compartment, then grabbing my wallet, tossing it in my bag. I pulled off, gripping the steering wheel so tight that I was practically cutting off the circulation in my hands. I kept my eyes on him in the rearview mirror as he followed me all the way up to the entrance of the Mall, then sped off. "Cracker bitch!" I said aloud pulling into the lot toward Nordstroms.

"You betta *work*, bitch!" Nygeria finger-snapped as I approached her. I smiled, knowing she'd love the outfit I was wearing: a beige diamond-print dress by Diane von Furstenberg, DKNY hosiery and a pair of brown Manolo Blahnik stilettos. My Louis Vuitton satchel hung in the crook of my left arm.

"I take it you like?" I asked, pulling my shades down.

She sucked her teeth, grinning. "I hate you." We exchanged air kisses, then headed inside the restaurant. Once seated, we looked over our menus then ordered. I ordered the Cajun Jambalaya pasta and she ordered the Steak Diane with a side order of sautéed spinach.

"Can I get you ladies something to drink while you wait for you order?" the waiter asked.

"Hmm. I'll have a Tropical Smoothie and a bottle of Pelligrino with lemon, please." Nygeria rolled her eyes. "What?" I asked.

"A *Tropical* Smoothie," she mocked. "I know you're not pregnant so—"

I looked up at the waiter. "On second thought," I said, cutting her off. "Let me have a Flying Gorilla." I rolled my eyes back at her. "Satisfied?"

She smiled. "Now, you're talking. And I'll have a Lemon Drop with an extra shot of Ketel One."

He smiled, taking our menus. "I'll be right back with your drinks," he said, walking off. We had chatted and laughed about everything under the sun through our entrées, and were on our third round of drinks when I decided to pull out the Platinum and diamond ring Mustafa had given me two nights ago. I slid it back on my finger, flashing it in Nygeria's face.

"Girl, don't tell me that's what I think it is?" she asked, almost indignantly, raising an eyebrow.

"Well, damn. I'd thought you'd be happy for me."

"I am. But, I mean. The last time we spoke, you were talking like you were ready to axe him if he didn't get his shit together."

"I was," I defended. "But . . ."

"Well, what's changed?"

Nothing really, I thought. I decided to keep that to myself, along with the fact that I had to stab his tires up and confront some chick. Along with the fact that he had climbed in bed and cried his eyes out, declaring his undying love for me. I had never seen him cry before. And it touched me. Softened my heart, if you will. And, yes—I believed him. I needed to. "I guess I've had a change of heart."

"Hmm."

"Is that all you can say?"

She reached for my hand, offering a slight smile. "It's gorgeous, girl," she said, inspecting the perfectly clear stone. She let my hand go. "But, I'll be lying if I didn't say I'm a bit taken aback. I mean, a few weeks ago, you had Autumn and I over talking about how you felt Mustafa was cheating on you and how you had a problem with him hustling. Now you're sitting here showing me an engagement ring."

"Well, I'm just as surprised. Believe me. But Mustafa is adamant that this is what he wants. He loves me, girl. And you know how I feel about him."

"So, you're saying he's not cheating on you? And he's outta the game?"

"Well, no. I'm not saying that. I mean. Well, with the cheating thing, it was just my gut. It's not like I had any proof or anything. And I'm not going to let my wandering mind get the best of me. I have to trust that he's being straight with me. And as far as him stacking his paper, I've decided to let him just do him."

"Hmm. Well, that's a switch in gears."

I shrugged my shoulders. "I know."

"So have you set a date?"

"No. Not yet. I mean. I just got the ring. But, I've been thinking about a winter wedding."

"Hmm," she said, pursing her lips. "Sounds cute. And when were you thinking of having this glorious event?"

"Not until next year. Maybe, December 2006."

We sat in silence for a while, neither of us speaking. Just sipping on our drinks.

"So, have you at least done what I suggested?" she finally asked, closing the space between us. I gave her a quizzical look. "Did you at least listen to his messages?"

"Yeah," I admitted.

"And?"

"Nothing," I lied. "For the last two weeks, there've been no calls from any other females." Well, that part was true. She stared at me. Blinked real hard. She seemed apprehensive. "What?"

She shook her head, "Nothing."

"Say it."

She took a deep breath. "You're my girl and all. And you know I got your back. I didn't really wanna tell you this. But, now that you're talking about getting married I think you should know . . ."

"Know what?"

" . . . Well, I think Mustafa is dealing with some chick in New Brunswick."

For a split second, it felt as if my heart stopped. Thinking was not the same as knowing. But it warranted my attention. "What do you mean by 'dealing with'? And where'd you get this information from?"

"Well," she sighed, clasping her hands on the table. "Last week, I was sitting in Weaves and Wonders enjoying the cocktails and ambiance of the place while waiting to get my hair done when these two chicks come in . . . " she paused, gauging my response.

"And?" I asked, feeling myself getting impatient.

"Well, they both sat down across from me, and I noticed one of the chicks had on a bangin' pair of heels. And you know me and shoes." I rolled my eyes. She ignored my growing irritation and continued, "So, I complimented her on them. And she smiled, then said 'thank you'. Well, I was gonna leave it at that. But the chick with her decides to add, 'It took my man almost a year before he kicked out dough to buy me a pair of shoes. And this heifer gets a shopping spree in a matter of months. So I asked her how long they'd been together, and she says 'almost two months'. Then I was like, two months and he's already buying you gifts. He sounds like a good catch. She agreed. And I smiled, wanting to know more. So I asked how the two of them met. And she tells me on a chat line. Then they both giggle, and high-five each other. Then clicked their glasses together, gulping down their drinks. I just kind of gave them both strange looks. After that, they went into some idle chitchat. And I continued flipping through my *Essence* magazine, and sipping on my champagne. Then the chick with the bangin' shoes cell goes off; she picks up, says a few things. Then hangs up.

"Then she turns to her friend, and says 'that was just him'. And, then goes into this story about planning a weekend trip to South Beach. Then chick with her says, 'well let me know when you and Mustafa'—right then, my ears perked up—'are going because me and Tru were thinking about going to.' Well, homegirl rolls her eyes, saying the trip is on hold because *he* has to be in Maryland. And that's what that call was about."

I focused my attention on the drink in front of me and then at Nygeria's silly ass before I spoke. I was beginning to believe Autumn when she said Nygeria was a confabulator, especially when she's tossed a few drinks. She was really letting her imagination get the best of her. "Ny, what does this have to do with me?"

"Girl, how many Mustafa's you know go to Maryland?" I shrugged my shoulders. "Now it could have been a quirk. But it wasn't."

"And how do you know that?" I asked, feeling myself get more annoyed by the moment.

"Because I asked—" she paused. I waited for her to finish taking a sip of her drink—"I asked her if that's where her man was from. And she said *no.* She said he was from East Orange; but had family in Maryland. I put two and two together. This chick was talking about your . . . Nia, girl, are you alright?" Nygeria could come up with some of the craziest shit. Like the time she had sworn she had seen Mustafa in Atlantic City. And the whole time he was . . . in Maryland. No. There's more than one Mustafa in the world. And I was sure there was more than one living in East Orange with all the wanna-be Muslims in the area. So, *no*, I wasn't buying into this foolishness. *But how many go to Maryland?*

I closed my eyes, squeezing them tight, and then opening them. I swallowed the knot in my throat, freeing my airway so I could finally speak. "I'm fine," I said, taking a long sip of my drink, then sitting it down. I parted a smile. "Why wouldn't I be?"

"I don't know. For a moment, it looked like you were about to faint."

"Girl, please" I said, waving her on. "Sounds more like a coincidence to me, than a situation for alarm." I leaned in, then steeple my hands in front of me. "I'm not saying Mustafa isn't capable of creeping. Anything is possible. We both know no one is exempt from that happening. But hooking up with some chick on a chat line is stretching it. There's no way he'd go there."

"I guess," she said, giving a disappointed sigh. "It just sounded too close for comfort. And you know I wouldn't have said anything if it didn't sound legit to me. I mean. It may not be him. However, I just thought you should know. Just in case." She smiled, patting my hand. "We, girls. And, you know I'm gonna always have your back. "

Yeah, I thought, *just like you thought you saw him dancing with some other chick.* I nodded, looking around for the waiter. I was ready to go. "I appreciate that," I said evenly. I started to ask her what this chick looked like, or if she knew her name, but decided against it. It would have only given credence to what she had already told me. I was determined to not believe any of this nonsense. I glanced at my watch. It was already five o'clock.

When the waiter came with our check, I paid the bill, then told her I had to get home to meet Autumn. Glancing at her watch, she indicated she had to get home as well because her and Devon had plans to go into the City. Once we got outside to the parking lot, I thanked her for doing lunch, gave her a hug, then strutted to Mustafa's car, taking in slow, deep breaths.

By the time I drove into my driveway—pulling up behind my truck, I had managed to erase most of what Nygeria had shared. But there were pieces that remained stuck in my head. *He said he had to go to Maryland. They met on a chat line. How many Mustafa's do you know from East Orange who goes to Maryland?* I stuck my key in the door, turned the knob and walked in, shaking the conversation from my mind.

The aroma of barbequed chicken greeted me as I stepped through the door. Lenny William's "Cause I Love You" blared through the house. I loved that song. It was just something about the words that touched me. I hummed along, walking into the kitchen.

A smile found its way on my face, seeing Mustafa in his boxers and bare-chested, busying himself over the stove. He was one sexy sight. "Hmm," I said, walking over to him. "What a nice surprise." I kissed him on the lips. Suddenly, the day's events seemed to fade away.

He smiled. "Hey, baby.

"Smells good. What's for dinner?" I asked, peeking in one of the pots. Fresh string beans with smoked turkey were simmering.

"And there's potato salad, sweet potatoes and baked macaroni to go with that," he stated proudly.

"Wow," I replied, smiling. I didn't have the heart to tell him I had just eaten a big lunch, and was stuffed. I prayed I'd be able to make room for everything. "I'm impressed."

"Yeah, I bet you didn't think I had skills, did you?"

"You're just full of secrets, huh?" I asked in a tone filled with connotation.

"It's all good," he replied, kissing me again. This time deep, more intense. "Why don't you go on up and take a shower? Dinner won't be ready for another half hour or so."

"Hmm. That doesn't sound like a bad idea," I replied.

"And when you come back down, come down naked."

I raised my eyebrow.

He flashed a wide smile. "Tonight, dinner will be served in the nude."

"Hmm. And what's for dessert?" I asked, tipping my head coyly to the side.

"Me," he replied, winking, then kissing me on the tip of my nose.

I smiled, grabbing at his crotch. He was already hard. "How 'bout we skip dinner—" I dropped to my knees—"and go straight for the dessert?" I finished, unleashing his big, beautiful dick, then slowly taking it in my mouth. He moaned. And I sucked him with everything that was in me, swallowing down all the bad vibes, and angst that seemed to keep rising in the pit of my stomach. *They met on a chat line. Just thought you should know. Just in case.*

Eighteen

Autumn

If I told you I wasn't shocked to hear Mustafa had bought Nia an engagement ring, I'd be lying. I wanted nothing more than for Nia to be happy. But I had to wonder if Mustafa would be able to bring her the kind of bliss she sought. I mean. Happiness should come from within. Shouldn't it? Happiness was a choice. Wasn't it? But, for Nia, Mustafa seemed to be her everything. She seemed to be, bit by bit, losing herself in him. My beautiful cousin seemed to be clinging, holding onto something she'd never really have with Mustafa. Or would she? Maybe it was just my imagination, or my over protectiveness. However, I believed in my heart if things didn't work out the way she hoped, dreamed—it would destroy her. And that worried me. It worried me that her heart, what she felt, would one day betray her. It would be another devastating loss that would surely strangle her spirit. No, I wanted nothing more than to be happy for her. She deserved it. We both did.

From out of nowhere, I heard Nana and smiled. "Love is, what love does. Don't ever forget that," Nana had said the night before she took her final breath. "Let faith and the good Lord's will guide your heart. But the journey won't always be easy. Sometimes you have to go through some trials and tribulations to understand what real love is; but when you find it, embrace it. Hold on to it. And never let it go. You hear me?" Nia and I nodded, between the sobs, and the aching reality that the one person who loved us unconditionally was about to leave us. She was a mother to our mothers, and then—faced with tragedy—had become a mother to her granddaughters, loving us as if she had carried us in her womb and birthed us. She was a God-

"I heard you the first time," I responded. "Should I bring something?"

"Nope," she replied. "Just your pretty face."

I laughed. "You're so silly."

"Just make sure you're here."

"I said I'd be there," I sighed, wondering why she was so anxious for me to come over. "What's the occasion?"

"Nothing," she said. "Mustafa has been asking about you and I just thought it would be nice if you came over and had dinner with us."

"Hmm. . . . hold on," I said, getting up from the sofa. "Someone's at my door."

I looked through the peephole, then opened the door. "May I help you?"

"I have a delivery for a Miss Autumn Brimmington," the deliveryman said.

"That would be me."

"Please sign here," he said, handing me his electronic board. I signed my name, then he handed me a box." I checked it for a return address. There was none.

I opened the package, and inside was a signature TIFFANY & CO box. I pulled open the box and gasped. "Oh. My. God!"

"What is it?" Nia asked.

"I just got another package. And you're not going to believe what it is this time," I said, pulling out an eighteen karat gold lock pendant. It was beautiful.

"Well, don't keep me in suspense," she said. "What is it?"

"A gold lock on a sixteen-inch chain. From Tiffany's."

"Tiffany's? You go, girl. And you still have no idea who is sending you these expensive gifts?"

"None, whatsoever," I admitted. Almost every day for the last two weeks, I've received a package from one delivery service or another. And have come home to boxes on my doorstep. From flowers and candy to fruit baskets and

fearing woman; kind, gentle and humble. The woman who hummed lullabies and tucked us in, even as teenagers; the woman who had showered us with warm kisses, and sweet hugs was gone; yet, still lingered in the corners of my heart and mind. *I miss you so much, Nana,* I thought, closing my eyes, allowing tears to ease the pain. The fleeting pain, the ephemeral agony that reminded me of just how empty life could be without love.

I hadn't meant to fall asleep but when I glanced at my watch, it was 6:30 P.M. I got up and went into the kitchen, fixing myself a pot of herbal tea. When it was ready, I poured myself a cup, then came back and curled up on my sofa, taking slow, deliberate sips, allowing it to warm me—soothe me, thinking about nothing in particular. When I heard the sound of a car pulling up, I got up to peek out the side of my curtain. *Shit!* I spotted his truck, and couldn't believe my damn eyes. Morris was sitting outside in my driveway. I watched him get out of his truck, look around, then look up at my bedroom window. Not knowing what state of mind he was in, I started to call the police. But then decided against it. I went to my hall closet, pulled a jacket off the hanger and wrapped it around my shoulders. Then took a deep breath, swinging my door open to confront him. I was stunned to see him already on my doorstep, preparing to ring the bell.

"What are you doing here?"

"I needed to see you," he answered tenderly.

"You shouldn't be here," I responded, folding my arms in front of me. I thought about the court hearing, and how the Judge had asked me if I wanted to pursue a restraining order against Morris. But I declined. I told him it wouldn't be necessary. I just wanted to go on with my life and didn't feel Morris was any real threat to me. But now, seeing him standing in my doorway, I wasn't so sure.

"Can I come in . . . just for a minute."

Reluctantly I stepped back, opening the door wider—against my better judgment, allowing him into my space. "Only for a minute," I said, pulling my jacket tighter against my flesh as if a chill had swept through me.

"I just want you to know that I'm really sorry for what I did."

"You've already apologized."

"I just need to know what I can do to make it right? How can I fix the wrong I've done?" The Judge had ordered Morris to participate in an "Alternatives to Abuse" program, a twenty-six week domestic violence intervention for offenders. As long as he completed the program, the assault charge would be dismissed. And I was okay with that. I didn't want to see him with a police record. I just wanted him to take responsibility for what he did, learn from it, and—hopefully, never raise his hand to another woman.

For the first time, since I've known him, he looked worn. Crushed by the weight of shame. Maybe he was remorseful. Maybe. But, I'd never know. Not in this lifetime. The only thing I knew was what was deeply embedded in my memory; what lied dormant in the crevices of my heart. Painful flashes of my mother, followed by flashes of myself: Autumn, the daughter of a woman killed by a man; Autumn, the little girl haunted by the screaming and the yelling; the bruises. The police. The never-ending merry-go-round of make-up's and break-ups. *Don't ever go back. Promise me.* I looked at him sympathetically. "You can't, Morris. You put your hands on me, and that's not something that will ever change."

His eyes darted around the room, and then an awkward silence stood between us. The room grew suddenly warm, and I felt the sweat of something final roll down my back. I removed my jacket, draping it over my arm. We gave each other one final glance, then looked away, drifting to some far place neither of us could see in the other. It seemed as if time was standing still—waiting.

Morris looked down, staring at his Timberland-clad feet. "I love you, Autumn," he finally said in a voice so soft, I almost didn't hear him. But when he said it, I knew it was the only thing spoken. He looked back up, gazing deep into my eyes, searching for something lost. Something treasured, but never again to be found. Then repeated, "I love you." If only he had shown m this gentleness before. If only he had opened up his heart and let me in. Mayb I could have felt something different for him. But he hadn't. And I didn't. Those three words could have made a world of difference if things were different, if life hadn't dealt another hand of cards—only if he had been the man for me.

I reached out and stroked his cheek, a sad smile formed on my lips.

"Please, don't come here again. It's over between us."

He nodded. Resignation filled his eyes. I watched his face drop, felt his regret. "I know," he softly replied, taking my hand and pressing his lips int my open palm. "I know." I stared at him, allowing him to kiss what was an would never be, then pulled away. Slowly, I opened the door, watching hir step out into the night, and out of my life—for good.

The next day, I called Verizon and Cingular Wireless and had my pho numbers changed. I wanted to make sure Morris didn't have any way of contacting me, or me being tempted speak to him if he did.

"Girl, are you still coming over for dinner, Saturday?" Nia asked. Truth told, I had forgotten all about it. She had called me the other day and in me over. I wasn't really feeling up to it, but she sounded so full of excit I just couldn't decline.

"Yes, Nia. I'll be there. What time would you like me there?"

"Six o'clock."

"Okay, I'll see you then."

"Six o'clock, Autumn."

Morris looked down, staring at his Timberland-clad feet. "I love you, Autumn," he finally said in a voice so soft, I almost didn't hear him. But when he said it, I knew it was the only thing spoken. He looked back up, gazing deep into my eyes, searching for something lost. Something treasured, but never again to be found. Then repeated, "I love you." If only he had shown me this gentleness before. If only he had opened up his heart and let me in. Maybe I could have felt something different for him. But he hadn't. And I didn't. Those three words could have made a world of difference if things were different, if life hadn't dealt another hand of cards—only if he had been the man for me.

I reached out and stroked his cheek, a sad smile formed on my lips. "Please, don't come here again. It's over between us."

He nodded. Resignation filled his eyes. I watched his face drop, felt his regret. "I know," he softly replied, taking my hand and pressing his lips into my open palm. "I know." I stared at him, allowing him to kiss what was and would never be, then pulled away. Slowly, I opened the door, watching him step out into the night, and out of my life—for good.

The next day, I called Verizon and Cingular Wireless and had my phone numbers changed. I wanted to make sure Morris didn't have any way of contacting me, or me being tempted speak to him if he did.

"Girl, are you still coming over for dinner, Saturday?" Nia asked. Truth be told, I had forgotten all about it. She had called me the other day and invited me over. I wasn't really feeling up to it, but she sounded so full of excitement, I just couldn't decline.

"Yes, Nia. I'll be there. What time would you like me there?"

"Six o'clock."

"Okay, I'll see you then."

"Six o'clock, Autumn."

"I heard you the first time," I responded. "Should I bring something?"

"Nope," she replied. "Just your pretty face."

I laughed. "You're so silly."

"Just make sure you're here."

"I said I'd be there," I sighed, wondering why she was so anxious for me to come over. "What's the occasion?"

"Nothing," she said. "Mustafa has been asking about you and I just thought it would be nice if you came over and had dinner with us."

"Hmm. . . . hold on," I said, getting up from the sofa. "Someone's at my door."

I looked through the peephole, then opened the door. "May I help you?"

"I have a delivery for a Miss Autumn Brimmington," the deliveryman said.

"That would be me."

"Please sign here," he said, handing me his electronic board. I signed my name, then he handed me a box." I checked it for a return address. There was none.

I opened the package, and inside was a signature TIFFANY & CO box. I pulled open the box and gasped. "Oh. My. God!"

"What is it?" Nia asked.

"I just got another package. And you're not going to believe what it is this time," I said, pulling out an eighteen karat gold lock pendant. It was beautiful.

"Well, don't keep me in suspense," she said. "What is it?"

"A gold lock on a sixteen-inch chain. From Tiffany's."

"Tiffany's? You go, girl. And you still have no idea who is sending you these expensive gifts?"

"None, whatsoever," I admitted. Almost every day for the last two weeks, I've received a package from one delivery service or another. And have come home to boxes on my doorstep. From flowers and candy to fruit baskets and

Reluctantly I stepped back, opening the door wider—against my better judgment, allowing him into my space. "Only for a minute," I said, pulling my jacket tighter against my flesh as if a chill had swept through me.

"I just want you to know that I'm really sorry for what I did."

"You've already apologized."

"I just need to know what I can do to make it right? How can I fix the wrong I've done?" The Judge had ordered Morris to participate in an "Alternatives to Abuse" program, a twenty-six week domestic violence intervention for offenders. As long as he completed the program, the assault charge would be dismissed. And I was okay with that. I didn't want to see him with a police record. I just wanted him to take responsibility for what he did, learn from it, and—hopefully, never raise his hand to another woman.

For the first time, since I've known him, he looked worn. Crushed by the weight of shame. Maybe he was remorseful. Maybe. But, I'd never know. Not in this lifetime. The only thing I knew was what was deeply embedded in my memory; what lied dormant in the crevices of my heart. Painful flashes of my mother, followed by flashes of myself: Autumn, the daughter of a woman killed by a man; Autumn, the little girl haunted by the screaming and the yelling; the bruises. The police. The never-ending merry-go-round of make-up's and break-ups. *Don't ever go back. Promise me.* I looked at him sympathetically. "You can't, Morris. You put your hands on me, and that's not something that will ever change."

His eyes darted around the room, and then an awkward silence stood between us. The room grew suddenly warm, and I felt the sweat of something final roll down my back. I removed my jacket, draping it over my arm. We gave each other one final glance, then looked away, drifting to some far place neither of us could see in the other. It seemed as if time was standing still—waiting.

fearing woman; kind, gentle and humble. The woman who hummed lullabies and tucked us in, even as teenagers; the woman who had showered us with warm kisses, and sweet hugs was gone; yet, still lingered in the corners of my heart and mind. *I miss you so much, Nana,* I thought, closing my eyes, allowing tears to ease the pain. The fleeting pain, the ephemeral agony that reminded me of just how empty life could be without love.

I hadn't meant to fall asleep but when I glanced at my watch, it was 6:30 P.M. I got up and went into the kitchen, fixing myself a pot of herbal tea. When it was ready, I poured myself a cup, then came back and curled up on my sofa, taking slow, deliberate sips, allowing it to warm me—soothe me, thinking about nothing in particular. When I heard the sound of a car pulling up, I got up to peek out the side of my curtain. *Shit!* I spotted his truck, and couldn't believe my damn eyes. Morris was sitting outside in my driveway. I watched him get out of his truck, look around, then look up at my bedroom window. Not knowing what state of mind he was in, I started to call the police. But then decided against it. I went to my hall closet, pulled a jacket off the hanger and wrapped it around my shoulders. Then took a deep breath, swinging my door open to confront him. I was stunned to see him already on my doorstep, preparing to ring the bell.

"What are you doing here?"

"I needed to see you," he answered tenderly.

"You shouldn't be here," I responded, folding my arms in front of me. I thought about the court hearing, and how the Judge had asked me if I wanted to pursue a restraining order against Morris. But I declined. I told him it wouldn't be necessary. I just wanted to go on with my life and didn't feel Morris was any real threat to me. But now, seeing him standing in my doorway, I wasn't so sure.

"Can I come in . . . just for a minute."

perfume to—now, jewelry. "And, it's starting to get kinda spooky. For the life of me, I can't figure out who would be spending all this money on *me* "

"Girl, enjoy them. Its probably just some secret admirer tryna woo you."

"Or some nut"—I said aloud, more to myself—"preparing to kill me." I peeked out the side of my curtains, then pulled them shut. Thoughts of someone lurking in the bushes watching, lying in wait to attack or rape me heightened my concern, frightened me. Then I thought about purchasing a firearm—just in case. "I'm wondering if I should call the police and inform them."

"Call the police? Girl, please. What do you think they're gonna do?"

I sighed. "I don't know. Maybe, they'll be able to track down who's sending these things to me before something happens. Perhaps I should purchase some surveillance equipment, just in case. "

"Autumn, please," she said, letting out an exasperated sigh. "You've been watching too much *CSI*."

"No, Nia. I'm dead serious. This person—whoever it is—knows where I live, and could be watching everything I do, every time I leave my house, every time I come home. They know I'm here alone. Anything might happen. I should see about getting a gun for protection."

"Autumn, don't talk like that. You make it sound like danger was just on the horizon, or something."

"You never know. I don't mean to sound like a prophet of doom or anything, but there are a lot of crazy people out here doing bugged out things. Men beating, killing, then chopping up their wives, or burying their girlfriends bodies in concrete. Girl, anything's possible."

"I wouldn't worry if I were you," she said, sounding uncharacteristically unfazed about my fears. "In time, all things will be revealed."

I sucked my teeth. "Spoken like a true psychic," I said, trying to lighten my mood. "So tell me, what else do you see in your crystal ball?"

"Dinner at six," she said, chuckling. "And bring that locket so I can see it. If you don't want it, I'll be more than happy to wear it for you."

I rolled my eyes. "Yeah, I bet you would. Bye."

"Love you."

I smiled. "Love you back."

Saturday at six P.M., I arrived at Nia's wearing the locket around my neck. I had to admit, it was simply stunning. Mustafa opened the door, giving me a hug.

"Hey, stranger," he said, closing the door behind me. "Long time, no see."

I smiled. "I know. How are you?"

"Fine, now that you're here," he said, chuckling. "You're cousin's been working me like a slave. Word up. A brotha can't even get his chill on around here."

"Poor thing," I said, handing him my coat. "Well, how 'bout you go on and do what you do, and I'll go help the Massa."

He chuckled. "True that," he said, hanging up my coat, then heading up the stairs. "Let her know, you've set me free."

Nia appeared in the doorway of the kitchen, wearing a red apron with ESSENCE MUSIC FESTIVAL, NEW ORLEANS 2002 written across the front in black lettering. Even with her face flushed from the heat of the stove, she glowed.

"I thought I heard Mustafa in here talking to someone. Where'd he run off to anyway?" she asked, placing a hand on her hip.

"Upstairs. Said he needed a break."

She rolled her eyes. "Yeah, right. Whateva. Well, you might as well come in and help me."

"I thought I was an invited guest," I said, sucking my teeth, following her into the kitchen. "My goodness, looks like you cooked for an army. Who else you expecting?"

"Don't worry about all that. Just help me finish cutting up these vegetables for the salad."

I washed my hands, then dried them with a paper towel. "You know Shoprite had Dole salads on sale," I offered, jokingly. "It would have saved you a lot of time."

She cut her eyes at me, frowning. "Tonight doesn't call for bagged salad, okay. Now get to slicing." I laughed. Then began my task at hand. When I was done, I placed everything in a glass salad bowl, wrapped it with foil, then placed it in the refrigerator. "Ooh girl, let me see that necklace"—I walked over, allowing her to inspect it—"That's gorgeous," she said, grinning. She glanced up at the clock.

"What's so funny?"

"Nothing," she responded, handing me a tray of shrimp. "Sit these out on the coffee table for me."

"Who is all this stuff for?" I asked again, eyeing her suspiciously.

"Stop asking so many questions."

"Whatever," I snapped, walking out into the living room.

Suddenly, the doorbell rang.

"Autumn," Nia called out, "answer the door."

I sucked my teeth, rolling my eyes. "Who do I look like, Hazel the daggone Maid? First you got me helping you set things out. Now I'm answering doors. What in the world will be next?" I asked sarcastically, going toward the door. I opened it . . . and almost fainted.

There he stood. The color of dark chocolate with thick lashes wrapped around coal black eyes; a perfectly trimmed goatee framed his succulent lips, and his baldhead was as smooth as a baby's bottom. He was everything I remembered. Everything I tried to forget. I stood in the doorway, shocked.

He smiled. "Well, are you gonna invite me in?" The lusciousness of his voice caused something buried deep within me to erupt.

"Quasheem," I gasped, taking a step back before I fell over.

"How have you been?" he asked, walking in. The crisp scent of his cologne greeted me.

I nervously cleared my throat. "Fine. And you?"

"I've been making it," he stated, checking me out from head-to-toe. "You haven't changed a bit."

"Neither have you," I said, shifting my weight from one foot to the other. My heart thumped. He was always good looking. But I didn't remember him being this *fine*. This polished. It was obvious that he worked out—his muscular arms, broad shoulders and chiseled chest were practically bulging out of his black V-neck cardigan. He was stylishly dressed in all black. I glanced down at his feet, and noticed he was wearing an expensive pair of loafers. Gucci, I think.

As if on cue, Nia walked in like the cat that had swallowed a canary. "Quasheem," she sang, giving him a hug. "I'm so glad you were able to come." I gave her an under-eyed glare. "Please, come in."

"Thanks for inviting me," he said, handing her a bottle of champagne. "Veuve Clicquot okay?"

"It's perfect. One of my favorites." *Oh, please,* I thought with a silent roll of my eyes. Nia fluttered around the room. "Qua, have a seat. Dinner is almost ready. Can I get you something to drink while you wait?"

"No, I'm fine," he said, taking a seat on the sofa. "Nice spot."

"Thanks."

Mustafa finally came downstairs freshly showered and dressed in a pair of Polo carpenter jeans, a red and blue Polo jersey and some leather Timbs. Quasheem stood, and extended his hand.

"Yo, Money," Mustafa said, giving him a brotherly handshake. "What's poppin'?"

"I can't call it," Qua responded. They both took a seat across from each other.

"Mu," Nia offered, "Quasheem owns Sigma Cuts."

"Oh, word?" Mustafa replied, nodding his head. "That's wassup."

"Thanks, man. It definitely keeps me busy."

"I feel you, yo. You have a couple of shops, right?"

"Yeah, four."

"Yeah, that's what I thought. One of my mans and his son get their haircut over at the one on South Orange Avenue."

"Oh, aiight. Yeah, that one opened about six months ago." He had shops located in Englewood, Fort Lee, and Newark and had been featured in *Vibe* Magazine as one of hip-hops hottest spots for the best cuts. But, of course, I wouldn't have known that since I'm not a subscriber—or a reader of it, for that matter.

"So, you just doin' it up, huh?"

Quasheem grinned sheepishly. "Somethin' like that," he answered, stealing a peek at me as I sat and watched the exchange between the two of them like a tennis match.

"I'll have to come down and check you out."

"And when you do, just let whatever barber hits you up know you on the house."

"Word. Good lookin' out."

Nia came back out from the kitchen with a tray of cheese and crackers, then sat down beside Mustafa, avoiding my stare.

"So, Qua," she said. "What have you been up to?"

"Just tryna make it."

"Well, I have to say. I'm really impressed. Who woulda thought you'd be this big time entrepreneur."

He smiled. "Nah, I'm just tryna eat. That's all."

Mustafa's cell went off, he looked at the number, getting up. "Yo, excuse me, one minute. I gotta take this." He went into the dining room, speaking in a hushed tone, then returned to his place beside Nia. She cut her eyes, keeping her smile in place.

Finally catching my gaze, I narrowed my eyes, giving her the "let me have a word with you in private" look. She got the hint, and excused herself with me on her designer heels, leaving Mustafa and Quasheem behind us.

As soon as we got out of earshot, I dug into her. "What in the world is *he* doing here?" I asked through clenched teeth. I'm not sure why I was angry; but I was. I felt like my space had been invaded without my permission.

"I invited him," she said casually.

"No shit, Sherlock," I hissed. "For what purpose?"

"Autumn, I know you're shocked—"

"You think," I snapped sarcastically.

"And probably mad at me. But, I thought it was time the two of you saw each other. And, since you refused to call him, I decided the next best thing would be to get the two of you in the same room."

I folded my arms across my chest. "That was my choice. A decision I made so why the hell would you go against that?"

"I don't see why you're getting all bent outta shape about it. Its just dinner, Autumn."

"Because, you had no right. That's why," I argued, trying to keep my voice down.

"Do you mean to tell me you're still *that* upset over what he did to you?"

I couldn't believe she was standing there asking me that. She knew how bad he had hurt me, getting not one—but two chicks pregnant. I even had a fight over him. I cried for weeks over him. Thought about him constantly. Saw bits of him in every man I had dated—well, with the exception of Morris. Still, he was always somewhere in my mind, hiding. I had given my heart, and my virginity to him. And he . . . stole my innocence. But, that was years ago. I was over him. *Wasn't I?* Yes! I had moved on with my life. Hadn't I? Of course, I had. He was my past. *Then why does it feel like he still has something that belongs to me?* The question nagged at me, demanding an answer—an answer I was unable to give. "Why didn't you tell me you had spoken to him, and invited him over?"

"Would you have still come over?"

"No. I wouldn't have."

"Exactly," she replied.

I rolled my eyes.

"Autumn, he just wants to talk to you," she responded. "He still cares for you."

"I told you, we have nothing to talk about. What happened between the two of us is in the past."

"Is it really?" she asked, eyeing me doubtfully.

"Of course it is," I snapped, hoping I sounded convincing.

She pursed her lips. "Then it shouldn't kill you to have dinner with someone you're over, now should it?"

I sucked my teeth. "Answer me this, Nia: who in the hell appointed you the Queen of deciding what's best for me?"

She stared at me, tilting her head, ignoring the question. "You know, Autumn. Sometimes the hardest thing in life is learning to follow the prodding's of ones own heart. You can hide behind that brick wall if you want, but eventually it'll all come tumbling down. Especially when you're not being honest with yourself." And with that, she waltzed back into the living room, leaving me standing there, wondering what the hell that was supposed to mean.

Dinner was absolutely delicious. As ill at ease as I was, I had to give it to Nia. She had really outdone herself. After dinner, we returned to the living room, sipped on champagne, and listened to music. Of course I offered to help Nia with the dishes but she refused, insisting Mustafa would help her. I in turn, interpreted that as being her way of leaving me alone with Quasheem since I had hardly said more than ten words to him the whole night. What was there to say? I hadn't seen him in years. So much time had come and gone between us. Though he was someone I once knew, once loved, he was like a stranger to me. "Wild Is The Wind" played, and I closed my eyes, absorbing her melodic voice. For some reason, the words seemed fitting in an odd kind of way.

"Randy Crawford, right?" he asked, pulling me back into his space.

I smiled, nodding. We both took slow sips of our drinks, listening. Shifting our eyes from each other. I wondered what he was thinking. Was he really listening to the words?

"So, how are your kids?" I inquired, trying to close the chasm that was slowly spreading between us. But, asking the question seemed to open unhealed wounds.

"They're fine. Thanks for asking."

"What, they're like"—I counted in my head—"twelve now?"

He nodded. "Yeah," reaching into his pocket and pulling out a piece of candy. He offered me a piece. I shook my head, watching him pop the round ball in his mouth. "They'll be thirteen in a five months."

I smiled, knowingly. Thirteen years? I couldn't believe how fast time had flown. I let my thoughts stroll down memory lane. I was fifteen, he sixteen—when I had finally given myself to him. After three years of dating, of kiss-filled promises, I had allowed him to enter the depths of my being. Allowed him to make love to me. Unencumbered. Flesh to flesh. I let myself feel. Taste. Touch. That afternoon—in his twin bed, I felt something magically wonderful. And as awkward and nervous and unsteady as I was, I gingerly, methodically, accepted his entrance. And with each thrust, I felt an awakening. As I pushed against him, and him against me, I knew no one would ever touch me the way he had. No matter what happened from that point forward, nothing for me would ever be the same. I knew I would never give my heart to anyone else the way I had given it to him. And now, almost thirteen years later, he had found his way back into my life.

"Are those the only two you have?" I finally asked.

"Yeah, for now," he said, taking me in with his gaze. "One day, I'd like to have more," he offered. I shifted my eyes. "What about you? You have any children?"

His question caused a wave of sadness to spread over me. Somewhere in my fantasies, I had hoped to have a husband and children by the time I was thirty. I had three more years to go. But, by the looks of things, that wasn't going to happen. My dreams had been stolen a long time ago. And I had to accept there'd be no fairytales of a happy ending. I shook my head, suddenly feeling my biological clock ticking. I wondered if he heard it.

"Not at the moment," I said, getting up from my seat and walking over to the window, wondering what my life would have been like had I not miscarried. Wondering what kind of mother I would have been. I stared out into open space, slowly sipping the remainder of my drink.

Quasheem sauntered over, stood in back of me, leaned in, and then whispered, "I've never stopped thinking about you."

I turned to face him. We were standing face-to-face. I could almost taste his mint-flavored breath. A million butterflies freed themselves inside my stomach as I looked up into his eyes. I stepped back. Smiled nervously. *Sometimes the hardest thing in life is learning to follow the prodding of ones own heart.*

I opened my mouth to speak, but he pressed a finger to my lips. "You were my first love, Autumn. You still are. No one has ever been able to fill that void. When I ran into Nia, everything I've ever felt for you came back. I wanted to hear your voice. Wanted to know that you were okay. That someone loved you, maybe not as much as me but loved you enough. Made you happy. But when Nia told me you weren't involved with anyone. I knew it was my second chance. I knew I had to see you."

"Qua, I—"

"Sshh. Let me finish," he whispered, gazing into my soul. "I know I hurt you. But, I hope you know it was never intentional. I was so young. And dumb. I thought having more than one girl was what being a man was about. I believed I was a player, but in the end I got played. I lost you. I've never stopped loving you, Autumn. You got to believe me. I tried to find what we had in other females, but none could ever measure up to you. Somehow, I always ended up comparing them to you. My son's mothers, I never loved. Could never love. They were just pawns in my lonely quest for something I never really fully understood, until I became much older, and matured. You, Autumn, have been everything I've been searching for. Everything I've needed. And I want another chance with you."

"I don't know," I finally said, finding my voice. I looked away. "I don't have any room for chances."

"All I'm asking is to be your shelter in the rain. That's all." He gently lifted the gold pendant hanging around my neck, and kissed the lock, then pressed it against my lips. "Let me be the key that opens your mind and frees your heart, Autumn." I looked into his eyes, deeply. And saw, for the first time in my life, in a rainbow of colors, streaks of something beautiful. And it frightened me.

Slowly, everything that I was sure of was no longer a certainty. Everything I was—everything I used to be—seemed to collide, causing tiny pieces of my life to burst before my eyes. My emotions were slipping out of my grasp. I was losing myself to something much greater than my resolve to walk away. And I wasn't sure what to do. Maybe it was the alcohol. Maybe it was the nagging voice that said, "Let love find it's way to you." Whatever it was, I knew if I crossed this threshold, nothing would ever be the same. From somewhere deep in the core of me, something stirred, wrapped in a feeling I thought was long gone. A feeling I wasn't sure I could deny. *Fate or instinct?* He reached for me, and before I knew what was happening, I did the unthinkable . . . I stepped into his embrace.

Nineteen

Nia

Today, this moment . . . I . . . don't think I can handle any disappointments or unexpected surprises. That's what I was thinking when Mustafa walked out of the bathroom, fully dressed, and announced he had to go back to Maryland. *For a few days,* that's what he said. "Excuse me?" I asked, not wanting to embrace the statement. But it pierced the air, and pierced every fiber of my being. Something was slowly beginning to feel amiss. And I needed answers to bring some clarity to that which I was unable to see, that which I didn't want to believe. There was something, somewhere down in the pit of my gut that made me question him, that made me suspicious. Despite the sudden attentiveness, despite the ring, despite his undying profession of love for me, despite the tears and the toe-curling lovemaking, it was at that moment that his announcement demanded answers. Demanded understanding. Unfortunately—I got neither.

He said he had to go to Maryland. They met on a chat line. Just thought you should know. I pursed my lips, staring at him—through him, trying to conjure up a reasonable explanation as to why *my* man was off to Maryland again. Without facts, I didn't want to keep accusing him, assuming. *How many Mustafa's do you know who live in East Orange and have family in Maryland?*

"You alright?" he asked, sitting on the bed beside me.

I blinked real hard, held onto hope. Took in a breath. Deep. Controlled. Forced a smile. "I'm fine."

He kissed me on the side of my head. "You need some money?" he asked, digging in his front pocket and pulling out a wad of hundreds.

I shook my head. "I don't *need* money," I answered, turning my attention to him. "I need to know why you're going back to Maryland."

"I'm going down to meet Janice," he replied. "You know she's been really stressed about this whole court shit with Shari."

"Yeah, I know that's what you've said."

"Come on," he said, getting up from the bed, "you act like I'm making this up or something."

"I didn't say that."

"Well, that's how you're acting."

"Hmm. Well, are you?"

"Hell, no," he snapped, twisting his face up. "Why the hell would I do some crazy shit like that?"

I shrugged my shoulders. "I don't know. You tell me."

"Yo, don't tell me you 'bout to start buggin' again. You need to quit."

"Whose condoms are in your glove compartment?" I asked, watching him intently. Nothing unbalanced showed in his expression. Nothing about him seemed unfamiliar.

"What condoms?"

"The two boxes of Trojans in your glove compartment."

"I don't know anything about no boxes of condoms. I don't even use condoms"—I narrowed my eyes, tilting my head—"I mean, I don't have any reason to use them. You know what I mean."

"Actually I don't."

He frowned. "Yo, what the hell you snooping around in my glove compartment for anyway."

I smiled. Remained calm. "I wasn't *snooping*, as you call it. I got pulled over last week, and came across them when I was looking for the registration and insurance cards."

"And you just now saying something."

"It totally slipped my mind until now. So if you're not using them, then who is?"

He shook his head. "Yo, I have no idea. They're not mine."—He snapped his fingers—"Oh, damn. I told that nigga don't leave them in my car. Those are Malik's. I forgot all about him putting them in there."

"Malik's?" I questioned, furrowing my brows.

"Yeah. He bought them a while back. As a matter of fact, it was the last time—" I folded my arms across my chest, turning my lips up. I thought back on the time I was in his bedroom, looking around, of course, and found two used condoms in his trashcan. Don't ask me what possessed me to look in his trash, or what I was looking for 'cause I couldn't tell you. But I did it. And was sick to my damn stomach. Anyway, I confronted him and he swore they weren't his, giving me some story about catching his sixteen-year old nephew in his bedroom screwing some girl. And when I asked him what the hell his nephew was doing fucking some fast-assed girl in his room, he shrugged his shoulders like it was no big deal. "He was just doing what boys his age do. Hell, since you snooping and shit, you should know those little ass condoms wouldn't fit me. Besides, do you think I'd be dumb enough to leave that shit in my trash if they were mine?" That's what he said to me. I couldn't believe that mess. I don't know about you. But, if I walked in and caught my niece or nephew—or anyone else for that matter—having sex in my room, or in my damn bed, I'd beat them senseless. But, that's me. Anyway, I just rolled my eyes and left. Disgusted.

"So what you're saying is, your brother bought them.

"True."

"Isn't he married?" I asked.

"Yo, listen. I don't get in that man's business. What he does is what he does. I ain't got nothing to do with that."

"Call him," I demanded.

"Say what?"

"Call him. I wanna ask him myself."

He sucked his teeth. "Yo, you buggin'. Word up."

"Well, if they're not yours then he should be able to claim them, right?"

He stood there, staring at me.

I tilted my head, and waited.

He flipped open his cell, and dialed his number. "Yo, Malik. What's good, nigga? Nah, I can't call it. Listen, Nia wants to speak to you. Yeah nigga . . . Right . . . Oh, aiight. Hold on."—He handed me the phone—"here."

"Hey, Malik," I said, eyeing Mustafa.

"Yo, baby girl. What's poppin'?"

"Do you know anything about these condoms in Mustafa's glove compartment?"

He paused. "Oh, shit, yeah. Those are mine. Why, what's up?"

"What's up is you were about to get your brother smacked up in here." Mustafa rolled his eyes, shaking his head.

"Nah, nah. It's all good. That's my work."

"Oh, aiight." I said, keeping my stare on my Mustafa. "I just wanted to make sure before I went the hell off in here."

He laughed. "Nah, don't do that."

"Well, here's your brother."

"Aiight, baby girl. You be easy."

"You too," I said, handing Mustafa back his phone.

"Yo, nigga, I'm gonna get up with you lata."—He let out a sigh—"Yeah, right. Aiight. One." He hung up, then shot me a look. "Yo, you satisfied. Damn, girl. You be on some real extra shit."

Ask him only once, I heard Nygeria repeat in my head. I got up, walked over to him, and draped my arms around his neck, pressing my nude body into him. He stood there, trying to act annoyed. I looked up at him, staring him directly in his eyes, carefully studying his face. "Mustafa, I'm gonna ask you something. And I'm gonna ask you one time. And after this, I'm gonna dead it."

"Yeah, aiight," he said, eyeing me cautiously.

"Are you cheating on me?" I pressed my finger up to his mouth, as he opened it to speak. "Please think about the question before you answer it."

"There's nothing to think about," he said. "No, I'm not cheating on you."

"Have you ever been on a chat line?"

"A what line?" he asked, looking at me dumbfounded.

"A *chat* line," I repeated.

He scrunched his face up. "Nah. I ain't beat for that shit."

I smiled. "Good." I walked away from him, getting back into bed.

"Yo, where these questions coming from?"

"I just asked. That's all."

"Come on now. I know you. You just not gonna ask no shit like that out the blue unless you gotta reason."

"I just asked, Mustafa. 'Cause I wanna make sure you're not playing me."

"Yo, how many times we gotta go through this?"

"At the moment, I'm done with it. You said, *no*. And I'm gonna leave it at that. And for your sake, I hope that's what it is because I'm giving you an opportunity to come clean. 'Cause at the end of the day, I don't want there to be any surprises."

"Yo, where's this talk coming from?" he asked.

"I just wanna be clear. And I'm not gonna play games with you. Like I said, if you got somebody else, this is the time to bring it to the table."

"I told you no, so why you trippin'? I mean, damn. What more do you want from me? You need to stop being so insecure."

"I'm not trippin', Mustafa. And, I'm not being insecure. I just don't want there to be any room for confusion. That's all. I just want you to be honest. That's it."

"And I am. Listen, baby,"—he paused, then let out a sigh—"you're gonna have to start having some faith in me. If there's no trust between us, then we're gonna keep going around in circles with this. I told you, you're number one in my life. I put that big ass rock on your finger so I'm not going anywhere. And that's what it is, feel me?"

I felt the urge to snicker at his statement. In my head I heard the laughter. It's absurdity. *Trust you. Have faith in you. Yeah, okay.* As convincing as he sounded, I didn't know whether to believe him, but I had no real reason not to. So I decided to hold my tongue and keep my thoughts to myself—for now.

"I hear you. Now, let me get a thousand dollars," I said, plopping two pillows in back of me. "I might wanna go shopping later."

He dug in his pocket and peeled off ten one-hundred-dollar bills, tossing them on the nightstand. "You something else," he remarked, shaking his head.

I thought about his assessment for a moment, then parted a smile. "I'm glad you realize that." He stood there, with both hands on his hips, staring. Trying to figure me out. "What? Is there something you wanna say to me?"

"Nah," he said, rubbing his chin. His cell phone rang. He glanced at the number, ignoring it as he walked over and gave me a kiss. A kiss of deception, I thought. "I gotta get going. I'll hit you up lata."

"Have a safe trip, Mustafa." I yawned, and stretched, feeling mentally exhausted from pretending.

Our eyes met. And I gazed at him for a moment, taking him in. At that moment—in his eyes, I saw the reflection of my own apprehension, and wondered if he knew what I was thinking. *Liar.*

"I love you," he stated, leaning in to kiss me on the lips again.

"Hmm, hmm." I said, nodding. I watched him walk out the bedroom, heading down the stairs and finally out the door. I sat stone still and listened for the sound of his engine, then pressed my eyes shut when I heard him pulling off. Disappearing into the throes of distrust. My happiness seemed to evaporate, then vanish in thin air right before my eyes. I pulled the sheets up over my head, and steadied my breathing. Slowly, unintentionally, sleep came in vibrant, constantly changing colors. And a dream so real took shape. Swirled. Shifted. Collided and mixed in its own kaleidoscope.

They were sitting on the sofa with Mustafa's thick arm draped around her shoulder, while he played between her legs with his free hand. His jeans were unfastened and his stiff dick stuck out like a sword. She threw her head back and let out a moan. Then placed her face in his lap, slipping his dick in and out of her mouth. I stood in the window, peering in with disbelief on my face. I heard the screams in my head. Opened my mouth to let them out, but nothing came. She licked the sides of his dick, twirled her tongue around its head, then swallowed it greedily until he bucked, shivered, and unleashed his lust in her mouth. She licked her lips, stuck her fingers in her pussy, then slipped them in his mouth. I watched their illicit act like a Peeping Tom. Remained glued in one spot, letting the scene play out. I blinked. I couldn't move. Couldn't breath. I blinked again. She lifted up from the sofa, taking Mustafa by the hand and leading him upstairs. His dick was still wet from her lips, and the remnants of his nut. Glistening in the dim light. I waited. Wanted to weep. But the tears wouldn't fall. Instead, I grabbed my bat, walked to the back of the house, then slipped in through the backdoor. Dirty dishes were in the sink.

The garbage overflowed. A green notepad was sitting on the counter. On it was scribbled, Hair appointment. Cleaners. Meet Mu. I made my way to the living room and climbed the stairs. Slowly. Took one step at a time. Tiptoed down the hall. The door to the bedroom was shut. I reached for the knob, hesitated. I listened, pressed my ear tight to the door, then knocked softly instead. No answer. I knocked again and when there was still no answer, I opened the door and quietly went in. Music was playing. Candles were burning. Clothes were strewn across the floor. I followed the sounds coming from the bathroom. Moans. My breath came to a painless; yet, complete stop in my throat. The door was cracked. I peeked through the narrow space. Except for her four-inch heels, she was naked and was sitting up on the edge of the counter with her thick legs wrapped around Mustafa's waist. He was pounding in and out of her voraciously. The smell of sex was heavy enough to be licked off the air. I gagged. Felt my stomach bubble, twisting in knots.

"Damn, baby. You tight. This pussy's real wet. Just how I like."

"Hmm. Hmm. Oooh, oh, baaaby."

"Yeah, baby. That's it. Show daddy how much you missed this dick."

Slowly, I pushed the door open. Stood in the doorway. Half-shocked, half-disgusted. Pain stricken. I opened my mouth to speak but nothing would come out. The words stuck in the back of my throat. Clung against my tonsils. I gripped the neck of my bat, raised it over my head, then smashed him in the back of the head. "You fucking bastard!" I screamed hysterical. Pounding him. Beating him for every lie, every tear shed. Thrashing him until he collapsed. Until he felt the magnitude of what he had done. I was crushed. Had fallen apart. And there was nothing that could be done to mend what had been broken—my heart.

Somewhere in the middle of my frenzy, I realized his jumpoff had escaped. She had run out the house butt-naked, screaming for her life. But what did it matter to me. She wasn't my target. She wasn't the one who'd hurt me. On my way out the bedroom, I knocked over every candle around the room. The curtains caught fire, then the floral bedspread. The room quickly went up in flames, engulfing my soul in its blaze as I closed the door and walked out leaving my man there to burn to death.

A relentless buzzing caused me to jerk awake; my body bathed in sweat. A hand clenched around the neck of an imaginary bat. It was my alarm. I glanced at the digital clock on the nightstand, then reached over and pressed the annoying sound away. It read: 1:30 P.M. I sat up, propped on my elbows, breathing in harsh gasps. "Pull yourself together, girl," I said aloud. "You're gonna let this man drive you crazy." *If you don't trust him, why stay?* It was just a bad dream. More like a damn nightmare, I answered in my head. Then why the hell do I feel so betrayed? It was the same recurring nightmare that crept up in my sleep, suffocating me. No matter how hard I tried to shake the thought out of my head, it always made its way back to me. "Oh, the hell with this," I snapped aloud, looking over at the crisp bills on the nightstand. "A day at Short Hills is just what the doctor ordered." I peeled myself out of bed, deciding a new Louis bag or pair of shoes would chase my doubts away. I pulled my hair back, steamed up the shower, then jumped in. Turning the dial on the pulsating setting, I let the pulsing stream flow over me like a river. Tension rippled through me, then slowly out of me. When I was done, I stood at the sink and brushed my teeth, staring at myself in the foggy mirror as I did it. I took my damp towel and wiped what appeared before me: The reflection of someone slowly becoming undone. I knew it, but couldn't—or didn't want to—see it for what it was. I blinked, and then saw Nana. Heard her voice. *Patience is a virtue. Everything done in the dark comes to the light. Trust me. The truth will be revealed, sweet child. It always does. You just need to be still, and it'll come.* I swallowed hard at Nana's confession. "Please don't let it be what I think," I said into the mirror, pushing the thought out of my mind. But the feeling was in my bones, ran through my blood.

Stepping out of the bathroom into to my bedroom, I dried myself off. My nipples hardened from the chill and I took both breasts in my hand, letting my towel drop to the floor, and squeezed. Kneaded. Pinched. Caused currents to move through my body like electricity, shocking every nerve. Everything tingled. I was so horny. And didn't know why. I watched myself in my mirror, admired my smooth flawless body—cantaloupe-sized breasts, small waist, round hips, firm thighs—getting turned on at my naked image. I slid two fingers across my clit. Pushed on it like a buzzer, then slipped them inside of me, allowing my hips to move against my hand. Rhythmically finger-fucked myself. Clutched. Shuddered. Moaned. Groaned. Then allowed a heavy orgasm to flow. After I was done, I washed my hands, and got dressed. Glancing at the clock, I grabbed my satchel, and headed for the door.

Thirty-five minutes later, I was pulling into the parking garage. It was strangely quiet in the mall for a Friday evening; but I was okay with that. I made my way up the escalator, stopping into the Gucci store before making my way to my final destination. I purchased a black monogrammed silk scarf and a pair of black pumps. With a little over three hundred dollars to spare, I decided to go into Illuminations and pick up some candles, then go down to Sephora's to pick up a bottle of Thierry Mugler's Angel Star. Yes, I know it was a hundred-and-seventy-dollars; but it smelled nice. And I wanted it. So I bought it. Anyway, with seventy-seven dollars left, it was time to go. So, I strutted through the mall with my bags, making my way to the exit. Two cats were walking toward me, one of them looked vaguely familiar. When I got up closer, I recognized him as one of the Mustafa's boys.

He smiled, stopping in front of me. His man dipped into Barnes and Nobles. "Yo, what's good, Ma?"

I hated when niggas called me *Ma*. It was just annoying. *Do I look like your damn, mother?* I thought, pasting a smile on my face. "My name is Nia," I politely corrected.

"Mu's girl, right?"

I nodded. "Yeah."

"I see you doin' your thing. Looking fly as always," he said, letting his eyes linger over my body.

I ignored the hunger in his gaze. "Thanks."

He licked his lips. "So where's Mu at?"

"He's out of town."

For a moment, I thought I saw something glimmer in his eyes. "Oh, word. When is he due back?"

I shrugged my shoulders. "In a few days, I guess."

"Is that right," he said, grinning. "So what you getting into tonight."

I raised my eyebrow. *No this nigga's not tryna holla at me.* "In my bed—alone," I stated, tilting my head. He got the hint, changing the nature of his conversation.

"I feel you. Tell Mu to hit me up when he touches."

"And your name, again?" I asked.

"Haneef."

"I will," I said, glancing at my watch. "Well, Haneef. It was nice talking to you."

"You be easy."

"You too," I said, preparing to walk away. His man came out of the store, empty-handed of course.

"Yo, you bad as hell," he said, staring into my eyes. You gotta man."

"Yes, I do," I said with attitude, dismissing his comment.

"Yo, nigga. This Mu's girl," Haneef stated.

"Which one?"

I raised my brow, and frowned. *Which one?* I didn't like the sound of that. Haneef shot him a look. "*Nia,* nigga," he snapped, placing emphases on my name, leading me to believe that I had been a topic of discussion at one time or another.

"Oh, my bad. You wifey."

The way he said that made the hair on the back of my neck stand up. "No," I snapped, raising my brow, "I'm his fiancée. So what did you mean by 'which one'?"

Haneef gave him an evil stare. "Yo, don't pay this cat no mind."

"I was just fuckin' with you," he offered, letting a sly grin curl his mouth.

I stared at him, pursing my lips, shifting my weight from one foot to the other. He was trying to clean it up, but I wasn't buying it. He was full of shit. I knew it by the way he said it. Smelled it a mile away. "If you say so. Well, let me get out of here."

"Be safe, pretty."

"Thanks," I said, ignoring the 'pretty' remark, walking off. I overheard his partner say, "Damn, she fine as hell." I glanced over my shoulder, letting him know I heard him, catching them both staring at my ass, grinning. No good, niggas. But, who cared. The only thing ringing in my ear was, *Oh, you wifey.*

By the time I got home, my thoughts were scattered like leaves being tossed around in the wind, drifting. I didn't want doubt to consume me. But, somehow, it had. In my head I could see Mustafa. And I was mentally drained and wanted, needed, a distraction. No matter how slight. I dialed Nygeria's number. "Hey heifer," she said, picking up on the third ring. "Where the hell you been? I've called you mad times today." I looked over at the caller ID, pressed the button and saw that she had called six times.

"I went shopping," I stated. "Why didn't you call me on my cell?"

"I did. But you didn't have it on. I just figured Mustafa was there digging your back out."

I sucked my teeth. "Please. He's in Maryland."

"Hmm." In my mind's eye I could see her rolling her eyes in her head. "I take it he's still hustling."

"Yep," I offered, picking at my cuticles. I made a mental note to get myself a manicure.

The silence between us told me she wanted to say something more, knowing I wouldn't want to hear it. Instead, she smacked her lips. "So where'd you go?"

"Short Hills."

"I should have known," she said, laughing. "I don't even know why I asked that stupid ass question." I chuckled. "So, what'd you buy?"

I walked into the living room, plopping on my sofa. I kicked off my shoes and put my feet up on my glass table. "Don't worry about it," I snapped, laughing. "You'll see when I serve you."

She sucked her teeth. "What . . . *ever*. Well, who was out there? Any fly niggas?"

"You know I don't be looking at none of them fools. And you shouldn't be either."

"Says who?"

"Says me. Aren't you still going hot and heavy with Devon?"

"Yeah, and? Ain't nothing wrong with looking. Please. Niggas do it all the time." I was amazed that she was still dealing with him 'cause the girl went through men like underwear.

"Hmm. I'm impressed," I stated. "It's going on what, five months? And you haven't given him his walking papers."

"Something like that," she said, chuckling. "Let's just say his dick still feels good in me. And I'm in love with his paper."

I rolled my eyes. "Girl, please. You big on his ass, so don't even front."

"Maybe. Maybe not."

"Whatever, ho. Anyway, do you know some cat named Haneef?"

"What he look like?"

"Tall, brown-skinned with slanted eyes. And a head full of waves."

"Hmm-hmmm," she purred. "He's from Paterson. Why?"

"'Cause he was tryna get his rap on. And I looked at him like he was crazy."

"Humph. Chile, I heard that nigga got a big ass dick, but he broke as hell."

"Well, that doesn't matter to me 'cause I wasn't interested."

"I heard that. So what was he talking about?"

I leaned back on the sofa and recapped the whole Mall encounter. "I couldn't get over his obnoxious ass boy, talkin' 'bout 'oh you wifey'. What kind of shit is that?"

"Sounds like he was tryna tell you something on the sly."

"And you know I'm not even tryna go there."

"I feel you. Well, have you been checking his messages?"

"No, not lately. Why?"

"Nia, I know you love Mustafa and all, but he's got a lot of shit with him. And that's all I'm gonna say."

"And what's that supposed to mean?"

"It means just keep your eyes and ears open."

"You're right. I do love him. But, I'm not gonna let him play me either."

"Well, I'm gonna tell you like this, Niggas come a dime a dozen. If Mustafa isn't gonna treat you right. There's someone out here who will," she stated, snapping her fingers. "Do *not* let him steal your joy. You're too damn fly to be stressing."

"You're right."

"I know I am. With or without him, you will be just fine." The way I was feeling, I wasn't sure if what she said was an afterthought or a true statement. But one thing was for certain: I didn't want to find out. However, somewhere deep down in the center of my being, I knew her words would somehow become my reality.

Twenty

Autumn

Get a hold of yourself, girl, I said to myself, daydreaming. A whole week had gone by since dinner at Nia's, and I was still wondering how I could still feel Quasheem's arms wrapped around me. I was trying to figure out how in the world I let myself get caught up in the moment like that. But, the man sure did feel good. Humph. And smelled good too. I always try to be a lady, but the freak in me would have done him right there in the middle of Nia's living room if I hadn't come to my senses. It had been a long time since I had some good, body-rocking, tear-jerking, all night lovin'. And when I felt his hardness pressed up against me, my panties moistened. Yes, I'm truly embarrassed to say, I gotta little ho in me. Well, I guess you figured that out the night I let Morris have a taste in the parking lot, after a few drinks and several dances later. Oh, well. Anyway, over the years I had convinced myself that I was over Quasheem Daniels. But now, after seeing him, I wasn't so sure. And I didn't know what to do about it. After I stepped into his arms, I realized what I had done and quickly pulled away, walking back over to the sofa, taking my seat. And when he wasn't stealing glances at me, I was able to take a few deep breaths to keep myself from falling, slipping into his dreamy eyes. But, it was so damn hard to concentrate. He was like a chocolate bar waiting to be sucked, slowly. *Melts in your mouth, not in your hands.* I found myself toying with the locket hanging around my neck, absently putting it up to my lips. And he watched me, intently, leaning back in his seat. When I noticed his gaze, I shifted uncomfortably, and pretended to be looking at its inscription on the back, TO MY ONLY LOVE.

"So I take it you like the chain?" he asked.

I tilted my head, then shook my head. "Don't tell me. You're my secret admirer?"

He grinned. "In the flesh." There was no need asking him how he had gotten my address. When the answer was in the other room, washing dishes. *That damn busybody, Nia,* I thought.

"You spent a small fortune on me," I acknowledged.

"You're worth every dime spent Autumn, and then some." And here I couldn't even get a decent meal out of Morris's lame behind. Humph, as far as I was concerned, I knew my cootie-box was worth more than a damn night at the Ponderosa or Golden Corral. Dumping him was the best thing I could have done.

"Well, I'm flattered. But, you didn't . . . I mean, you shouldn't have."

He smiled again. "I wanted to."

"Thank you. But, I have to say, for a moment there, I thought it might have been a nut sending all those expensive things."

He laughed. "Nah, just me," he rubbed his chin. "Then again, I've been considered a little nutty at times."

Thick, and gooey, I quickly shook the thought from my mind. "Hmm. I bet," I stated, letting his comment take on a meaning of it's own.

"So, tell me. Miss Lady, what have you been up to the last twelve years?"

"Working," I offered. I didn't think it was necessary to share every aspect of my life, not now, anyway. "And trying to stay focused. What about you?"

"Just tryna pay my taxes on time and stay black." I smiled. He continued by stating after he graduated from Orange High School he moved to Hampton, Virginia with his parents, and ended up attending Hampton University where he received a bachelor's degree in business management. After graduation, he applied to graduate schools, got accepted to Ohio State and earned his MBA, then landed a job working for American Express as a financial analysts but became bored with it after a year. So, he returned to Jersey and opened up his first barbershop two years ago. "I just couldn't see working for someone else. I needed my own, if you know what I mean."

I shook my head, knowing all too well. "I'm impressed," I stated, honestly. With the plight of so many brothas falling victim to the streets, it was good seeing a young, educated black man doing his thing, positively. It was a beautiful thing. And being *fine* didn't hurt.

"Well, I owe it to my parents; if they hadn't stayed on my back, I'd probably have ended up on the block, or in prison somewhere. Getting up outta Jersey was the best thing they could have done."

"Change is always good."

"So, what's a pretty lady like you still doing single?"

His question surprised me. I sighed, shrugging my shoulders. "I don't know. I guess I keep being in the wrong places, at the wrong times, running into the wrong men." That was as much as I was willing to offer. There was no need to rattle off my dossier that listed deadbeats, and duds.

He stared into my eyes. "Well, maybe we need to do something about that."

I shifted in my seat. Not ready to go there with him. I glanced at my watch. It was going on ten o'clock. I looked around the living room, then toward the kitchen. "It looks like Nia and Mustafa have abandoned us," I said, changing the subject. Two hours had gone by and neither one of them came out once to check on us. "What lousy hosts."

He chuckled. "Looks that way. I take it you didn't know I was going to be here."

"Was it that obvious?" I asked.

"Just a little." He leaned in, staring at me. Then offered a smile. "If you'd known would you have come?"

"Honestly?" I asked. He nodded, waiting for me to answer. "Nope."

He laughed.

"What's so funny?"

He shook his head. "I figured that."

I shrugged my shoulders. "Well, you asked."

"That I did." He glanced at his watch. "I guess I better get ready to hit the road."

"Well, I'll get your coat," I said, getting up and heading for the closet.

He stood as well. "Dag," he said, placing his hand against his chest. "You sure know how to deflate a brotha's ego. And here I thought you were enjoying my company."

"I did, I mean . . . I was," I stammered, handing him his butter-soft leather jacket.

He put his coat on, then opened his arms. "Well, can I get a hug goodbye?" I gave him a quick hug, then stepped back. "It was good seeing."

I smiled. "You too."

"So, am I going to be able to see you again?"

"Who knows, it's a small world. I'm sure we'll run into each other again."

He nodded. "That it is. Tell Nia, and Mustafa, I said goodnight. And thanks for everything."

"I will."

I closed the door behind him, then headed for the kitchen to check on the host and hostess.

The doorbell rang and, absent-mindedly, I opened the door without looking through the peephole. "Quasheem," I said, taking in his strength. "What are you doing here?"

"Well, are you gonna invite me in, or do I have to stand outside in the cold?"

I pulled my robe tight, stepping aside to let him in. "Now, what are you doing here?"

"I was in the neighborhood and thought I'd stop by."

I tilted my head, narrowing my eyes. "You were just in the neighborhood?" I sucked my teeth, trying to suppress a smile. "I thought you lived on the other side of town."

He grinned. "I do. I decided to take the scenic route, and to deliver these to you," he stated, handing me a bouquet of red roses.

"You didn't have to do that," I said, taking them from him. "Thank you. They're beautiful."

"Not as beautiful as you."

A slight smile crept up on me, despite myself. No, Autumn, I said to myself. But right at that very moment, I was fifteen—again, in a twenty-seven-soon-to-be-twenty-eight year old body, blushing. Embarrassment quickly found me, causing me to regain my composure. "You shouldn't be here."

"Why, do you have company or something?" he asked, looking over my shoulder.

"No, I don't."

"Good," he said, closing the door behind him and removing his coat. "Then you won't mind if I come in and have a seat."

"Actually," I said, placing the palm of my hand in the center of his chest to stop him, "I *do* mind."

He stared at me, placing his warm hand over mine. Something about his touch weakened me. Broke my resolve. His heartbeat was heavy, strong, and I could feel the stirring between my legs match its beat. I quickly pulled my hand away.

"Why?"

"Because you weren't invited. And I don't like announced guest."

"Well, if I would have had your number I would have called first, and announced myself."

"You should have gotten it from Nia," I said sarcastically.

"She wouldn't give it to me. Said you'd have her head."

I laughed. "But she gave you my address."

He chuckled. "I know, right. And I had a hard time getting that from her. I had to practically beg it out of her." He had gotten it from her after she called him and told him I wouldn't be calling, and decided to send me gifts—first, until he could summon up the nerve, the courage, to knock on my door. But, then Nia had the bright idea to play matchmaker by inviting him over, deciding, without asking, that I needed to see him. That we needed to talk because that's what *he* wanted. Damn what I wanted. To hell with what mattered to me. Crazy thing, I wasn't even sure what I wanted.

"Well, you still shouldn't be here."

"But I am. And you mean to tell me, you're going to put me out in that night air without even offering me something warm"—he licked his lips, eyeing me seductively—"to drink?" I tightened the belt of my robe around my waist, feeling naked under his gaze.

"I have nothing warm . . . I mean, there's nothing warm for you to drink."

"It's chilly out there," he said, feigning a pout, pointing towards the door. "I just want to talk. That's all."

"You can't."

"Why?"

"I already told you."

"No, you didn't."

"Because I said so."

"That's not a good enough answer."

"Well . . . too bad." *Great comeback,* I thought. "Any way, Mr. Man. The last time I checked, my name was on this mortgage, so I don't owe you an explanation, or a reason for that matter." *Yeah, that's telling him. You go, girl.*

"True. But why are you being hard on a brotha?"

"I'm not trying to be hard. I'm just not up for company. That's all."

"And it has nothing to do with me?"

"Nope. I just don't think you should be here."

"Then come take a ride with me."

"Do you see what time it is?" I asked, pointing over at the wall clock. "I have to go to work in the morning."

He furrowed his brow. "And you're going to bed at seven o'clock at night?"

"No, I mean, yes. I go to sleep early," I lied. I didn't want to tell him, he was breaking one of my house rules. No unannounced guest, especially a man. But he wasn't just *any* man. He was . . . he was, um, someone I knew. He was someone who had captured my heart. Someone who had touched me in ways no one else had. Standing before me—in my present—was my past. And at that very moment, I wanted to slap him for sleeping with those girls, and getting them pregnant. Those should have been my babies. I should have birthed and nursed them; not those tramps he laid with. And I wanted to slap the piss out of him for robbing me of that, for stealing my heart, for living in my memory; and for hurting me—intentional or not. I stood, defiantly, facing him. And I wanted to slap him for awakening these feelings. Feelings of anger, and hope, and desire all mixed up, turning and twisting. My emotions were tossed every which way. And I was mad at him, and myself for feeling—for wanting, for needing. I wanted to say all this to him; but I didn't.

He folded his arms, and waited. "Well?"

"Well, what?"

"Are you gonna offer me a seat, or do I have to stand here?"

"I told you, you couldn't stay. So no, I'm not."

"Then I guess I'll just stand here and stare at your beautiful face."

I shook my head. "Why are you trying to make this difficult?"

"I should be asking you that. All I'm trying to do is talk to you, but you're acting like I'm some mass murderer or something."

"You hurt me," I snapped. My confession startled me. Freed me. "And I haven't let that go. I thought I did. But seeing you, opens up old wounds for me. And I don't know what to do about it."

"How 'bout you start by offering me a seat, and we talk about it. I'm a good listener."

"I don't know if I'm ready to talk about it. I mean. It's my stuff. Not yours. You've gone on with your life. And I thought I had too. But, obviously I've still held onto some things that I need to work on."

"I told you I never meant to hurt you. And I really am sorry about how things ended with us. Like I told you the other night, I was young and dumb. I was just a horny kid willing to stick anything moving. And I definitely wasn't thinking about how that would affect the rest of my life. But I didn't care about any of them. Hell, I was too young to know what love was back then."

"And now you do?" I asked.

He nodded. "I know what it isn't."

"And what's that?"

"It's not feeling empty, or alone. And I've felt very empty without you." I felt the sharp edges of anger begin to smoothen. He sighed. "I'll be the first to admit, I've made some mistakes in my life, Autumn. And I'm far from perfect. I ran behind the wrong women, all for the wrong reasons. And the only thing I regret is hurting you. Losing you. I have two beautiful sons, who I love deeply. But I've missed you. I never stopped thinking about you. And I only want a chance to make it up to you."

"And what makes you think you can?"

"I don't know. But all I know is I wanna try. If you'd just let me."

"I'm not who I was twelve years ago, Qua."

"And neither am I."

"I hope not," I stated. "But you need to understand, I've had some losses, and learned some valuable lessons that have made me a very different kind of woman. I don't look at life the same way I once did."

"Neither do I," he offered. "I'm a man, baby, who doesn't want to waste a moment of his life holding on to past hurts or disappointments. Life is too short. I want to be happy. And I want to know that my presence makes someone else happy. I want that someone to be you. I want to love and be loved. And I'm here because I want that with you."

I let his words linger, cling in the air before I opened my mouth to say anything. And, when I did, the only thing I could come up with was, "Hmm."

He smiled, glancing at his watch. "So, are you tired of standing, yet?"

I shook my head. "Nope."

"So, I guess that means you're still not going to offer me a seat."

"Offering you a seat would mean I wanted you to stay, which I don't. And I don't want you trying to get comfortable, then I might not be able to get rid of you."

He smiled. "You know, Autumn. I know enough to know that if you *really* wanted me to leave you'd already have put me out. So, that says you really don't want me to. But, I'm cool with standing."

I rolled my eyes. But he was right. There was this fleeting part of me that didn't want him to go. But, I wasn't going to make it easy for him. "So, what's your relationship with your son's mothers?" I questioned, letting my mind travel around the horizon of what ifs. What if he comes with a lot of baby momma drama? What if he's just looking to get custody of his sons and wants a surrogate mother for them while he runs the streets? What if he's still sleeping with them on the side? The last thing I wanted to do is be tangled up in a bunch of craziness by a man with a trunk load of baggage when I have my own stuff to deal with. Before I made any decision, one way or the other, I needed know. The last thing I was interested in was dealing with some man who still had dealings with the mothers of his children, or the drama of either one of them still wanting him. I wasn't built for that madness, and I definitely wasn't going to be fighting either one of them over him. Not this time, not *if* I decided to trek down this road again. Besides, I wasn't even sure if I wanted to deal with a man with an already made family. Or if looking in their innocent faces wouldn't be a constant reminder of what he had done.

"I take good care of my son's that's it. I'm far from a deadbeat dad if that's what you're asking."

"No. That's not what I was asking. The question was . . . is, are you still messing with either one of them?"

He frowned his face up. "Hell no," he snapped. "I haven't dealt with my son's mothers in years. And I have no interest in them, and the feelings are mutual. Candice and Javon live in Atlanta. Been there for the last four years. And Jackie and Qaadir moved to Willingboro about two years ago. They have their lives, and I have mine. I have my boys three months out of the year, and alternating holidays. And I'm cool with that."

"So, what do you want from me?" I asked.

"To spend a little time with you. Take you out. Get to know you."

"And what if that isn't possible? What if that's not what I want?"

"Then at least I can walk away knowing I tried. But I don't think that's what you want."

"And what makes you think that?"

"Because I feel it in here," he answered, pointing at his heart, then walking over and touching the space between my breasts. "And I know you feel it to. No matter how hard you fight it, I know it's what you want to. And I'm here to give it to you."

Without warning, he scooped me in his arms and kissed me. His aggression caught me off guard, and I fought hard to catch my breath. Tried to stop him. Or did I? But he eased his warm tongue into my mouth, pressing himself against me. His lips were lethal. And I was melting. "You taste . . . so sweet," he whispered lushly, slowly running his fingers across my lower back. "Damn, Autumn. You feel so good. I've been standing here wanting to do this since I walked through the door." I was losing myself. *Oh, God, Autumn. No. Yes. No. Yes. Noooooo. Yessss.* I felt a tingling within my loins. He was awakening the starving beast between my legs—an insatiable monster of lust. Its mouth was opening, slowly watering. Dripping. Forming puddles in the center of my panties. As good as he felt, as much as I wanted to be held, I had to get control of myself before . . . before I ended up doing something I'd regret in the morning.

Finally I found the strength to break away, collecting myself. "You do realize," I said, peeling myself from out of his strong arms. "This is a form of sexual assault."

"You're worth the jail time," he said, grinning. "Hell, as good as you feel, the judge can lock me up and throw away the key."

"You're crazy, you know that?"

"I'm crazy about you. Always have been."

"Qua," I said. "You can't just walk up in here and think we can pick up where we—" he interrupted me with another kiss, sending sparks through me. Setting my senses ablaze. I was on fire. When he pulled away, I was . . . speechless.

"I'm going to make you love me all over again, Autumn. If it's the last thing I do, you are going to know how much I've loved you. How much I've needed you. Missed you."

"You really need to go."

"Can I at least call you?"

"No," I said, gazing at him.

"Then I'll be knocking on your door again."

"And maybe I'll let you in, and maybe I won't."

"Then I'll wait outside, all night if I have to."

"That's considered stalking."

"Says who?"

I smiled, opening my door. "Have a goodnight Qua."

He grabbed his coat, slipping it on, then started for the door. He stopped and turned back and said, "Umm. I was wondering. I mean. Your birthday is next month. And I was hoping I could take you out." *He remembered. After all these years, and he still remembered.*

"Are you asking me out on a date?" I asked, suppressing a giggle.

He grinned. "Definitely."

"Hmm," I said, smirking. "Maybe." He stepped back into my space to kiss me again, and this time I didn't try to stop him. I welcomed the taste of his sweet, delicious lips—if only for one night.

"Goodnight," he finally said, pulling away from me. In his eyes, I saw something . . . the roots of possibility, the blooming of a new beginning. I closed the door behind him, then braced myself against it. The scent of his cologne lingered on my robe, and instinctively I brought the fabric to my nose and inhaled. I closed my eyes and slowly exhaled. *Let love find you.* "Maybe," I whispered with the hint of a smile on my heart.

Twenty-One

Nia

Always trust your instincts. That's what my mother used to always say. But I didn't want to trust them—not this time. I wanted to shut out the painful truth—again. I wanted to close my eyes and wake, believing that my nagging suspicions were just a bad dream. If I could just stop the clock and rewind time, maybe, everything would be the same. Maybe everything would be the way it was supposed to be. But it wasn't. And I knew it wouldn't be. Three days had gone by and Mustafa still hadn't returned from his so-called trip to Maryland. I called him numerous times, and kept getting his voicemail. So, after the ninth time calling him, I punched in his password, and retrieved his messages. There were three messages from some lunatic chick, screaming into the phone about how she was sick of his shit. Sick of him standing her up, and that he'd never sniff her pussy again. Then she took it a step further by asking, demanding to know, "which one of your *bitches* you laid up with tonight?" My head hurt. Felt like someone had taken a sledgehammer, and bashed my brains in. *Which one?* I kept playing each one over and over, trying to make some sense out of them. When I had had enough, when I knew what I needed to know, I kindly did him a favor, and saved them. At that moment—in a frenzy—I jumped up, running upstairs, then swung open the doors to my closet, ripping clothes off of hangers, snatching everything that belonged to him, and throwing them in a pile. "Fuck you, Mustafa!" I screamed, running through the house. "You can't fucking call. You can't pick up your fucking phone. You want to fucking play me. Fuck you, your lies, and your cheating ass. Fuck you!" Then—like a mad woman—I hurled drawers out of the dresser, and dumped boxers, socks, and undershirts in the middle of the floor. "You finger-fucking the wrong bitch, nigga!" I yelled, swinging his belonging all over the room. Smashing cologne bottles in the bathroom. Ripping up pictures.

I went down to the kitchen got a large garbage bag then returned to my room, and filled the bag with all of his shit, along with his toothbrushes, deodorant and razors. I wanted everything—anything that remotely belonged to him—out of my fucking house. I dragged the bag to my car, threw it in the backseat, then hopped in my truck. I was dropping his shit off to his sister's.

I was so damn pissed, I couldn't think straight. My hands were shaking and my heart was racing so bad I had to sit, try to pull myself together before I ended up killing myself—or someone else—behind the wheel. Then just as I was about to pull out of my driveway, something caught my attention: A white envelope on the side of the driver's seat. I didn't remember it being there a few days ago. Then again I wasn't paying any attention. I picked it up. It was from Cingular Wireless, addressed to Mustafa. How in the world did this get in here? I wondered. Then it dawned on me that Mustafa had had my truck before he left for Maryland. Anyway, I thought it might have been a welcome package, or something because it wasn't a typical envelope for a bill. But, me being who I am, I just had to go looking for shit. I pulled out the contents and almost gagged. It was a thirty-page phone bill, with over four-hundred-and-thirty-six phone calls. Everything in me went limp. I felt pains in my chest. Felt like my heart was being stabbed with a thousand needles. I steadied my breathing, skimming each page. Numbers with area codes from 516, 973, 908, 201, 732, 301, 215, 718, 304, 864 and 856 filled the pages. I reached for my satchel and remembered I had left it in the house. I got out taking the phone bills with me back inside.

Once inside, I went into the kitchen, sat at the table, and slowly, like an investigator, seeking clues to a crime, took a yellow highlighter and highlighted the numbers that were called the most. Numbers that had been called all hours of the day, all hours of the night; numbers dialed at midnight, two in the morning, three in the morning, four in the morning. Numbers that had thirty, sixty, and seventy, to one-hundred-and eighty minutes talked. I took a deep breath. *Guide my fingers*, I said to myself as I started dialing. *Give me the answers I seek.* I took a deep breath, then dialed. First number: 973-854-7766. A recorded message picked up. "You have reached Talkee.com . . . a party line . . .This company does not allow hard-core chat . . . we have three rules: Never give out your phone number, never give out your address, and you must be over eighteen . . . if you are willing to play by these rules, press seven." I hung up, then ran over to my sink and threw up—weeping. Gagging. Coughing. Screaming. *They met on a chat line . . . They met on a chat line . . . They met on a chat line . . .* The words pounded in my head, beating like angry drums.

I blew my nose, and then returned to my task at hand, dialing numbers until two o'clock in the morning. Some answering machines picked up, others were answered by females—all of whom knew Mustafa in one way or another. But only two admitted to dealing with him. "Hello," the voice on the other end answered.

"Hello," I said. "You're number is constantly on my phone bill, and I'm trying to figure out who it belongs to. Do you know Mustafa?"

"Yes. Why?"

"Because your number is on my phone bill."

"Okay. And?"

"And. I want to know your relationship with him."

"He's my friend."

"Friend, like in *friend.* Or friend like in dealing with him."

"Like in dealing," she answered.

"And how long have you been *dealing* with him?"

"Why?"

"Because, like I said, your number is on my phone bill."

"And who are you?"

"I'm his girl," I snapped. "And I wanna know how long you been dealing with my man."

"Obviously, he ain't really your man 'cause if he was, he wouldn't be with me," she snapped back.

"Did you know he had a woman?"

"Yeah. And?"

"And. When I see you. I'm gonna go in your mouth."

"Yeah, whatever!" *Click.* I put a star by her name as a reminder to track her down.

The next number I called. "Hello."

I repeated my initial greeting, then asked, "Do you know Mustafa?"

Silence.

"Yes," she finally said. "And who's this?"

"His sister," I lied. "Are you one of his women?"

"I *am* his woman," she stated.

I slowed my breathing. "Oh, that's nice. He's never mentioned you. What's you're name?"

"Melinda."

"Well, hello Melinda. I apologize for calling you. But, like I said, I see all these phone numbers on my cell bill, and I'm just trying to figure out who all these numbers belong to. And unfortunately, I haven't been able to get up with Mustafa. Have you seen him?"

"Yeah. I was with him a few days ago."

"Oh, so you must have seen him before he went to Maryland?" I probed.

"I didn't know he was in Maryland. He said he had some business to take care of in Miami. Which sister are you?" she asked. "Because I met Janice and Trisha."

Miami. *She said they were planning a trip to South Beach. But it was on hold.* I felt the air around me thin. Slowly, the room began to spin. "I'm Samantha," I offered, keeping the rage that spread threw me like wildfire contained. "His half-sister. When did you meet Janice and Trisha?"

"Oh," she said. "Umm. I had dinner at Janice's house about a month ago. Interestingly, she wasn't too friendly. She seemed pissed about something."

"Is that so?"

"Yeah, she kept cutting her eyes at Mustafa the whole night."

"Hmm. Do you have feelings for him?" I asked.

"Yes. I care about him. We've been talking about having a baby."

A baby? I muted the wailing in my head. *Are you fucking crazy!* "How old are you?"

"Twenty-four."

"Did you know he's engaged?" I questioned, holding my breath.

"No," she said. "I wasn't aware of that." I could hear the disappointment in her voice. Felt her pain. "How long has he been engaged?"

"A month or so. But they've been together for almost five years."

"I see."

I closed my eyes, pressing back tears. "Do you mind if I ask you something?"

"No, not at all."

"How did you meet *my* brother?"

A deadly silence entered the space between my ear and the phone. A trickle of sweat slid down my spine. Hurt, and fear, and mistrust crept down the center of my chest and clung to my shirt. A sick sensation whirled in the pit of my gut. My stomach began to heave. *Please, God. Don't let it be so.*

"On a chat line," she finally said. Oh my God! She wasn't the only female he met over the phone—on a fucking chat line.

"Thank you," I said, hanging up. I sat with the phone in my hand, dazed, feeling detached, and beaten down with disbelief. I screamed into my hands. Cried until my chest felt like it would collapse. My eyes were sore from crying. My throat was raw from screaming at the top of my lungs like a deranged woman. I needed to pull myself together.

I dialed the 301phone number and got a female's voice on an answering machine. I hung up. I thought about calling Mustafa, demanding answers. But I knew I wouldn't believe anything that came out of his mouth. I knew he'd lie. *Think, Nia. Think.* Finally, I decided what I was going to do. I put a star by her number, then went back out to the car, pulled out the overstuffed plastic bag, dragging it back in the house, then put everything back in its place. The love, the years wasted, along with the pain—memories all wrapped in contradictions. And it hurt like hell. But I was so damn confused. Nothing made any sense to me. But the only thing I was certain of, Mustafa was up to no fucking good. Anger surged through me like a tidal wave. "You are going to fucking pay, Mustafa!" I yelled. "I promise you. When you least expect it, you are going to fucking pay!" I threw myself across my bed and cried myself to sleep.

Seven A.M. I was still lying in bed, staring up at the ceiling, feeling like shit, wondering what the hell Mustafa was doing, who he was doing it with and where. Bastard. I wondered if I would have been in all this mess, getting caught up in relationships with wrong men, if I had known my own father. I saw him once when I was five years old, and again when I was nine. And both times, like now, his image was one big blur. Anytime I asked about him, my mother would brush me off, dodging my questions like stray bullets. And I never understood why. Eventually, I accepted his absence. Accepted being fatherless. But, there was still that little girl inside of me who dreamt about him being in my life. Acknowledging me. Loving me. Protecting me. I don't think men realize the importance of them being in their children's lives. I don't think they understand the value of having them around, no matter how slight. It makes a world of difference. Having a father's love. Then again, even if he had been in my life, I had to wonder if he'd be another man to let me down. What could he have really taught me about men since he didn't live by any moral code of standards? He was a married man, sneaking around with my mother up until the time she got pregnant with me. It's obvious he didn't respect his vows, or his commitment to his wife. Yet, my mother knew his situation, and knew there was no future with him, still she allowed herself to get knocked up by him. A part of me wondered if she did it purposefully in some desperate attempt to keep him, or force him to be with her. Or did he fill her head with a bunch of empty promises? Whatever the case, I still felt deserted by him. I still felt as if he had left her to raise me—his daughter—alone. Sadly, outside of my own experiences, what little I did learn about men was through my grandmother's advice. "How you get him, is how you'll keep him. Remember that. Pay close attention to how a man treats his mother. If he doesn't respect her, chances are he won't know how to respect you."

However, my mother, who always seemed to involve herself with men who had other women, seemed to rationalize it by saying, "it's in a man's nature to have more than one woman. Besides, men are like buses, one comes every fifteen minutes. You get tired of one ride, you can get off and catch another." And she seemed content with that, parading around with someone else's man. Riding men like they were a means to an end. Or was she? Somehow I refused to believe she was okay with being the other woman. Then again, there were many women out there who were. Women who didn't mind playing the mistress or spending the holidays alone, waiting by the phone, hoping. Whining and pleading for him to leave his family for her. Well, I wasn't one of them. And I'd be damn if I would become one. Or had I grown to be one without even realizing it?

I remembered before I got all caught up in Mustafa how I could dismiss a brotha without missing a beat. I didn't, wouldn't dare, settle for any nonsense. The minute you got on some bullshit, I'd axe your ass without giving it a second thought. But, Mustafa did something to me. He came into my life and opened the doors to my heart. And, yet, with all these red flags flapping in my damn face, it was hard for me to close it, and let him go.

And now it had come to this. Crying over a man.

Disgusted, I swung my feet over the edge of the bed and reached for the phone. First I called out sick from work, and then, intuitively, something compelled me to dial Janice's number. I went to the window, pulled the drapes open, looked out, and waited. *She's probably still in Maryland,* I thought. I glanced over at the clock and decided it was still early for her if she was home. She was probably still sleeping. I thought about hanging up. But it was too late—someone had already picked up.

"Hello," she answered.

I grabbed a lock of my hair and twisted it around my finger, walking back over to my bed and sitting on the edge. "Janice?" I asked, shocked to hear her voice.

"Yeah. Who's this?"

"It's Nia."

"Oh, hey, girl," she said, sounding surprised. "What's up?"

"Nothing much. I was just calling to see how you've been doing since it's been a while since we've talked."

"Girl," she chuckled. "I've been running ragged between work and these kids. I guess you heard about Shari?"

"Yeah. I did. I'm so sorry. I've been meaning to call you. When'd you get back?"

"Get back? I haven't gone anywhere. I've been right here. Chile please. No need to be sorry. It's her life. Like I told her fast ass when she wanted to go down to Maryland and live with her father, if you get pregnant don't think you coming back here 'cause I ain't taking care of no babies."

Pregnant? I know I didn't hear her correctly. I was silent for a moment. What if she just didn't want to talk about her incarceration? Mustafa never said anything about her being pregnant. Maybe he didn't know. Or perhaps it slipped his mind. Yeah, that had to be it. I tried to shake the thoughts from my head. Oh God. What if . . . Mustafa had made this whole story up? No, no. He wouldn't do something like that. Would he? "She's pregnant?" I asked softly.

"Hmm-hmm. Four-months. And her sorry-ass father got the nerve to be calling me, talking about he can't do a damn thing with her. Sneaking boys in and out of the house. Staying out all hours of the night. Shit. I asked his ass what the hell he was calling me for. When she was here acting up, he was jumping all over me like I was supposed to be superwoman or something. Now he sees it ain't as easy as he thought. And the thing that really wrecks my nerves is the fact that the damn child doesn't even know who the father is. Well, that's what she says. Humph. How the hell you not going to know who the hell you fucking? I'm so damn disgusted. That's my child, and I love her dearly, but it looks like she done got down there and turned into a regular 'ole ho."

I didn't want to believe what I was hearing. "What a minute," I said, trying to regroup. I was so startled I almost dropped the phone. "I thought Shari was locked up."

"Locked up? Girl, where in the world you hear that mess? That's where her hot ass needs to be. But no, she's down in Maryland running wild."

Silence. If my heart sunk any further it'd be in my lap. I crossed my leg, bouncing it. My head was starting to hurt. Suddenly, I realized that I was sitting so far on the edge of my bed that I would damn near fall over. I sat back, staring around the room in disbelief.

"When's the last time you spoke to Mustafa?" I asked, squeezing the phone until my fingers ached.

"He stopped by here just before he went to Mi . . ." she stopped, realizing she was saying more than she was supposed to. She lightly laughed it off. "Girl that fool is always on the move. He blows in and out of here like the wind. Can't no body ever seem to pin him down long enough to have a decent conversation with him."

I swallowed hard. Remained calm. "Do you know a Melinda?"

"No," she responded, quickly, "I don't think I do. Why?"

"Well, she said she and Mustafa had dinner at your house last month."

"Unh-uh. Mustafa didn't bring any Melinda here. I know someone in a truck came by, and he went outside and talked to whoever it was for a while. But he didn't bring no female up in here. That's my brother and all, but he knows I don't play that shit."

"Oh. I could have sworn she said she met you and Trisha," I offered, imagining them all sitting around the table laughing and eating like one big happy family.

"Girl, please. I'd definitely have remembered that. Like I said, I don't play that."

"Hmm. Well, I was just wondering."

An awkward silence filled the room.

"Listen, girl. Don't pay them stupid ass chicks any mind. You know someone always tryna throw salt in the game."

"Yeah, I guess," I replied. *This is a bunch of bullshit*, I thought. I needed to end this conversation before I said something I'd regret. "Well, I just wanted to give you a call to let you know I was thinking about you."

"Girl, I appreciate that. We'll have to get together before the holidays. Maybe do drinks."

"That sounds good," I said, frowning into the phone. I looked down at the diamond on my left ring finger. Despite its sparkle against the bright morning light, the room felt utterly dim. A feeling of sadness washed over me as I held the phone against my ear. The realization that Mustafa had been lying all along about his niece being locked up, and going to trial made me sick to my fucking stomach. How crazy was that? *My God*, I thought. *If he'd make up something like that, what else is he capable of lying about?* Was he really going to Maryland all those times or was he somewhere else? Who the hell was he with? Would I really ever be able to trust him in this relationship? Why was I putting up with his shit? Or was FOOL stamped across my damn forehead? *Aw, hell no!* I screamed in my head. *This nigga really thinks he's slick.* The real question was, what the hell was I going to do about it?

I knew Janice was covering up for Mustafa; but I wasn't going to call her on it. Out of his three sisters, she and I had a pretty decent relationship. However, I knew where her loyalties were. And I had to respect that. So, I decided it best not to dig any deeper. But, little did she know, she had helped open a gaping hole of uncertainty into a wide crater without trying. One thing was for sure, if I wanted to get to the bottom of what Mustafa was up to, I was going to have to look elsewhere. *Sit and be still. What you seek will come.* Somehow I knew my lack of patience wouldn't allow me to sit and be still long enough to let it—whatever *it* was—come on its own. I was going after it.

Twenty-Two

Autumn

"Good morning. American Financial, Autumn Brimmington speaking. How can I help you?"

"Autumn—" she said, in a depressed tone.

"Nia?"

"Yeah."

"What's wrong?" I asked, feeling alarm catch in my throat. "Is everything alright?"

"Yeah," she said, unconvincingly. "I need you to do me a favor."

"What?"

"I need you to run some numbers for me and tell me who they belong to."

I sighed. "What's going on? Numbers for what?"

"Please, Autumn. I don't want to go into right now."

"Alright," I said, sensing her impatience. "Hold on. Let me call you right back."

"Alright," she responded. I hung up, then called her on my cell. I didn't want to chance the call being listened in on. It would just be my luck I was being screened for quality assurance taking phone numbers. She picked up on the first ring. "Hello."

"Okay. Give me the numbers," I said, taking a pen and jotting them down. "I wanna know what is going on?"

"I can't talk about it right now. Just run those numbers for me."

"Are you about to do something crazy," I asked.

"No. I just need to know whom those numbers belong to. That's all."

I pursed my lips, not totally convinced. "Alright. I'll call you back in a few."

I punched the first number into my computer system. It belonged to a Samantha James in Irvington. The next number was listed to Nyeemah Paterson in Linden. The third number was listed to a Keyonna Leonard in Largo, Maryland. I wrote down the addresses each number was listed under, then buzzed my supervisor.

"Stanley speaking."

"Hi, Stan. This is Autumn."

"Hey. What can I do for you Autumn?"

"I have a family emergency. And I need to leave for the day."

"No problem. I hope everything is okay." he said, sounding genuinely concerned.

"Me too," I answered, hanging up, then grabbing my things and heading for the door.

I knew in my heart what brought me to her. I sensed the hidden message. During our childhood and into our teens, we knew instinctively when the other was hurting. Knew without words ever being spoken the depths of our own hearts; knew each other's fears and secrets. We were connected by our own uncertainties. I pulled up in her driveway, then turned off my ignition.

When I got to the front door, I took a deep breath, then rang the doorbell. No answer. I banged on the door. "Nia, girl . . . open this door or I will beat it down." Finally it opened. "Girl, what in the world is going on?" I asked, walking in. I stood there for a moment, shaking my head. Then noticed her swollen, bloodshot eyes. "Oh, no . . . you've been crying!"

"Well, hello to you, too," she lamented, plopping down on her sofa. "And no I haven't been *crying*," she stated flatly, shifting her eyes from me.

"Don't give me that. Those heavy lids are the sign of someone whose been crying. And not tears of joy." I studied her. And in her face, in the shifting of her eyes, came clarity. "Forget it. What'd he do to you?"

"What makes you think *he* did anything?"

I threw my pocketbook and coat in the leather recliner and placed my hands on my hips. "Oh, no Sweetie, those swollen eyes are the Mustafa-did-something-wrong eyes. So talk to me, Nia."

"Damn it, Autumn. Can you please just drop it? I really don't want to talk about it. Not right now."

"Uh-oh," I said, sitting down beside her. "This is big. And you know I'm not going anywhere until you dish the dirt. And don't give me that 'he didn't do anything' crap. 'Cause I know better." She looked the other way, shaking her head. "Wait a minute. This has something to do with those numbers you asked me to track for you, doesn't it?"

She stared at me blankly, ignoring the question. "Did you get what I asked for?"

"Yeah," I said, getting up to retrieve the information out of my pocketbook. Against my better judgment, I handed them to her. "What are you going to do with it?"

"I don't know," she said, studying the names and addresses. Her eyes welled up with tears, and she broke down crying. "I love him"—she waved the paper, shaking it as if she were trying to put out a fire—" but *this* shit is killing me." She got up and went into the kitchen, then returned with a stack of papers and some pictures. She tossed them on the coffee table. I picked up the seven photos and flipped through them. They had been taken in what looked like a motel room; and some doe-eyed, brown-skinned female—sporting a short pixie cut with gold toned highlights—was sitting on the bed with the covers up over her breasts. She had a big greasy grin, an I-just-finished-sucking-a-dick smile—painted across her face. At the foot of the bed was a pair of Timbs, Mustafa's I guessed. The next photo was of the same chick, lying on her side, showing off a butterfly tattoo on the lower part of her back. I said nothing. Just kept looking at them as Nia paced the room. Another one was of her standing in the doorway of the motel bathroom in just her pink panties, posing, showing off her saggy breasts and stretch marks. She was mediocre in looks, but stood, posturing, like she was a fly girl. *Humph,* I thought. I had enough. I tossed them back on the table, picking up the papers. They were highlighted pages of a phone bill. I shook my head disgusted. I understood the source of my cousin's pain, felt her despair. Lying and cheating were the two things I promised myself I'd never again take from any man. "I'm going to fuck him up, Autumn. I swear I will. The minute he walks through this fucking door, I'm going to kill him."

I shook my head. "No, Nia. You can't."

"And why can't I? That motherfucker is out here fucking around on me. Playing me like I'm some stupid bitch. Well, I got his bitch, Autumn." Her eyes narrowed with enmity. "I hate him. With everything in me, I am going to fuck him up."

"Nia," I said softly, "it's not worth it . . . he's not worth it. Just let him go."

"Just like that"—she snapped her fingers—"I'm supposed to just let him go on about his fucking life. Just let him get away with fucking me over. Fuck that! I've been nothing but good to him. So no, I'm not just going to let him get away with fucking me over. I've been so damn stupid. I knew he was fucking around on me. I just didn't want to believe it. But my gut . . . my gut told me. Everything he did was suspect. I asked him, practically begged him, to tell me. Be truthful. But, *noooo*! This motherfucker looked me in my damn face, and told me to stop trippin'. Told me I was buggin'. Even after I got that fucking yeast infection, I still tried to give him the benefit of the doubt. Still tried . . . wanted . . . to believe his grimy ass. I *never* get fucking yeast infections. Never!" I gave her a quizzical look. "Yes, you heard me. I know that black motherfucker gave it to me. I don't care what anyone says. I never said anything about it. Because I didn't want to . . .

"Four fucking years, Autumn. Four, long, fucking years, I stood by his ass. Waited for his ass. Stayed true to his ass. And this bitch gets out and fucks everything moving. Then comes here and crawls up in my motherfucking bed, and gives me a goddamn yeast infection. And still . . . I . . . let him convince me that I was overreacting. Being fucking dramatic. And all along I knew. But I just couldn't—didn't want to—accept it. Because I knew it would fucking hurt! So I closed my eyes, and tried to ignore it."

I knew better than anyone what Nia was capable of. Her hostility erupted like an angry volcano. And I knew I needed to find a way to deescalate her without underplaying the seriousness of what she was feeling. I needed to choose my word wisely, carefully. I lowered my voice. "I know you're hurting, Nia. But, you can't let him do this to you."

"He's already done it. The damage has already been fucking done!"

"Nia, sweetheart. You can't let him have this kind of emotional control over you."

"It's too fucking late. He has it. Everything. My heart. My spirit. My damn soul."

"I know," I said sorrowfully. I looked away. And now he was slowly robbing her of her sanity. *Love*, I thought, *should have no expectations*. Expectations limit you. Confine you. Keeps you shackled to false hopes. And opens the doorway to heartache. I turned my attention back to her. "But, you can move on from this. You're strong. Beautiful. And, one day, somebody worthy of your love will come, and give you what you deserve. You just have to hold on."

"I can't be strong. I don't know how to be. I mean. I used to. But, now, I'm so fucking drained. I feel like a fucking shell, empty."

"Nia, don't. You have to try to be rational, otherwise you'll end up regretting—"

"My only regret is loving him," she snapped. "And for being so fucking dumb." She broke down, and wept. "A lie hurts worse than any fucking truth. All he had to do is be honest with me, Autumn. That's all. Was that asking too much? This hurts so fucking bad." I got up and walked over to her, and wrapped my arms around her, rocking her. Slowly she sank into my embrace, and sobbed into my chest.

"No, it wasn't," I said, rubbing her back. "But some people just don't have it in them to be honest. No matter how hard they try, they just can't—"

"He's meeting bitches on chat lines and shit," she stated, cutting me off. "Can you believe that? Fucking pages and pages of calls to a goddamn chat line. You mean to tell me, he's that hard-pressed for some pussy. I suck his dick and fuck him any time he wants, any way he wants, letting him stick his dick in my ass. Giving him every ounce of me. And he has to be on a motherfucking phone line bagging pussy."

"Sometimes, Nia. It's not always about what you give them, or how much you give them. It's never gonna be enough. They'll always want more. The more you give, the more they want—the more they take."

She pulled away from me, wiping her eyes with the back of her hand. "Then that's too bad. And oh, so, fucking sad. But I'm not the one. And I warned him." Her voice seethed with anger.

"Nia, you can't compromise who you are," I said, taking her by the hands. "In the end, he'll get just what he deserves. What goes around . . . comes around. Not on your terms, though. Let it take its course. Trust me, what's coming to him will catch up to him. Come on, let me fix you some tea," I said guiding her toward the kitchen.

Nia sat down at the table while I busied myself around her kitchen. She lowered her head and covered her face with her hands, and cried as she had earlier—loud and hard. Her sobs reverberated in my ears, echoed through my body, bounced off the walls of my heart, then down into the pit of my stomach. The vociferousness of her pain was deafening. In my mind's eye, an image formed, took up space in my imagination—a woman lost in love, withering from a broken spirit; crushed by the deceptiveness of what her heart would not allow her to see. The truth. *Love is not pain.* I watched Nia intently, as I waited for the kettle to blow, letting her get it out. From somewhere deep, someplace buried in my soul, I heard my mother's voice in the whistling of the teapot. "Most men ain't shit. You can't trust them as far as you can see the sun from the moon. Most of 'em think with the head swingin' between their legs. They'll take all you have to give 'em. Then when you're all used up, when they've drained you, stolen everything you're worth, they'll toss you out like yesterday's news." And when I asked her why she stayed—why she held on, she bitterly answered, looking at me through vacant eyes, "Because sometimes you have to take what you can get until something better finds you." Sadly, for her, it never did. I reflected on my relationships with Morris, and Trevor, and the few men in between, and wondered if I had taken what I could get, if I had settled—waiting and hoping, for something better to discover me. *Let love find you.* My thoughts rested on Quasheem, and I wondered. Could I rewind the clock and recapture what used to be? Could I really allow him back into my heart and move forward? Only time would tell.

Finally, her crying subsided. She sat with her back stiff. I placed a cup of green tea sweetened with honey and a splash of lemon on the table in front of her, then took a seat across from her. She gazed at the steaming cup, absently. I reached over and patted, then squeezed her hand in a slight attempt to let her know everything would be okay. It had to be. For her sake, and his.

"I hate him," she finally said, swiping the tears from her face.

"No you don't," I said, gently. "You're hurt, and disappointed. But you don't hate him, Nia. I know you. You care deeply for him. And it's not your fault for him being who, or how, he is. You took a chance and fell in love. Unfortunately he's just not for you. He's not deserving of someone like you."

Her lips trembled, and then she began to cry, softly at first, and then in sobs that shook her body, and went through me like a knife, cutting deep. I got up and went into the powder room and brought back a box of Kleenex. "And he hurt me. And I *hate* him for that." I stooped down in front of her, took some tissue and wiped the tears from her face.

"Some people, no matter how hard you love them, can't always love you back in the way you want them to. Accepting that reality isn't always easy. It hurts. But it's not your fault. You expected him to give you what you had given him. And he didn't. But those expectations were yours—not his. And it's okay. Yes, it hurts, right now. But you will grow from this. And learn—"

"To never trust another fucking man," she snapped, "as long as I live."

"No," I corrected, lifting her chin. "That loving someone comes with no guarantees. It's a risk we all take each time we let someone into our space; each time we open our hearts to them. And sometimes we end up loving the wrong person."

"Well, he fucked over the wrong one."

"And, it's his lost. He'll have to live with that."

"You're right," she said, narrowing her eyes. "I want him to live with the consequences of his actions. Feel just what I feel. I want him to feel how it is to hurt."

"It won't change what's been done," I reasoned. "You have to find a way to let him go. Otherwise, it's going to eat you up."

She pursed her lips, wandering off. She inhaled deeply, then exhaled. "You know. I packed all his shit up last night in a plastic bag, then turned around and put everything back."

"Why?" I asked.

She shrugged her shoulders, slowly shaking her head. "I don't know."

Silence came between us. Both of us pulled our lips in, wondering what brought us to this point. Pain had a way of connecting us; keeping us tied to unpleasant memories. And if left unchecked, it could eat away at your existence, spreading like cancer. *How can you see what's going on in the present if you so busy looking in the past? You got to push forward.*

"You need to make some decisions," I finally said.

She sighed. "I know." She looked off into space, then finally picked up her cup and took a measured, deliberate sip, then peered over the rim of her cup. "For the sake of not losing what's left of my mind, I'm going to let him go. I have to. But he's going to pay before I do. And I promise you that, Autumn."

I gazed at her long and hard, considering what she had just said. Absorbed the meaning buried in her words, then shook my head. "No," I said. "You don't have to do anything to him to—"

"You're right," she stated, eerily. "I don't. He did it to himself."

We sat in stillness, sipping our tea as I tried to think of something to say to soothe her aching soul. I searched for the right words—but could find none. I watched her take another sip from her cup. Defeat was in her eyes. It tore me up to see her like this. Yet, I knew this was a journey she'd have to travel, and it'd be one hell of a ride. However, I'd be with her every step. The sound of the telephone jolted us both. She painstakingly pushed up from her chair, dragging her feet. She looked at the caller ID. I saw dots of hurt swell into balls of rage. Right at that moment, I knew. I was stuck in the middle, spinning in the eye of a dangerous storm.

Twenty-Three

Nia

"Hello," I snapped into the phone.

"Hey, sexy," he replied in a singsong tone. The minute I heard his voice, I felt every thing in me stiffen. I pulled in a deep breath, and summoned the strength to keep from screaming on him. My jaws tightened.

"Where. Are. You?"

"I'm still in Maryland."

I bet you are. "And you just now getting around to calling me?"

"Sorry, baby," he said. Things have been hectic. I think they're gonna try Shari as an adult. This whole court thing has us all fucked up."

He is really gonna play this lie out to the end, I thought, rolling my eyes upward. *Go along with his little game, Nia.* I took a deep breath. "So what does that have to do with you finding time to pick up the fucking phone? Court isn't all day and night."

"Come on, baby. I'm sorry."

I sucked my teeth. "When you coming back?"

"Probably Thursday."

"And why you staying down there so long?"

"I told you. Court."

"Humph."

"What's that supposed to mean?"

"Nothing."

"Come on. Don't start."

"Don't start what, Mustafa?"

"You know," he said, pausing. "Listen. I apologized for not hitting you up sooner. If you wanna . . . "

"Do I wanna what?" I interrupted, bracing myself for the surge of curses that were about to leave my mouth. I felt them rumbling, crashing against my tongue. I swallowed hard; pushing everything I wanted to say to the back of my throat. *Not yet, Nia.*

He sucked his teeth. "If you wanna beef, then go 'head. Get it off your chest. Just know you still my baby."

I rolled my eyes, and took another deep breath. "Is there anything you wanna tell me Mustafa?"

"Like what?"

"Please, don't play stupid. I'm really getting tired of your games. So you need to really let it go."

"I don't know what you're talking about."

"Yeah, right!"

"I said I apologize for not calling. Damn. What more do you want?"

I listened for as long as I could with him apologizing and giving me lame-assed excuses. None that mattered or made any damn sense. How his sister needed him. How she was stressed out. How every time he thought to call he got sidetracked. Bullshit! Lies. Lies. And more lies. Finally I couldn't take it anymore, and went off. "You are a motherfucking liar! And I don't wanna hear no more of your shit. So kiss my motherfucking, black ass."

"Yo, why you snappin'. I said I was sorry. Damn!"

"Whateva, nigga! I don't wanna hear it."

"I see you wanna beef 'n shit. I'll get up with you later."

"Don't do me any fucking favors, nigga."

"Yo," he snapped, "what the fuck is up with you? Where the fuck is all this hostility coming from? I'm telling you shit has been hectic, and you wanna be on some other shit. I apologize, damn. If I don't call, it doesn't mean I'm not thinking about you. You know I've always got you on the brain. What the fuck!"

"Mustafa, you know what?" *No, girl. Not over the phone. Keep it together.*

"What?"

"Nothing," I said, catching Autumn's stare. "Listen. I'm going to be out of town for a few days. So, get at me when you can."

"Where you going?" The nerve of him!

"Why should it matter? You out doing you."

"What the fuck you talking 'bout. I'm in Maryland dealing with some family shit."

"Well, good for you," I snapped. "That's what your mouth says. So, since Maryland is where you're spending so much time, nigga, do us both a favor and just keep your ass there. 'Cause I'm not the one."

"Yo, whatever man."

"I know it's 'whatever'. I'm tired of your shit."

"What are you talking about?"

Silence.

"Nia?"

"Nothing. Just forget it."

Silence.

"Why you trippin'?"

Silence.

"Yo, you be buggin'. Word up. And I ain't beat for that shit right now. I got a lotta shit on my mind. And I need your support. Not you beefin' about shit you got made up in your damn head. You sit around with your little girlfriends, listening to their sad, fucked up lives, 'cause they ain't got a nigga holding them down, and you start taking that shit out on me. You need to check yourself. For real."

I laughed hysterically. "Mustafa, you crack me the hell up. You need a damn Emmy for best Performing Actor, nigga, with all of your damn lies. But it's all good."

"I have no reason to lie to you," he offered.

"Bullshit," I snapped. "But don't sweat it. Like I said, I'm going to be out of town. And everything you're fucking doing is going to come out. So get ready. 'Cause I'm about to blow your lying ass out the motherfucking water."

He sucked his teeth. "What the hell you talking about? Ain't nobody lying to you."

"Like I said, that's what your mouth says. But I know better, Mustafa. So, I'm gonna ask you one more time. Is there anything you want to tell me? Speak now or forever hold your peace."

"Nah." He sucked his teeth. "You be on some real extra shit sometimes."

"Oh, well. It is what it is. And you ain't got to deal with it. Trust me."

"I love you, Nia," he said, sighing. "I know I do some fucked up shit, and sometimes I just don't give a fuck . . . "

"So, is that supposed to be some sort of confession?"

"There's nothing to confess. I'm keeping shit real with you.

"Oh, please," I snapped. "Give me a fucking break."

"Yo, I don't know how many times I gotta tell you, you got my fucking heart, girl. Do you need to hear it every single day? Do I have to engrave the shit in the fucking wall for you to get it through your head?"

"Whatever, Mustafa."

"Yo, you need to chill out. Word up. You don't make shit easy for me with all your bitching, and always accusing me of shit."

"Well, if you weren't out doing shit you shouldn't, I wouldn't be bitching. But, trust me. Everything is about to come to an end. And I mean that."

"What are you talking about?" he asked, sounding frustrated.

"Figure it out," I snapped, hanging up in his ear. "That fucking bastard!" I screamed. "Calling here like shit's all sweet." He called back. I picked the phone up, then slammed it onto the receiver. He called again, and I let it ring until it went into voicemail.

I went back to the table, and plopped down in my seat, swiveling side-to-side in my chair.

Autumn eyed me, putting her elbows on the table. "You okay?"

"No, I'm not. But I will be. I'm going to be A-motherfucking-okay. Trust me. As good as my name is Nia, that dirty motherfucker is gonna regret the day he laid eyes on me. He's lucky I don't slice his fucking dick off."

She sighed. I could tell my cursing was disturbing her, maybe even offending her. Oh well. Given my level of aggravation, I didn't care. She'd get over it. "So, where you going?" she asked.

I stopped swinging in my chair, looking at her. "I think I need to get my head together," I answered, running my hands through my hair up, then pulling it up in a ponytail. "You know, get away for a few days."

She nodded. "I understand. Sounds like a good idea. You want me to come with you?"

I shook my head. "Thanks. But I need to do this alone."

"I can respect that," she said, standing up. "Well, I guess I'd better get going."

I agreed. Although I appreciated her coming over the way she did, and letting me scream, and cry my eyes out, there really was nothing more for her to say, or nothing else she could do. I needed time. Time to think. Time to plan. And time to . . . get even. *Payback is bitch!* I nodded, getting up. She hugged me, kissing me on the cheek. "You sure you don't want me to stay?"

I shook my head. "No. I'll be fine."

She grabbed her pocketbook, slipping it onto her shoulder. At that moment I began to feel teary-eyed again. Maybe I didn't want her to leave after all.

I wasn't ready to see her go. My chest began to feel heavy as I held back my tears, thinking to myself. *I'm not going to cry. Not again. Not right now.*

"If you need me, call."

"I will. Thanks for getting those addresses for me, and for being here."

She smiled. "It was nothing," she stated, spreading open her arms. "Give me a hug." I walked to her, and we embraced each other hard. Long. "I love you, girl."

"I love you too. Drive safe."

I stood in the doorway, watched her back out of the driveway, then waved. When she was half way down the street, out of view, I closed the door behind her, locked it, then ran upstairs to my computer, pulling out the information she had given me.

My palms grew sweaty, and adrenaline pumped through me as the Department of Corrections website came up. I accepted its disclaimer, then double clicked on OFFENDERS SEARCH. My fingers trembled as I typed in the last name: Leonard, then the first name: Keyonna. I waited, knees together, ankles crossed, and heart beating strong before I clicked the SUBMIT button. I held my breath when her name popped up, and I clicked on her SBI number. Her photo came up, and I almost gagged. Girlfriend wasn't what I expected. Actually, I don't know what I expected her to look like, but she wasn't bad looking—okay, okay, she was a cute chick. Damn. Anyway, she had a forehead like Sade and sort of reminded me of her with her hair pulled back the way it was. I stared at her photo for several seconds, maybe minutes, before I started to read her socio-demographical-criminal history.

Race:	Black
Ethnicity:	Black
Sex:	Female
Hair Color:	Black
Eye Color:	Brown
Height:	5'8"

Weight:	140 lbs.
Birth Date:	June 28, 1973
Admission Date:	November 10, 2001
Current Facility:	Paroled

My stomach churned as I thought back on those letters I found, reflecting. Bringing her words—this convict, this parolee, this chick who my man was fucking—back to life in my head. *Hey sweetness. How's my baby doing? Last night I had my first wet dream about us. I miss you so much, baby. I can't wait to feel you inside me again.* I scrolled down and continued reading.

Offense: CDS/Distribute Drugs on School Property; Offense Date: November 16, 1999.
Offense: 2 count CDS/Manufacture, Distribute, Dispense; Offense Date: November 16, 1999.

I would have never imagined she was a chick pushing weight. But by the looks of things she was. Or maybe she was just someone who had gotten caught up loving the wrong nigga and took the fall—out of love, out of loyalty. Who knows? I'd heard of many stories about chicks who went to prison for their men, or withheld evidence because they didn't want to be labeled a snitch. So they did the time. While he remained out—free as a bird, doing him. Go figure. It could never be me. *I don't know what your deal is, but I'm about to find out,* I thought, printing her page, then exiting the website. I glanced at the paper with her address on it, then went on Mapquest. I printed out the directions from my house to hers in Maryland, then typed in the information for the other two chicks. Before I left for Largo, I intended on doing a drive-by to pay that chick in Irvington—you know, the one who tried to talk slick, a visit. Yes, I was ringing her damn doorbell, and going in her mouth. I thought about bringing Nygeria with me—for back up. *Then again, I'll handle her ass on my own,* I thought.

I went to the closet, pulled the door open, and felt sick to my stomach. How could this bastard play me like this? I questioned, snatching his clothes off the hangers again. "The nigga had an EZ pass to my damn pussy, fucking me anytime he wanted and that wasn't enough!" I yelled out loud, tossing his boxers, shorts, socks and T-shirts back out of drawers. "I asked you, nigga," I said aloud, throwing his shit around the room and in the middle of the floor, "if you had somebody else, gave you a fucking opportunity to come clean. But *nooooooo!* You try to make me think I'm fucking crazy. Acting like I was some jealous, insecure, dumb ass. I'll show you a crazy bitch. I'll show you jealous, nigga." I couldn't stop crying and screaming long enough to think straight. I just kept yanking anything and everything that belonged to him down off hangers, throwing boxes of sneakers and boots out of the smaller closet. Then I went back into my walk-in closet and snatched down his large Prada duffle bag off the top shelf, then started stuffing his belongings in it. And when it was full, I retrieved the trash bag that had held his things the night before, and began dumping the rest of his shit in it. When I was done, I dragged the trash bag and duffle bag down the stairs, and slung them both toward the front door. *I should haul everything out to the fucking curb,* I thought, heading back upstairs to take a shower. As I stood under the showerhead scrubbing my body, a fury blazed through me at the thought of him looking me in my face everyday, lying and cheating.

Twenty minutes later, I was standing in my closet trying to figure out what I was going to wear. I decided on a black jumper and a pair of stiletto boots. I topped it off with a black leather blazer, then stuffed my hair underneath its matching hat. I decided I wasn't going to be caught looking sloppy when I rang this chick's doorbell. I'd save the jeans and Timbs for that snotty bitch from Irvington when I got back.

I backed out of my driveway, wheels spinning and screeching, flying down the street. I stopped at the Exxon, got gas, then headed for the Garden State Parkway to New Jersey Turnpike South. Two and a half hours, and six CD's, into my drive I was approaching the Fort McHenry Tunnel. I paid my toll, zoomed through the tunnel then veered off toward the ramp for 295. I got off my exit, traveled along Route193, then made a right onto Lottsford, then another right into a housing development. Swampfire Estates. I almost gagged when I approached the entrance to these grand homes with the cascading waterfalls. This nigga was laying up with some chick resting in fucking estate homes. I was hot.

When I found the street and house number, I pulled into the circular driveway, turned the ignition off, then checked myself in my mirror. A part of me had hoped Mustafa's car would have been there, that would have given me more reason to show out. But it wasn't. And I had decided on my drive down to conduct myself as a lady. Well, to be as ladylike as I could be, considering my state of mind. I knew I wasn't being rational. But I didn't give a fuck.

I walked toward the stone and stucco palace, took the three steps to the door, then rang the bell. Finally the door opened. I couldn't believe my fucking eyes. Standing in front of me was this model-type chick with skin the color of cinnamon. I checked her out from head to toe before I finally opened my mouth to speak. From the wavy, brown hair flowing down her back to her light brown eyes, she was . . . almost exotic looking; and definitely prettier than she looked in that DOC picture. And she had body for days. The sparkle of large diamond studs in each ear caught my attention. This was the villainess. The drug-dealing chick who was fucking my man. I was ill. Her black Dolce & Gabbana shirt clung to her breasts.

"Is your name Keyonna?" I asked.

"Yeah," she replied thick with attitude. "Do I know you?"

"No, actually you don't," I stated, matching her stance. "Where's Mustafa?"

"He's not here. So, how can I help you?"

"You can't," I snapped. "When do you expect him?"

"I don't know. Why?"

"Does he live here?" I asked, looking her dead in her eyes.

"Yeah, why?"

"When's the last time you saw him?"

"Why?"

"Listen," I said, getting ready to go off. "I just found out who you were, and I initially drove down here to beat your damn ass." She crossed her arms, raising her eyebrow. I continued, ignoring her glare. "Yes, you heard me correctly. I planned on giving you a buck fifty, right across your damn face." I slipped my hand in my coat pocket for effect. I didn't give a shit about her having been in prison, I'd cut her so clean and quick she wouldn't know what hit her until she dropped. Not only was my knuckle game nice, I also knew how to work a blade if necessary. And if she tried it, she'd find out. She must have seen the glazed look in my eyes 'cause she didn't leap. So, I removed my hand from my pocket and continued, "But, when I got here, I decided it wasn't worth it. So, here is Mustafa's shit. When you see him, you let him know I was here." I tossed his bags at her feet. "You can have him. 'Cause I'm done with him," I snapped turning to leave.

"Wait a minute," she called out, glancing down at the bags in front of her, then back at me. "Who are you?"

I turned back around, facing her. "He'll know, when he sees those things."

She frowned, looking over my shoulder toward my truck. "Where you from?"

"Jersey."

"And how do you know Mu . . . I mean, Mustafa?"

"I've been with him for five damn years. That's how I know him. And you've been *fucking* him for almost two, right?"

She gave me a shocked look. "We've been doing more than *just* fucking," she spat, twisting her lips. "You must be Nia," she said.

"So you know about me?" I asked.

"Yeah, Mu mentioned something about you. But he said it was over between the two of you."

"Well, mighty funny I didn't get the memo about it being over; but, trust and believe, it is now."

"Then I guess your business is done here," she said, eyeing me. "So, I'd appreciate it if you don't come back here. You said what you had to say, and now you can go on your merry way."

Nygeria's motto: *Beat the bitch down* came to mind. I quickly dismissed the idea, but knew I would if I had to. "Listen, Keyonna," I said tersely. "My beef isn't with you. It's with Mustafa. And he's lucky I didn't catch him here, because I would have busted his fucking face in for tryna play me . . ." She craned her neck to look behind her. Then brought her attention back to me. "I hope you don't think your pussy is all that Sweetie, 'cause he's got his dick stuck in more than one hole. Trust."

"Well, it must be," she snapped. "'Cause he's here with me."

"Well, I hope you don't think you got yourself a prize—"

She gave me an evil sarcastic grin. "Obviously, you must think I do, otherwise you wouldn't be standing here tryna claim it."

I felt myself beginning to snap. No, this was no longer concerning Mustafa. This was about to be about me. And her. In a flash, I saw my two hands around her neck choking her. Stomping that smug ass look off her damn face. But I caught myself when I heard the screams of someone crying, the sounds of a child. That's what brought me back to my senses. I felt a knot in my stomach.

"Is that your baby crying?" I asked.

"Yeah, and?"

I swallowed hard. "Mustafa's baby?"

Before she could open her mouth to reply, her answer rolled up in the driveway—live and direct, pulling behind my truck. I looked at Keyonna, then narrowed my eyes on Mustafa slowly getting out of his car.

He was taken aback. "Yo, Nia—wh-what," he stammered, walking toward the house. "What are you doing here?

"Surprise, motherfucker!" I snapped, walking up on him and slapping his face. I attacked him with everything in me, scratching, punching and clawing him up. "You fucking liar," I cried in an exasperated fury. He tried to grab my arms. "How long has this shit been going on? Hunh, nigga?"

Blood dripped from his face and neck. We wrestled for what seemed like forever before he was finally able to get me in a standing restraint with both my arms crisscrossed tight over my chest. "Yo, let me explain." He looked over his shoulder, "Key, go in the house, and shut the door."

"You sure?" she asked worriedly.

"Go 'head," he commanded, trying to catch his breath. "I got this." She went in like a good little girl, closing the door behind her.

"Get the fuck off me," I screamed, trying to break loose. I rammed my heel into his shin, then onto his foot. He tried to wrap his leg around mine, to keep me from ramming his legs and stomping on his feet. But I was out of control. I bit him on his hand.

"Shit!" he yelped, letting me go. "If you'd calm down, and let me explain. It's—"

"You can't explain shit to me. I wasted five fucking years of my life on your lying, cheating ass. And I am fucking through."

"This is just business. I'm tryna make shit happen for us, and you coming down here blacking about shit you know nothing about."

I let out a disgusted laugh. "Give. Me. A. Fucking. Break. You need to stop with your damn lies. You've been sneaking down here, lying to me. Fucking everything moving. And you talkin' 'bout it's business. And you doing it for *us*. Nigga, please! You must have bumped your fucking head if you think I'm that damn silly to believe that shit."

"Well, you can believe what you want—"

"Exactly. And I believe you ain't no fucking good."

"Why the fuck you down here, Nia, huh?"

"I came down here to catch your black ass, that's why I'm here. You left your phone bill, in my car nigga. And I called all your bitches. And when I get back to Jersey, I'm gonna fuck them all up."

He sucked his teeth. "Listen to yourself. You sound crazy as hell."

"You right," I snapped. "I am crazy. I'm crazy for getting myself all caught up in your ass. And I was crazy for putting up with your shit and believing in your black ass. I was crazy for giving you the fucking time of day. See. Mustafa. Loving you, needing you, was my biggest mistake. And I am fucking done with you. But, I promise you this, you better watch your fucking steps 'cause the minute you trip and fall, nigga, I'm gonna be there to spit all over you."

He waved his arm nonchalantly. "Whatever," he snapped, turning his back to go toward the house where Keyonna stood in the doorway, holding a screaming ass toddler.

"I know it's whatever, motherfucker," I screamed at his back, then ran up behind him and punched him in the back.

He turned around and grabbed me, balling his fist. "You got one more time to put your hands on me, and I'm gonna forget you a female and lay your ass out."

"Yeah, nigga," I spat in his face. "I want you to hit me, bitch. Go 'head."

He gave me a long, hard stare, then let me go. "You ain't worth it," he snapped, pushing me back. "Go the fuck home." He walked back toward the house. Leaving me standing there as if I never mattered to him. As if I were some stranger, intruding on his personal space.

"Fuck you, Mustafa! You ain't shit, nigga." I stormed over to my car, snatching the door open. I looked over at his chick. "Like I said, you can have him. 'Cause he ain't nothing but a fucking dog! "

I thought I saw her smirk. "He said you was a crazy bitch," she snapped. "Now get the fuck off our property before I call the police." I heard him tell her to close the door, and she did, leaving me standing there dumbstruck.

Get the fuck off our *property.* Now why in the world did she say that? I felt something take over me as if I was possessed. I felt like I was having an outer body experience, floating. Seeing everything from the outside. I was clearly going out of my mind, and at that point I didn't care. He had crossed me. I caught sight of the bat in my backseat, pulled it out, and charged back over to Mustafa's shiny Lex. And went off. I smashed his windshield in, then the passenger side window. His alarm went off, and the door flew open. "I don't give a fuck about you calling the cops," I screamed, running over and smashing the driver's side window. "Call 'em."

Mustafa ran back outside. "Yo, what the fuck!" he screamed, coming at me with clenched fists. "Take your ass back to fucking Jersey Nia. I swear to fucking God if you don't stop, I'm gonna fuck you up." I swung the bat like a wild woman. He tried to block the blow. But it crashed into his elbow. He screamed in pain. "Oww! Shit!"

"You already did that," I yelled, hitting him again, this time alongside his ribs. "With your lies. I hate you!" I hit him again, this time in his face. Blood splattered everywhere. "I'll fucking kill you for tryna play me!" In the corner of my eye I saw Keyonna standing in the doorway with the phone to her ear, screaming. "Hurry," I heard her yelling. But I didn't care. I was a scorned woman. And this man—the one I gave myself to, loved, and stayed true to—had hell to pay. And going to jail was of no consequence to me. I didn't give a fuck. When Mustafa hit the ground. I hit him again, then walked back to my car, opened up the trunk, and pulled out the can of gasoline, and doused him and his car up. Tears ran down my cheeks. This wasn't how I had planned it, but there was no turning back.

"Nooooo," she screamed, running out of the house. "What the fuck are you doing?!"

"This is between Mustafa and me, bitch. So you stay out of it or you'll get it too," I threatened, tossing gasoline in her direction. She backed away.

"Ni-Nia," he stammered, rolling around on the ground. Blood streamed down his face, and out of his mouth. "Let me explain. It's not what—" The funny thing, every part of my body trembled and my hands were shaking uncontrollably, but I wasn't afraid. He tried to lift his arms in surrender, knowing, sensing, I had lost my damn mind. I saw his eyes open wide with fear. I saw the terror on his face. He opened his mouth to speak, and I kicked him in his nuts. He let out a fierce scream, twisting in agony. "Awwww!"

I was hysterical. "You should have never lied to me, Mustafa. All you had to do is be honest. Why'd you have to hurt me like this? I did nothing but love you." In the background I heard the sirens approaching, and could see the blue and red lights bouncing and flashing like flares. I struck the match on his car, then struck another one and tossed it on the inside of his interior. It went up like an inferno. I sobbed.

Oh, you wifey.

They met on a chat line.

I'm just one of many.

Obviously, he ain't really your man.

I heard the voices, taunting me. Reminding me of my painful reality. I tossed the rest of the gasoline on him. "I loved you Mustafa. And all you had to do was just let me go, if you wanted to do you. But you didn't. You wanted your cake and eat it too. Well you got a mouthful, this time. motherfucker." I could see the cop cars coming toward the house, ripping down the street in a fury. I struck another match, tossing it on the man I loved, watching him roll and shriek in pain. I was supposed to be his one and only, but somehow I felt like I had been the other woman all along. And it hurt. Nothing would ever be the same for me. There was nothing the police could do that Mustafa hadn't already done. There was nothing that they could take from me that hadn't already been taken. As far as I was concerned, I had already lost everything that really mattered.

Twenty-Four

Autumn

I was curled up on the sofa engrossed in the *Season's of Beento Blackbird* when I heard a vehicle pulling up in my driveway, then an engine shut off. I glanced at the clock. It was eight-fifteen P.M. I placed the novel facedown on the sofa, then stood up and parted the drapes, peeking out. I couldn't believe my eyes. It was Morris getting out of his truck. What in the world is he doing here? I wondered, opening the door before he could ring the bell. "Why are you here?" I asked, trying to keep my tone in check.

"I was thinking about you. And just wanted to stop by to see how you were doing. I would have called but you've changed your numbers." He smiled. I crossed my arms around my waist. "Can I come in for a minute?"

I blinked and tried to keep the look of disgust off my face. Morris was really a nice-looking man. But that's all he had going for him. He smelled like he had been drinking. "No, you cannot," I stated, flatly. "You shouldn't even be here."

"I know. But, you've been on my mind. And I just wanted to see you."

"Well, now that you've seen me, you need to leave. And not come back here. *Please.*" Maybe I would have to get a restraining order if he couldn't get the hint, and stay the hell away from me. I really didn't want to have to go there.

"I've missed you."

I shrugged my shoulders. "And what's that supposed to mean to me?"

"I was hoping you . . . I mean, we, could maybe try again. Maybe go away somewhere. I know your birthday is coming up, and I'd like to do something special with you."

Like what, I thought. *Take me back down south to visit those country coons he calls family.* Give me a break. I couldn't believe my ears. He wanted *me* to go away somewhere with him. He must have been out of his drunken mind. Please. After what he did, I think not! He'd probably take me someplace, out in the woods, and try to kill me. Who knew what was going through his mind. I didn't trust him as far as I could throw him, and that wasn't far.

"I know I fucked things up between us, but I'd really like to be friends. If possible."

"It's not," I said firmly. "

He moved toward me, trying to shorten the space between us. He was in my face, so close I could almost taste the liquor off his breath.

I frowned, then stepped back, tapping my foot.

"I can understand if you're still angry with me. But, do you think you'll ever be able to forgive me?"

In all honesty, I already knew that if I did nothing else, I'd have to have forgiveness in my heart in order to get on with my life. Otherwise, I'd be held hostage in the past. That wasn't an option. I understood hanging on to negative attachments would only bring me misery. I was responsible for my own happiness so relationships that no longer had a place in my life had to be permanently let go of, starting with this one.

I let out a deep sigh. "Morris, it's not about me forgiving you. I don't harbor any ill feelings toward you. I just don't want anything to do with you. And as far as us being—or becoming—friends, that will never be a possibility. The day you put your hands on me was the day that I knew you were not worthy of my respect, my love, or my friendship. You don't fit my definition of a friend. So, *no,* we can never be friends. If you see me out and you want to speak, that's fine. But other than that,"—I shook my head—"I'd rather you keep it moving. If you really care about me like you say, then you'll go on with your life, and let me go on with mine."

"I'm trying. But it hasn't been easy. I constantly think about you."

"Well, you really need to try harder. Because there's no chance in hell that I'd ever let you back in my emotional or physical space. I don't know how else to put it. But, you truly need to get over it."

He stared at me, almost through me, as if he were trying to bury his gaze into my soul. I looked away, glancing over at the clock, then looked back at him—matching his stare.

"You need to leave," I said, narrowing my eyes. "And not come back here."

He nodded. "Just know I'm really sorry for how things turned out."

"So am I."

"I wish things would have been different for us."

I shrugged. "They were the way they were supposed to be. There's nothing you, or I, can do about it now. What's done is done. And I really have no interest in holding onto it."

He looked down at his feet. "I've started that group counseling. And I realize I do have some things I need to work on . . . " He paused, waiting for my reaction. I had none.

I clasped my hands in front of me. "That's good to know. I hope everything works out for you."

He forced a pained smile. "Yeah, me too." He stuck his hands in his pockets. "I want you to know, you were the best thing that ever happened to me."

For some reason I believed him. But its too bad people don't appreciate what they have—or had—until it's gone. However, as far as he and I were concerned, it would have never lasted. Morris was all wrong for me. There was just no substance in what we had. I wanted bigger and better things for myself. I wanted someone I could grow with—emotionally, mentally and spiritually. Truth be told, I wanted love. And not from someone I knew wasn't right for me. I refused to delude him, or myself, to think otherwise. "I wish I could say the same," I said, standing in the doorway. "But one day I'm sure you'll find someone who will feel the same way you do. And be able to give you the things you need to grow. That just will . . . could . . . never be me. Everyone deserves someone special. And I hope when she comes into your life, you love her and treat her well."

He shook his head. "You're really one helluva woman."

I smiled. "You take care of yourself."

"Yeah, you too." He turned away. I waited for him to get in his truck and back out of my driveway before I finally closed the door. I inhaled, exhaled, feeling relieved. He was a part of the past. And that chapter of my life was finished.

I sat back down on my sofa and returned to my place in my book, enjoying the splendor of Akosua Busia's writing style. Her descriptions were colorful and her words flowed beautifully.

Hmm, I could go for a nice glass of wine, I thought, getting up to head for the kitchen. The doorbell rang, and I stopped in my tracks. I glanced at the clock, wondering who was at my door now. Hoping it wasn't Morris again. I looked through the peephole, then opened the door, trying to keep a smile from parting my lips.

"Quasheem."

"Hey, Pretty. Hope I'm not disturbing you," he said apologetically.

"No . . . no. I was just getting ready to go out," I lied. I was standing there, wearing a pair of Hunter College sweats and a too small T-shirt. He looked down at my bare feet, then stared at me, smiling. I folded my arms across my breasts. "I, um, was just getting ready to put some clothes on to run out to the store."

"Oh, yeah."

I nodded. "What brings you by?"

"I was thinking about you," he said. "And thought I'd come by on my way home. Since I don't have a way to call you. I stopped by and left several messages on your door, asking you to call me. But I guess the wind must have blown them away." There was a hint of sarcasm in his tone.

I laughed, nervously. Now it was my turn to apologize. "I got them, along with the cards. Thanks. I've been meaning to call, but I've been sidetracked."

"I feel you," he said, staring into my eyes. "I kinda figured that. That's why I decided to swing by, hoping to catch up with you. Do you mind if I come in?"

I shook my head, stepping aside. "No, not at all."

He smiled. "And do I get a seat this time?"

"Sure," I said, returning his smile. He removed his jacket. Damn, he was sexy. "But don't get too comfortable."

He chuckled. "Only if you wanted me to."

I ignored his comment, sitting in a chair across from him. "So how have you been?" I asked.

"I'm cool. Just thinking about you," he stated.

I've been thinking about you too, I thought. Thinking about our first sexual encounter. Remembering being in his arms, feeling his lips—again. Thoughts I knew I shouldn't have been entertaining. "Oh yeah? What were you thinking about?" I questioned, sheepishly.

That you wanna get in my drawers . . . "That I can't wait to spend some time with you. I'm glad Nia set it up for me to see you."

I smiled. "So am I," I said, honestly.

He stared at me.

"What?" I asked.

He shook his head. "You still fine as hell and . . . them lips are still sweet."

I blushed. "Thanks."

He glanced down at his watch. "Take a ride with me."

"I can't go out with you. I'm not dressed."

"But you were getting ready to go to the store. Remember?"

I hoped he didn't notice the flicker of deceit that crossed my face. "Oh, that's right I was."—I chuckled—"I almost forgot."

"Go get dressed. I'll take you."

"Oh, that's okay," I stated, shifting in my chair. "It wasn't that important."

"I still want you to take a ride with me," he said, eyeing me seductively. *Oh, if you only knew how bad I want to ride you,* I thought. And, against my better judgment, I went upstairs and changed into something more presentable. Ten minutes later, I was sitting in the passenger seat of his Range Rover. And we were on our way.

"Nice truck," I said, feeling a nervousness take over me.

"Thanks. I just picked it up today."

"Hmm. Must be nice to be able have such luxuries."

"Life is too short not too. I work hard, and like to spend my money on nice things."

"Hmm. I see." I took a deep breath, wondering if he was an impulsive spender, or someone who knew how to save. "If you don't mind me asking, what else do you do with your money?" I asked.

"Take care of my son's, invest, and save for a rainy day. I have a pretty decent portfolio. And an excellent credit score, if that's what your wondering."

I sighed a sweet sigh, then smiled. *A man after my own heart*, I thought.

Twenty minutes later, we were in Maplewood. I was surprised to be pulling up in his driveway. The garage door opened, and he drove in. Then got out, and opened my side of the door. He closed it when I got out. "Come on in." I followed behind him, not knowing what to expect.

"Want something?"

Yes, you. I shook my head, trying to figure out what the heck I was doing there, standing in the middle of his kitchen. "No, I'm fine. Thanks." I looked around the gourmet-style kitchen, taking in the stainless steel appliances, bamboo wood floor and floor-to-ceiling windows. For a bachelor's pad, it was spotless. "You have a nice place."

"Thanks. I just bought it a few months ago. Let me give you the grand tour." He walked me through his house, showing me around. His living room was open and airy with white leather furniture. It reminded me of a museum with artwork and Masaai statues neatly placed around the room. He even had some Woodrow Nash pieces. I was impressed. Downstairs was a game room and flat screen television and a CD and DVD collection that covered one long wall. Upstairs were four bedrooms, and two bathrooms. "And here's my bedroom," he said, flipping on the light. A king-size bed sat in the middle of a master bedroom with a fireplace and an adjoining sitting room where he had another flat screen. "I'm still trying to fix it up," he offered, shutting off the light and closing the door.

"Everything's so nice. Do you have a housekeeper?" I asked following him back downstairs to the kitchen.

"Yeah. I have someone who comes in once a week and takes care of me."

I raised my brow. "Is that so?"

He must have caught how what he said sounded. "I meant takes care of the cleaning. She's an older woman from the islands."

I shrugged.

Suddenly Quasheem leaned back against the counter, and pulled me into his arms. Before I could take a step back, his lips were on mine, then lightly along the side of my neck. "I've been wanting to do this all night," he mumbled in between kisses, placing his hands along the small of my back. His lips found their way up from my neck to my ear. He nibbled my earlobe tenderly. Flicked his tongue in my ear, grinded himself into me. I moaned. He kissed my eyelids, my nose, and my lips. Leaving a trail of soft, warm, wet kisses. I shivered. But I wasn't cold. There was a warm current—electricity, creeping through my body. Shaking my stomach lining, rattling my uterus—causing my vaginal walls to constrict. The scorpion in me was ready. Curiosity and lust was quickly getting the best of me. I reached down and felt the length of him, his thickness. I knew what I needed. He knew what I needed. I closed my eyes and said a quick, silent prayer. Asking for the strength to not throw him down on the kitchen floor and ride him like a rogue wave: steep and cresting. I opened, then shifted my eyes and pulled away from him, slowly. This was moving way too fast.

"Sorry about that," Quasheem whispered. "I couldn't help myself."

"I think we should take it slow."

"I'm cool with that," he said. "No pressure. But I do want to spend some time with you."

"I'd like that. But I can't guarantee you anything."

"Fair enough," he said, licking his lips. "Let's just see where things go."

I nodded in agreement. "Let's."

He glanced at his watch. "Well, I better get you back home before I end up . . . humph. You're something else. I want you bad as hell."

I smiled. "Well, good things come to those who wait. I've made some bad choices when it comes to men, and relationships," I said, looking up at him. "I haven't always used good judgment. But I know what I want."

"And what's that?" he asked.

"To be loved and to know that the right person is capable of loving me back. So, trust me. The next man I give myself to, he is going to be more than a good lay. He'll be my husband."

He reached for my hand. "I like the sound of that," he said, softly kissing the inside of my hand. "And I'm willing to wait for you. Now let me get you outta here before I change my mind."

I took in a deep breath, then slowly blew it out. I was thankful Quasheem had willpower because if he didn't I know where I would have ended up. Wrapped up in his arms, basking in his nakedness. Probably regretting my actions.

He dropped me back off at my house, walking me to my front door. He leaned in and kissed me again. "So am I gonna get your number? Or do I have to keep popping up at your doorstep?"

This time I decided to give it to him. I fished out a black marker from the bottom of my purse, then grabbed his hand and wrote my number in his palm. He looked at it, committing it to memory, then balled his hand into a fist. "I'll call you tomorrow. Maybe we can catch a movie or something."

"I'd need to check my schedule first," I said, grinning.

He grinned back at me. "Yeah, you do that."

"Goodnight, Qua."

"Goodnight, baby."

I closed the door behind me, then braced myself against it. I took a deep breath. I couldn't believe I had almost slept with him. I turned on the lamp, and glanced at the clock. It was almost midnight. I picked up the phone and decided to call Nia to check in on her. And tell her about my night. When she didn't answer I left a message. Just as I was about to go upstairs, take a shower, then go to bed, the phone rang. I hoped it was Nia calling back. I glanced at the caller ID, then frowned. It was Nygeria. What in the world does this child want, I wondered, picking up.

"Autumn, Nia has gotten herself in some serious trouble."

My heart caught in my throat. "Say what? Trouble how? Where?"

"She went to Maryland and confronted some chick Mustafa was messing with, and attacked him. And now she's in Prince George's County Detention Center. She's been trying to call you all night. She needs you to go down there and get her out. I'm worried about her." She was talking a mile a minute. Clearly upset

"Nygeria," I said. "I need you to slow down and tell me what happened."

"All I know is, she burned Mustafa's car up and tried to set him on fire—"

"OhmyGod!" I exclaimed. "When?"

"Sometime today. I mean, last night. She was crying hysterically. I couldn't understand a word she was saying. I think she's really lost it. All I know, she's in some serious shit."

I plopped down in my chair, then leaned back, breathless. Somehow I felt responsible. *I should have never given her those addresses,* I thought, staring at the walls in disbelief. I shook my head. No, no. This had to be a mistake. Nygeria was saying that Nia had gotten herself arrested. She set Mustafa, and his car, on fire. "This . . . this doesn't make sense. I was just with her this morning. I mean—"

"Autumn, first thing in the morning we have to get her a lawyer, and get her outta there."

"I'll see what I can do." I hung up.

Tomorrow was Saturday. If she really did what Nygeria said she had done, there was no way she was getting released over the weekend. Particularly, not being from out of state. I closed my eyes, hoping whatever trouble Nia had gotten herself into we could get her out of. But my fear was she'd need more than an attorney to do it. *Why couldn't she just let him go?* I thought, holding my head in my hands. "Because her heart wouldn't let her," I answered aloud. A tear escaped from eyes, sliding down my cheek.

Twenty-Five

Nia

And so it began, the beginning of my end. Or should I say this is how my life ended and began. Behind bars. How ironic is that? The night of my arrest, I remember standing in the middle of the driveway with the bat in one hand and the empty gasoline can in the other. But I don't remember setting Mustafa's lower body or his car on fire. Nor do I remember pulling out my blade and slicing his face. But the reports said I did. And the evidence proves I did. My attorney has tried to call it passion provocation. But, the knife, the bat and gasoline showed my behavior wasn't in the heat of the moment. No, I wasn't in the throes of passion. Yes, I had slipped into a moment of insanity. But, I had given thought to what I was going to do. From the time I got into my truck and hopped on 95, I knew. I was cognizant. I understood where I was headed. I was conscious of who I was going to confront. And I was fully aware Mustafa was going to catch hell. I just didn't know I'd wake up and my life would become one big blur. There's no need for a trial, or any long proceedings. I just want to get it over with. So, I sit and wait for my sentence. Crazy thing, almost two months after my rampage, I'm still sitting and waiting. In jail is where I've spent my twenty-eighth birthday. And Thanksgiving. And this is where I'll spend my Christmas, and New Years. Funny thing, I'm not upset or stressed about it. The judge has denied my bail twice because of the seriousness of my charges. Arson. Attempted murder. And two counts aggravated assault. And this hick ass prosecutor feels, given my mental state, I'm a flight risk. Go figure. I know I'm guilty as charged. I take full responsibility for my actions. And I accept my consequences. So where the hell am I going? As far as I'm concerned, the real crime was that I loved the wrong man, and was too caught up in the trappings of what I wanted love to be and got hurt in the process.

Anyway, today, despite it being the middle of December, the sun is shining. And with my face pressed against my window, I'm letting its rays warm me. Even in the face of overcasts, sunlight finds its way to me. Greets me regularly. Awakens me. And sometimes I just want to reach out and touch it. I close my eyes and let my imagination take me to faraway places with sandy white beaches, crystal blue waters and lots of golden sunshine. Sometimes I visit Bermuda. Other times St. Lucia. Fortunately, I have one of the better cells in the building and I can see as far out as my thoughts will allow. My mind's eye transfixes me to serene places. Keeps me sane in an insane world of shackles and chains. Despite concrete walls and steel doors, I find peacefulness in an unpleasant state of being. This is what my time behind bars has become. Imagery coalescing.

Dressed in a jailhouse jumpsuit, I sit and wait for my visit. Visits and mail from Autumn and Nygeria are the only things that keep me going. Sometimes they drive down together, other times separately. But, faithfully, I'm called out for a visit. Or there's a letter or card waiting for me when I return to my cell from mess or some other activity. Every time Autumn comes here, she breaks down and cries. Seeing me in prison garb is hard for her. But I tell her it's okay. I know this isn't the life she wanted for me. Hell, it's not what I wanted for myself. But, it's what has become of my existence. And if I'm to survive this, I need to believe. Thankfully, I have them both to see me through this. It's funny how the two of them have found a way to get along. They've made a truce for my sake. Have become connected through my circumstances. It's amazing how life throws you a curve ball. Just when you think you have everything figured out, you wake up and realize nothing is what you thought it was. Right now, my thoughts and memories are what keep me from slipping into a depression. Sometimes I sit by my thick, barred window, looking out remembering the days of pigtails and catholic school uniforms, the innocent days of hopscotch and double-Dutch; the parties and shopping sprees, and wonder how I allowed myself to get caught up in this predicament.

Sometimes, I close my eyes, and see my Nana busying herself in the kitchen, making her homemade cinnamon rolls and whipped sweet potatoes. And I can almost hear her soft voice sharing her lessons on life, and love. Everything seems so long ago. But the recollection—the sounds and the smells are so real. And bring a smile to my face. I wish I woulda listened.

Had I just been patient; sat still and waited. Mustafa would have gotten what he had coming to him. Come to find out, the police had him under surveillance for months building a case to take him down. But, I beat them to the punch. Not only was he in violation of his parole for crossing state lines without permission; he had two secret indictments. Isn't that something? Three weeks after I attacked him, they had already gathered enough evidence to bag him. It was just a matter of time. Now, it looks like he'll be locked down for a long time. Humph. They swarmed all over that spot here in Maryland like roaches. In one big swoop, they tore up his little happy home. Seizing everything. They dug up the whole backyard and found guns, coke and over four hundred thousand dollars in cash. And now he's lying in a building across from me—burned up, and stitched up—waiting for trial. I can only shake my head. He's guilty as sin, and he's still tryna lie his way out of shit. Some things will never change. But, that's not my problem. Anyway, last week, I got a letter from him stating he hopes I'll be able to live with myself for what I did to him. I cracked the hell up at that shit. I'm convinced he's nuts. Nigga, puh-leeze!

Of course I wrote him back, and said, "You shitted on me. And, as far as I'm concerned, you got what you deserved. If you had any regard for me, or what he had, you wouldn't have been out there slinging your dick in everything moving. You wouldn't have had your ass stretched out in a motel room, taking pictures of some damn greasy-lipped chick who just sucked your dick or who you just fucked. Fucking those chicks raw, then coming up in my bed was downright disrespectful and grimy as hell. You should have kept shit real, and stepped off so you could do you. But you wanted your cake and eat it too. I rode shit out with you nigga. Did your whole bid with you faithfully, and you tried to play me for a damn fool. So, yes, I can live with myself. "

His response, "Just because I cheated on you, doesn't mean I didn't love you. You're the one I wanted to spend my life with." I laughed, tearing his letter up in tiny pieces, tossing his lies up in the air like confetti. It's over. Sadly, it ended long before it ever got started. But I refused to accept it, didn't want to believe it. Anyway, I said I'd never do another bid with Mustafa. And I meant that. Crazy thing, I never thought in a million years that I'd be doing one along with him. Let's see who holds him down now.

You know, I found out he was lacing Keyonna the whole time he was home. She was in the drug game with him, down for whatever. His ride or die chick. Humph. And the crazy shit is he was playing daddy to a child that's not even his. It's some other nigga's. Another cat she was fucking in the halfway house. But she wasn't sure who the father was so she pinned it on his ass. How trifling is that? He was so busy tryna play me, and keeping her from blowing up his spot that he got played. But the truth always comes out. Like the saying goes, you lie down with dogs you wake up with fleas. And he has a bed full of them. Whatever. Now she's turning State's evidence against him just to save her own ass. Oh, she's here too, waiting to be extradited on parole violations and some other drug-related offenses. How stupid is that? Not that what I did was any smarter; but I don't have a child that's going to be affected by all this—without a mother.

Anyway, I fought her. Not over Mustafa, though. I promised myself I would never fight a chick over a man again. And I meant that. No. She came up in here tryna jump bad, blaming me for bringing heat to her life. Popping off at the mouth. So, I beat her down in the library real good. Then I let her know she could have him, and all of his madness. Please. Anyway, now they have a "keep separate" stamped on both of our files. Something they should have done from gate. But they didn't. Oh, well.

And, on top of all this other mess, news has it that Mustafa has contracted genital herpes from the chick Nygeria was telling me she had met at Weaves and Wonders. Come to find out, the night he pulled up behind my truck, he had just gotten back from Miami with her. Had fucked her raw, and now he has the blisters to remind him of what he did. Nasty dog! Good for his sneaky ass. Supposedly, the condom broke. Yeah, right! Luckily, he didn't give that shit to me. And for that, I'm grateful. If I didn't learn anything else in life, I've learned that everything happens for a reason. Had I stayed with him, continued to turn my head to his lying, and cheating ways, there's no telling what he might have given me. And, then I'd be in this piece for a body. I would have killed him for sure, and thought nothing of it. I just shake my head. There's just too much going on with him. Do I have any regrets? Yeah some. But, I'm not gonna spend my time, or my energy, thinking about them. I can't. What's done is done. And there's nothing that can change that. So, I try to move on. Embrace my life with a sense of purpose. Something I really didn't have before because I was so wrapped up in love. I was so caught up in my own fantasies and insecurities that I ignored the damn truth. Refused to see things for what they were. An illusion. Oh, well. You live and learn.

Anyway, my attorney believes my charges might get downgraded. But, it doesn't matter. I'm not going to hold my breath. It's not like I'm going anywhere any time soon. They can give me a life sentence as far as I'm concerned. Either way, I finally feel liberated. I've accepted my choices—be they right, wrong, or indifferent. They were mine, and mine alone. And I'm okay with it. I was responsible for letting Mustafa in my life, and I was responsible for keeping him there. And I'm accountable for my actions. I could have just let him go. I could have just packed his bags and went on my merry way. But I didn't. Something in me wouldn't let me. So, I deal with whatever happens. As far as I'm concerned, it's the first day of the rest of my life. And I'm okay. Being behind bars is forcing me, teaching me, to live day by day. Each day, I'm learning that we must first see the flaws in ourselves before we can see the beauty in others. So many times we go through life so busy looking down that we don't take time to look up to see what's going on around us. Jail is teaching me that. And it has forced me to accept the things I cannot change. Nothing in life is guaranteed. Promises are made and broken. Expectations aren't always met. So, I no longer worry about being let down. I'm learning to accept people for where they're at in their lives. It doesn't make them good or bad. It just means I don't have to accept it in mine.

This place forces me to take a long, hard look at myself without the stiletto heels or designer wears. Without expensive jewelry or fly hairdos. And sometimes I don't like what I see: a lonely girl lost in a woman's body; a woman who has cried a thousand times over a man. I see the scars of my mistakes. So I have no use for a mirror. I know who I am. And what I've become. Being around a bunch of chicks, there's no need to try to keep up with what's hot and what's not. So, I've had no choice but to let it go. There's no need to be pretentious. Who do I have to impress? At the end of the day, we're all in here, waiting, doing time. Or letting time do us.

Consequently, everyone here has a story to tell. Some share fairytales that turned into nightmares. Some give narratives of life gone wrong. Some give accounts of broken promises, and broken spirits. And, then there are others who choose to hold onto false hopes. Dreams of a happily-ever after that will never come true. Not in this lifetime. But, their fantasy is their reality and it's what gets them through their own personal hell. Sadly, I know I'm not the first—nor will I be the last, woman to look for love in all the wrong places, and faces. So who am I to judge? I have my own story. I have my own hurts. And disappointments. And I shed my own tears. Sometimes outwardly, other times I keep them buried deep in the crevices of my heart.

But that's neither here or there. I accept my reality. I acknowledge my faults. And if people can't take me as I am, if they can't love me for all that I am, then I don't need them in my life—particularly a man. As we all know, people come and go for whatever reasons. And every time you open your heart to them, you take a chance. Loving them becomes a gamble. You either win or lose. And sometimes you give more than what is given. Nana always said, "Love is what love does." I should have lived by that.

Regretfully, I had been emotionally chained, a prisoner of my own feelings, trying to hold onto a man who didn't want to be held. I had hoped Mustafa would have seen the love I had for him reflected in my eyes. But, he didn't. And you can't make someone who doesn't love you love you back. Or should I say, love you the way you want them to. It took all of this—the tears, the drama, the lies, everything—for me to see what he was really made of. And he wasn't, will never be, the man for me. Sadly, I lost myself, became disillusioned, in someone that wasn't for me. I loved someone more than I loved myself. But at the core of all this madness, I'm learning that my existence as a woman isn't—was never—contingent on Mustafa, or any other man, loving me, or wanting me. And this self-discovery is liberating.

So, again, I ask. Have you ever loved someone so much that it hurt? Have you ever loved someone so much that you were willing to ignore the gut-wrenching truth that he was no good for you? Have you ever compromised yourself for the sake of being loved? And, instead of just letting go, you held on—hoping, wishing, praying, that things would get better. Out of fear of being alone. Out of desperation. Out of some false belief that you could change him. Out of some sick, twisted need to prove you were the better woman. That no one else could love him better than you. Well, take it from me—it ain't worth all the heartache and trouble. Believe me. The dishonesty and betrayal will destroy you. I just hope you're smart enough to find a way to set yourself free from all the drama before it cripples you. Suffocates you. And kills your spirit.

I'll tell you this much: I may be locked down. And I may not ever live to see another day. But I'm thankful. I know I am worthy of love. Of being loved. I deserve honesty and trust. Something I didn't get from Mustafa. And I know now, with everything that is in me, Love isn't pain. And it definitely isn't a bunch of lies and drama. Trust me. I'm finally trying to find a way to take back what belongs to me, what had been stolen from me—my self-worth. My dignity. Yes, I'm reclaiming me. I'm restoring my faith in me. And I'm slowly healing. Bit by bit, behind these walls, I am trying to find ways to reconstruct me. Redefine me. And, more importantly, love me. Don't get me wrong. I'm not saying it's easy. And I know I have a long way to go. But, for the sake of saving myself, it's a process I must commit to; must endure. I don't know what tomorrow holds for me. And at this point, it's unimportant. All I know is that, no matter what happens, I'm going to be okay. Because—at this very moment—despite everything that has happened in my life, today is definitely a damn good day.

About the Author

Dywane D. Birch, a graduate of Norfolk State University and Hunter College, is the author of *Shattered Souls* (2000) and *From My Soul To Yours* (2004). He is also a contributing author to the intriguing compilation, *Breaking The Cycle* (2005), edited by Zane—a collection of short stories on domestic violence, which won the 2006 NAACP Image Award for outstanding literary fiction; and a contributing author to the anthology *Fantasy* (2006), a collection of erotica short stories. He has a master's degree in psychology and is a clinically certified forensic counselor.

A former director of an adolescent crisis shelter, he continues to work with adolescents and adult offenders. And currently speaks at local colleges on the issue of domestic violence while working on his fourth novel and a collection of poetry. He divides his free time between New Jersey and Maryland.